Brazilian
ESCAPE

ESCAPE
COLLECTION

Lynne *Jennie* *Melanie*
GRAHAM LUCAS MILBURNE

Greek
ESCAPE

April 2017

Carol *Maisey* *Catherine*
MARINELLI YATES MANN

Spanish
ESCAPE

May 2017

Jessica *Helen* *Liz*
GILMORE BROOKS FIELDING

Italian
ESCAPE

June 2017

Ally *Amy* *Michelle*
BLAKE ANDREWS DOUGLAS

Australian
ESCAPE

July 2017

Barbara *Christy* *Robin*
McMAHON McKELLEN GIANNA

French
ESCAPE

August 2017

Carol *Sandra* *Tara*
MARINELLI MARTON PAMMI

Brazilian
ESCAPE

September 2017

Brazilian
ESCAPE

Carol   Sandra   Tara
MARINELLI MARTON PAMMI

Published in Great Britain 2017
By Mills & Boon, an imprint of HarperCollins*Publishers*
1 London Bridge Street, London, SE1 9GF

BRAZILIAN ESCAPE © 2017 Harlequin Books S.A.

Playing the Dutiful Wife © 2013 Carol Marinelli
Dante: Claiming His Secret Love-Child © 2004 Sandra Myles
A Touch of Temptation © 2013 Tara Pammi

ISBN: 9-780-263-93105-1

09-0917

PLAYING THE DUTIFUL WIFE

CAROL MARINELLI

Carol Marinelli is a Taurus, with Taurus rising, yet still thinks she is a secret Gemini. Originally from England she now lives in Australia and is a single mother of three. Apart from her children, writing romance and the friendships forged along the way are her passion. She chooses to believe in a happy ever after for all and strives for that in her writing.

CHAPTER ONE

'I'M GOING TO have to go,' Meg said to her mother. 'They've finished boarding, so I'd better turn off my phone.'

'You'll be fine for a while yet.' Ruth Hamilton persisted with their conversation. 'Did you finish up the work for the Evans purchase?'

'Yes.' Meg tried to keep the edge from her voice. She really wanted just to turn off the phone and relax. Meg hated flying. Well, not all of it—just the take-off part. All she wanted to do was close her eyes and listen to music, take some nice calming breaths before the plane prepared for its departure from Sydney Airport— except, as usual, her mother wanted to talk about work. 'Like I said,' Meg said calmly, because if she so much as gave a hint that she was irritated her mum would want to know more, 'everything is up-to-date.'

'Good,' Ruth said, but still she did not leave things there.

Meg coiled a length of her very straight red hair around and around one finger, as she always did when either tense or concentrating.

'You need to make sure that you sleep on the plane, Meg, because you'll be straight into it once you land. You wouldn't believe how many people are here. There are so many opportunities…'

Meg closed her eyes and held on to a sigh of frustration as her mum chatted on about the conference and then moved to travel details. Meg already knew that a car would meet her at Los Angeles airport and take her straight to the hotel where the conference was being held. And, yes, she knew she would have about half an hour to wash and get changed.

Meg's parents were prominent in Sydney's real estate market and were now looking to branch into overseas investments for some of their clients. They had left for Los Angeles on Friday to network, while Meg caught up with the paperwork backlog at the office before joining them.

Meg knew that she should be far more excited at the prospect of a trip to Los Angeles. Usually she loved visiting new places, and deep down Meg knew that really she had nothing to complain about—she was flying business class and would be staying in the sumptuous hotel where the conference was being held. She would play the part of successful professional, as would her parents.

Even though, in truth, the family business wasn't doing particularly well at the moment.

Her parents were always very eager to jump on the latest get-rich-quick scheme. Meg, who could always be relied on for sensible advice, had suggested that rather than all of them flying over maybe just one of them should go, or perhaps they should give it a miss entirely and concentrate on the properties they already had on their books.

Of course her parents hadn't wanted to hear that. This, they had insisted, was the next big thing.

Meg doubted it.

It wasn't that, though, which caused her disquiet.

Really, when she had suggested that only one of them go—given that she dealt with the legal side of things—Meg had rather hoped they might have considered sending only her.

A week away wasn't just a luxury she required—it was fast becoming a necessity. And it wasn't about the nice hotel—she'd stay in a tent if she had to, just for the break, just for a pause so that she could think properly. Meg felt as if she were suffocating—that wherever she turned her parents were there, simply not giving her room to think. It had been like that for as long as she could remember, and sometimes she felt as if her whole life had been planned out in advance by her parents.

In truth, it probably had.

Meg had little to complain about. She had her own nice flat in Bondi—but, given that she worked twelve-hour days, she never really got to enjoy it, and there was always something at work that needed her attention at weekends: a signature to chase up, a contract to read through. It just never seemed to end.

'We're actually going to look at a couple of properties this afternoon…' Her mum carried on talking as there was a flurry of activity in the aisle beside Meg.

'Well, don't go agreeing to anything until I get there,' Meg warned. 'I mean it, Mum.'

She glanced over and saw that two flight attendants were assisting a gentleman. His face was blocked from Meg's vision by the overhead lockers, but certainly from his physique this man didn't look as if he required assistance.

He was clearly tall and extremely fit-looking, and from what Meg could see he appeared more than capable of putting his own laptop into the overhead locker, yet the attendants danced around him, taking his jacket and offering their apologies as he went to take the seat beside Meg.

As his face came into view Meg, who was already struggling, completely lost her place in the conversation with her mother. The man was absolutely stunning, with very thick, beautifully cut black hair worn just a little too long, so that it flopped over his forehead. He had a very straight Roman nose and high cheekbones. Really, he had all the markings of a *very* good-looking man, but it was his mouth that held her attention—perfectly shaped, like a dark bruise of red in the black of his unshaven jaw, and even though it was a scowling mouth, it was quite simply beautiful.

He threw a brief nod in Meg's direction as he took the seat beside her.

Clearly somebody wasn't very happy!

As he sat down Meg caught his scent—a mixture

of expensive cologne and man—and, though she was trying to focus on what her mother was saying, Meg's mind kept wandering to the rather terse conversation that was taking place beside her as the flight attendants did their best to appease a man whom, it would seem, wasn't particularly easy to appease.

'No,' he said to the attendant. 'This will be sorted to my satisfaction as soon as we have taken off.'

He had a deep, low voice that was rich with an accent Meg couldn't quite place. Perhaps Spanish, she thought, but wasn't quite sure.

What she *was* sure of, though, was that he demanded too much of her attention.

Not consciously, of course—she just about carried on talking to her mother, her finger still twirling in her hair—but she could not stop listening to the conversation that was none of her business.

'Once again,' the flight attendant said to him, 'we apologise for any inconvenience, Mr Dos Santos.' Then she turned her attention to Meg, and although friendly and polite, the flight attendant was not quite so gushing as she had so recently been to Meg's fellow passenger. 'You need to turn off your phone, Ms Hamilton. We are about to prepare for take-off.'

'I really do have to go, Mum,' Meg said. 'I'll see you there.' With a sigh of relief she turned off her phone. 'The best part of flying,' she said as she did so—not necessarily to him.

'There is nothing good about flying' came his brusque response as the plane started to taxi towards the runway. Seeing her raised eyebrows, he tempered his words a little. 'At least not today.'

She gave him a small smile and offered a quick 'Sorry,' then looked ahead rather than out of the window. After all he could be in the middle of a family emergency and racing to get somewhere. There could be many reasons for his bad mood and it was none of her business after all.

She was actually quite surprised when he answered her, and when she turned she realised that he was still looking at her. 'Usually I do like flying—I do an awful lot of it—but today there are no seats in first class.'

Niklas Dos Santos watched as she blinked at his explanation. She had very green eyes that were staring right at him. He expected her to give a murmur of sympathy or a small tut tut as to the airline's inefficiency; those were the responses that he was used to, so he was somewhat taken aback at hers.

'Poor you!' She smiled. 'Having to slum it back here in business class.'

'As I said, I fly a lot, and as well as working while flying I need to sleep on the plane—something that is now going to be hard to do. Admittedly I only changed my plans this morning, but even so...' He didn't continue. Niklas thought that was the end of the conversation, that he had explained his dark mood well enough. He hoped that now they could sit in mutual silence, but before he could look away the woman in the seat next to him spoke again.

'Yes, it's *terribly* inconsiderate of them—not to keep

a spare seat for you just in case your plans happen to change.'

She smiled as she said it and he understood that she was joking—sort of. She was nothing like anyone he usually dealt with. Normally people revered him, or in the case of a good-looking woman—which she *possibly* was—they came on to him.

He was used to dark-haired, immaculately groomed women from his home town. Now and then he liked blondes—which she was, sort of. Her hair was a reddish blonde. But, unlike the women he usually went for, there was a complete lack of effort on her part. She was very neatly dressed, in three-quarter-length navy trousers and a cream blouse that was delicate and attractive. Yet the blouse was buttoned rather high and she wore absolutely no make-up. He glanced down to nails that were neat but neither painted nor manicured and, yes, he did check for a ring.

Had the engines not revved then she might have noticed that glance. Had she not looked away at that moment she might have been granted the pleasure of one of his very rare smiles. For she seemed refreshingly unimpressed by him, and Niklas had decided she was not a *possibly* good-looking woman in the least...

But she spoke too much.

He would set the tone now, Niklas decided. Just ignore her if she spoke again. He had a lot of work to get through during this flight and did not want to be interrupted every five minutes with one of her random thoughts.

Niklas was not the most talkative person—at least he did not waste words speaking about nothing—and he certainly wasn't interested in her assumptions. He just wanted to get to Los Angeles with as much work and sleep behind him as possible. He closed his eyes as the plane hurtled down the runway, yawned, and decided that he would doze till he could turn on his laptop.

And then he heard her breathing.

Loudly.

And it only got louder.

He gritted his teeth at her slight moan as the plane lifted off the runway and turned to shoot her an irritated look—but, given that her eyes were closed, instead he stared. She was actually fascinating to look at: her nose was snubbed, her lips were wide and her eyelashes were a reddish blonde too. But she was incredibly tense, and she was taking huge long breaths that made her possibly the most annoying woman in the world. He could not take it for the next twelve hours, and Niklas decided he would be speaking again to the flight attendant— someone would have to move out of first class.

Simply, this would not do.

Meg breathed in through her nose and then out through her mouth as she concentrated on using her stomach muscles to control her breathing as her 'fear of flying' exercises had told her to do. She twisted her hair over and over, and when that wasn't helping she gripped onto the handrests, worried by the terrible rattling noise above her as the plane continued its less than smooth climb. It really was an incredibly bumpy take-off, and she loathed this part more than anything—could not relax until the flight stewards stood up and the seatbelt signs went off.

As the plane tilted a little to the left Meg's eyes screwed more tightly closed. She moaned again and Niklas, who had been watching her strange actions the whole time, noted not just that her skin had turned white but that there was no colour in her lips.

The minute the signs went off he would speak with the flight attendant. He didn't care if it was a royal family they had tucked in first class; someone was going to have to make room for him! Knowing that he always got his way, and that soon he *would* be moving, Niklas decided that for a moment or two he could afford to be nice.

She was clearly terrified after all.

'You do know that this is the safest mode of transport, don't you?'

'Logically, yes,' she answered with her eyes still closed. 'It just doesn't feel very safe right now.'

'Well, it is,' he said.

'You said that you fly a lot?' She wanted him to tell her that he flew every single day, that the noise overhead was completely normal and nothing to worry about, preferably that he was in fact a pilot—then she might possibly believe that everything was okay.

'All the time,' came his relaxed response, and it soothed her.

'And that noise?'

'What noise?' He listened for a second or two. 'That's the wheels coming up.'

'No, that one.'

It all sounded completely normal to him, yet Niklas realised *she* probably wasn't quite normal, so he continued to speak to her. 'Today I am flying to Los Angeles, as are you, and in two days' time I will be heading to New York...'

'Then?' Meg asked, because his voice was certainly preferable to her thoughts right now.

'Then I will be flying home to Brazil, where I am hoping to take a couple of weeks off.'

'You're from Brazil?' Her eyes were open now, and as she turned to face him she met his properly for the first time. He had very black eyes that were, right now, simply heaven to look into. 'So you speak...?' Her mind was all scrambled; she could still hear that noise overhead...

'Portuguese,' he said and, as if he was there for her amusement—which for a moment or two longer he guessed he was—he smiled as he offered her a choice. 'Or I can speak French. Or Spanish too, if you prefer...'

'English is fine.'

There was no need to talk any more. He could see the colour coming back to her cheeks and saw her tongue run over pinkening lips. 'We're up,' Niklas said, and at the same time the bell pinged and the flight attendants stood. Meg's internal panic was thankfully over, and he watched as she let out a long breath.

'Sorry about that.' She gave him a rather embarrassed smile. 'I'm not usually that bad, but that really was bumpy.'

It hadn't been bumpy in the least, but he was not going to argue with her, nor get drawn into further conversation. And yet she offered her name.

'I'm Meg, by the way.'

He didn't really want to know her name.

'Meg Hamilton.'

'Niklas.' He gave up that detail reluctantly.

'I really am sorry about that. I'll be fine now. I don't have a problem with flying—it's just take-off that I absolutely loathe.'

'What about landing?'

'Oh, I'm fine with that.'

'Then you have never flown into São Paulo,' Niklas said.

'Is that where you are from?'

He nodded, and then pulled out the menu and started to read it—before remembering that he was going to be moving seats. He pushed his bell to summon the stewardess.

'Is it a busy airport, then?'

He looked over to where Meg sat as if he had forgotten that she was even there, let alone the conversation they had been having.

'Very.' He nodded, and then saw that the flight attendant was approaching with a bottle of champagne. Clearly she must have thought he had rung for a drink—after all, they knew his preferences—but as he opened his mouth to voice his complaint Niklas conceded that it might be a little rude to ask to be moved in front of Meg.

He would have this drink, Niklas decided, and then he would get up and go and have a quiet word with the attendant. Or an angry one if that did not work. He watched as his champagne was poured and then, perhaps aware that her eyes were trained on him, he turned, irritated.

'Did you want a drink as well?'

'Please.' She smiled.

'That is what your bell is for,' he retorted. She didn't seem to realise that he was being sarcastic, so he gave in and, rolling his eyes, ordered another glass. Meg was soon sipping on her beverage.

It tasted delicious, bubbly and icy-cold, and would hopefully halt her nervous chatter—except it didn't. It seemed that a mixture of nerves about flying and the fact that she had never been around someone so drop-dead gorgeous before resulted in her mouth simply not being able to stop.

'It seems wrong to be drinking at ten a.m.' She heard her own voice again and could happily have kicked herself—except then he would perhaps have her certified. Meg simply didn't know what was wrong with her.

Niklas didn't answer. His mind was already back to thinking about work, or rather thinking about all the things he needed to get finalised so that he could actually take some proper time off.

He *was* going to take some time off. He had not stopped for the last six months at the very least, and he was really looking forward to being back in Brazil, the country he loved, to the food he adored and the woman who adored him and who knew how it was…

He would take two or perhaps three weeks, and he was going to use every minute of them indulging in life's simple but expensively prepared pleasures—beautiful women and amazing food and then more of the same.

He let out a long breath as he thought about it—a long breath that sounded a lot like a sigh. A bored sigh, even—except how could that be? Niklas asked himself. He had everything a man could want and had worked hard to get it—worked hard to ensure he would never go back to where he had come from.

And he *had* ensured it, Niklas told himself; he could stop for a little while now. A decent stretch in Brazil would sort this restless feeling out. He thought of the flight home, of the plane landing in São Paulo, and as he did he surprised himself. His champagne was finished. He could get up now and have that word with the flight attendant. But instead Niklas turned and spoke with *her*.

With Meg.

CHAPTER TWO

'SÃO PAULO IS very densely populated.'

They were well over the water now, and she was gazing out at it, but she turned to the sound of his voice and Niklas tried to explain the land that he loved, the mile after mile after mile of never-ending city.

'It is something that is hard to explain unless you have seen it, but as the plane descends you fly over the city for very a long time. Congonhas Airport is located just a couple of miles from downtown...'

He told Meg about the short runway and the difficult approach and the physics of it as she looked at him slightly aghast.

'If the weather is bad I would imagine the captain and crew and most *paulistanos*...' He saw her frown and explained it a little differently. 'If you come from Sao Paulo or know about the airport then you are holding your breath just a little as the plane comes into land.' He smiled at her shocked expression. 'There have been many near-misses—accidents too...'

What a horrible thing to tell her! What a completely

inappropriate thing for him to say at this moment! And she had thought him so nice—well, nice-looking at least. 'You're not helping at all!'

'But I am. I have flown in and out of Congonhas Airport more times than I can remember and I'm still here to tell the tale… You really have nothing to worry about.'

'Except that I'm scared of landing now too.'

'Don't waste time in fear,' Niklas said, and then stood to retrieve his computer. He did not usually indulge in idle chatter, and certainly not while flying, but she had been so visibly nervous during take-off, and it had been quite pleasant talking her around. Now she was sitting quietly, staring out of the window, and perhaps he did not have to think about moving seats after all.

The flight steward started to serve some appetizers, and Meg had an inkling that Mr Dos Santos was being treated with some tasty little selections from the first-class menu—because there were a few little treats that certainly weren't on the business class one—and, given that she was sitting next to him, by default Meg was offered them too.

'Wild Iranian caviar on buckwheat blinis, with sour cream and dill,' the flight attendant purred to him, but Niklas was too busy to notice the selection placed in front of him. Instead he was setting up a workstation, and Meg heard his hiss of frustration as he had to move his computer to the side. Clearly he was missing his first-class desk!

'There is no room—' He stopped himself, realising

that he sounded like someone who complained all the time. He didn't usually—because he didn't have to. His PA, Carla, ensured that everything ran smoothly in his busy life. But Carla simply hadn't been able to work her magic today, and the fact was between here and LA Niklas had a lot to get done. 'I have a lot of work to do.' He didn't have to justify his dark mood, but he did. 'I have a meeting scheduled an hour after landing. I was hoping to use this time to prepare. It really is inconvenient.'

'You'll have to get your own plane!' Meg teased. 'Keep it on standby...'

'I did!' he said. Meg blinked. 'And for two months or so it was great. I really thought it was the best thing I had ever done. And then...' He shrugged and got back to his laptop, one hand crunching numbers, the other picking all the little pieces of dill off the top of the blinis before eating them.

'And then?' Meg asked, because this man really was intriguing. He was sort of aloof and then friendly, busy, yet calm, and very pedantic with his dill, Meg thought with a small smile as she watched him continue to pick the pieces off. When the food was to his satisfaction there was something very decadent about the way he ate, his eyes briefly closing as he savoured the delicious taste entering his mouth.

Everything he revealed about himself had Meg wanting to know more, and she was enthralled when he went on to tell her about the mistake of having his own plane.

'And then,' Niklas responded, while still tapping

away on his computer, 'I got bored. Same pilot, same flight crew, same chef, same scent of soap in the bathroom. You understand?'

'Not really.'

'As annoying as your chatter may be...' he turned from his screen and gave her a very nice smile '...it is actually rather nice to meet you.'

'It's rather nice to meet you too.' Meg smiled back.

'And if I still had my own plane we would not have met.'

'Nor would we if you were lording it in first class.'

He thought for a moment. 'Correct.' He nodded. 'But now, if you will forgive me, I have to get on with some work.' He moved to do just that, but just before he did he explained further, just in case she had missed the point he was making. 'That is the reason I prefer to fly commercially—it is very easy to allow your world to become too small.'

Now, that part she *did* understand. 'Tell me about it.' Meg sighed.

His shoulders tensed. His fingers hesitated over the keyboard as he waited for her to start up again.

When she inevitably did, he would point out *again* that he was trying to work.

Niklas gritted his teeth and braced himself for her voice—was she going to talk all the way to Los Angeles?

Except she said nothing else.

When still she was quiet Niklas realised that he was actually *wanting* the sound of her voice to continue their conversation. It was at that point he gave up working for a while. He would return to the report later.

Closing his laptop, he turned. 'Tell *me* about it.'

She had no idea of the concession he was making—not a clue that a slice of his time was an expensive gift that very few could afford, no idea how many people would give anything for just ten minutes of his undivided attention.

'Oh, it's nothing...' Meg shrugged. 'Just me feeling sorry for myself.'

'Which must be a hard thing to do with a mouthful of wild Iranian caviar...'

He made her laugh—he really did. Niklas really wasn't at all chatty, but when he spoke, when he teased, when she met his eyes, there was a little flip in her stomach that she liked the feeling of. It was a thrill that was new to her, and there was more than just something about him...

It was *everything* about the man.

'Here's to slumming it,' Niklas said. They chinked their glasses and he looked into her eyes, and as he did so somehow—not that she would be aware of it— Niklas let her in.

He was a closed person, an extremely guarded man. He had grown up having to be that way—it had meant survival at the time—yet for the first time in far too long he chose to relax, to take some time, to forget about work, to stop for a moment and just be with her.

As they chatted he let the flight steward put his

laptop away. They were at the back of business class, tucked away and enjoying their own little world.

The food orders were taken and later served, and Meg thought how nice Niklas was to share a meal with. Food was a passion in waiting for Meg. She rarely had time to cook, and though she ate out often it was pretty much always at the same Italian restaurant where thcy took clients. They'd chosen different mains, and he smiled to himself at the droop of her face when they werc served and she found out that steak tartare was in fact raw.

'It's delicious,' he assured her. 'Or you can have my steak?'

At the back of her mind she had known it was raw, if she'd stopped to think about it, but the menu had been incredibly hard to concentrate on with Niklas sitting beside her, and she had made a rather random selection when the flight steward had approached.

'No, it's fine,' Meg said, looking at the strange little piles of food on her plate. There was a big hill of raw minced steak in the middle, with a raw egg yolk in its shell on the top, surrounded by little hills of onions and capers and things. 'I've always wanted to try it. I just tend to stick to safe. It's good to try different things...'

'It is,' Niklas said. 'I like it like this.'

Something caught in her throat, because he'd made it sound like sex. He picked up her knife and fork, and she watched him pour in the egg, pile on the onions and capers, and then chop and chop again before sliding the mixture through Worcestershire sauce. For a fleeting moment she honestly thought that he might load the fork and feed her, but he put the utensils down and returned to his meal, and Meg found herself breathless and blushing at where her mind had just drifted.

'Good?' Niklas asked when she took her first taste.

'Fantastic,' Meg said. It was nice, not amazing, but made by his hands fantastic it was. 'How's *your* steak?'

He sliced a piece off and lifted the loaded fork and held it to her. This from a man who had reluctantly given her a drink, who had on many occasions turned his back. He was now giving her a taste of food from his plate. He was just being friendly, Meg told herself. She was reading far, far too much into this simple gesture. But as she went to take the fork he lifted it slightly. His black eyes met hers and he moved the fork to her mouth and watched as she opened it. Suddenly she began to wonder if she'd been right the first time.

Maybe he *was* talking about sex.

But if he had been flirting, by the time dessert was cleared it had ended. He read for a bit, and Meg gazed out of the window for a while, until the flight attendant came around and closed the shutters. The lights were lowered and the cabin was dimmed and Meg fiddled with her remote to turn the seat into a bed.

Niklas stood and she glanced up at him. 'Are you off to get your gold pyjamas?'

'And a massage,' Niklas teased back.

She was half asleep when he returned, and watched idly as he took off his tie. Of course the flight attendant rushed to hold it, while another readied his bed, and then he took off his shoes and climbed into the flight bed beside her.

His beautiful face was gone now from her vision, but it was there—right there—in her mind's eye. She was terribly aware of his movements and listened to him turn restlessly a few times. She conceded that maybe he did have a point—the flight bed was more than big enough for Meg to stretch out in, but Niklas was easily a foot taller than her and, as he had stated, he really needed this time to sleep, which must be proving difficult. For Niklas the bed was simply too small, and it was almost a sin that he sleep in those immaculate suit trousers.

She lay there trying not to think about him and made herself concentrate instead on work—on the Evans contract she had just completed—which was surely enough to send her to sleep. But just as she was closing her eyes, just as she was starting to think that she might be about to drift off even with Niklas beside her, she heard him move again. Her eyes opened and she blinked as his face appeared over hers. She met those black eyes, heard again his rich accent, and how could a woman not smile?

'You never did tell me...' Niklas said, smiling as he invited her to join him in after hours conversation. 'Why is your world too small?'

CHAPTER THREE

THEY PULLED BACK the divider that separated them and lay on their sides, facing each other. Meg knew that this was probably the only time in her life that she'd ever have a man so divine lying on the pillow next to hers, so she was more than happy to forgo sleep for such a glorious cause.

'I work in the family business,' Meg explained.

'Which is?'

'My parents are into real-estate investments. I'm a lawyer...'

He gave a suitably impressed nod, but then frowned, because she didn't seem like a lawyer to him.

'Though I hardly use my training. I do all the paper-work and contracts.'

He saw her roll her eyes.

'I cannot tell you how boring it is.'

'Then why do you do it?'

'Good question. I think it was decided at conception that I would be a lawyer.'

'You don't want to be one?'

It was actually rather hard to admit it. 'I don't think I do...'

He said nothing, just carried on watching her face, waiting for her to share more, and she did.

'I don't think I'm supposed to be one—I mean, I scraped to get the grades I needed at school, held on by my fingernails at university...' She paused as he interrupted.

'You are *never* to say this at an interview.'

'Of course not.' She smiled. 'We're just talking.'

'Good. I'm guessing you were not a little girl who dreamed of being a lawyer?' he checked. 'You did not play with wigs on?' His lips twitched as she smiled. 'You did not line up your dollies and cross-examine them?'

'No.'

'So how did you end up being one?'

'I really don't know where to start.'

He looked at his watch, realised then that perhaps the report simply wasn't going to get done. 'I've got nine hours.'

Niklas made the decision then—they would be entirely devoted to *her*.

'Okay...' Meg thought how best to explain her family to him and chose to start near the beginning. 'In my family you don't get much time to think—even as a little girl there were piano lessons, violin lessons, ballet lessons, tutors. My parents were constantly checking my homework—basically, everything was geared towards me getting into the best school, so that I could get the best grades and go to the best university. Which I did. Except when I got there it was more push, push, push. I just put my head down and carried on working, but now suddenly I'm twenty-four years old and I'm not really sure that I'm where I want to be…' It was very hard to explain it, because from the outside she had a very nice life.

'They demand too much.'

'You don't know that.'

'They don't listen to you.'

'You don't know that either.'

'But I do.' He said. 'Five or six times on the telephone you said, "Mum, I've got to go." Or, "I really have to go now…"' He saw that she was smiling, but she was smiling not at his imitation of her words but because he had been listening to her conversation. While miserable and scowling and ignoring her, he had still been aware. 'You do this.' He held up an imaginary phone and turned it off.

'I can't.' she admitted. 'Is that what you do?'

'Of course.'

He made it sound so simple.

'You say, *I have to go*, and then you do.'

'It's not just that though,' she admitted. 'They want to know everything about my life…'

'Then tell them you don't want to discuss it,' he said. 'If a conversation moves where you don't want it to, you just say so.'

'How?'

'Say, *I don't want to talk about that*,' he suggested.

He made it sound so easy. 'But I don't want to hurt them either—you know how difficult families can be at times.'

'No.' He shook his head. 'There are some advantages to being an orphan, and that is one of them. I get to make my own mistakes.' He said it in such a way that there was no invitation to sympathy—in fact he even gave a small smile, as if letting her know that she did not need to be uncomfortable at his revelation and he took no offence at her casual remark.

'I'm sorry.'

'You don't have to be.'

'But…'

'I don't want to talk about that.' And, far more easily than she, he told her what he was not prepared to discuss. He simply moved the conversation. 'What would you like to do if you could do anything?'

She thought for a moment. 'You're the first person who has ever asked me that.'

'The second,' Niklas corrected. 'I would imagine you have been asking yourself that question an awful lot.'

'Lately I have been,' Meg admitted.

'So, what would you be?'

'A chef.'

And he didn't laugh, didn't tell her that she should know about steak tartare by now, if that was what she wanted to be, and neither did he roll his eyes.

'Why?'

'Because I love cooking.'

'Why?' he asked—not as if he didn't understand how

it was possible to love cooking so much, more as if he really wanted her tell him why.

She just stared at him as their minds locked in a strange wrestle.

'When someone eats something I've cooked—I mean properly prepared and cooked...' She still stared at him as she spoke. 'When they close their eyes for a second...' She couldn't properly explain it. 'When you ate those blinis, when you first tasted them, there was a moment...' She watched that mouth move into a smile, just a brief smile of understanding. 'They tasted fantastic?'

'Yes.'

'I wanted to have cooked them.' It was perhaps the best way to describe it. 'I love shopping for food, planning a meal, preparing it, presenting it, serving it...'

'For that moment?'

'Yes.' Meg nodded. 'And I know that I'm good at it because, no matter how dissatisfied my parents were with my grades or my decisions, on a Sunday I'd cook a meal from scratch and it was the one thing I excelled at. Yet it was the one thing they discouraged.'

'Why?' This time he asked because he didn't understand.

'"Why would you want to work in a kitchen?"' It was Meg doing the imitating now. '"Why, after all the opportunities we've given you...?"' Her voice faded for a moment. 'Maybe I should have stood up to them, but it's hard at fourteen...' She gave him a smile. 'It's still hard at twenty-four.'

'If cooking is your passion then I'm sure you would be a brilliant chef. You should do it.'

'I don't know.' She knew she sounded weak, knew she should just say to hell with them, but there was one other thing she had perhaps not explained. 'I love them,' Meg said, and she saw his slight frown. 'They are impossible and overbearing but I do love them, and I don't want to hurt them—though I know that I'll probably have to.' She gave him a pale smile. 'I'm going to try and work out if I can just hurt them gently.'

After a second or two he smiled back, a pensive smile she did not want, for perhaps he felt sorry for her being weak—though she didn't think she was.

'Do you cook a lot now?'

'Hardly ever.' She shook her head. 'There just never seems to be enough time. But when I do...' She explained to him that on her next weekend off she would prepare the meal she had just eaten for herself and friends...that she would spend hours trying to get it just right. Even if she generally stuck with safer choices, there was so much about food that she wanted to explore.

They lay there, facing each other and talking about food, which to some might sound boring—but for Meg it was the best conversation she had had in her life.

He told her about a restaurant that he frequented in downtown São Paulo which was famed for its seafood, although he thought it wasn't actually their best dish. When he was there Niklas always ordered their *feijoada*, which was a meat and black bean stew that tasted, he told her, as if angels had prepared it and were feeding it to his soul.

In that moment Meg realised that she had not just one growing passion to contend with, but two, because his gaze was intense and his words were so interesting and she never wanted this journey to end. Didn't want to stop their whispers in the dark.

'How come you speak so many languages?'

'It is good that I do. It means I can take my business to many countries…' He was an international financier, Niklas told her, and then, very unusually for him, he told her a little bit more—which he never, ever did. Not with anyone. Not even, if he could help it, with himself. 'One of the nuns who cared for me when I was a baby spoke only Spanish. By the time I moved from that orphanage…'

'At how old?'

He thought for a moment. 'Three, maybe four. By that time I spoke two languages,' he explained. 'Later I taught myself English, and much later French.'

'How?'

'I had a friend who was English—I asked him to speak only English to me. And I—' He'd been about to say looked for, but he changed it. 'I read English newspapers.'

'What language do you dream in?'

He smiled at her question. 'That depends where I am—where my thoughts are.'

He spent a lot of time in France, he told Meg, especially in the South. Meg asked him where his favourite place in the world was. He was about to answer São Paulo—after all, he was looking forward to going back there, to the fast pace and the stunning women—but he paused for a moment and then gave an answer that surprised even him. He told her about the mountains away from the city, and the rainforests and the rivers and springs there, and that maybe he should think of getting a place there—somewhere private.

And then he thanked her.

'For what?'

'For making me think,' Niklas said. 'I have been thinking of taking some time off just to do more of the same...' He did not mention the clubs and the women and the press that were always chasing him for the latest scandal. 'Maybe I should take a proper break.'

She told him that she too preferred the mountains to the beach, even if she lived in Bondi, and they lay there together and rewrote a vision of her—no longer a chef in a busy international hotel, instead she would run a small bed and breakfast set high in the hills.

And she asked about him too.

Rarely, so rarely did he tell anyone, but for some reason this false night he did—just a little. For some reason he didn't hold back. He just said it. Not all of it, by any means, but he gave more of himself than usual. After all, he would never see her again.

He told her how he had taught himself to read and write, how he had educated himself from newspapers, how the business section had always fascinated him and how easily he had read the figures that seemed to daunt others. And he told her how he loved Brazil—for there you could both work hard and play hard too.

'Can I get you anything Mr Dos Santos…?' Worried that their esteemed passenger was being disturbed, the steward checked that he was okay.

'Nothing.' He did not look up. He just looked at Meg as he spoke. 'If you can leave us, please?'

'Dos Santos?' she repeated when the steward had gone, and he told her that it was a surname often given to orphans.

'It means "from the Saints" in Portuguese,' he explained.

'How were you orphaned?'

'I don't actually know,' Niklas admitted. 'Perhaps I was abandoned, just left at the orphanage. I really don't know.'

'Have you ever tried to find out about your family…?'

He opened his mouth to say that he would rather not discuss it, but instead he gave even more of himself. 'I have,' he admitted. 'It would be nice to know, but it proved impossible. I got Miguel, my lawyer, onto it, but he got nowhere.'

She asked him what it had been like, growing up like that, but she was getting too close and it was not something he chose to share.

He told her so. 'I don't want to speak about that.'

So they talked some more about her, and she could have talked to him for ever—except it was Niklas who got too close now, when he asked if she was in a relationship.

'No.'

'Have you ever been serious about anyone?'

'Not really,' she said, but that wasn't quite true. 'I was about to get engaged,' Meg said. 'I called it off.'

'Why?'

She just lay there.

'Why?' Niklas pushed.

'He got on a bit too well with my parents.' She swallowed. 'A colleague.' He could hear her hesitation to discuss it. 'What we said before about worlds being too small...' Meg said. 'I realised I would be making mine smaller still.'

'Was he upset?'

'Not really.' Meg was honest. 'It wasn't exactly a passionate...' She swallowed. She was *so* not going to discuss this with him.

She should have just said so, but instead she told him that she needed to sleep. The dimmed lights and champagne were starting to catch up with both of them, and almost reluctantly their conversation was closed and finally they slept.

For how long Meg wasn't sure. She just knew that when she woke up she regretted it.

Not the conversation, but ending it, falling asleep and wasting the little time that they had.

She'd woken to the scent of coffee and the hum of the engines and now she looked over to him. He was still asleep, and just as beautiful with his eyes closed. It was almost a privilege to examine such a stunning man more intently. His black hair was swept back, his beautiful mouth relaxed and loose. She looked at his dark spiky lashes and thought of the treasure behind them. She wondered what language he was dreaming in, then watched as his eyes were revealed.

For Niklas it was a pleasure to open his eyes to her.

He had felt the caress of her gaze and now he met it and held it.

'English.' He answered the question she had not voiced, but they both understood. He had been dreaming in English, perhaps about her. And then Niklas did what he always did when he woke to a woman he considered beautiful.

It was a touch more difficult to do so—given the gap between them, given that he could not gather her body and slip her towards him—but the result would certainly be worth the brief effort. He pulled himself up on his elbow and moved till his face was right over her, and looking down.

'You never did finish what you were saying.'

She looked back at him.

'When you said it wasn't passionate...'

She could have turned away from him, could have closed the conversation—his question was inappropriate, really—only nothing felt inappropriate with Niklas. There was nothing that couldn't be said with his breath on her cheek and that sulky, beautiful mouth just inches away.

'I was the one who wasn't passionate.'

'I can't imagine that.'

'Well, I wasn't.'

'Because you didn't want him in the way that you want me?'

Meg knew what he was about to do.

And she wanted, absolutely, for him to do it.

So he did.

It did not feel as if she was kissing a stranger as their lips met—all it felt was sublime.

His lips were surprisingly gentle and moved with hers for a moment, giving her a brief glimpse of false security—for his tongue, when it slipped in, was shockingly direct and intent.

This wasn't a kiss to test the water, and now Meg knew what had been wrong with her from the start, the reason she had been rambling. This thing between them was an attraction so instant that he could have kissed her like this the moment he'd sat down beside her. He could have taken his seat, had her turn off her phone and offered his mouth to her and she would have kissed him right back.

And so she kissed him back now.

There was more passion in his kiss than Meg had ever tasted in her life. She discovered that a kiss could be far more than a simple meeting of lips as his tongue told her exactly what else he would like to do, slipping in and out of her parted lips, soft one minute, rougher the next. Then his hand moved beneath the blanket and stroked her breast through her blouse, so expertly that she ached for more.

Meg's hands were in his hair and his jaw scratched at her skin and his tongue probed a little harder. As she concentrated on that, as she fought with her body not to arch into him, he moved his hand inside her top. Now Niklas became less than subtle with his silent instructions and moved his hand to her back, pulling her forward into his embrace. She swallowed the growl that vibrated from his throat as beneath the blanket he rolled her nipple between his fingers—hard at first, and then with his palm he stroked her more softly.

To the outside world they would appear simply as two lovers kissing, their passion indecent, but hidden. Then Niklas moved over her a little more, so all she could breathe was his scent, and his mouth and his hand worked harder, each subtle stroke making her want the next one even more. Suddenly Meg knew she had to stop this, had to pull back, because just her reaction to his kiss had her feeling as though she might come.

'Come.' His mouth was at her ear now, his word voicing her thought.

'Stop,' she told him, even if it was not what she wanted him to do, but she could hardly breathe.

'Why?'

'Because,' she answered with his mouth now back over hers, 'it's wrong.'

'But *so* nice.'

He continued to kiss her. Her mouth was wet from his but she closed her lips, because this feeling was too much and he was taking her to the edge. He parted her lips with his tongue and again she tried to close them, clamped her teeth, but he merely carried on until she gave in and opened again to him. He breathed harder, and his hand still worked at her breast, and she was fighting not to gasp, not to moan, to remember where they were as he suckled her tongue.

Meg forced herself not to push his hand far lower, as her body was begging her to do, not to pull him fully on top of her as Niklas made love to her with his mouth.

She hadn't a hope of winning.

He removed his hand from her breast and prised her knotted fingers from his hair. Then he moved her hand beneath his blanket, his body acting as a shield as he held her small hand over his thick, solid length. Her fingers ached to curl and stroke around him, but he did not allow it. Instead he just flattened her palm against him and held it there. His mouth still worked against hers, and she tried to grumble a protest as her hand fought not to stroke, not to feel, not to explore his arousal.

He won.

He smothered her moan with his mouth and sucked, as if swallowing her cry of pleasure, and then, most cruel of all, he loosened his grip on her hand and accepted the dig of her fingers into him. He lifted his head and watched her, a wicked smile on his face, as she struggled to breathe, watched her bite on her lip as he too fought not to come. And he wished the lights were on so he could watch her in colour, wished that they were in his vast bed so the second she'd finished they could resume.

And they would, he decided.

'That,' Niklas said as he crashed back not to earth but to ten thousand feet in the air, 'was the appetiser.'

She'd been right the first time.

He *had* been talking about sex.

She put on a cardigan and excused herself just as the lights came on.

As she stood in the tiny cubicle and examined her face in the mirror she fastened her bra. Her skin was pink from his prolonged attention, her lips swollen, and her eyes glittered with danger. The face that looked back at her was not a woman she knew.

And she was *so* not the woman Niklas had first met.

Not once in her life had she rebelled; never had she even jumped out of her bedroom window and headed out to parties. At university she had studied and worked part-time, getting the grades her parents had expected before following them into the family business. She had always done the right thing, even when it came to her personal relationships.

Niklas had been right. She hadn't wanted her boyfriend in the way she wanted Niklas, and had strung things out for as long as she could before realising she could not get engaged to someone she cared about but didn't actually fancy. She had told her boyfriend that she wouldn't have sex till she was sure they were serious, but the moment he'd started to talk about rings and a future Meg had known it was time to get out.

And *that* was the part that caused her disquiet.

She wasn't the passionate woman Niklas had just met and kissed—she was a virgin, absolutely clueless with men. A few hours off the leash from her parents and she was lying on her back, with a stranger above her and the throb of illicit pulses below. She closed her eyes in shame, and then opened them again and saw the glitter and the shame burned a little less. There was no going back now to the woman she had been, and even if there were she would not change a minute of the time she had spent with Niklas.

She heard a tap against the door and froze for a second. Then she told herself she was being ridiculous. She brushed her teeth and sorted her hair and washed in the tiny sink, trying to brace herself to head back out there.

As she walked down the aisle she noticed her bed had been put away and the seats were up. She attempted polite conversation with Niklas as breakfast was served. He didn't really return her conversation. It was as if what had passed between them simply hadn't happened. He continued to read his paper, dunking his croissant in strong black coffee as if he *hadn't* just rocked her world.

The dishes were cleared and still he kept reading. And as the plane started its descent Meg decided that she now hated landing too—because she didn't want to arrive back at her old life.

Except you couldn't fly for ever. Meg knew that. And a man like Niklas wasn't going to stick around on landing. She knew what happened with men like him, wasn't naïve enough to think it had been anything more than a nice diversion.

She accepted it was just about sex.

And yet it wasn't just the sex that had her hooked on him.

He stretched out his legs, his suit trousers still somehow unrumpled, and she turned away and stared out of the window, trying not to think about what was beneath the cloth, trying not to think about what she had felt beneath her fingers, about the taste of his kisses and the passion she had encountered. Maybe life would have been easier had she not sat next to him—because now everything would be a mere comparison, for even with the little she knew still she was aware that there were not many men like Niklas.

Niklas just continued reading his newspaper, or appeared to be. His busy mind was already at work, cancelling his day. He knew that she would have plans once they landed. That she probably had a car waiting to take her to her hotel and her parents. But he'd think of something to get around that obstacle.

He had no intention of waiting.

Or maybe he would wait. Maybe he'd arrange to meet up with her tonight.

He thought of her controlling parents and turned a page in the paper. He relished the thought of screwing her right under their nose.

She, Niklas decided, was amazing.

There was no *possibly* about it now.

He thought of her face as she came beneath him and shifted just a little in his seat.

'Ladies and gentlemen…' They both looked up as the captain's voice came over the intercom. 'Due to an incident at LAX all planes are now being re-routed. We will be landing in Las Vegas in just over an hour.'

The captain apologised for the inconvenience and they heard the moans and grumbles from other passengers. They felt the shift as the plane started to climb, and had she been sitting next to anyone else Meg might have been complaining too, or panicking about the prolonged flight, or stressing about the car that was waiting for her, or worried about what was going on...

Instead she was smiling when he turned to her.

'Viva Las Vegas,' Niklas said, and picked up her remote, laid her chair flat again and got back to where he had left off.

CHAPTER FOUR

'IT WAS A false alarm.'

They were still sitting on the plane on the tarmac. The second they had landed in Vegas Niklas had pulled out his phone, turned it on and called someone. He was speaking in Portuguese. He had briefly halted his conversation to inform Meg that whatever had happened in Los Angeles had been a false alarm and then carried on talking into his phone.

'Aguarde, por favour!' he said, and then turned again to Meg. 'I am speaking with my PA, Carla. I can ask her to reschedule your flight also. She will get it done quickly, I think.'

And make sure he'd sit next to her too, Niklas decided.

'So?' he asked. 'When do you want to get there?'

Of course the normal response would be as soon as possible, but there was nothing normal about her response to him. Niklas was looking right at her, and there was undoubtedly an invitation in his eyes, but there was something he needed to know—somehow she had to tell him that what had happened between them wasn't usual for her.

To put it mildly.

Except Niklas made her stomach fold into herself, and his eyes were waiting, and his mouth was so beautiful, and she did not want this to end with a kiss at an airport gate. She did not want to spend the rest of her life regretting what would surely be a far more exciting choice than the one she should be making.

He made it for her.

'It sounds as if there is a lot of backlog. The airport will be hell with so many people having to re-route. I could tell her to book our flights for tomorrow.' Niklas had already made the decision. He had not had twenty-four hours to himself in months, had not stopped working in weeks, and right now he could think of no one nicer to escape the world with.

'I'm supposed to be...' She thought of her parents, waiting for her at the conference, waiting for her to arrive, to perform, to work twelve-hour days and accept weekends constantly on call. Hers was a family that had every minute, every week, every year of her life accounted for, and for just for a little while Meg wanted to be able to breathe.

Or rather to struggle to breathe under him as he kissed her and took her breath.

He looked at her mouth as he awaited her answer, watched the finger that twirled in her hair finally pause as she reached her decision, saw her tongue moisten her lips just before she delivered her answer.

'Tomorrow,' Meg said. 'Tell her tomorrow.'

He spoke with Carla for a couple more moments, checked he had the right spelling of her surname and date of birth and passport number, and then clicked off his phone.

'Done.'

She didn't know what his life was like—didn't really understand what the word *done* meant in Niklas Dos Santos's world...

Yet.

They waited for their baggage and she got to kiss him for the first time standing up, got to feel his tall length pressed against her. He loaded their bags onto one trolley and then he did a nice thing, a very unexpected thing: he stopped at one of the shops and bought her flowers.

She smiled as he handed them to her.

'Dinner, breakfast, champagne, kisses, foreplay...' God, he didn't even lower his voice as he handed her the flowers. 'Have I covered everything?'

'You haven't taken me to the movies,' Meg said.

'No...' He shook his head. 'There was a movie on. You chose not to watch it. I cannot be held responsible for that...'

Oh, but he had been. She felt the thorns of the roses press in as he moved closer again and crushed the flowers.

'Consider yourself dated.'

There was no waiting in long queues for Niklas. Customs was a very different thing in his world, and as his hand was holding hers, she too was processed quickly. Suddenly they had cleared Customs and were walking out—and it was then she got her first glimpse of what *done* meant in a world like Niklas's.

Carla must have been busy, for there was already a driver waiting, holding a sign with 'Niklas Dos Santos' written on it. He relieved them of their bags and they followed him to a blacked-out limousine. She never got a glimpse of Vegas as they drove to the hotel, just felt the brief hit of hot desert sun.

No, she never saw Vegas at all.

She was sitting on his lap.

'I'm going to be the most terrible let-down…' She peeled her face from his.

'You're not,' he groaned.

'I am…' God, her head was splitting just at the attempt to be rational. 'Because I have to ring my mum…'

Her hands were shaking as she dialled the number, her mind reeling, because she *had* to tell him she was a virgin. Oh, God, she really was going to be a let-down! His fingers were working the buttons on her trousers now, his hand slipping in and cupping her bum. His mouth was sucking her breast through her blouse as she was connected to her mother, and she heard only smatters of her conversation.

'Yes, I know it was a false alarm…' She tried to sound normal as she spoke with a less than impressed Ruth. 'But all the flights are in chaos and tomorrow was the earliest I could get.' No, she insisted for a third time, there was simply nothing she could do that would get her there sooner. 'I'll call you when I've sorted out a hotel and things. I have to go, Mum, my battery's about to go flat.'

She clicked off the phone and he turned her so that she was sitting astride him. Holding her hips, he pushed her down, so she could feel what would soon be inside her, and for the first time she was just a little bit scared.

'Niklas…'

'Come on…' He did her blouse up. 'We are nearly there.'

She made herself decent, slipped her cardigan over her blouse to hide the wet patch his mouth had made, and found out once again what it was like in his world.

They breezed through check-in, and even their luggage beat them to their huge suite—not that she paid any attention to it, for finally they were alone. As soon as the door shut he kissed her, pushing her onto the bed. He removed his jacket and pulled condoms from his pocket, placing them within reach on the bedside table, and then he removed her trousers, taking her panties with them at the same time.

God, he was animal, and he moaned as he buried his face in her most private of places. Meg felt the purr of his moan, and this new experience coupled with her own arousal terrified her.

'Niklas…' she pleaded as his tongue started to probe. 'When I said my relationship wasn't passionate…'

'We've already proved it had nothing to do with you.' His words were muffled, but he felt her tense and as he looked up he met anxious eyes.

'I haven't done this before.' She saw him frown. 'I haven't done anything.'

There was a rather long pause. 'Good. I will look after you…'

'I know that.'

'I *will*.'

And then his mouth resumed, and she felt his breath in places she had never felt someone breathe before, but still the tension and fear remained. Niklas must have sensed it too, as he raised himself up on his elbows and looked down at her beneath him, her face flushed.

Niklas was a very uninhibited lover; it was the only piece of himself that he readily gave. Sex was both his rest and recreation, and with his usual lovers there was no need for long conversation and coaxing, no need for reticence or taking his time. But as he looked down at her flushed cheeks he recalled their long conversations on the plane, and the enjoyment of spending proper time with another person. He thought of all the things he had told her that he never usually shared with anyone, and he realised he liked not just the woman who lay beneath him but the words that had come from her mouth.

He kissed it now, as if doing so for the first time.

Not their first kiss. Just a gentle kiss—albeit with his erection pressing into her as he thought about what to do.

His first intention had been to push her on the bed and take her quickly, just so that they could start over again, but he really liked her, and he wanted to do this well.

Thoroughly.

Properly.

'I know…'

He sounded as if he'd had an idea, and he stopped kissing her, smiling down at her before rolling off and picking up the phone. He told Meg that a bath would relax her, and as they waited for a maid to come and run it he wrapped her in a vast white dressing gown. She lay on the bed, watching him as he went through his case, and then he joined her on the bed and showed her some documents, his fingers pointing to the pertinent lines, which she read, frowning.

'I don't get this.'

'I had to get a check-up when I was in Sydney, for my insurance…' he explained.

'So?'

'I wasn't worried about the results. I always use protection…' He was so completely matter-of-fact.

'I'm not on the pill,' Meg replied as she understood his meaning, and she saw his eyes widen just a little as she dampened his plans.

'But still…' He stopped himself, shook his head as if to clear it. What the hell had he been thinking? For a second a baby had seemed a minor inconvenience compared to what they might miss out on. He was, Niklas decided, starting to adore her, and that always came with strong warnings attached—that was always his signal to leave.

'Niklas…am I making a big mistake?'

He was as honest with Meg as he was with all

women, because his was a heart that would remain closed. 'If you are looking for love, then yes,' Niklas said. 'Because I don't do that.'

'Never?'

'Ever,' Niklas said. He could not bear even the thought of someone depending on him, could not trust himself to provide for another person, just could not envisage sharing, yet alone caring—except already a part of him cared for *her*.

'Then I want as long as we've got,' Meg said.

When the maid left he took her by the hand and led her to the bathroom. The bath was sunken, and as she slid into the water he undressed, and she was looking up at his huge erection, her cheeks paling in colour. Niklas found himself assuring her that nothing would happen between them just yet—not until she was sure she was ready. The need to comfort her and reassure her was a new sensation for him, and as he looked down at her he decided that for the next twenty-four hours he would let himself care.

He climbed into the water with her and washed her slowly, sensually, smoothing the soap over her silky skin. He dunked her head in the water too, just so he could see the red darken.

'Your last boyfriend—did he try…?' Niklas asked as he soaped her arms, curious because he wondered how any man could resist the beautiful woman he held in his arms.

'A bit…' Meg said.

Even her arms blushed, he noted.

'I just…'

'What?' He loved her blushing, and found himself smiling just watching her skin pinken, feeling the warmth beneath his palms as she squirmed.

'I told him I didn't want to do anything like that till we were really serious. You know…'

His eyes widened. 'Married?'

'Engaged,' she corrected.

'Do people really say that?' He sounded incredulous, his soapy hands moving lower, past her breasts and down to her waist. 'How would you know if you wanted to marry someone if you hadn't—?'

'That had nothing to do with it. I wasn't demanding a ring. I realised I was just making up excuses…'

'Because?' He was sliding his soapy hands between her legs now, and she didn't know how to answer. 'Because?' he insisted.

'Because I didn't have any compulsion to sit in a bath with him and let him wash me *there*…' She couldn't believe he expected her to speak as he was doing what he did. 'And then he started talking rings.'

'I bet he did,' Niklas said, because, naked with her like this, what man wouldn't want his ring on her finger?

Suddenly his brain went to a place it should not, and Niklas tried hard to shut it down. This had to stay as just sex between them. He pulled her straight over to him, hooked her legs over his and kissed her shoulder.

'I loved flying with you…' He said it like a caress

as he lifted her hair, and his mouth moved to the back of her neck and sucked hard.

She closed her eyes at the bruise he was making, and then felt his hand move up her thigh. It was his neck she was now kissing, licking away the fragrant water just to get to his skin. As they continued to nip and kiss each other Niklas moved his hand, his finger slipping inside, and when she felt a moment's pain she sucked harder on his neck. He pushed in another finger, stretching her, and again she bit down on his shoulder as pain flashed through her body. She knew he had to stretch her—she had seen that he was huge and this was her first time after all—but he did it with a gentleness that moved her.

He continued to slide his fingers in and out, and then kissed her breast, sucking on her wet nipple. She began to moan and lift herself to his fingers as pleasure washed over her. Niklas realised that things were moving rather faster than he had intended. He wanted her on the bed—or rather they needed to get back to the condoms.

'Come on...' He moved to stand, except her hand found him first and, yes, she deserved a little play too.

He liked being touched by a woman. He had just never expected to enjoy it as much as he did now. Had never expected the naked pleasure in her eyes and the tentative exploration of her hands, just her enjoyment of him, would make him feel as it did.

For enjoy him, Meg did. It was bliss to hold him, huge and slippery and magnificent in her hands, and she was still scared, but rather more excited at the prospect of him being inside her.

'Like this?' she checked, and he closed his eyes and leant his head back on the marble wall behind him.

'Like that,' he said, but then changed his mind. 'Harder.' And he put his hand over hers and showed her—showed her a little too well.

'Come here.' He pulled her up over him. He was seconds away, had to slow down, but he had to have her. He was rubbing himself around her and she was desperate for him to be inside her too.

'We need…' It was him saying it, and he knew he should take her to bed and slip on a condom, but he wanted her this moment, and for once in his life he was conflicted. He knew he could have her now, that he was the only one thinking, and he wanted the pleasure. But as he looked at her, hovering over him, Niklas knew he wouldn't have a hope of pulling out in time.

Her hands were on his shoulders and he was holding her buttocks, almost fighting not to press her down. He wanted to give in, to drive her down and at the same time lift his hips, and he would have—absolutely he would have, in fact—had her phone not rung.

He swore in Portuguese, and then French, and then Spanish at the intrusion.

'Leave it,' he said.

But it rang again, and for a brief moment common sense returned. He stood, taking her wet hand and helping her out as they headed for the bed. He turned off her phone, and checked that his was off too, for he was tired of a world that kept invading his time. Then he looked at the shiny foil packets and realised that the last thing he wanted was to be sheathed when he entered this woman.

'I want to feel you,' he said. 'I want you to feel me.'

And his mind went to a place he never allowed it to go.

He'd been told by plenty of people that he was damaged goods, that a man with his past was not capable of a stable relationship.

Yet he wanted to be stable for a while.

He was tired of the noise and the endless women. Not once had he considered commitment, and he didn't fully now, but surely for a while longer he could carry on caring? He had amassed enough that he could trust himself to take care of another person for a while at least, and if there were consequences to his reckless decision then he could take care of that too.

He could.

In that moment he fully believed that he could.

He would.

No, he did not want others around him today—did not want his thoughts clouded. Usually, to Niklas, rapid thoughts were right, and they were the ones that proved to be the best. He looked at her, pink and warm and a virgin on his bed, and decided he would do this right.

Thoroughly.

Properly.

'Marry me.'

She laughed.

'I'm serious,' he said. 'That's what people do when they come to Vegas.'

'I think they usually know each other first.'

'I know you.'

'You don't.'

'I know enough,' Niklas said. 'You just don't know me. I *want* to do this.'

And what Niklas Dos Santos wanted he usually got.

'I'm not talking about for ever—I could never settle with one person for very long, or stay in one place— but I can help you sort out the stuff with your family. I can step in so you can step back...'

'Why?' She didn't get it. 'Why would you do that?'

He looked at her for a long time before answering, because she was right. Why *would* he do that? Niklas had had many relationships, many less than emotional encounters, and there had been a couple of long high-maintenance ones. Yet not once in his life had he considered marriage before. Not once had he wanted another person close. He had actually feared that another person might depend on a man who had come from nothing, but as he looked at her for the first time he wasn't daunted by the prospect at all.

Around her—again for the first time—he trusted in himself.

'I like you.'

'But what would you get out of it?'

'You,' he replied, and suddenly it seemed imperative that he marry her—that he make her his even if just for a little while. 'I like sorting things out...and I like you. And...' He gestured to the condoms on the bedside table. 'And I don't like them. So,' he said, reaching for the hotel phone, 'will you marry me?'

There was nothing about him she understood, but more than that there was nothing about herself she understood any more, for in that moment his proposal seemed rather logical.

A solution, in fact.

'Yes.'

He spoke on the phone for just a few moments and then turned and smiled at his bride-to-be.

'Done.'

CHAPTER FIVE

IT WAS THE quickest of quick weddings.

Or maybe not.

They were in Vegas, after all.

Niklas rang down to the concierge and informed them of their plans, telling him how they wanted them executed.

'Do you want them to bring up a selection of dresses?' he asked Meg. 'It's your day; you can have whatever you want.'

'No dress.' Meg smiled.

But there were *some* traditional elements.

He ordered lots of flowers, and they arrived in the room along with champagne, and there was even a wedding cake. Meg sat at a table trying on rings as the celebrant went through the paperwork.

He'd arranged music too, but Niklas chose from a selection already on his phone, and Meg found herself walking at his side to music she didn't know and a man she badly wanted to.

The bride and groom wore white bathrobes, and she

stood watching as the titanium ring dotted with diamonds she had chosen was slipped onto her finger. Perhaps bizarrely, there was not a flicker of doubt in her
mind as she said yes.

And neither was there a flicker of doubt in Niklas's
mind as he kissed his virgin bride and told her that he
was happy to be married to a woman he had only met
yesterday.

'Today,' Meg corrected and, yes, because of the time
difference between Vegas and Australia it *was* still the
day they'd first met.

'Sorry to rush you.' He grinned.

There was a mixture of nerves and heady relief when
everyone had left.

He undid her robe and took off his, and then he
pulled her onto the bed.

'Soon,' Niklas promised as his hands roamed over
her, 'you will be wondering how you got through your
life without this.'

'I'm wondering now,' Meg admitted, and she wasn't
just talking about the sex. She was talking about him
too. She had never opened up more fully with another
person, had never felt more like herself.

Niklas's kiss was incredibly tender—a kiss she
would never have expected from him. He kissed her
till she almost relaxed, and then his mouth became more
consuming. He needed to shave, but she liked the roughness, liked his naked body wrapped around hers.

She was on her back, and he was on top as he had so
badly wanted to be on the plane. He could not wait—

not for a moment longer. His knees nudged hers apart and he slipped his fingers briefly in, checking she was ready for him, finding that she was.

And now there was nothing between them.

And he was no longer patient.

He warned her it would hurt.

He watched her face as she blanched in pain, then kissed her hard on the mouth.

As he drove into her she screamed into his mouth, because that first thrust seemed to go on for ever, and every part of her felt as if it was tearing just to accommodate his long, thick length. He tried to be gentle, but he was too large for that. But once he had ripped off that Band-Aid he kept moving within her, kept on kissing her mouth, her face, giving her no choice but to grow accustomed to the new sensations she was feeling. He moved within her as his tongue had earlier described that he would, moving deep till he had driven her wild. He wasn't kissing her now, and she looked up to see his face etched with concentration, his eyes closed, his body moving rapidly as hers rose to meet him.

Now it was Meg's hands urging him on, digging her fingers into his tight buttocks, whimpering as she sought relief, and then he opened his eyes and let her have it, spilled every last drop deep into her. Her orgasm followed quickly after, and she was frenzied as she came, almost scared at the power of her body's response, at the things he had taught her to do.

And then he collapsed on top of her, his breathing heavy, and although it felt like a dream somehow it was real. Meg realised that he had been right—she had no idea how she'd got through her life without this.

Without him.

'Shouldn't we be regretting this by now?' Meg asked.

They were lying in a very rumpled bed and it was morning. Her body ached with the most delicious hurt, but Niklas had assured her for this morning's lesson she would need only her mouth.

'What's to regret?' He turned on the bed and looked over to her.

He didn't do happiness, but he felt the first rays of it today. He liked waking up to her, and the rest was mere detail that he would soon sort out.

'You live in Brazil and I live in Australia...'

'As we both know, there are planes...' He looked across the pillow. 'Do you worry about everything?'

'No.'

'I think you do.'

'I don't.'

'So how shall we tell your parents?'

He saw her slight grimace.

'They might be pleased for you.'

As the real world invaded so too did confusion. 'I doubt it. It will be a terrible shock.' She thought for a moment. 'I think once they get used to the idea they'll be pleased.' And then she swallowed nervously. 'I *think*.'

He smiled at her worried face. 'First of all *you* need to get used to the idea.'

'I don't know much about you.'

'There isn't much to know,' Niklas said.

She rather doubted that.

'I don't have family, as I said, so you have avoided having a mother-in-law. I hear from friends they can sometimes be a problem, so that's an unexpected bonus for you!'

He could be so flippant about things that were important, Meg thought, and there was so much she wanted to find out about him. She wondered how he had survived without a family, for a start, how he had made such a success of himself from nothing—because clearly he had. But unlike their wedding some things, Meg guessed, had to be taken more slowly—she couldn't just sit up and fire a thousand questions at him. Somehow she knew it wasn't something he would talk about easily, but she tried. 'What was it like, though?' Meg asked. 'Growing up in an orphanage?'

'There were many orphanages,' he said. 'I was moved around a lot.' Perhaps he realised he wasn't answering her question, because he added, 'I don't know, really. I try not to think about it.'

'But...'

He halted her. 'We're married Meg. But that doesn't mean we need every piece of each other. Let's just enjoy what we have, huh?'

So if he didn't want to talk about himself she'd start with the easier stuff instead. 'You live in São Paulo?'

'I have an apartment there,' Niklas said. 'If I am working in Europe I tend to stay at my house in Villefranche-sur-Mer. And now I guess I'll have to look for somewhere in Sydney...' His smile was wicked. 'If your father gets really cross, maybe I can ask if he knows any good houses—if he would be able to help...'

Meg started to laugh, because it sounded as if he did understand where she was coming from. Niklas was right—a nice big commission would certainly go a long way towards appeasing her father. She realised that the shock would wear off eventually, and that her rather shallow parents would be delighted to find somewhere for their rich new son-in-law to live.

As Meg lay there, and the sun started to work its way through the chink in the curtains, she started to realise that this was the happiest she had been in her life. But even with that knowledge there was one part about last night that had been unjustifiably reckless.

'I'll go on the pill...' she said. 'If it isn't already too late.'

He had said this wasn't for ever, and the wedding ring that had seemed a solution yesterday was less than one now.

'If last night brings far-reaching consequences you will both be taken care of.'

'For a while?'

He looked over and knew that, unlike most women, Meg wasn't talking about money. But his bank account was the only thing not tainted by his past.

'For a while,' Niklas said. 'I promise you—we'll be arguing within weeks, we'll be driving each other insane—and not with lust...' He smiled in all the wrong places, but he made her smile back. 'You'll be glad to see the back of me.'

She doubted it.

'I'm hard work,' he warned.

But worth it.

Though she *was* going on the pill.

And then he looked over to her again, and for as long as it was like this she could adore him.

'I am going to write to the airline tomorrow and thank them for not having a first-class seat,' he said.

'I might write and thank them too.'

'It will be okay,' he told her. 'Soon I will ring Carla and I will have her re-schedule things. Then we will meet with your parents and I will tell them.' He grinned at her horrified expression.

'*I'll* speak to my parents.'

'No,' Niklas said. 'Because you will start apologising and doubting and I am a better negotiator.'

'Negotiator?'

'How long do you want off for our honeymoon?' Niklas said. 'Of course you will want to give them notice—you don't want to just walk out—but for now we should have some time together. Maybe I'll take you to the mountains…' There was no gap between them now, so he pulled her across. 'And I will also tell them that we will have a big wedding in a few weeks.'

'I'm happy with the wedding we had.'

'Don't you want a big one?'

Her hand slid down beneath the sheet and she loved it that he laughed, not understanding that laughter was actually rare for him. Then her mouth followed her hands, and he lay there as she inexpertly woke another part of him.

'Don't you want a proper wedding, with family and dancing?'

'I hate dancing...' She kissed all the way down his length and she felt his hand in her hair, gently lifting her to where he wanted more attention.

'I do too.'

'I thought all Brazilians could dance?'

'Stop talking,' Niklas said. 'And I never said I couldn't. I just don't.'

She looked up at the most stunning, complicated man who had ever graced her vision and thought of his prowess and the movement of his body. All of it had been for her, and she shivered at the thought of the days and nights to come, of getting to know more and more of him. Already she knew that she was starting to want for ever, but that wasn't what this was about.

And then she tasted him again.

His hands moved her head as he promised she would not hurt him and told her exactly what to do with her mouth. She was lost in his scent, the feel of him in her mouth, and the shock of his rapid come was a most pleasant surprise. It was a surprise for Niklas too, but this was how she moved him.

He did not want to get out of bed—did not want to get back to the world. Except no doubt it was screaming for him by now—he had never had his phone turned off for so long.

He climbed out of bed and she lay there, just staring at the ceiling, lost in thoughts of him and the time they would take to get to know the other properly.

And Niklas was thinking the same. He had been looking forward to some time off, had been aware that he needed some, now he could not wait to take it.

He showered quickly and considered shaving, and then he picked up his phone, impatient to speak to Carla, to change his plans yet again. He grimaced when he saw how many missed calls he'd had, how many texts, and then he frowned—because there were hundreds. From Carla, from Miguel, from just about everyone he knew...

It was his first inkling that something was wrong.

Niklas had no family, and the only person he had ever really cared about was in bed in the next room, so he didn't have any flare of panic, but there was clearly a problem. Problems he was used to, and was very good at sorting them out.

It just might take a little time, that was all, when really he would far rather be heading back to bed. He dialled Carla's number, wondering if he should tell Meg to order some breakfast. He would just as soon as he made this call.

She could hear him in the lounge, speaking in his own language into his phone. She lay there for ages, twisting her new ring around her finger. Then, as he still spoke on the phone, she realised she wasn't actually terrified at the prospect of telling her parents, and even if this wasn't the most conventional of marriages, even if he had warned her it would end some day, she was completely at peace with what had occurred.

The only thing she was right now, Meg realised, was starving.

'I'm going to ring for breakfast,' she said as he walked back into the room, and then she looked over and frowned, because even though he had been gone ages she was surprised to see that he was dressed.

'I have to return to Brazil.'

'Oh.' She sat up in the bed. 'Now?'

'Now.'

He was not looking at her, Meg realised. What she did not realise was that precisely two seconds from now he was going to break her heart.

'We made a mistake.'

As easily as that he did it.

'Sorry?'

'The party's over.'

'Hold on…' She was completely sideswiped. 'What happened between there and here?' She pointed to the lounge he had come from. 'Who changed your mind?'

'I did.'

'What? Did you suddenly remember you had a fian-cée?' Meg shouted. 'Or a girlfriend…?' She was start-ing to cry. 'Or five kids and a wife…?' It was starting to hit home how little she knew about him.

'There's no wife…' he shrugged '…except you. I will speak with my legal team as soon as I return to Brazil, see if we can get it annulled. But I doubt it…'

He didn't even sit on the bed to tell her it was over,

and she realised what a fool she had been, how easily he had taken her in.

'If it cannot be annulled they will contact you for a divorce. I'll make a one-off settlement,' he said.

'Settlement?'

'My people will sort it. You can fight me for more if you choose, but I strongly suggest that you quickly accept. Of course if you are pregnant...'

He stood there with the sun streaming through the curtains behind him, and all she could see was the dark outline of a man she didn't know.

'It might be a good idea to think about the morning-after pill.'

And then there was a knock on the door and it was a bellboy to take his case.

'I've asked for a late check-out for you, if you want to reschedule your flight. Have breakfast...' he offered, as if this was normal, and then he tipped the bellboy, who left with his luggage.

'I don't understand...' She was turning into some hysterical female, sitting screaming on a bed as her one-night stand walked off.

'This is the type of thing people do in Vegas. We had fun...'

'Fun!' She couldn't believe what she was hearing.

'It's no big deal.'

'But it is for me.'

'It's about time that you grew up, then.'

She had never expected him to be cruel, but she had

no idea what she was dealing with. Niklas could be cruel when necessary, and today it was.

Very necessary.

He could not look at her. She was sitting on the bed in tears, pleading with him, and also, he noted, growing increasingly angry. Her voice rose as she told him that *he* was the one who needed to grow up, that *he* was the one who needed to sort out his life, and her hands were waving. Any minute now he thought she would rise and attack him. He wanted to catch her wrists and kiss the fear away, wanted to feel just for a moment her body writhing in anger and to reassure her—except he had nothing he could reassure her with. He knew how bad things would be shortly, so he had to be cruel to be kind.

'What did you have to marry me for?' she shouted. 'I was clearly already going to sleep with you...'

She was about to lunge at him, Niklas knew. She was kneeling on the bed, still grabbing the sheet around her for now, but in a moment it would be off. Her green eyes were flashing, her teeth bared and with his next words he knew he would end this.

'I told you yesterday.' He went to the bedside and flicked a few foil packets to the floor. 'I don't like condoms.'

He took the clawing to his cheek, stood there as she sprang towards him, then caught and held her naked fury by the arms for a moment. And then he pushed her back on the bed.

And as simply as that he was gone.

* * *

A minute ago the only things on her mind had been breakfast and making love with her new husband.

Now they were talking annulments and settlements.

Or rather they weren't talking.

He was gone.

He had left with cruel words and livid scratches on his cheek and she just lay there, reeling, her anger like a weight that did not propel her, but instead seemed to pin her down to the bed. It was actually an achievement to breathe.

A few minutes later Meg realised she was breathing in through her nose and out through her mouth, as she had done on the plane during take-off. Her own body was rallying to bring her out from the panic she now found herself in. Still she lay there and tried to make sense of something there was no sense to be made of.

He had played her.

Right from the start it had all been just a game to him.

Except this was her life.

Maybe he was right. Maybe she did need to grow up. If a man like Niklas could so easily manipulate her, could have her believing in love at first sight, then maybe she *did* need to sort herself out. She curled into herself for a moment, breathed for a bit, cried for a bit, and then, because she had to, Meg stood.

She didn't have breakfast.

She ordered coffee instead, and gulped on the hot

sweet liquid in the hope that it would warm her, would wean her brain out of its shock. It did not.

She showered, blasting her bruised, tender body with water, for she could not bear to step into the bath where they had kissed and so nearly made love.

Sex, Meg reminded herself. Because as it turned out love at first sight had had nothing to do with it.

She dressed quickly, unable to bear being in a room that smelt of them, and then she looked at the rumpled and bloodstained sheet on the bed where he had taken her and thought she might throw up.

Within an hour she was at the airport.

And just a little while later she was sitting on a plane and trying to work out how to get her life back to where it had been yesterday.

Except her heart felt as bruised and aching as the most intimate parts of her body, and her eyes, swollen from crying, felt the same.

Meg ordered a cool eye mask from the attendant. Before putting it on she slid off her wedding ring and put it on a chain around her neck, trying to fathom what had happened.

She couldn't.

She did her best with make-up in the toilet cubicle just before they came in for landing. She lifted her hair and saw the bruise his mouth had left on her neck and felt a scream building that somehow she had to contain. She covered her eyes with sunglasses and wondered how she would ever get through the next few hours, days, weeks.

'Thank God...' Her mum met her at the baggage carousel. 'The car's waiting. I'll bring you up to speed on the way.' She peered at her daughter. 'Are you okay?'

'Just tired,' Meg answered, and then she looked at her mum and knew she could never, ever tell her, so instead she forced a smile. 'But I'm fine.'

'Good,' said her mum as they grabbed her case and headed for the car. 'How was Vegas?'

CHAPTER SIX

MEG STOOD IN her office, looking out of the window, her fingers, as they so often did, idly turning the ring that still, almost a year later, lived on a chain around her neck.

She wasn't looking forward to tonight, given what she had to tell her parents.

It had nothing to do with Niklas. There had been eleven months of no contact now. Eleven months for Meg to start healing. Yet still she didn't know how to start.

She couldn't bear to think about him, let alone tell anyone what had happened.

And even though she could not bear to think about him, even though it actually hurt to do so, of course all too often Meg did.

It hurt to remember the good bits.

The bad bits almost killed her.

Surprisingly, she couldn't quite work out if she regretted it.

Niklas Dos Santos, for the brief time he had appeared

in it, had actually changed her life. Meeting him had changed her. Hell *did* make you stronger. This was her life and she must live it, and Meg had decided that she was finally going to follow her dreams and study to be a chef. Now she just had to tell her parents. So in a way tonight did in fact have something to do with him.

The strange thing was, she wanted to tell Niklas about her decision too—was fighting with herself not to contact him.

As painful as it was to remember, as brutal as his departure had been, still a part of her was grateful for the biggest mistake of her life and, fiddling with his ring as she so often did, Meg felt tears sting her eyes.

That was the only thing that was different today.

She hadn't cried for him since that morning. Actually, she had, but it had only been the once—the morning a couple of weeks later when she had got her period. Meg had sunk to her knees and wept on the toilet floor, not with relief, but because there was nothing left of them.

Nothing to tell him.

No reason for contact.

Apart from the paperwork it was as over as it could be.

So for the best part of a year she had completely avoided it. Had tried not to think of him while finding it impossible not to.

Every day had her waiting for a thick legal letter with a Brazilian postmark and yet it had never arrived.

Every night was just a fight not to think.

Sometimes Meg was tempted to look him up on the internet and find out more about the man who she could not forget—yet she was scared to, scared that even a glimpse of his face on her computer screen would have her picking up the phone to beg.

That was how much she still missed him.

Sometimes she grew angry, and wanted to contact him so that they could initiate the divorce, but that would be just an excuse to ring him. Meg knew she didn't need to speak with him to divorce him, yet she had not even started the simple process, because once she started down that path it would stop being a dream—which sometimes she thought it must have been...

Then her fingers would move to the cool metal of his ring and she'd find out again it was real.

She looked up at the clock and saw that it was time for lunch. Grateful for the chance of some fresh air while she worked out exactly how to tell her parents she was leaving the family business, Meg was tempted to ignore the ringing phone.

She wished she had when she answered it, because some new clients had arrived and were insisting that they be seen immediately.

'Not without an appointment.' Meg shook her head. She was fed up with pushy clients and the continual access she was expected to provide. 'I'm going to lunch.'

'I've told them that you're about to go for lunch.' Helen sounded flustered. 'But they said that they would wait till you get back. They are adamant that they see you today.'

Meg was sick of that word—everyone was *adamant* these days, and because there wasn't much work around her parents insisted more and more that they must jump to potential clients' unreasonable demands.

'Just tell them that they need to book,' Meg said, but as she went to end the call she froze when she heard a certain name.

A name that had her blood running simultaneously hot and cold.

Cold because she had dreaded this day—dreaded their worlds colliding, dreaded the one mistake in her crafted life coming back to haunt her—but at the same time hot for the memories the name Dos Santos triggered.

'He's here?' Meg croaked. 'Niklas is here?'

'No,' Helen answered, and Meg was frustrated at her own disappointment when she heard that it wasn't him. 'It's *regarding* a Mr Dos Santos, apparently, and these people really are insistent…'

'Tell them to give me a moment.'

She needed that moment. Meg really did.

She sank into her chair and poured a drink of water, willed herself to calm down, and then she checked her appearance in the mirror that she kept in her drawer. Her hair was neatly tied back and though her face was a touch pale she looked fairly composed—except Meg could see her own eyes were darting with fear.

There was nothing to fear, Meg told herself. It wasn't

trouble that had arrived. It had been almost a year after all. No doubt his legal team were here to get her signature on divorce papers. She closed her eyes and tried to calm herself, but it didn't help because all she could see was herself and Niklas, a tangle of legs and arms on a bed, and the man who had taken her heart with him when he left. Now it really was coming to an end.

She stood as Helen brought her visitors in and sorted out chairs for them. Then Helen offered water or coffee, which all three politely declined, and finally, when Helen had left and the door was closed, Meg addressed them.

'You wanted to see me?'

'First we should introduce ourselves.'

A well-spoken gentleman started things off. He introduced himself and his colleague and then Rosa, a woman whom Meg thought might be around forty, took over. It was terribly difficult to tell her age. She was incredibly elegant, her make-up and hair completely immaculate, her voice as richly accented as Niklas's had been, and it hurt to hear the familiar tone—familiar because it played over and over each night in her dreams. But she tried not to think of that, tried to concentrate on Rosa as she told Meg that they worked at the legal firm Mr Dos Santos used. She went through their qualifications and their business structure, and as she did so Meg felt her own qualifications dissolve beneath her—these were high-end lawyers and clearly here to do business. But Meg still didn't understand why Niklas had felt it necessary to fly three of his most powerful lawyers all the way to Australia, simply to oversee their divorce.

A letter would have sufficed.

'First and foremost,' Rosa started, 'before we go any further, we ask for discretion.'

They were possibly the sweetest words that Meg could hope to hear in this situation.

'Of course' was her response, but that wasn't enough for Rosa.

'We *insist* on your absolute discretion,' Rosa reiterated, and for the first time Meg felt her hackles rise.

'I would need to know what you're here in regard to before I can make an assurance like that.'

'You are married to Niklas Dos Santos?'

'I think we all know that,' Meg said carefully.

'And do you know that your husband is facing serious charges of embezzlement and fraud?'

Ice slid down her spine. Her hackles were definitely up now, and Meg thought for a moment before answering, 'I had no idea.'

'If he is found guilty he will probably never be released.'

Meg ran her tongue over her lips and tasted the wax of the lipstick she had applied earlier. She could feel beads of sweat breaking out on her forehead and felt nauseous at the very thought of a man like Niklas confined and constricted. She felt sick, too, at the thought of what he must have done to face serving life behind bars.

'He is innocent.' The man who had first introduced

them spoke then, and Meg couldn't help raising one of her eyebrows, but she made no comment.

Of course his own people would say that he was innocent.

They were his lawyers after all.

She didn't look at Rosa when she spoke. Instead she examined her nails, tried incredibly hard to stop her fingers from reaching for her hair. She did not want to give them any hint that she was nervous.

'We believe that Niklas is being set up.'

What else would they say? Meg thought.

'I really don't see what this has to do with me.' Meg looked in turn at each of the unmoved faces and was impressed by her own voice when she spoke. She possibly sounded like a lawyer, or a woman in control, though of course inside she was not. 'We were married for less than twenty-four hours and then Niklas decided that it was a mistake. Clearly he was right. We hardly knew each other. I had no idea about any of his business affairs. Nothing like that was ever discussed…'

Rosa spoke over her. 'We believe that Niklas is being set up by the head of our firm.'

It was then that Meg started to realise the gravity of the situation. These people were not just defending their client, they were implicating their own principal.

'We have had little access to the case, which in something as big as this is unusual, and without access to the evidence we cannot supply a rigorous defence. For reasons we cannot yet work out, we believe Miguel is intending to misrepresent Niklas. Of course we cannot let our boss know that we suspect him. He is the only one who has access to Niklas while he is being held awaiting a trial date.'

'He's in prison now?'

'He has been for months.'

Meg reached for her water but her glass was empty. Her hands were shaking as she refilled it from the jug. She could not stand the thought of him locked up, could not bear to think of him in prison, did not want those thoughts haunting her. She didn't like the new night-mares these people had brought, and she wanted them gone now.

'It really is appalling, but...' She didn't know how she could help them—didn't know the Brazilian legal system, just didn't know why they were here. 'I don't see how it has anything to do with me. As I said, I'm not involved in his business...' And then she started to panic, because maybe as his wife she had a different involvement with Niklas that they were here to discuss.

'We have made an application of behalf of Niklas for him to exercise his conjugal rights...'

Meg could hear her own pulse pounding in her ears as Rosa continued speaking and she drained her second glass of water. Her throat was still impossibly dry. Her fingers moved to her hair and she twirled the strand around one finger, over and over.

'Niklas is entitled to one phone call a week and a two-hour conjugal visit once every three weeks. He is being brought before the judge in a fortnight for the trial date to be set and we need you to fly there. At your visit with him on Thursday you are to tell him that only when he is in front of the judge he is to fire his lawyer. Before that he is to give no hint. Once he has fired Miguel we will step in for him.'

'No.' Meg shook her head and pulled her finger out of her hair. She was certain of her answer, did not need to think about this for a moment. She just wanted them gone.

'The only way we can get in contact with him is through his wife.'

'I'll phone him.' It was the most she would do. 'You said that he was entitled to a weekly phone call...' And then she shook her head again, because of course the calls would be monitored. 'I can't see him.' She could not. 'We were married for twenty-four hours.'

'Correct me if I am wrong...' Rosa was as tough with the truth as she was direct. 'According to the records we have found you have been married for almost a year.'

'Yes, but we—'

'There has been no divorce?'

'No.'

'And if Niklas was dead and I was here bringing you a cheque would you hand it back and say, *No, we were only married for twenty-four hours? Would you say, No, give this to someone else. He had nothing to do with me...?*'

Meg's face was red as she fought for an answer, but she did not know that truth—not that it stopped Rosa.

'And because you have not screamed annulment I am assuming consensual sex occurred.'

Meg felt her face grow redder, because sex had been the only thing they had had between them.

'If you had found yourself pregnant, would you not have contacted him? Would you have told yourself it did not count as you were only married for twenty-four hours? Would you have told your child the same...?'

'You're not being fair.'

'Neither is the system being fair to my client,' Rosa said. 'Your husband will be convicted of a crime he did not commit if you do not get this message to him.'

'So I'm supposed to fly to Brazil and sit in some trailer or cell and pretend that we're...?'

'There will be no pretending—you *will* have sex with him,' Rosa said. 'I don't think you understand what is at stake here, and I don't think you understand the risks to Niklas and his case if it is discovered that we are trying to get information in. There will be suspicions if the bed and the bin...'

Thankfully she did not go into further detail, but it was enough to have Meg shake her head.

'I've heard enough, thank you. I will start preparing the paperwork for divorce today.' She stood.

They did not.

'Marrying Niklas was the biggest mistake of my life,' Meg stated. 'I have no intention of revisiting it and I'm certainly not...' She shook her head. 'No. We were a mistake.'

'Niklas never makes mistakes,' Rosa countered. 'That is why we know he is innocent. That is why we have been working behind our own principal's back to ensure justice for him.' She looked to Meg. 'You are his only chance, and whether or not it is pleasant, whether or not you feel it is beneath you, this *must* happen.'

She handed her an envelope and Meg opened it to find an itinerary and airline tickets.

'There is a flight booked for you tomorrow night.'

'I have a life,' Meg flared. 'A job, commitments...'

'A visit has been approved for Thursday. It is the only chance to make contact with him before the pre-trial hearing in two weeks' time. After you have seen him you can go to Hawaii—though we might need you to go back for another visit in three weeks, if things don't go well.'

'No.' How else could she say it? 'I won't do it.'

Rosa remained unmoved. 'You may want this all to go away, but it cannot. Niklas deserves this chance and he will get it. You will see, when you check your bank account, that you are being well compensated for your time.'

'Excuse me?' Meg was furious. 'How dare you? How on earth did you...?' But it wasn't about how they had found out her bank details. It wasn't that that was the problem right now. 'It's not about money...'

'So it's the morality of it, then?' Rosa questioned. 'You're too precious to sleep with your own husband even it means he has to spend the rest of his life behind bars?'

Rosa made it sound so simple.

'For the biggest mistake of your life, you chose rather

well, did you not?' Rosa sneered. 'You are being paid to sleep with Niklas—it's hardly a hardship.'

Meg met her eyes and was positive that he and Rosa had slept together. They both stared for a moment, lost in their own private thoughts. Then Rosa stood, a curl on her lip, and another sassy Brazilian gave her opinion of Meg as she upended her life.

'You need to get over yourself.'

CHAPTER SEVEN

When they had gone, Meg did what she had spent a year avoiding.

She looked up the man she had married and found out just how powerful he was—or had been before he had been charged. She understood now that the Niklas Dos Santos she was reading about would be less than impressed to find himself in business class. And then she read about the shock his arrest had caused. Niklas might have a reputation in business as being ruthless, but he had always seemed honest—which was apparently why it had made it so easy for him to con some high-flying people into parting with millions. They had believed the lies that had been told to them. His business peers' trust in him had made them gullible, and despite Rosa's and her colleagues' protestations of his innocence, for Meg the articles cast doubt.

She knew, after all, how effortlessly he had read *her*, how easily he had played *her*. Meg had seen another side to Niklas and it wasn't one she liked.

And yet, as Rosa had pointed out, he was her husband, and she was apparently his one hope of receiving a fair trial.

And then Meg clicked on images and wished she had not.

The first one she saw was of him handcuffed and being bundled into a police car.

There were many more of Niklas, but they were not of the man she knew. The suit was on and the tie was beautifully knotted, the hair was as she remembered, but not in one single image did she see him smiling or laughing. Not one single picture captured the Niklas she had so briefly known.

And then she found another image—one that proved the most painful of all to see.

His arrogant face was scowling, there were three scratches on his cheek that her nails had left there, and a deep bruise on his neck that her mouth had made. Meg read the headline: *Dos Santos vira outra mulher!* Meg clicked for a translation. She wanted to know if he had returned that morning and been arrested—wanted to know if that was the reason he had been so cruel to her. Had he known he was about to be arrested and ended it to protect her? She waited for the translation to confirm it, held her breath as it appeared: *Dos Santos upsets another woman!*

And even in prison, even locked up and a world away, somehow he broke her heart again.

There was a knock at the door. Her mother didn't wait for an answer, just opened it and came in. 'Helen said you had visitors?'

'I did.'

'Who were they?'

'Friends.'

She saw her mum purse her lips and knew she would not leave until she found out who her friends were and what they wanted. Even without the arrival of her visitors Meg remembered she had been due for a difficult conversation with her parents today, and now seemed like a good time to get it over with.

'Can you get Dad...?' Meg gave her mum a pale smile. 'I need to speak to you both.'

It didn't go well.

'After all we've done for you' was the running theme, and the words Meg had expected to hear when she told them that she had chosen not to continue working in the family firm.

She didn't mention Niklas. It was enough for them to take in without giving them the added bonus of a son-in-law! And one in prison too.

It should have been a far harder conversation to have, yet she felt as if all her emotions and fears were reserved for the decision that was still to come, and Meg sat through the difficult conversation with her parents pale and upset, but somehow detached.

'Why would you want to be a chef?' Her mother simply didn't get it—didn't get that her daughter could possibly want something that had not been chosen for her. 'You're a lawyer, for God's sake, and you want to go and work in some kitchen—?'

'I don't know exactly what I want to do,' Meg broke in. 'I don't even know if I'll be accepted…'

'Then why would you give it all up?'

And she didn't know how to answer—didn't know how to tell them that she didn't feel as if she was actually giving up *anything*, that she was instead taking back her life.

Just not yet.

She told them she was taking a holiday, though she still wasn't sure that she was, but even without Niklas looming large in her thoughts taking a few weeks off while her parents calmed down seemed sensible.

'And then I'll come back and work for a couple of months,' Meg said. 'I'm not going to just up and leave…'

But according to her parents she already had.

Later, as she sat on the balcony of her small flat and looked at the stunning view, Meg thought about her day. What should have been a difficult conversation with her parents, what should have her sitting at home racked with guilt and wondering if she'd handled things right, barely entered her thoughts now. Instead she focused on the more pressing problem looming ahead.

Quietly she sat and examined the three things she had that proved her relationship with Niklas had actually existed.

She took the ring from the chain around her neck and remembered the certainty she had felt when he had slipped it on—even though he had told her it could never be for ever, somehow she had felt it was right.

And then she picked up the marriage certificate she

had retrieved from her bedside table and examined the dark scrawl of his signature. *Niklas Dos Santos*. She saw the full stop at the end of his name and could even hear the sound his pen had made as he'd dotted the document.

Finalised it.

And then she examined the third thing, the most painful thing—a heart that even eleven months on was still exquisitely tender.

There had been no one since, no thought of another man since that time. She felt dizzy as she peered into her feelings, scared as to what she might find. The truth was there waiting and she hadn't wanted to see it. It hurt too much to admit it.

She loved him.

Or rather she had.

Absolutely she had, or she would never have married him. Meg knew that deep down. And, whether or not he had wanted it, still that love had existed. Her very brief marriage with him had for Meg been the real thing.

And, as Rosa had pointed out, they *were* still married.

It was getting cool, so Meg went inside and read the itinerary Rosa had handed her. Then she looked up the prison he was being held at and could not believe that he was even there, let alone that on Thursday she might be too.

Would be.

Meg slid the ring back on her finger.

A difficult decision, but somehow easily made. Yes, Rosa was right. In legal terms he was still her husband.

But it wasn't in legal terms only that she made her choice. There was a part of herself that she must soon sort out, must work out how to get over, but for now at least, in every sense, Niklas was still her husband.

Though her hotel and flights had been arranged, any problems had to be dealt with by the travel agent, Rosa had told her. Meg must not, under any circumstance, make contact with them. She must not be linked to them in any way—not just to protect them, or even Niklas, they had warned her, but to protect herself.

And she registered the danger but tried not to dwell on it, just tried to deal with a life that had changed all over again.

There was another row with her parents—a huge one this time. They had no comprehension as to why their usually sensible daughter might suddenly up and take off to Brazil.

'Brazil!' Her mother had just gaped. 'Why the hell do you want to go to Brazil?'

They didn't come to the airport to say goodbye. Still, there was one teeny positive to the whole situation: Meg barely noticed the plane taking off. Her thoughts were too taken up with the fact that she was on her way to see Niklas.

And she barely noticed it a second time, when she transferred at Santiago and knew she was on the last leg of her journey to see him. Shortly after take-off the stewards stood, and after a little while she was offered a drink.

'Tonic water...' Meg said, and then changed her mind and added gin.

'Off on holiday?'

She turned to her friendly fellow passenger, an elderly lady who had cousins in São Paulo, she told Meg.

'Yes...' Meg said. 'Sort of.'

'Visiting family?'

'My husband.' How strange it felt to say it, but she was, after all, wearing his ring, and her documents were in her bag, and she might have to say the same thing at Customs, so maybe she'd better start practising.

'Brazil first and then three weeks in Hawaii...'

'Lovely.' The old lady smiled and Meg returned it. Just as Niklas had that first day, she wished her neighbour would just keep quiet.

She could hardly tell her the real purpose for her visit!

Instead she ordered another gin.

It didn't help.

She cried as they descended over São Paulo—she had never seen anything like it. Stretched below her was a sea of city, endless miles of buildings and skyscrapers. The population of this city alone was almost equivalent to the entire population of Australia, and never had Meg felt more small and lost.

The final approach was terrifying—more so because of all he had told her about it, more so now that she could see just how closely the cars and the planes and the city co-existed, more so because she was actually here.

Bizarrely, her eyes searched for him after she'd cleared Customs—a stupid flare of hope that this was a strange joke, that he was testing her, that he might be waiting with flowers and a kiss. Perhaps she might once more feel the thorns press into her skin as he teased her about the lengths she'd go to for just a couple of hours with him.

It wasn't a joke, though. It wasn't a game. There was no one here to greet her.

Meg exited the airport and tried to hire a taxi, but she had never seen a taxi queue like this one. She was exhausted and overwhelmed as once again Niklas pushed her out of her comfort zone.

The driver's music was loud, his windows were down, and he drove her through darkening streets into Jardins. Everything was loud there too. The city pulsed with life. There were food stalls on the streets—unfamiliar scents came in through the windows of the car whenever they stopped at traffic lights—and it was more city than she could deal with. Which made sense, Meg thought with a pale smile. After all it was the city Niklas was from.

All Meg wanted to do was to get to her room.

Dishevelled, confused, *tired*, after they pulled up at a very tall hotel Meg paid the taxi driver. The second she stepped inside she knew she was back in his world.

Modern, cosmopolitan, with staff exquisite and beautiful.

It was a relief to get to her room and look out of the window at the bewildering streets below, to fathom that she was actually here—that tomorrow she would be taking another taxi to visit Niklas in prison.

Meg scanned the confusing horizon, wondered as to his direction, wondered if he had any inkling at all that she was even here.

Wondered all night how she could stand to face him tomorrow.

'Hi, Mum…' She rang not because they had insisted she did—they were hardly talking, after all—she rang because, despite their problems, Meg loved her parents and wanted the sound of normality tonight.

'How's Brazil?' Her mother's voice was terse, but at least she spoke.

'Amazing,' Meg said. 'Though I haven't seen much of it…'

'Have you booked any trips?'

'Not yet,' Meg said, and was quiet for a moment. She didn't like lying, especially to her parents, but she found herself doing it at every turn. Tomorrow she would be ringing her parents again to tell them that she had changed her mind about Brazil and was going to spend the rest of her vacation in Hawaii—how would they react to that?

More than anything Meg just wanted tomorrow over with, so that she could lie on a beach and hopefully heal once and for all. She hadn't dared risk putting her divorce application in her luggage in case it caused questions at Customs, but the second she landed home it would be posted.

Her heart couldn't take any more of him.

'How's Dad?'

'Worried,' her mum said, and Meg felt her heart sink—because she hated that they were worried about her. 'It's going to cost an arm and a leg to hire a new lawyer...'

Meg knew her mum didn't mean to hurt her, but unintentionally she had. The business was always the biggest thing on their minds.

'I've told you that I'll work for a couple of months when I get back. You don't have to rush into anything. And you don't need a full-time lawyer; you can contract out. We'll go through it all properly when I get back.'

'You *are* coming back?'

And Meg gave a small unseen smile, because maybe it wasn't just about the business. As difficult as they could be at times, they did want what they thought was best for her, and they did love her—that much Meg knew.

'Of course I am. I'm just taking a few weeks to sort out my head—I'll be back before you know it.'

It was impossible to sleep. She was dreading tomorrow and seeing him again, dreading the impact of seeing him face to face. It was emotionally draining just thinking about him, let alone seeing him.

Let alone having sex with him.

If Meg slept, she didn't sleep much, and she was up long before her alarm call. She ordered breakfast, but her stomach was doing somersaults and she could hardly manage to hold down a small piece of bread and grilled cheese.

The coffee she was more grateful for.

Had she not loved him, she doubted she could do this.

But had she not loved him she would not have married him in the first place and wouldn't be in this mess.

Except she remembered his cruel words from that morning long ago and knew that love had no place in this.

She gave up on breakfast and lay in the bath, tried to prepare herself for what lay ahead, but had no idea how. As she picked up a razor and shaved her legs she did not know if her actions were for his pleasure or for her pride. It was the same with the body oil she rubbed in. She wore simple flesh-coloured underwear and an olive green shift dress with flat leather sandals. Her hand was shaking too much to bother with make-up so she gave in.

Rosa had given her the name of a good car company to use, rather than getting a taxi, and the desk rang to tell her that her driver was here. As she left the room she glanced around and wondered how she would feel when she returned. This time tomorrow she would be on a plane on her way to Hawaii. This time tomorrow it would be done—for despite what Rosa had said she would not be returning to him.

Once was enough.

Twice might kill her.

So she looked at her room and tried not to think too much about what had to happen before she returned.

They drove through the most diverse of cities, passed the Court of Justice, where in two weeks Niklas would be, and in daylight Meg saw more of this stunning city. There was beauty and wealth, and such poverty too. She thought of Niklas growing up on the streets, and of how much he had made of himself only to fall. She didn't know enough to believe in his innocence. She might be a fool for love, but she wasn't a blind fool. Still, he deserved a fair trial.

Meg had never known such fear in her life as they approached the jail. The sight of the watchtower, the sounds when she entered, the shame of the examination... Her papers were examined and her photograph taken and she was told her rights—or rather her husband's rights. She could return in three weeks; she could ring him once a week at a designated time and speak for ten minutes. And although Meg took the paper with the telephone number on it, she knew that she would never use it.

Then a female guard examined her for contraband and Meg closed her eyes, thinking she would spit at her if she ever faced Rosa again, before being allowed to pull her knickers back up. Maybe she did need to get over herself, but as she was led through to an area where two guards chatted she heard the Dos Santos name said a few times, and even if Meg didn't understand precisely what they were saying she got their lewd drift. As she stood waiting for Niklas to arrive Meg knew that, yes, she might have to get over herself—but right about now she was completely over *him*.

CHAPTER EIGHT

THE SLOT ON the door opened and lunch was delivered. Niklas ate beans and rice. It was tepid and bland and there were no herbs to pick out, but he was hungry and cleared his plate in silence.

His cellmate did the same.

It was how they both survived.

He refused to let the constant noise and shouts from other inmates rile him. He made no comment or complaint about the bland food and the filth. From the first day he had arrived here, apart from the odd necessary word, he had been silent, had conformed to the system though some of the guards had tried to goad him.

As he had entered the jail they had told him of the cellmate they had for him, of the beatings he could expect. They'd told the rich boy just how bad things would be in there for him as he'd removed his suit and shoes and then his watch and jewellry before they searched him and then hosed him.

Niklas had said nothing.

He had been hosed many times before.

There was no mirror to look in, so after his hair was shaved he'd just run a hand over his head. He wore the rough denim without real thought. He had worn harsher clothes and been filthier and hungrier than this on many occasion.

Niklas was streetwise. He had grown up in the toughest place and survived it. He had come from nothing and he'd returned to nothing—as he had always silently feared that he would. This anonymous, brutal world was one that he belonged in, and the one he truly deserved. Perhaps this was actually his home, Niklas had realised—not ten thousand feet in the air, swigging champagne as caviar popped in his mouth; not considering a home in the mountains and a family to take care of. He had been a fool to glimpse it, a fool to let down his guard, for those things were not his to know.

Assets frozen, friends and colleagues doubting him... The eventual snap of cuffs on his wrists had provided temporary relief as Niklas went back to the harsh world he had known one day would reclaim him. He'd returned to another system and navigated it seemingly with ease. But the temporary relief had soon faded and a sense of injustice had started to creep in. His head felt as if it would explode at times, and his body was so wired that he was sure he could rip the bars from the cell window with his bare hands or catch bullets with his teeth—but then, as he had long ago taught himself to, he simply turned those thoughts off.

Not for a second did he show his anger, and rarely did he speak.

His cellmate was one the most feared men in the prison. He ran the place and had contacts both inside and out. The guards had thought it would be like two bulls put in the same paddock. The motto of São Paulo was *I am not led. I lead.* So they had put the rich boy who led the business world in with the man who led the inmates and had waited for sobs from Dos Santos. But Niklas had held Fernando's eyes and nodded when he had been placed in his cell. He had said good evening and got no answer, and from that point on Niklas had said nothing more to him. He had ignored his cellmate—as suited Fernando, as suited him—and over the months the tension had dissipated. The silence between the two inmates was now amicable; both men respected the other's privacy, in a friendship of no words.

Niklas finished his lunch. He would exercise soon.

They had not been let out to the yard in over a week, so in a moment he would use the floor to exercise. He paced himself, sticking to routines to hold onto his mind. For while he slotted in with the system, while he followed the prison rules, more and more he was starting to reject them. Inside a slow anger had long been building and it was one that must not explode, because he wanted to be here when his trial date was set—did not want solitary till then.

He lay on his bunk and tried not to build up too much hope that he might be bailed in a fortnight, when he appeared for the pre-trial hearing. Miguel had told him that he thought bail was unlikely—there were too many high-profile people involved who did not want him to have freedom.

'But there is no one involved,' Niklas had pointed out at their last meeting. 'Because I did not do anything. That is what you are supposed to prove.'

'And we will,' Miguel said.

'Where's Rosa?' Niklas had asked to see Rosa at this visit. He liked her straight talking, wanted to hear her take on things, but yet again it was Miguel who had come to meet with him.

'She...' Miguel looked uncomfortable. 'She wants to see you,' he said. 'I asked her to come in, but...'

'But what?'

'Silvio,' Miguel said. 'He does not want her in here with you.'

And Niklas got that.

Rosa's husband, Silvio, had complained about Rosa working for him. Niklas and Rosa had once been an item for a few weeks, just before she had met Silvio, and though there was nothing between them now, her working for Niklas still caused a few problems.

As he lay there replaying conversations, because that was all he was able to do in this place, Niklas conceded that Silvio was right not to want Rosa to visit him here.

Nothing would happen between them, but it was not just Rosa's sharp insight he wanted. The place stank of testosterone, of confined angry male, and Rosa was open enough to understand that his eyes would roam. She would let them, and he knew that she would dress well for him.

He tried not to think of Meg—did not want even an image of her in this place—but of course it was impossible not to think of her.

As his mind started to drift he turned those thoughts off and hauled them back to his pre-trial hearing. His frustration at the lack of progress was building—his frustration at everything was nearing breaking point.

He climbed down from his bunk and started doing sit-ups, counting in his head. And then he changed to push-ups, and for those he did not bother to count. He would just work till his body ached. But anger was still building. He wanted to be on the outside—not just for freedom but because there he could control things, and he could control nothing here except his small routines. So he kept on doing his sit-ups and as a guard came to the door Niklas carried on, ignoring the jeering, just kept on with his workout.

'Lucky man, Dos Santos.'

He did not miss a beat, just continued his exercise.

'Who did you pay?'

Still Niklas did not answer.

'You have a beautiful wife.'

Only then did he pause, just for a second, mid-push-up, before carrying on. The guard didn't know what he was talking about. No one knew of Meg—they were winding him up, messing with his head, and he chose not to respond.

'She's here waiting to see you.'

And then the slot in the door opened and he was told to get up. There was no choice now but to do as he was told. So Niklas stood, met Fernando's eyes for just a second, which was rare. The change in routine was notable for both of them.

Niklas put his hands through the slot and handcuffs were applied, then he pulled his cuffed wrists back as the cell door was opened. He walked along the corridor and down metal steps, heard the jeers and taunts and crude remarks as he walked past. There were a couple of shoves from the guard but Niklas did not react, just kept on walking while trying to work things out.

Miguel must have arranged a hooker, finally pulled a few strings.

Thank God.

Maybe now his mind would hold till the trial date.

Not that he showed any emotion as they walked. He'd learnt that many years ago.

Show weakness and you lose—he'd learnt that at eight.

He had walked through the new orphanage he'd been sent to—he had been on his third orphanage by then—and this one was by far the worst. Still, there was good news, he had been told—his new family were waiting to meet him. A beautiful family, the worker had told him. They were rich, well fed and well dressed and had everything they wanted in the world except children. More than anything they wanted a son and had chosen Niklas.

His heart had leapt in hope. He'd hated the orphanage, a rough home for boys where the staff were often cruel, and he had been grinning and excited as the door had been pushed open and he had prepared himself to meet his new family.

How the workers waiting for him in there had laughed at his tears—how they had jeered him, enjoying their little joke long into the night. How could he have been so bold as to think that a family might want him?

It was the very last time that Niklas had cried.

His last display of true emotion.

Now he kept it all inside.

He would not give the prison guards the same pleasure. Whatever their plan, he would not give them the satisfaction of reading his face.

But then he saw her.

It had not properly entered his head that it might actually be Meg.

He had not allowed it to.

She did not belong in here. That was his first thought as he saw her dressed in a linin shift dress. Her hair burned gold and copper, the colour of the sun at night through his cell window, and then he saw the anxiety in her eyes turn to horror as she took in the shaved head and the rough clothing. A lash of shame tore through him that he should be seen by her like this, and his expression slipped for just a second. He stared ahead as his cuffs were removed, and though he remained silent his mind raced. To the left was Andros, the guard he trusted the least, and he thought again how Meg did not belong here. He wanted to know who the hell had arranged this, who had approved this visit, for even though he was confined and locked up he still had a system in place, and he had told Miguel that everything was to be run by him.

He could feel Andros watching as she walked towards him, heard the fear and anxiety in her voice as she spoke.

'I've missed you so much.'

She was playing a part. Niklas got that. But as her lips met his cheek it did not matter. Her touch was the first reprieve for his senses in months. Her skin on his cheek was so soft that the contact actually shocked him. He wanted to know the hows and whys of her visit here, wanted to know exactly what was going on, yet his first instinct was not to kiss her, but to protect her—and that meant that he too must play a part, for Andros was watching.

It was a kiss for others, and his mind tried to keep it at that—except her breath tasted of the outside and he drank her in. The feel of her in his arms allowed temporary escape and it was Meg who pulled back.

Meg stood with her cheeks burning red, tears of shame and hurt and anger in her eyes, and her lips pressed closed as one guard said something that made the other laugh. Then a door opened and they walked into a small, simply furnished room. The guard shouted something to them, and whatever language you spoke it was crude, before closing the door behind them. Meg stood and then realised that she couldn't stand for very much longer, so she sat on a chair for a moment, honestly shaken.

It wasn't just shock at the sight of him—seeing Niklas with his hair cropped almost as short as the dark stubble on his chin, dressed in rough prison denim. Even like this he was still the most beautiful man she had ever seen. It was not just the shock that she had again tasted his mouth, felt his skin against hers, relighting all those memories from their one night together. It was everything: the whole journey here, the poverty in the streets she had driven through, the sight of the prison as she had approached, the watchtower and the guns on the guards and the shame of the strip-search. Surely all of those things had severed any feelings she had for him?

But, no, for then she'd had to deal with the impact of seeing him again, of tasting him. For a moment she just sat there and wondered how, after all she had been through, she could still hear her heart hammer in relief to be back at his side. She wanted to be over him—had to be for sanity's sake—so she tried not to look at him, just drank from the glass of water he offered her.

He stood and watched her and saw her shock, saw what just a little while in this place had done to her, and thought again how she did not belong here.

'Why?' He knelt down beside her and spoke in a rough whisper. 'Why would you come here?'

She didn't answer him—Meg couldn't open her mouth to speak.

'Why?' he demanded, and then she looked at him and he was reminded of the last time he had seen her. Because even with the absence of her bared teeth he could feel her anger, could see her green eyes flash with suppressed rage and hear the spit of her words when finally she answered him.

'You're *entitled* to me, apparently.'

Niklas remembered the first time he had met her. She had been anxious, but happy, and he knew that it was he who had reduced her to this. He could see the pain and the disgust in her eyes as she looked at the man she had married, as she saw the nothing he really was.

And he did not want her charity.

'Thanks, but no thanks.'

He moved to the door, preparing to call for the guards. He might regret it later, but he did not want a minute more in this room.

As he moved to go he heard her voice.

'Niklas.' She halted him. This was not about what had happened between them, not about scoring points, she was here for one reason only. 'Your people told me...' He turned to face her. 'I'm to tell you...'

He silenced her by pressing his finger to his lips and nodded to the door. He trusted no one—never had in his life, and wasn't about to start in here. But then he closed his eyes for a second, for that was wrong. Because for a while he had trusted *her*, and did still. He came over to her, knelt down again and moved his head to her mouth, so she could quietly tell him the little she knew.

'Miguel is working against you. You are to ask for a change of representation at your trial...'

His head pulled back and she watched as he took in the news. Quietly she told him the little she knew. His face was grey and his eyes shone black. He swallowed as if tasting bile and she heard his rapid angry breathing. His whisper was harsh when it came.

'*No.*'

It had to be a lie, because if his own lawyer was working against him he was here for life.

She *had* to be lying.

'How?' he demanded. 'Why?'

'I don't know anything more than that,' Meg said. 'It's all I've been told.'

'When?' he insisted, his voice an angry whisper. 'When were you told?'

And she told him about the visit—how on Monday morning Rosa and her colleagues had arrived at her place of work. He thought of her momentarily in Sydney, getting on with her life without him, and now here she was in Brazil.

'They should never have sent you...' He was livid. 'It's too dangerous...'

'It's fine...'

It was so *not* fine.

'Niklas...' She told him *all* they had told her—that they had to have sex, about the bed and the bin, and that the guards could not know she was here for any other reason.

He saw her face burn in shame, and she saw his disgust at what he had put her through.

'It's fine, Niklas,' she whispered. 'I know what I'm doing...' She could feel his fury; it was there in the room with them.

'You should not be here.'

'It's my decision.'

'Then it's the wrong one.'

'I'm very good at making those around you, it would seem. Anyway,' she whispered harshly, 'you don't have to worry—you're paying me well…'

'How much?'

She told him.

And he knew then the gravity of his situation, understood just how serious this was—because he had no money any more. Everything had been frozen. He thought of his legal team paying her with money of their own and it tempered the bitterness that sometimes consumed him a little. Then he looked at the woman he might even have loved and tasted bitterness one again, for he hated what the world had done to him.

'So you're not here out of the goodness of your heart?'

'You've already had that part,' Meg said. 'So can we just get it over with?'

She looked over to the bed and he saw the swallowing in her throat, knew that she was drenched in fear. He looked to the door again, knowing there was a guard outside, one he did not trust, who must never get so much as a hint as to the real reason she was here.

Paid to be here, Niklas reminded himself.

He trusted no one again.

He stood and ripped the sheet from the bed, and she sat there as he twisted it in his hands before throwing it back. She heard his anger as he took the bedhead in angry hands and rocked the bed against the wall. He felt his anger building as he slammed the bed faster and faster. He had never paid for sex in his life. Yes, he'd have been grateful for a hooker, but he'd never taken Meg as one and his head was pounding as the bed hit the wall again and again. He did not know who to believe any more, and as the bed slammed faster he shouted out.

Meg sobbed as he shouted, but it did nothing to dissipate the fury still building, and then he picked up the condoms by the bedside and went to the small wash area and got to work to make sure evidence of their coupling was in place. Meg sat there, listening and crying. She understood his anger but she did not understand her own self, for even here, amidst this filth and shame, she wanted him. So badly she wanted to be with the man she had so sorely missed. Not just the sex, but the comfort he somehow gave.

'Niklas...' She walked into the washroom and ignored him when he told her, less than politely, to go away. His back was to her. She moved to his side and saw his fury, saw his hand working fast. He repeated his demand for her to leave him, and when it was clear that she didn't understand just how much he meant the words he told her in French and then Spanish.

'How many ways do you need to hear it...?'

How deep was his shame to be seen like this, to be reduced to this? His back had been to Meg, for he could not face her, yet she'd slipped into the space between him and the wall and her mouth was on his. One of her hands joined his now.

'Leave me.'

'No.' She stroked him too.

'Leave me,' he said as her other hand slipped off her panties.

'No.'

And she put her hands around his neck and pressed herself against him, tried to kiss him. He spat her out.

'You don't know the fire you are playing with.'

'I want to, though.'

She wanted every piece of him—wanted a little more of what she could never fully have. Because a man like Niklas could only ever be on loan to her. She had flown to him not because she had to, not for the money, and not for the morality of doing the right thing by her husband. Purely because of him, and not once did his anger scare her.

Not once, as rough hands pulled her dress up, did she fear him.

He lifted her up and onto him and positioned her, pulling her roughly down to him. The most basic sex was their only release and she wrapped her legs tight around him, locked her arms around his neck. His kiss was violent now, and she felt the clash of their teeth and tongues and the rapid angry stabs of him. The rough feel of denim on her thighs was nothing compared to the roughness deep inside, and her back was hard against the wall. Meg could feel his anger, it blasted deep inside her, and it let Meg be angry too—angry at so many things: that she was here, that she still wanted him, even that this man still moved her so.

Her moans and shouts that he blocked with his mouth

shocked Meg even more—scared her, almost—but she was not scared of him as he pulled her down on him, as she felt the bruise of his fingers in her hips. She could feel her orgasm building rapidly, as if she had waited eleven months just to come to him, as if her body had been waiting for him to set it free.

There was a flash of confusion for Niklas too, for her cries and the grip of intimate muscles, the arch of her back and the spasm of her thighs, could never be faked. He had thought this was charity, a paid act at best, a sympathy screw at worst, but she was craving him again, the way she once had, and as he shot into her he remembered all the good again—the way they had been. He never cried, but he was as close to it now as he had ever been. They were both drenched in brief release and escape and his kisses turned softer now, to bring her back to him. Then he heard the drizzle of the tap and his eyes opened to his surroundings, to the reality they faced. There were no more kisses to be had and he lifted her off.

Stood her down.

But she would not lose him to his pride and she carried on kissing him, opened his shirt and put her palms to his chest. He felt as if her hands seared him, for there had been no contact, no touch of another on his skin for many months, and he loathed the exposure, the prying of her hands. It was just sex he wanted, not her, but her hands were still moving, exploring the defined muscles. Her fingers were a pleasure and he did not want her to be here—yet he wanted her for every second that they had.

There would be hours later for thinking, for working out what to do about Miguel. For now he wanted every minute he had left with her.

He took her to the bed and undressed her, took his clothes off too, and she looked at all the changes to his body. He was thinner, but more muscled, and his face wasn't the one she had turned to on the plane—it was closed and angry, and yet she had felt his pain back there, felt him slip into affection, and for a small moment had glimpsed the man she had once met.

'Is that why you ended things?' She looked over to him as he joined her on the bed, but he just lay and looked up at the ceiling. 'Did you find out the trouble you were in?'

'I didn't know then.' It would be easier for her if he lied.

'So what happened that morning to change things?'

'I spoke to my people at work, realised how much I had on...'

'I don't believe you.'

'Believe in your fairytale if you want.' Niklas shrugged.

'Are you going to tell me to grow up again?' she asked. 'Because I grew up a long time ago—long before you met me. I've realised that I wasn't being weak staying in my job—I simply won't ride roughshod over the people I care about. And I don't believe that you would either and,' she finished, 'I *do* believe that you cared about me.'

'Believe what you want to.'

'I will,' Meg said. 'And I care about you.'

'It makes no difference to me.'

She had been paid plenty to be here with him so he should turn and start things. She had told him what she had came to say and the clock was counting down. He should use every minute wisely. They should not bother with talking—there were more basic things to be getting on with. Except this was Meg, and she didn't know how to separate the two.

'How are you dealing with being in here? How—?' she started, but he soon interrupted.

'I was right the first time.' He turned to look at her face—the face he had first seen on a plane. 'You talk too much. And I don't want to talk about me.' But before he moved to kiss her he allowed himself the luxury of just one question. 'Are you still working for your parents?'

'I resigned...' Meg said. 'I'm trying to choose my course at the moment...'

'Good,' Niklas said. He should push her hand down to where he was hardening again, but first there was something else he wanted to know. 'Are you okay?'

'Of course.'

'Are you happy?'

'Working on it.'

'Do your parents know you are here?'

'They know that I am in Brazil...' he saw tears pool

in her eyes '…they don't know I have a husband that I'm visiting in prison.'

'You need to get away from here,' Niklas said. 'As soon as this visit is over.'

'I fly to Hawaii tomorrow.'

'Okay.' Tomorrow should be okay, he told himself, but he wasn't sure. 'Maybe change it to tonight…'

'I fly out at six a.m.'

He saw her grimace at the thought, remembered the first time they had met and the conversation they had had.

'How was your landing?' And for the first time he smiled. He didn't care how much they'd paid her, that she'd flown into Congonhas was enough for him to know that this had nothing to do with money.

'It wasn't so bad…' she attempted, and then told him the truth. 'I was petrified. I thought I was going to throw up. Although,' she added, 'that might have been the gin!'

He laughed, and so did she. He hadn't laughed for almost a year, but this afternoon he did. She kicked him and they fought for a bit—a nice fight, a friendly fight—and he took her back to when they'd been lovers so easily, far, far too easily. But, given this was the last time she would be here, she let him. No one could kiss like he did. It was quite simply perfect, and the feel of him hard in her hands was perfect too.

This time he would be gentle, Niklas decided, worried that he had been too rough before. He didn't just kiss her mouth, he kissed her everywhere—her hair and her ears and down to her neck, breathing in her scent. He kissed down to her waist and then further, to where he wanted to be. He had been too rough, for she was hot and swollen, but Meg lay there and felt his soft kiss and was lost to it.

When he couldn't hold on any more he reached for the condom that was a requirement in here. Her hands reached for it too, and he let her put it on, but before she did she kissed him there, and he closed his eyes as she did so. Two hours could never be enough for all they wanted to do. She slid it on. He should roll her over and take her, but he let her climb on top of him, because if he looked up to her hair and her body for a little while he could forget where he was.

And she looked down as she moved on him and knew exactly why she was here. She loved him. Still. Her real fear at coming here had nothing to do with the flight or the prison or the danger, it was *him*—because she'd known all along that this was the only way she would ever be over him.

She should be grilling him about his involvement in the charges, insisting she find out, or just lying on her back martyred as he took her, ready to get the hell out once he'd finished. Instead she'd told him she cared about him. Instead she was riding him, and his hands were busy elsewhere, roaming her body. He was watching her. She was moaning, and he told her to hush, for he would not give the guards the turn-on of the sounds that she made. He put his hand over her mouth and she licked it, bit it, and he pushed his fingers into her mouth.

He was coming, and so was she, and when the moment finally came she folded on top of him, buried his face with her hair, and he felt the silent scream inside her as she clutched him tightly over and over till it ended.

That was when she told him she loved him.

'You don't know me,' he said.

'I want to, though.'

'Divorce me,' he said, still inside her, and pulled her close. 'Send the papers to Rosa and I'll sign them.'

'I don't want to.'

'You do.'

She didn't.

'I can see you again in three weeks…' She was drunk on him. 'I can come to the trial.'

'You are to *leave*!'

'I can ring you on Wednesday each week…'

He was scared now as to what he'd unleashed. Scared not of her passion, but that she might stay.

'No.'

'I can. I'm allowed one phone call a week.'

He looked up at her and all he knew was that she was not coming back here. With his own lawyer working against him he was probably done. Here was where he would always be and he would not do this to her. Even with new lawyers, trials took for ever in Brazil. Even with the best legal team he would be here for years at best. He lifted her off him and swore in three languages when he saw the condom was shredded. 'Get the morning-after pill and when I speak with my new lawyers I will have them file for divorce…'

'No…'

'You are to go to Hawaii.'

'Niklas—'

The guards were knocking at the door. Their time was up. He stood and threw her clothes at her, telling her to dress quickly for he did not want them getting one single glimpse of her. She continued to argue with him as he picked up her bra and clipped it on her, before lifting each leg into her panties, followed by her dress, and even as he zipped it up still she argued.

'We're finished,' he told her.

And he wasted time telling her that they *had* to be over when he should have told her how dangerous this was, just how little he knew about what was going on, and that he was scared for her life. But the guards were here now and he could not say.

He gave her a brief kiss, his eyes urging her. 'Have a safe flight.'

CHAPTER NINE

SHE DIDN'T WANT to lie on a beach in Hawaii.

There could be no healing from him.

She wanted to be close to him, wanted to be there for his trial hearing at least. She hoped for a miracle.

He would not want her there. Meg knew that.

But he was her husband, and she could at least be here in the city for him. Could watch it on the news, could be close even if he didn't know it.

And then she could visit him again before she left. She did not want a divorce from him now, and she wanted one more visit to argue her case.

She was probably going insane, Meg realised as she cancelled Hawaii and stayed on in Brazil, but that was how he made her feel.

She ventured out onto the busy streets and toured the amazing city. The sights, the smells, the food, the noise—there was everything to meet her moods.

And without Niklas she might never have seen any of this—might never have visited the Pinacoteca, a stunning art museum, nor seen the sculptured garden beside it.

At first Meg did guided tours with lots of other tour-
ists around her, but gradually she tuned in to the energy
of the place, to the smiles and the thumbs-up from the
locals and ventured out more alone. She was glad to
be here—glad for everything she got to see, to hear, to
feel. Every little thing. She could have lived her whole
life and never tasted *pamonah*, and there were vendors
selling them everywhere—from the streets, from cars,
ringing triangles to alert they were here. The first time
Meg had bought one and had sunk her teeth into the new
taste of mashed and boiled corn she had been unable to
finish it. But the next day she had been back, drawn by
the strange sweet taste—inadvertently she'd bought sa-
voury, and found that was the one she liked best.

There were so many things to learn.

So badly she wanted to visit the mountains, to take
a trip to the rainforests Niklas had told her about, yet
it felt too painful to visit the mountains without him.

She didn't dare ring him that first week. Instead
when six p.m. on Wednesday neared she sat in a restaurant the concierge had told her was famed for its seafood
and ordered *feijoada*. Maybe it wasn't the same restaurant Niklas had told her about, but she felt as if angels
were feeding her soul and that she was right to be there.

As the days passed she fell more and more in love
with the city—the contrasts of it, the feel of it and the
sound of it. The people were the most beautiful and elegant she had seen, yet the poverty was confrontational.
It was a world that changed at every turn and she loved

the anonymity of being somewhere so huge, loved being lost in it, and for two weeks she was.

As instructed, she did not contact Rosa. The only people she spoke to were her parents, and she gave Niklas no indication that she was there until the night before his trial date.

His face was on the TV screen, a reporter was already outside the court, and Meg had worked out that *amanhã* meant tomorrow. Until *amanhã* she simply could not wait. She just had to hear his voice. She had fallen in love with a man who was in prison and she should be signing paperwork, should be happily divorced, should be grateful for the chance to resume her life—but instead she sat in her hotel room, staring at the phone...

Confused was all she was without him. The passion and love she felt for him only made real sense when he was near her and she had an overwhelming desire to talk to him. She counted down the moments until she could make that call.

He knew that she would call.

Niklas could feel it.

Andros came and got him from his cell and he sat by the phone at the allotted time. The need for her to be safe overrode any desire to hear her voice.

His teeth gritted when he heard the phone ring, and he wondered if he should let it remain unanswered, but he needed her to get the message—to get out of his life and leave him the hell alone.

And then he heard her voice and realised just how much he craved it, closed his eyes in unexpected relief just to hear the sound of her.

'I told you not to ring.'

'I just wanted to wish you good luck for tomorrow.'

'It is just to arrange a trial date...' He did not trust the phones. He did not trust himself. For now he wanted her to visit him again. He wanted her living in a house in the mountains right behind the prison and wanted her to ring him every Wednesday, to come in to see him every three weeks. What scared him the most was that she might do it. 'You did not need to ring for that. It will all be over in ten minutes.'

She understood the need to be careful. 'Even so, I hope they give you a date soon.'

'What are you doing now?'

'Talking to you.'

'Is everything okay?'

She knew what he was referring to—had seen his face when he'd removed the condom.

'It's fine.'

'Did you go to a *pharmacia*?'

He closed his eyes when she didn't answer, thought again of her in a home in the mountains, but this time he pictured her with his baby at her side and selfish hope glimmered.

'How's Hawaii?'

He heard her pause, heard that her voice was a little too high as she answered him. 'You know...' She attempted. 'Nice.'

'I *don't* know,' Niklas said, and it was not about what he wanted, it was not about him, it was about keeping her safe. His words were harsh now. 'I've never been and I want a postcard,' he said. 'I want you, *tonight*, to write me a postcard from Hawaii.'

He was telling her what to do and she knew it.

'Niklas,' she attempted, 'I still have some holidays left. I thought maybe next week…'

'You want to be paid again?'

'Niklas, please—' She hated that he'd mentioned money. 'I just want to see you.'

'You've already earned your keep…go spend your money on holiday.'

'Niklas…I know you don't mean that.'

'*What* do you know?' His voice was black. 'We were married for one day; we screwed an awful lot. You know nothing about me.'

'I know that you care. I know when you saw me—'

'Care?' he sneered down the phone. 'The only way I can get sex in here is if they bring in my wife—that's it. I am sick of conversations, and you seem to want just as many of those as you give of the other.'

'Niklas, please…'

But he would not let her speak. He had to get her away from here. Did she not get that she could be in danger? He had no idea what was happening on the outside, had no idea what was going on, and he wanted her safely away—had to make sure she was safe.

So again he drowned her with words.

'Meg, if you want to come back and suck me, then do. But just so long as you know you mean nothing to me.'

He slammed down the phone—not in fury but in fear. He put his hands through the door and felt the cool of the cuffs. His mind was racing. Since her visit, since getting the information that Miguel was working against him, his mind had been spinning, trying to work out what the hell was going on, trying to figure things out. But now he had a head full of *her*, and he had more to be concerned with than that she was still here in Brazil.

He needed to speak with Rosa—had to work out what the hell was going on.

As he was walked back to his cell his face was expressionless, but his mind was pounding like a jackhammer and he cursed under his breath in Portuguese as Andros made some reference to his wife, about his nice little family, and asked how scum from the streets had managed that. Then Andros pushed him up the stairs and Niklas cursed again, but in French this time.

'Watch it, Dos Santos…' Andros told him, sensing his prisoner's rising anger and slamming him up against the wall.

The move was not meant to overpower him, Niklas realised, simply to provoke him, because Dos Santos was an orphan's name. Niklas went to swear again, in Spanish, but his brain was working quickly, far more quickly than his mouth, and in that second he knew what was happening.

Dos Santos meant something different in Spanish.

And it was a Spanish nun who had named him.

Dos Santos in Spanish meant two saints.

He had a twin.

In that very second it was as if a bomb had exploded in his brain and he worked it all out. He knew instantly how he had got to be here. Knew that his double was out there and had been working with Miguel against him. And with a lurch of fear that was violent to his soul he knew that Meg was in serious danger.

Niklas said nothing when Andros jeered again, just stood silent against the wall as Andros spoke filth about his wife. He stood still and refused to react as another guard came over. A decent guard this time, because there were plenty of them around.

'Trouble?' the guard asked.

'No trouble,' Niklas said, because he did not want to go to solitary tonight. He really needed to get to his cell.

He stood compliant as his cuffs were removed and went quietly into his cell. There he met the eyes of Fernando, and for the first time since his arrival he spoke with the other man.

'I need your help,' Niklas said, for he had worked out what was happening and urgent help was required. 'I need you to make contact on the outside.'

CHAPTER TEN

ANOTHER NIGHT CRYING over Niklas Dos Santos and Meg swore it would be the last.

Part of her could almost convince herself that he was just trying to get her to leave, that that was the reason behind his cruel words, but the more sensible part of Meg soon talked herself round. Her sensible side reminded her that this was a man she knew nothing about—a man who had caused her nothing but heartache and trouble since the day that they had met.

Hawaii sounded pretty good to Meg right now.

A week lying on the beach concentrating on nothing but how best to forget him.

It was well after lunchtime now, and Meg was *still* waiting for the travel agent to return her call. When she did, Meg would ask to be booked onto the earliest flight that could be arranged, and she packed her suitcase in preparation. Very deliberately she did not turn on the vast television to see how his trial was going, or to catch a glimpse of him on the news, because one glimpse of Niklas and she was lost to him—that much she knew.

She wanted her divorce now, wanted to be the hell away from him, would not waste even one more single minute on him.

But as she packed up her toiletries Meg threw tampons into her make-up bag and suddenly realised that it might be rather more complicated than that.

She looked at the unopened packet, an Australian brand because she hadn't bought any since she had arrived here, and tried to remember when she'd last had a period.

She tried to remember the days in Australia before her life had been changed so dramatically by the visit from Niklas's lawyers. No, she hadn't had her period for a while.

There should be the reassurance that they'd used condoms, but the last one hadn't held.

Could she be pregnant?

Would she tell him if she was?

Meg looked in the mirror and decided that, no, she could not deny him that. Even if his life was to be spent on the inside, he would have to know the truth, and it wasn't the kind of news she could reveal in a letter—maybe she would have to visit him again.

Maybe not.

A letter was probably more than he deserved.

But first she had to know for sure.

She was probably overreacting, Meg told herself as she headed out of her hotel room and to the elevators. Worrying too much, she tried to convince herself as she headed onto the street. With all that she'd been through these past weeks it was no wonder that her period was late.

The streets were busy, as always—the cars jammed together, horns blaring, and sirens blazing as police tried to thread their way through the impossible madness that was downtown São Paulo. She found a *pharmacia* and inside it was the same as the world over, with numerous pregnancy testing kits sitting on the shelves. Meg didn't need to speak the language to know she was making the right purchase.

What was different from Australia, though, was that instead of being pounced on by an assistant the second she entered the store, here Meg was pretty much ignored. Even when she tried to pay the pharmacist and his checkout assistants were all taking an impromptu break and watching the television, and Meg could feel mounting impatience. She really had to know now if she was pregnant. Had to make the decision of facing Niklas and telling him while she was still here.

Finally someone came over to serve her, still talking to her colleagues, and Meg froze when she heard one of them shout the name Dos Santos. She felt sweat bead on her forehead as she paid, because despite herself— despite all this—she wanted to turn the television on, wanted to know how he was.

She almost ran back to the hotel, terrified of her feelings for him, that even a mention of his name could reduce her to this petrified state.

It was blissfully cool and quiet in her room—such a contrast to the chaos down below. She fought not to turn on the television, picked up the remote and hurled it, tried not to look where it landed. The light on the phone said she had a new message. She hoped it was the travel agent and played it back, but heard her mum's voice instead. Meg honestly didn't know how she could ever begin tell her parents all that had happened. She had always hoped she would never have to, but if this test proved positive...

She could feel the tears starting again but refused to give in to them—just bit them back and headed to the bathroom, put her purchase in its bag on the bench, ready to find out. Then there was a knock on the door and Meg assumed it was the cleaner. She didn't want her coming in now. She wanted privacy for this at least.

So she went to tell them. She didn't even look through the peephole, just opened the door, and what was left of the sensible part of her mind struggled to remain calm because standing at her door was Niklas. She froze for a moment, unable to respond to seeing him in such an ordinary setting. She wanted to sob at him, to rage at him, to ask him how on earth he was here—except she just stood there.

'It's okay...' He stepped in. 'I know it must be a shock to see me here.'

'I don't understand...'

'The judge understood,' he said. 'Didn't you see it all on the news?'

'I haven't been watching it.'

'That is good.' He gave her a smile. 'I get to tell you the good news myself.'

'I don't want to hear it.' She was so very angry with him, and now finally she could tell him. 'I haven't been watching it because I'm sick of this, Niklas. I'm sick of how you make me feel at times. I can't do this any more.'

'You're upset.'

'Do you blame me?' She looked at him. She could smell his cologne—the same cologne he had worn the day they had met. He was dressed in a stunning suit now, just as beautiful as the day they had met, just as cruel as the day he had ended things between them, but she wanted to know. 'You've been let off?'

'I've been bailed while they take some time to review new evidence.'

'Well, after the way you spoke to me last night I need some time for a review too,' Meg answered. She refused just to go back to loving him. He had hurt her too much. And she could not find out if she was pregnant while he was near. She needed to do that part alone.

'Come here...' He moved to pull her into his arms.

'Just leave.' It took everything she had to shake her head. 'Just go, Niklas. I'm doing as you told me. I'm going to Hawaii...'

'You're upset.'

'Why do you keep saying that? Of *course* I'm upset!' she flared. 'Did you think I wouldn't be? How the hell do you justify speaking to me like that?'

'Meg...'

He walked over and she did *not* want him to take her in his arms, did not want him to melt her all over again.

'I say stupid things at times. You know that...'

'Stupid things?' There were so many other ways she could describe his words. 'It was more than stupid, it was foul...' She would not be fobbed off. 'Why?' she demanded. 'Why did you speak to me like that?'

'I've said I'm sorry.'

'No, you haven't, and you're clearly not as sorry as I was to hear it.' She went to open the door, to tell him to get out of here, but he stopped her and wrapped his arms around her shoulders. Meg just stood there, tears rising, remembering the love they had made and all the ways he made her feel. But she could not go back there. 'Get out!' She pushed him off her. 'I mean it, Niklas...'

'Meg...' His mouth was on her cheek and she pulled her head away. His hands were in her hair but she brushed them off.

'Please,' she said, 'can you just leave me? I'll call you later. I'll—'

His phone rang then, and it annoyed her that he took the call. Yes, of course he was busy, she knew that, and maybe she should be flattered that he had come straight to her, but it annoyed her that in the middle of a row he could just stop and take a call. It made her even more angry, and she was tired of making excuses for him. She wanted him gone and she told him so when he ended his call.

'You are cross...' He smiled at her. 'You look beautiful when you are cross...'

He aimed his phone at her and she blinked at the flash. 'What the hell are you doing?'

'I've missed things like this. I want to capture everything…'

'I just you want you to leave.'

But he simply refused to listen. 'Let's go for a walk.'

'A walk?'

The last thing she wanted was a walk. She wanted him to leave. She looked at his lips and not even his beautiful mouth could silence her doubts now. She just wanted him gone.

'A walk to clear the air…' Niklas said.

'No.' She shook her head. 'I'm waiting for the travel agent to ring me back.'

'She'll call back if you're not here.' He shrugged. 'Come,' he said. 'I want to taste the fresh air. I want to feel the rain…'

She looked out of the window. Yes, it was raining, and she realised that he wouldn't have felt the rain in a long time. She was relieved that he wasn't all over her, trying to kiss her back to confusion as he so often did, but she didn't feel she knew him at all.

'Meg, after all we have been through will you at least come for a walk with me?'

'You hurt me last night.'

'I apologise.' His black eyes met hers. 'Meg, I truly apologise. We can start again, without all this hanging over us…'

But she was stronger than she'd thought she could be.

She looked into his eyes and quite simply no longer wanted him—didn't want to get back on the rollercoaster ride beside him. It was then that she made a decision that was surprisingly easy; she looked at the man who had broken her heart and knew that he would break it all over again. She simply refused to let him.

It was over.

Whatever the pregnancy test told her, Meg knew it was far better that she find out well away from him. She would fly to Hawaii today, search for the clarity he so easily clouded and make better decisions alone.

'Come...' he said. 'I want to taste my freedom.'

Maybe it would be easier to tell him that they were finished while they were walking. Maybe it would prove easier out there. Because she knew his kisses made her weak. So she nodded and she went to get her jacket, to comb her hair.

'Don't worry about that...' he said. 'Your hair is fine...'

Niklas was right. Her hair really didn't matter right now—it was her heart Meg had to worry about. They rode down in the lift together and Meg looked at him more closely. She hated her swollen eyes. Even more she hated that she had let him cause them.

They headed out through the foyer and into the street and she felt the warm rain that was so regular here. His hand reached for her, but she pulled hers back, refusing to give this man any more chances. He'd already used his last one with his filthy words to her the previous night and now his pathetic attempt at an apology.

'I'm ending it, Niklas.' He kept on walking. 'I'm going to file for divorce.'

'We'll go to a bar and talk about it.'

'There's nothing to discuss.' Meg stopped—which wasn't the most sensible thing to do on such a busy street.

There were moans from a few pedestrians and he took her hand and they kept walking. She really was sure that she was making the right choice, because she did not know him, and he did not know her, and a walk would not clear the air. Only his kiss could possibly have given them a chance, because sex was the only thing they had going for them. Maybe she was mad for thinking it, but shouldn't that be the way a man celebrated his freedom? If he loved her, if he wanted her, wouldn't the first thing he wanted be taking her to bed, not out for a walk?

'There's a bar up here that I know,' Niklas said. 'It's not far—just a couple of blocks away...'

'I don't want to go to a bar...'

'The street is too noisy. Come on, we can talk properly there.'

'I don't want to talk.'

Meg was starting to panic now, and she didn't really know why. His hand was too tight on her wrist, and he was walking her faster, and she had the most appalling thought then that he hadn't been bailed at all. There was an urgency in the steps he was taking. She looked over to him and his head was down, and it dawned on Meg that maybe he had escaped from jail. She recalled the screams of the police cars and bikes. They were screaming in the streets even louder now. She remembered too the pharmacy staff all huddled around the television, saying his name. Maybe it was because Niklas Dos Santos had escaped. Still he walked her ever faster.

'Niklas…'

She could hear the thud of music as they turned into a side street, could hear the clang of triangles and the smell of *pamonah*. There were so many people around; surely she was safe. She pulled her hand from his and stopped walking, but he turned and put a hand to her cheek. She shivered, but not with pleasure. There was something dark and menacing in his eyes. She was a fool to have got involved with this man, a fool to follow her heart, for look where it had led her—to a dingy side street in Brazil with a man she was now terrified of.

'Come,' he said. 'We will talk about where our relationship is going later. Right now I want to celebrate my freedom and I want you to celebrate it with me.' His hand was tight on her arm. 'You wouldn't deny me that?'

'I do,' she said. 'And I want you to let me go.'

'Don't spoil this day for me, Meg—it's been a hell of a long year for both of us. Now we can drink *cachaca*, unwind, dance. Later we can talk, but first…'

He lowered his head to kiss her, but it was too late for that and she moved her head back from his, suddenly confused. Because Niklas didn't dance. It was one of the few things that she *did* know about him—or had that been just another of his lies? Suddenly she was scared, and with real reason now.

Meg turned to go but he pulled her roughly back and

pushed her against the wall. Then he opened his jacket and she saw that he had a gun.

'Try to run and it will be the last thing you do…'

'Niklas…' she begged, and when Meg heard her own voice she heard the way she sounded when she pleaded for her life. She was trying to show him that she wasn't panicked, trying to reason with a man she absolutely didn't know, trying to get away. 'Why do you need me?' she said. 'If you've escaped…'

People were turning to look at them, maybe alerted by the panic in her voice even though she wasn't screaming. Or perhaps it was that if he had just escaped then his picture would be everywhere, being flashed over the news. Perhaps that was why he lowered his face to her.

'Why do you need me with you?'

'Because you're my last chance.'

And his mouth came down on hers.

She could hear a car pulling up beside them and Meg knew this was *her* last chance to get away. She knew instinctively that when the car doors opened she would be shoved in, that that was why he had taken the call—to arrange all this. Terrified, Meg did the only thing she could think of to survive. She bit hard on his lip with all she had—took that beautiful mouth and bit it as hard as she could. In the second when he recoiled, as he cursed her in Portuguese and reached for his gun, Meg ran—ran as she never had—ran and ran faster as she heard gunshots.

She kept running till rough arms grabbed her and pulled her down, slamming her to the ground. She felt her cheek hit the pavement and the skin leave her leg as she rose to run again, heard another volley of gunshots and looked behind her. She saw police cars screeching up. Whoever had shielded her from him had gone. Then she stared at the body on the ground and it was the only thing she could see.

'Niklas!' she screamed, and tried to run back to him, for she hated the man but it was agony to see him lying dead and riddled with bullets.

She could not stop screaming. Not even when other arms wrapped around her and her face was buried in rough prison denim and she smelt him again—not his cologne, but the scent of Niklas, her drug of choice, a scent that till now had been missing. She heard him saying over and over that she was safe, that he was here, that now it would all be okay, but she still did not believe it was him—until he lifted her face and she met his eyes, saw that the beautiful mouth had not been bitten and knew that somehow it was him.

That she was safe.

It was just her heart that was in danger again.

CHAPTER ELEVEN

MEG DID NOT get to see him again. Instead she was taken to a police station. There were press clamouring outside as she was taken in to give a statement, and while she was waiting for a translator Rosa arrived.

Meg gave her statement as best she could. They kept talking about twins, and although she had already worked that out when she was being held in Niklas's arms, her brain was so scrambled and confused that even with a translator she could hardly understand the questions, let alone answer them.

Every time she closed her eyes she saw Niklas—or rather the man she had thought was Niklas—lying there dead. The raw grief and panic, the *knowing* in that moment that she would never see him again, that the man she had fallen so heavily in love with was now dead, was not a memory or a feeling she could simply erase.

Fortunately Rosa had told the police she would return with Meg tomorrow, but that for now she needed peace, and thankfully they accepted that.

'We will return at ten tomorrow,' Rosa told her.

They stepped out into the foyer and she saw him standing there, still dressed in prison denim. He took her in his arms and she knew then that she had to be careful, because the one thing she had worked out before this embrace was that she wasn't strong around him—that she'd only been able to break up with Niklas when it hadn't actually been him.

'I'm still angry with you.'

'I thought you might be.' He kissed her bruised cheek and didn't let her go as he spoke. 'We can row in bed.'

Which sounded a lot more like the Niklas she knew. He held her tight and pressed his face into her hair and she could feel his ragged breathing. For a moment she thought he was crying, but he just held her a moment longer and spoke into her hair.

'The press are outside so we have to go out the back. I am taking you far away from here. I need to stay in the city, but—'

'*Não,*' Rosa said.

Meg heard the word *amanhã* again, and realised Rosa was telling him that Meg must return to the police tomorrow.

'I'll ring Carla, then.'

With his arm still around Meg he took Rosa's phone and started to dial the number. Whilst he was occupied Meg stepped out of his embrace, and a little later, when they climbed into a waiting car, she sat on the back seat far away from him, needing some time alone.

Even though they went out the back way the press still got some photos and it was horrible. They scrambled over to the car and blocked their exit, but the driver shook them off. Niklas told her it might be like this for a while, and that he was taking her to a hotel. He saw the start in her eyes.

'We're not going back *there*—I've asked Carla to book us into a different one.'

Us.

So easily he assumed.

They entered the new hotel the back way too, and were ushered straight to a waiting lift where Niklas pressed a high number. They stood in silence till Meg broke it.

'Did you get off?'

'I've been released on bail.'

'So why are you still wearing...?' And then she shook her head, because she was simply too tired for explanations right now.

They stepped out of the lift and there was hotel security in the corridor—'For the press,' Niklas said, but it felt a lot like prison to her, and no doubt to him too, but he said nothing, just swiped open a door, leading her into a plush suite.

Meg stood there for a moment, only knowing for certain the city she was in and that Niklas was alive. She remembered her feeling at seeing him dead, and the fear that had gripped her in the moments before, and started shaking.

'I wanted to take you away from the city tonight, but because we need to go back to the police station tomorrow it is better that we stay here. I've had your stuff packed up, but it is in the other place…you'll have to make do for now…'

It was hardly 'make do'; there was food and soon she would take a bath, and then she sat and had a strong coffee. Niklas offered her *cachaca*—the same drink she had been offered a little while ago—and she shuddered as she remembered. He opened the fridge and opened a bottle of champagne instead.

Which seemed a strange choice and was a drink she hadn't had it in almost a year.

Not since their wedding.

It was the drink they had shared on the day they had met, and he poured her a glass now, kissing her forehead as they chinked glasses and celebrated that somehow they were both here. It was a muted celebration, and there was still so much to be said, but Niklas dealt with the essentials first.

'You need to ring your parents.'

'I don't know what to say to them,' Meg admitted. She felt like crying just at the thought of them, was dreading the conversation that had to be had—and how much worse it was going to be now, after not telling them anything.

'Tell them the truth,' Niklas said. 'A bit diluted.' He nudged her. 'You need to speak to them now in case they hear anything on the news, or the consulate might contact them. Have they tried to ring *you*?'

'I didn't even bring my phone with me,' Meg said.

'It will be at the other hotel,' Niklas said. 'For now

they just need to know you are safe. I will speak to them if it gets too much.'

'No.' She shook her head—not at phoning them, but at the thought of him talking to them. She knew how badly things were going to go. 'I'll do it...'

'Now.'

'I still don't really know what happened.' But she took the phone, because he was right. They needed to know she was safe. 'Leave me,' she said, and was glad that he didn't argue.

Niklas headed into the bedroom and she dialled the number, then looked out of the window to a very beautiful, but very complicated city. She held her breath when she heard the very normal sound of her mum.

'How's Brazil?' Ruth asked. 'Or is it Hawaii this week?'

'Still Brazil,' Meg said, and because Ruth was her mum straight away she knew.

'What's wrong?'

It was the most difficult of conversations. First she had to tell her how Vegas had been and how she had married a man she had only just met. She diluted the story a lot, of course—an awful lot—but she still had to tell them how, the morning after their wedding, Niklas had upset her, how she had been trying to psyche herself up to divorce him.

And her mum kept interrupting her with questions that her father was shouting—questions that weren't really relevant because they still didn't know half of the story. So she told them she was here to visit him, that he had been arrested a while ago, but was innocent of all charges. Her mother was shouting and sobbing now, and her dad was demanding the phone, and they were simply getting nowhere, and then Niklas was back and she was so glad to hand the phone over to him.

She found out for certain then just how brilliant he was, how clever he was with people, for somehow he calmed her father down.

'My intention when I married your daughter was to take proper care of her. I was on my way to tell you the same when I found out that I was being investigated.'

He said a few more things, and she could hear the shouts receding as he calmly spoke his truth.

'I was deliberately nasty to her in the hope she would divorce me—of course she was confused, of course she was ashamed and did not feel that she could tell you. I wanted to keep her away from the trouble that was coming—in that I failed, and I apologise.'

They didn't need to know all the details, but he told them some pertinent ones, because as soon as they hung up they would be racing to find out the news for themselves. So he told them about the shooting, but he was brief and matter-of-fact and reiterated that Meg was safe. He told them that they could ring any time with more questions, no matter the time of day or night, and that he would do his best to answer them. Then he handed the phone back to Meg.

'You're safe,' her mum said.

'I am.'

'We need to talk…'

'We will.'

When she hung up the phone she looked at him. 'You could have told me the truth that day.' She was angry that he hadn't.

'What? Walk back in and tell you that I am being investigated for fraud and embezzlement? That the man you met twenty-four hours ago is facing thirty-five years to life in jail…?' He looked at her. 'What would you have said?'

'I might have suggested you didn't go back till you found out the case against you…' she flared. 'I might not be the best one in the world, but I *am* a lawyer…'

'My own lawyer was telling me to get straight back.' He kicked himself then, because had he confided in her—had he been able to tell her—he might not have raced back, might have found out some more information before taking a first-class flight to hell.

'I had to return to face it,' Niklas said. 'Would you have stood by me?'

'You never gave me that chance.'

'Because that was what I was most afraid of.' He was kneeling beside her and she could hear him breathing. 'You never asked if I did it.'

'No.'

'Even when you visited…even when you rang…'

'No, I didn't.'

'Did you believe I was innocent?'

'I hoped that you were.'

'There was too much love for common sense,' Niklas said.

She sat there for ages and was glad when he left her alone and headed to the bathroom. She heard his sigh of relief as he slipped into the bath water and thought about his words—because while she had hoped he was innocent, it hadn't changed her feelings towards him and that scared her. After a little while she wandered in to him.

'I am so sorry.' He looked at her. 'For everything I have put you and your family through.'

'It wasn't your fault.'

'No,' he said. 'But still, I have scared you, and nearly cost you your life…'

And then he looked at her and asked the question the police had asked her earlier.

'Did he do anything to you?'

'Apart from hold a gun at me…' she knew what he meant '…no.'

She watched him close his eyes in relief and knew then that he *had* cried.

'He wanted to walk,' Meg said. 'That was when I started to worry.' She gave him a pale smile. 'Not quite the Niklas I know.' And then there wasn't a pale smile. 'I'm still cross about what you said on the phone.'

'I wanted you to leave,' he said. 'I wanted you to be so angry, so upset, that you got on the next plane you could…'

'I nearly did.'

'Do you want me tell you what happened?'

She wanted to hear it now, and he held his hand out to her. Yes, he assumed she would join him—and for now he was right. Her clothes and her body were filthy, and she wanted to feel clean again, to hear what had happened, and she wanted to hear it as she lay beside him. So she took off her clothes and slid into the water, with her back to his chest, resting on him, and he held her close and washed all her bruises and slowly he told her.

'There was bedlam in court,' Niklas said as he washed her gently. 'The place erupted when I asked for a new lawyer, and then Rosa presented the evidence implicating Miguel. He was arrested immediately, but of course I had to go back to prison…I knew they were never going to release me just like that. I told them that you were in danger, but they would not listen, and then, as they were taking me back, *he* made contact with Carla, asking for money. He said that he had my wife and texted a photo. The police only believed me then that I had a twin.'

She frowned and looked up to him. 'You *knew* you had a twin?'

'I guessed that I did last night, after I spoke to you.'

'How?'

'It made sense. I knew I was innocent.'

'But how did you work it out?'

'I swear in several languages…' She smiled, because that *was* what he did. 'I was angry after speaking to you—worried that you would not leave—and I swore in Portuguese. The guard warned me to be careful, he called me Dos Santos and I heard the derision in his voice, in his tone. I thought he was referring to me hav-

ing no one, and I swore again, and then he said something about you. I went to curse again, but in Spanish…'

He was soaping her arms and his mouth was at her
neck—not kissing, just breathing.

'The first nun who looked after me, till I was three,
she taught me Spanish…'

Still Meg frowned.

'Dos Santos means something different in Spanish,'
Niklas explained. 'In Portuguese it means "from the
saints", in Spanish it means…'

'Two.' She turned and looked to him. '"Two saints".'

'There were two of us… That is why the Spanish
nun chose our surname. It made sense. Apparently in
the month before I was arrested I was having meals
and meetings with very powerful people, persuading
them to invest….'

'My God!'

'He and Miguel were rorting every contact I have
made. A couple of months before it happened I thought
I had lost my phone, but of course they had it and were
diverting numbers. Both of them knew that they didn't
have long before I found out, or the banks or the police
did, so they were busy getting a lot of money based on
my reputation. My lawyer had every reason to want
me to be convicted and spend life in jail—every reason not to tell me about the evidence that would con-
vict me. Because as soon as I saw it, I would know the
truth. It was not me.'

She felt him breathe in deeply.

'I can see how people were fooled. When I saw him

lying there I felt as if I was looking at me.' He elaborated on his feelings no more than that, and told her the little he knew. 'His name was Emilios Dos Santos. The police said he had lived on the streets all his life but had no criminal record—just a few warnings for begging. I guess he was tired of having nothing. When he found out Miguel had been arrested he must have seen you as his last chance to get money from me…'

'How did he know I was here? How did he know what hotel…?'

'The prison guards, maybe.' He shrugged. 'Miguel would have been paying someone to keep an eye on me. You would have had to give your address for the prison visitors' list.'

She knew then how dangerous it had been not to listen to him, not to leave when he had told her to.

'I should have gone to Hawaii.'

'Yes,' he said, 'you should have.' But then he thought for a moment. Because without her here, without his fear that she was in danger, he might not have worked things out.

'It doesn't matter anyway,' Meg said. 'It's over now.' He didn't answer, and she turned and saw the exhaustion and agony still in his face. She could have kicked herself, for at the end of the day he had lost his twin, and Meg knew that despite all that had happened it had to hurt.

'Maybe he did want to talk to you when he found out he had a twin—perhaps Miguel dissuaded him, saw the chance to make some serious money and told him it was the only way.'

'I don't want to speak about that.'

So quickly he locked her out.

And then the phone rang—trust the hotel bathroom to have one.

Niklas answered it.

'It's your father.' He handed it to Meg, and she spoke with her parents. Neither shouted this time, just asked more questions—and, more than that, they told her how much they loved her, and how badly they wanted her to come home as quickly as possible.

She was glad she was facing away from him, but glad to be leaning on him as they spoke and he held her. Later her father asked to speak with him, and he held out his wet hand for the phone and listened to what her father was saying.

'We have to give some more statements to the police, so Meg needs to be here for a few more days,' he said, 'but I will take her somewhere quiet.' He listened for a moment and then spoke again. 'She's tired now, but I will see what she wants to do in the morning, once she has spoken to the police.'

And then he said goodbye, and she frowned because they almost sounded a little bit friendly.

'He's coming around to me.'

It was, as Meg knew only too well, terribly easy to do so.

'They want you home, Meg.'

'I know that, but I want to be here with you.'

'Well, they need to see you,' Niklas said. 'They need to see for themselves that you are not hurt.'

'I know that…' She wanted him to say he'd come with her, wanted him to say he would never let her go, but he didn't. She wanted more from him, wanted to be fully in his life, but still he would not let her in.

She turned her head and looked at him—looked at this man who'd told her from the start that they'd never last.

'This doesn't change things, does it?'

He didn't answer.

She surprised herself by not crying.

'You'll never find another love like this.' She meant it—and not in an arrogant way—because even if he didn't accept it, even if he refused to believe it, whether he wanted it or not, this really *was* love.

'I told you on the first day that it would not be for ever.'

'We didn't love each other as much then.'

'I have never said that I love you.'

'You did earlier.'

'I said there was too much love for common sense,' Niklas said. 'Too much love for you to think straight…'

'I don't believe you.'

'Believe in fairytales if you want to.' He said it much more nicely than last time, but the message was the same. 'Meg, I told you I could never settle in one place, that I could not commit to one person for ever. I *told* you that.'

He had.

'And I told you that I don't do love.'

He had.

'You said you wanted this for as long as it lasted.'

His voice was the gentlest and kindest she had heard it.

'In a few days, once all the questioning is over, you need to go home to your family.'

And even if she'd promised herself not to cry she did a bit, and he caught her tear with his thumb before lowering his head and tasting it. She could hear the clock ticking, knew that every kiss they shared now might be their last, that soon it would be a kiss goodbye.

'It could last…' She pulled her head away and opened her mouth to argue, but he spoke over her.

'I don't want to wait for the rows and the disenchantment to kick in. I don't want to do that to us because what we have now is so good. But, no, it cannot last…'

Which was why she'd accept his kisses—which was why, tonight, she would shut out the fact that this was temporary. Because tonight maybe she just needed to escape, and maybe he did too.

And even if he wouldn't admit it, even if he chose not to share his feelings, Niklas felt as if he'd just stepped out of hell's inferno into heaven as his mouth met hers.

Her mouth was bruised, but very gently he kissed it. Her cheek was hurting and her legs were grazed where she'd fallen. She knew she could never keep him, that for now guilt and fear would drive his kisses, and that later this man she didn't really know would return to a life she had never really been in. This wasn't love they were making. It was *now*.

Over and over she told herself that.

She thought he'd make love to her in the water, but he took her wet to the bed and dried her with a towel, every inch of her, and then he kissed her bruises, up her legs, and he kissed her *there* till she was crying and moaning in frustration. His hand was over her mouth again, because there were still guards outside, but she wanted him—wanted all of him. Then he slipped inside her, and it was incredibly slow, a savour in each thrust, but the words she needed were not in her ears. She bit down as she came, and gave him her body while trying to claim back a heart this man didn't want but already had.

CHAPTER TWELVE

MEG WOKE IN the night, crying and scared, and Niklas held her tightly before he made love to her again.

And he would have had her again in the morning—was pulling her across the mattress when the phone rang to tell them that Rosa was on her way up.

'Later!' he said, and kissed her. 'Or just really, really quickly now?'

She looked into black eyes that smiled down at her and simply could not read him— couldn't be his sex toy any more.

'Later,' Meg said, and climbed out of bed.

She let Rosa in. She had brought fresh clothes for both of them. Surprisingly, she gave Meg a hug and told her that she would accompany them to the police station.

'I am very sorry for the way I spoke to you,' Rosa said.

'What way?' Niklas checked.

She looked at Niklas. 'I gave her a hard time.'

'You weren't the only one,' Meg said, and then went purple when Rosa laughed. God, was that the only place minds went in Brazil? 'What I meant,' she said in her best cross voice, 'was that I do understand why you said what you did.'

'I am grateful,' Niklas said to Rosa. 'To all three of you, but especially to you. I will repay you just as soon as I get my assets back.'

'Hopefully it won't be long now,' Rosa said, and then smiled as she scolded, 'But did you *have* to drink the most expensive champagne in the fridge? I just paid your room bill.'

'*You* paid?' Meg blinked. She wasn't talking about the champagne. 'That was your money?' Meg had assumed it came from Niklas's funds, but of course she now realised that while he was being investigated they would all be frozen.

'I put up my home,' Rosa said. 'I believed in him.'

'You're the richest one of us in the room,' Niklas said to Meg, and even Rosa laughed.

'I'll buy you all a coffee on the way to the station.' Meg smiled, but it was strained. She headed to the bathroom to get changed and thought about Rosa's belief in Niklas. It was clear to Meg that in the past Rosa and Niklas had slept together, but it wasn't that fact that riled her. It was the friendship they had that ate at her—a friendship that would not waver, one that would always last.

It was the longevity that riled her.

Meg opened the bag of fresh clothes and noticed that Rosa had chosen well for her. There was a skirt that was soft and long and would cover the grazes on her legs, a thin blouse and some gorgeous, albeit completely see-through, underwear. Meg inspected the underwear more closely and saw that there wasn't an awful lot of it, and when she pulled the knickers on she was silently mortified to realise that there was a hole in the middle—which was intentional. They were the most outrageous things she'd ever worn, but she could hardly complain to Rosa.

There were sandals too, because hers had broken yesterday.

She dressed and brushed her teeth, and combed her hair, and looked in the mirror and examined her solemn face. She should be happy and celebrating, except she couldn't quite rise to it. Memories of yesterday were still too raw, and she didn't understand how Niklas and Rosa could be smiling and chatting.

Didn't understand how Niklas could just turn his pain off.

But she had to learn how to, because soon she had to go home.

Had to.

She could not hang around and watch as his guilt for what he had put her through and the attraction he clearly had for her faded. She couldn't bear the thought of his boredom setting in as she waited for the news that she was to be dismissed from his life.

If Niklas didn't want for ever, then she couldn't carry on with it being just for now.

'Ready?' Niklas checked, looking over as she walked out of the bathroom.

'I guess so.' There was nothing to pack, after all.

'Do you want me to take your clothes and have them cleaned?' Rosa offered.

'I'll bin them.' Meg headed back to the bathroom to do so. 'I never want to see them again.'

'Okay.' Rosa hitched up her bag and headed off. 'I'll go and make sure the car is ready.'

When she'd left Meg picked up all the clothes from the wet bathroom floor and took them through to the bin in the lounge, but as she went to throw them in he stopped her.

'Not those.'

She looked at the denims he was retrieving and he turned and smiled.

'You might want me to shave my head again one day...'

She wasn't smiling back.

'It's all a game to you, isn't it?'

'No, Meg.' He shook his head, and he wasn't smiling now. 'It's not.'

But as they took the lift down she noted that he was holding a bag. He hadn't binned the denim clothes he'd worn in prison.

He pulled her into him and shielded her from the press as they left the hotel, did it again when they got to the police station, but she was actually shielding herself from him. He gave her a thorough kiss before she headed in to give her statement, but all it did was make her want to cry, because she wanted more than just sex from him.

'You'll be fine.' He wiped a tear with his thumb. 'Just tell them what happened. Rosa will be there…'

'I know.'

'It's nothing to be scared of,' he said. 'And then I'm going to get you right away from here—just us…' He smiled as he said it, gave her another kiss to reassure her.

She returned neither.

The statement was long and detailed, and she felt as if she were going over and over the same thing.

No, she had never met Miguel, and nor had Emilios mentioned him.

She didn't know who had called Emilios, but it had been after that call that he had suggested they go for a walk.

'They ask,' Rosa said, 'when did you realise it was not Niklas?'

'I never realised,' she said again.

'But you said you started to panic long before you saw the gun?'

She nodded, but Rosa told her she had to answer. 'Yes.'

They made her go over and over it, and she tried to explain things but it was so hard. It was hard to understand herself. She didn't want to say in the police station that she was surprised he hadn't taken her to bed, that perhaps that had been the biggest clue that it wasn't Niklas—which for Meg just rammed home how empty their relationship really was.

'So what made you panic?' Rosa checked again.

'I realised what a mistake I'd made marrying him,' Meg said, in a voice that was flat as she relived it. 'That there was no real basis for a relationship, that he'd always said it wouldn't last. All I wanted was to be away from him.'

'From Emilios?'

She shook her head. She remembered her swollen eyes and flinging things in a suitcase, the pleasure and pain of the last year, mainly the pain, and still, *still* he delivered it.

'From Niklas.' As she said it she saw Rosa's slight frown.

And then they took her further back, to her first meeting with Niklas on the plane and their late-night conversation.

'I asked how he'd been orphaned and he said he wasn't sure.'

'You asked if he had ever tried to look for his family?'

'Yes.'

'And what was his response?'

'He said that he had got Miguel, his lawyer, onto it, but he had got nowhere.'

'He said that?' the police officer checked via Rosa. 'He definitely said that?'

'Yes.'

The officer looked long and hard at her, and then Rosa asked if Meg was sure, as this was from a conversation a year ago. 'He asks if you are sure this is not the conversation you had with Niklas last night.'

Meg blinked.

'I told the police.'

'You remember this conversation exactly?' the officer checked, and she said yes, because she had been replaying every second of their time over and over for close to a year now.

'Exactly.' She nodded. 'And then I asked what it had been like, growing up in an orphanage, but he didn't respond,' Meg said. 'He told me he didn't want to speak about that sort of thing.'

But the police weren't interested in that part.

Only Meg was.

She went over and over everything again. She said that, no, she hadn't been aware she was being followed at the time, and looked to Rosa for explanation, but she gave a brief shake of her head. Then her statement was read back to her. She listened and heard that basically they had had an awful lot of sex and just a few conversations, but he had definitely mentioned that he had asked Miguel to look for his family. She signed her name to it.

'That is good,' Rosa said as they walked out. 'You have a good memory. They will jump on that part in court if Miguel denies that he was asked to find Niklas's family,' she warned. 'Just stay with that.'

'Am I free to fly home?' Meg asked. She saw the brief purse of Rosa's lips. 'My family's worried about me.'

'It might be better for Niklas's case if you were here.'

'What case?' Meg asked. 'It's clear he's innocent.'

'To you,' Rosa said. 'And it is to me. But dead men can't speak.' She gave a thin smile. 'I correct myself.

When I said that Niklas never makes mistakes, he has made one—he hired Miguel, and he is a brilliant lawyer. He might say it was both of them that were conning people. He might insist he believed it was Niklas giving him instructions, or that the directions came from both of them...'

'No!'

'Yes,' Rosa said. 'I will fight it, but it might look better for Niklas if his wife was here beside him—not back home, counting the money his legal team has placed in her account.'

'You know it isn't like that.'

'Tell the judge,' Rosa said, and she was back to being mean. 'I get that your family is worried about you, but if you can pretend for a little while longer that Niklas is a part of your family...'

'Niklas doesn't want me to,' Meg retorted. 'Niklas doesn't want a family...'

'He doesn't even know what one is!' Rosa shouted. 'Yet he has done everything right by you.'

'Everything *right* by me?' It was Meg who was shouting now. 'Are we talking about the same man?'

It wasn't the best choice of words, given the circumstances—especially as Niklas appeared then.

'My mother had triplets, maybe?' he quipped.

It was her poor choice of words, perhaps, but his response was just in bad taste. She did not understand how he could be so laid-back about it. How could he have his arm around her and be walking out of the police station as if the nightmare of the last year hadn't even happened?

It was the same circus of cameras as before, and then they left Rosa to give the press a statement. A car was waiting for them. It's driver handed the keys over to Niklas, who sat behind the wheel as Meg sat in the passenger seat. The moment she was seated Niklas accelerated away at speed—away from the crowds of press. After a while the car slowed, and the drive was a long one, taking them out of the city and through the hills. There was little conversation, just an angry silence from Meg, whereas with every mile the car ate up Niklas seemed more relaxed.

'You're quiet,' he commented.

'Isn't that what you want me to be?'

Sulking didn't work with Niklas. It didn't bother him a bit. He just carried on driving, one hand on the wheel, the other out of the window. Any minute now he'd start whistling, just to annoy her further. She was still bristling from Rosa's words. The first thing she would do when she got back to Sydney was send back all the money that she had been paid.

He looked over at her tense profile. 'We'll be there soon.'

She didn't answer him.

Nothing made sense: the policeman's questions had confused her, Rosa had angered her, and as for him... She turned and could not fathom how calm he was after all that had happened. He was fiddling with the sound system now, flicking through channels. She did not need background music, and her hand snapped it off.

'The police said I was being followed. That it wasn't the police who shot him…'

'It was a bodyguard.'

'Bodyguard?'

'Just leave it.'

'No,' Meg snapped. 'I will not.'

'He will not do any prison time. I have my lawyers working for him. I had a couple of people following you when I realised you were still here—when I guessed I had a twin. I did not know exactly what was happening, but I knew you would not be safe, so I arranged to have people protect you.'

'How?'

'I owe a favour to a very powerful man,' Niklas said. 'He got a message to the outside after you rang me.'

And then he stopped talking about it, and she felt his hand come to rest on her leg, and she could not understand how easily he dismissed the fact that it was a bodyguard *he* had arranged who had shot his twin.

Did nothing get to him?

He gave her thigh a squeeze, which she guessed meant they were nearly at their destination and would be off to look at another bedroom any time soon.

'We're here.'

It was the most stunning house she had ever seen, with dark wood, white furniture and screens on the windows so the sun and the sounds of the mountains could stream in. It was gorgeous and, Niklas said, the place he had dreamt of when he was on the inside.

'You like it?'

'It's gorgeous.'

'Look…'

He took her by the hand and led her to the bedroom, then walked and opened huge glass doors, revealing lush grass that rolled towards another mountain. The sound of birds was all that could be heard. In a place like this, Meg thought, you could start to heal.

'There are servants, but I have told them not to come till I call them. They've left us lots of food…'

And there were her things, hanging in the wardrobe, and there were his arms around her, and again he was holding her close.

She started crying and he didn't seem surprised at all.

'You're exhausted,' he said.

She was.

From nearly a year of loving him.

'Are you about to suggest we go to bed?'

'Meg…' He saw her anger and he didn't blame her. 'I don't care how cross you are. You deserve to be. If you want to shout, go ahead. I have put you through hell and I am just trying to make you feel better, to say the right thing. I'm probably getting it wrong, but for now you are here, and safe.'

It was the 'for now' part that was killing her, but she wasn't going to go there again. 'I don't know what's wrong,' she said. 'I'm so angry! I'm so confused…'

'It's shock,' he said. 'You were nearly kidnapped. You saw a man shot.'

'I saw your *twin* shot!' she shouted. 'I thought it was you.'

He did not react—he just held her.

'Shouldn't it be the other way round?' She pulled away from him, so angry. 'Shouldn't *you* be the one crying? He was your brother.'

'That's for me to deal with,' Niklas said.

'Can't you deal with it with me?'

'I prefer to do things like that alone.' He was nothing if not honest. 'I don't want to talk about me. Right now I want to be here for you.'

He said all the right things, but they were the wrong things too. He took all of her, but didn't give himself back, and maybe she had better just accept it. He felt nothing for anyone, and as she looked out to the mountains she hoped here she might find a little peace before she left him.

'I hope the press don't find us here.'

'Not a chance,' Niklas said. 'I told you that.'

'If they know that you own it they soon will.' She looked down the mountain and hoped there were no cars loaded with press following them up, because she was beyond tired now, could not face moving again. She just wanted a moment to gather her thoughts. 'They'll be going through all your assets...'

'I don't own it,' Niklas said. 'It's not listed in my assets. This is in your name...' He lifted up her face and kissed her frowning forehead. 'I bought this for you before I got arrested. I wanted the divorce, I knew I might be going away for a very long time, and this was to be part of your settlement. The sale went through the day before my finances were frozen...' He gave her a smile. 'They could not seize this because it is yours...'

'You bought this for me?'

'It is big enough for a bed and breakfast...' He shrugged. 'If that is what you want to do with it. I knew you would probably sell it...'

He had known he was about to be arrested and go to prison and yet he had still looked after her—had come to this place and chosen it. It was more than she could take in.

'Why are you crying?'

'Because of this.'

'I said I would take care of you.'

'And you have...'

He had kept every promise he had made, had listened to all her dreams.

They walked through the house and he showed her every room before he took her into the kitchen, with its massive ovens and benches, and huge glass doors that opened to let in the sound and the breeze of the mountains. He had chosen the perfect home—except he hadn't factored that he might live in it.

'I might have to stay here a while,' Niklas said. 'You can be my landlady.'

He came over for a kiss, because that was what he always did.

'I'll send you the rent I owe when I get it.'

'Send it?' Meg said.

'You need to go back.'

He did care about her. She knew it then—knew why he was sending her away. 'And you can't come with me.' It wasn't a question, she was telling him that she knew why.

He tried to hush her with a kiss.

'You can't come to Sydney even for a little while because you're still on bail.'

'Meg…'

When that didn't work, she was more specific. 'And you won't let me stay because you think you might go back to jail.'

'More than might,' Niklas said. 'Miguel is the best legal mind I have met…' He smiled. 'No offence meant.'

Always he made her smile, and always, Meg knew then, he had loved her—even if he didn't know it, even if he refused to see it. Rosa was right. He had always been taking care of her and he was trying to take care of her now.

'I'm on bail,' he said, 'and I doubt the charges will be dropped. Miguel will not simply admit his guilt. There will be a trial, there could be years of doubt, and then I might be put away again. You need to go back to your family.'

'*You're* my family.'

'No…' He just would not accept it. 'Because as much as I might want you here, as much as I thought of you here in this home while I was in that place, as much as a three-weekly visit might keep me sane, I will *not* do that to you.'

'Yes.'

'No,' Niklas said. 'We will have a couple of nights here and then, as I promised your father, I will make sure you get home. By the time you are there I will have divorced you.'

He was adamant.

And she both loved and loathed that word now. She wanted to kiss the man she was certain now loved her, yet she wanted to know the man she loved. He kissed her as if he would never let her go, yet he had told her that she must.

'You're so bloody selfish…' She could have slapped him. She pulled her head back, would not be hushed with sex. 'Why don't I get a say?' She was furious now, and shouting. 'You're as bad as my parents—telling me what I want and how I should live my life…'

'What?' he demanded. 'You *want* to be up here, living in the mountains, coming to prison for a screw every three weeks?'

'Your mouth can be foul.'

'Your life could be,' Niklas retorted. 'Barefoot and pregnant, with your husband—'

She didn't hear the next bit. It was then that Meg remembered—only then that she remembered what she had been preparing to find out before Emilios had come to her door. He watched her anger change to panic, and in turn she watched the fear that darted in his eyes when she told him that she might already be.

It was not how it should be. Meg knew that.

He just stood there as she walked off, as she walked into the bedroom and went through her things. Yes, there was her toiletry bag and, yes, Rosa had packed everything. The pregnancy testing kit was there.

She kicked off her shoes when she returned to the kitchen, because barefoot and pregnant she *was*.

'You need to go home to your family.'

'That's all you have to say?'

'That's it.'

She couldn't believe his detachment, that he could simply turn away.

'You'd let us both go, wouldn't you?'

'You'll have a far better life…'

'I probably would,' Meg said. 'Because I am sick of being married to a man who can't even talk to me, who sorts everything out with sex. Who, even if he won't admit it, *does* actually love me. I'm tired of trying to prise it out of you.'

'Go, then.'

'Is that what you want?' Meg persisted. 'Or are you telling me again what I *should* want?'

'I could come out of this with nothing!'

And if Meg thought she had glimpsed fear before, then she had no idea—because now that gorgeous mouth was strung by taut tendons. His black eyes flashed in terror as he saw himself searching bins for food—not just for himself but for the family she was asking him to provide for. Meg knew then that she had never known real fear…would never know the depth of his terror.

She would not die hungry.

She would not leave the earth unnoticed.

She would be missed.

'I might not be able to give you anything…'

She glimpsed the magnitude of his words.

'We might have nothing.'

'We wouldn't have nothing,' Meg argued, with this man who had no comprehension of family. 'We'd have each other.'

'You don't know what nothing is.'

'So tell me.'

'I don't want to discuss it.'

'Then I *will* leave, Niklas, and I *will* divorce you. And don't you dare come looking for me when the charges are dropped. Don't you dare try to get back in my life when you think the going can only be good.'

He just stood there.

'And don't bother writing to find out what I have, because if I walk out now I will do everything I can to make sure you can't find out. I will write "father unknown" on the birth certificate and you really will be nothing to your child.'

And she was fighting for the baby she had only just found out about, and the family she knew they could be, and as she turned to go Niklas fought for them too.

'Stay.'

'For what?' Meg asked. 'Shall we go to bed?' she demanded. 'Or shall we just do it here? Or…' she looked at him as if she'd had a sudden idea '…or we could talk.'

'You talk too much.'

He pulled her to him and kissed her mouth, running his hands over her, down her waist to her stomach. He pressed his hands into it for a second and then, as if it killed him to touch her there, he slid his hands between her thighs and moved to lift her skirt. He tried desperately to kiss her back to him, but she halted him and pulled her head away.

'And you don't talk enough.'

She would not let him go this time, and he knew he could not kiss her back into his life. And she *would* walk—he knew it. She was a thousand times stronger than she thought, and so must he be—for without her and his baby he was back to nothing.

'Don't waste time in fear, Niklas,' Meg said. 'You told me that.'

So he stood there and slowly and quietly told her what it had been like to be completely alone, to be moved on to yet another boys' home when he caused too much trouble, to boys' homes that had made living on the streets preferable.

And she *was* stronger than she'd thought she was, because she didn't cry or comment—just stood in his arms and listened. She'd asked for this, she reminded herself a few times at some of the harder parts.

'You would make a friend and then you would move on. Or he would steal from you and you would decide to go it alone. Then you might make another friend, and the same would happen again, or you would wake up and he would be lying dead beside you. But you keep on living, and you get a job, and it turns out you are clever—more clever than most—so you start to make money and you start to forget. Except you never do. But you make a good life for yourself, make new friends, and you would not change it, this new life, but still you taste the bitterness of your past. You make more money than you can spend because you're scared of having nothing again and, yes, you're happy—but it still tastes bitter.'

He didn't know how to explain it neatly, but he tried. He looked at her and could not fathom why she wanted to get inside his messed-up head.

'You never forget—not for one minute. You remember eating from bins and beatings, and running away, and the smell of sleeping on the streets, and you trust no one. You remember how people will take from you the second your back is turned—would steal from a beggar who sleeps on the streets. So you relish each mouthful you take and you swear you will never go back to being nothing. But always you fear that you will.'

And then he stopped.

'You want to hear the rest?'

'Yes.'

He paused, took a deep breath before continuing. 'Then you meet a woman on a plane, and this woman feels worried because in living her own life and following her dreams she might hurt her family, and you know then that there are people who do worry about others, who do care. And this woman changes your life.'

'I didn't.'

'More than that—you saved my life. Because when

I did go back to having nothing I survived. More than I should have, I thought of you. Every night I saw the sun, and it was the colour of your hair. Then last night I got to hold you, and look back, and I realised that it is a good world. There are people you cannot trust, but there are also people you can—people who help you even if you don't know it at the time.'

She didn't understand.

'That a woman you only dated for a while would put up her house...' He hesitated. 'Rosa and I...'

'I worked that out.'

'It was before she was married, and there has been nothing since, but her husband is still not pleased that she works for me. That she should go to him, that Silvio should trust her and me enough—that is real friendship,' he said. 'That does not let you taste bitterness.'

And that part she understood.

'Then you look back further and realise that the nun who taught you Spanish, the woman who named you, was the one good thing you can properly remember from your childhood and will end up saving the life of the woman you love—how can you not be grateful for that?'

'You can't not be.'

'And that woman you met on the plane—who your gut told you was right—who you married and then hurt so badly—would fly into Congonhas Airport to come and have paid sex with me...'

She thought of his anger in the prison, and the roughness of the sex, and then his tenderness afterwards, and she was so glad that he'd known he was loved, that she'd told him.

'I'd have done it for nothing.'

'I know,' he said, and he was honest. 'You loved me when I had nothing, and you will never properly appreciate what that means. But I might again have nothing, and I thought that was my worst nightmare, but to have nothing to give you or my child...'

'We've got a home that you chose for us,' Meg said. 'And I can work, and I have parents who will help me. Your child—our child—will never have nothing, and neither will you, so long as we have each other.'

He still could not really fathom it, but maybe he was starting to believe it.

'It might not mean prison...the charges could be dropped...' he said. 'Rosa thinks they have enough already to prove I was not involved. They are going through the evidence now.'

'And, unlike your wife, Rosa's got a good legal brain!' Meg said.

He didn't smile, but he gave a half-smirk.

'Rosa thinks it was Miguel who suggested the plan to my brother.' He tested this new thing called love. 'I want him to have a proper funeral. I want to find out more about him. I want to know about his life. Do you understand that?'

'Yes.'

'I might not talk about it without you.'

And still he said all the wrong things, but they were the right things for them.

'Whatever feels right for you.' And now she understood him a little better. She didn't have to know everything, didn't have to have all of him—just the parts that he chose to give. They were more than enough. And when he did choose to share, she could be there for him.

'Can you accept now that, even though I don't tell you everything, there are no secrets that might hurt you between us?'

'Yes.'

And then he did what Niklas did when he had to: he simply turned the pain of his past off. He smiled at her, held her, and then for the longest time he kissed her—a kiss that tasted deeper now, a kiss that had her burning.

But, unusually for Niklas, he stopped.

'And just to prove how much I love you,' he said, 'there will be no more sex for a while, so we can talk some more.'

'I didn't mean that.'

'No.' He was insistent. 'I can see what you were saying. We can go for a walk in the mountains.' He smiled and it was wicked. 'We can get some fresh air and we can talk some more...'

'Stop it.' His mouth had left her wanting.

She tried to kiss him, tried to resume, but Niklas shrugged her off and found a basket, started loading it from the fridge.

'We're going to have a picnic,' Niklas said. 'Is that romantic?'

He was the sexiest guy she had ever met, Meg realised, and she'd been complaining because they were having too much sex...

'Niklas, please.' She didn't want a picnic in the mountains, didn't want a sex strike from her Brazilian lover, and she told him so.

'Husband,' he corrected. 'I married you, remember?'

'Yes.'

'How can you say it was all about sex? I was nothing but a gentleman that day...I could have had you on the plane, but I married you first!'

'Hardly a gentleman,' she said. 'But, yes, you *did* marry me, and I get it all now. So can you put the basket down and...?'

'And what?' Niklas said.

Seemingly shallow, but impossibly deep, he was gorgeous and insatiable, and he was hers for ever.

His sex strike lasted all of two minutes, because now he was lifting her onto the kitchen bench even as he kissed her. His hands were everywhere and his mouth was too, but so were her hands before he slapped them away. '*I'm* doing this.'

He was the most horrible tease.

He whistled when he lifted up her skirt. 'What are you wearing?'

She writhed in embarrassment at his scrutiny. 'They're new.'

'You didn't buy these, though.' He smiled, because he couldn't really imagine his seemingly uptight girl buying knickers you didn't even have to take off.

'I might have.'

'Meg...' He was very matter-of-fact as he pulled down his zipper. 'You wore sensible knickers the day I met you. You even wore sensible knickers when you came to visit me in prison.' And then carefully he positioned her. 'Watch.'

And when he slipped straight into her the outrageous knickers she was wearing seemed like a sensible choice now.

'Never think I don't love you.' He would say it a hundred times a day if he had to. 'Never think that this is not love.'

And she knew then that he *did* love her, and that what they shared was much more than just sex. He was very slow and deliberate, and it was Meg who couldn't stop. He kept going as the scream built within her, and she waited for his hand to cover her mouth, waited for him to hush her—except they were home now, as he told her, and he pushed harder into her.

'We're home,' he said again, and moved faster, and for the first time she could scream, could sob and scream as much as she wanted, could be whoever and however she pleased.

And so too could he.

He told her how much he loved her as he came, and over and over he told her that he would work something out, he would sort this out.

And as he looked over her shoulder to the mountains he knew how lucky he was—how easily it could have been him lying dead on the pavement instead of his brother. His twin who must have tasted so much bitterness in his life too and been unable to escape as Niklas had done. When still he held her, when he buried his face in her hair and she heard his ragged breathing, for a moment she said nothing.

And then, because it was Niklas, he switched off his pain and came to her, smiling. 'Do you know what day it is today?'

'The day we found out we—' She stopped then, and blinked in realisation as her husband moved in to kiss her.

'Happy anniversary.'

CHAPTER THIRTEEN

SHE LOVED BRAZIL more and more every day she spent there, but it was the evenings she loved the most.

Meg lay half dozing by the pool, then stretched and smelt the air, damp from the rain that often came in the afternoon, washing the mountains till they were gleaming, and thought about how happy she was.

The charges had been dropped, but it had taken a couple of months for them to get back on their feet. They had paid Rosa back her money and lived off Meg's savings, but only when the nightmare of his returning to prison had stopped looming over them and Meg's pregnancy had started showing had Niklas really begun to think this was real.

There were now regular trips into São Paulo, and Niklas came to each pre-natal visit, and she loved that her family adored Brazil as much as Niklas did Australia when they were there.

She saw her parents often—they had only just left that day—and, thanks to a few suggestions and more than a little help from their new son-in-law, business was going well in Sydney.

They had surprised her—after the shock of finding out had worn off, they'd been wonderful. Niklas had flown them over to Brazil and the first day he'd met them he'd begun to work out why sometimes you couldn't just hang up the phone or shut someone out. He'd started to get used to both the complications and the rewards of family.

They hadn't shared their good news about Meg's pregnancy on that visit—it had seemed all too new and too soon to give them another thing to deal with, and there had also been a funeral to prepare for.

She had thought Niklas would do that on his own, except he hadn't.

Only a few other people had been invited. Meg had met Carla for the first time, and she was, of course, stunning, and there had been Rosa and her colleagues, and Rosa's husband Silvio too. And, even if they hadn't wanted to attend at first, her parents had come too, because they loved Meg and Niklas, and Niklas had told them how much it was appreciated. There had been flowers sent from Fernando—a fellow *paulistano* who knew only too well how tough it was on the streets, who knew that sometimes it was just about surviving.

Meg had been a bit teary, saying goodbye to her parents that morning, but they'd reassured her that they'd be returning in a month's time, so that they could be there for the birth of their grandchild.

If she lasted another month, Meg thought as she felt a tightening again and picked up her baby guidebook.

No, it wasn't painful, and they were ages apart. So she read about Braxton Hicks for a while. But then another one came, and this time she noted the time on her phone, because though it didn't quite hurt she found herself holding her breath till it passed. Maybe she should ring someone to check—or just wait because Niklas would be home soon? It probably was just Braxton Hicks...

Her pregnancy book said so...

Meg loved being pregnant. She loved her ripening belly, and so too did Niklas. And she loved *him* more than she had thought she was capable of.

No, she'd never fully know him. But she had the rest of her life to try and work out the most complicated man in the world.

The nightmares had stopped for both of them and life had moved on, and more and more she realised how much he loved her.

There was plenty of happiness—they had friends over often, and many evenings she got to do what she adored: trying out new recipes.

Meg looked at her phone. It had been ages since the last pain, so she should be getting started with dinner really. They had Rosa and her husband and a few other guests coming over tonight, to cheer Meg up after saying goodbye to her parents.

They had such good friends. She could even laugh at things now, and she and Rosa had become firm allies. Rosa would sometimes tease Meg about the earlier conversations they had shared—not to mention the outrageous knickers.

God, she'd been such an uptight thing then.

She lay blushing in her bikini at the thought of the lovely things they did, and then she felt another tightening. She looked at her phone again, noting the time. They were still ages apart, but as she heard the hum of the helicopter bringing Niklas home she was suddenly glad he was here. She walked across the lush grounds to meet him and picked a few ripe avocados from the tree to make a guacamole. As she did so she felt something gush.

It would seem the book was wrong. These weren't practice contractions, because there was real pain gripping her now—a tightening that had her blowing her breath out and feeling the strangest pressure.

Niklas saw her double over as he walked towards her. He could hear the chopper lifting into the sky and was torn between whether to ring and have the pilot return or just to get to her. He walked quickly, cursing himself because they had been going to move to his city apartment at the weekend, so that they could be closer to the hospital.

'It's fine...' He was very calm and practical when he found her kneeling on the grass. 'I'll get the chopper sent back and we will fly you to the hospital. Let's get you into the house...' He tried to help her stand but she kept moaning. 'Okay...' he said. 'I will carry you inside...'

'No...' She was kneeling down and desperate to push—though part of her told her not to, told her it couldn't be happening, that she still had ages, must keep the baby in. And yet another part of her told her that if she pushed hard enough, if she just gave in and went with it, the pain would be gone.

'It's coming!'

She was vaguely aware of him ringing someone, and frowned when she heard who it was.

'Carla?'

She wasn't thinking straight, the pain was far too much, but why the *hell* was he calling Carla?

'Done,' he said.

'Done?'

'Help is on the way...'

She could see him sweating, which Niklas never did, but his voice was very calm and he was very reassuring.

'She will be ringing for the helicopter to come back and for an ambulance...'

He saw her start to cry because she knew they would be too late—that the baby was almost here.

'It's fine...' He took off his jacket and she watched him take out his cufflinks and very neatly start to fold up his sleeves. 'Everything will be okay.'

'You've delivered a lot of babies, have you?' She was shouting and she didn't mean to.

'No,' he said, and then he looked up and straight into her eyes, and he turned her pain and fear off, because that was what he did best. 'But I did do a life-skills course in prison...'

And that he made her smile, even if she was petrified, and then she started shouting again when he had the gall to answer his ringing phone.

'It's the obstetrician.'

She must remember to thank Carla, Meg thought as he pulled down her bikini bottoms. From what she could make out with her limited Portuguese he was telling the doctor on speakerphone that, yes, he could see the head.

She could have told the doctor that!

But she was sort of glad not to know what was being said—sort of glad just to push and then be told to stop and then to push some more. She was *very* annoyed when he said something that made the obstetrician laugh, and she was about to tell him so when suddenly their baby was out.

'Sim,' he told the doctor. *'Ela é rosa e respiração.'*

Yes, her baby was pink and breathing. They were the best words in the world and, given he had said *ela*, it would seem they had a baby girl.

The doctor didn't need to ask if the baby was crying for it sang across the mountains—and Meg cried too.

Not Niklas—he never cried. Just on the day he'd found out she was safe she had seen a glimpse, and then the next day she had guessed he might have been, but he was in midwife mode now!

He did what the doctor said and kept them both warm. He took his shirt off and wrapped his daughter in it, and there was his jacket around Meg, and then he got a rug from beside the pool and covered them both with it. He thanked the doctor and said he could hear help arriving, and then he turned off his phone.

'She needs to feed,' he told her, and he must have seen her wide eyes. He was an expert in breastfeeding now, was he? 'The doctor said it will help with the next bit...'

'Oh...'

'Well done,' he said.

'Well done to you too.' She smiled at her lovely midwife. 'Were you scared?'

'Of course not.' He shook his head. 'It's a natural process. Normally quick deliveries are easy ones...'

He said a few other things that had her guessing he'd been reading her book—the bit about babies that come quickly and early.

'She's early...' Meg sighed, because she had really been hoping that this would be a very late baby, that somehow they could fudge the dates a little and she would never know she'd been made in prison.

'It will be fine,' he said. 'She was made with love. That's all she needs to know.'

They had a name for a boy and one for a girl, and he nodded when she checked that he still wanted it. She tasted his kiss. Then she saw him look down to his daughter and thought maybe she glimpsed a tear, but she did not go there—she just loved that moment alone, the three of them, just a few minutes before the helicopter arrived—alone on their mountain with their new baby, Emilia Dos Santos.

The Portuguese meaning, though.

From the saints.

* * * * *

DANTE: CLAIMING HIS SECRET LOVE-CHILD

SANDRA MARTON

Sandra Marton wrote her first novel while she was still in primary school. Her doting parents told her she'd be a writer some day, and Sandra believed them. In secondary school and college she wrote dark poetry nobody but her boyfriend understood – though, looking back, she suspects he was just being kind. As a wife and mother she wrote murky short stories in what little spare time she could manage, but not even her boyfriend-turned-husband could pretend to understand those. Sandra tried her hand at other things, among them teaching and serving on the Board of Education in her home town, but the dream of becoming a writer was always in her heart.

At last Sandra realised she wanted to write books about what all women hope to find: love with that one special man, love that's rich with fire and passion, love that lasts for ever. She wrote a novel, her very first, and sold it to Mills & Boon® Modern™ Romance. Since then she's written more than sixty books, all of them featuring sexy, gorgeous, larger-than-life heroes. A four-time RITA® award finalist, she's also received five *Romantic Times* magazine awards, and has been honoured with RT's Career Achievement Award for Series Romance. Sandra lives with her very own sexy, gorgeous, larger-than-life hero in a sun-filled house on a quiet country lane in the north-eastern United States.

CHAPTER ONE

DANTE Orsini was in the prime of his life.

He was rich, powerful and as ruggedly good-looking as a man could hope to be. He worked hard, played hard, and on those rare nights he went to bed alone, he slept soundly until morning.

But not tonight.

Tonight he was dreaming.

In his dream he walked slowly along a narrow road. It led to a house. He could hardly see it because of the heavy mist that hung over everything, but it was there.

His footsteps slowed.

It was the last place on earth he wanted to be. A house in the suburbs. A station wagon in the driveway. A dog. A cat. Two-point-five kids.

And a wife. One woman, the same woman, forever…

Dante sprang up in bed, gasping for air. A shudder racked his big, leanly muscled body. He slept naked, kept the windows open even now, in early autumn. Still, his skin was slick with sweat.

A dream. That's all it was. A nightmare.

The oysters last night, maybe. Or that brandy right before bedtime. Or…he shuddered again. Or just another resurfacing of that long-ago memory of what had happened when he was just eighteen, stupid and in love.

In what he'd thought was love.

He'd gone steady with Teresa D'Angelo for three months before he'd so much as touched her. When he finally did, one touch led to another and another and another....

Christmas Eve, he'd given her a gold locket.

She'd given him news that almost brought him to his knees.

"I'm pregnant, Dante," she'd whispered tearfully.

He'd been stunned. He was a kid, yeah, but he'd still known enough to use condoms. But he loved her. And she'd wept in his arms and said he'd ruined her life, that he had to marry her.

He would have.

He would have Done The Right Thing.

But fate, luck, whatever you wanted to call it, intervened. His brothers noticed how withdrawn he'd become. They sat him down, saw to it that he had enough beer to loosen him up a little and then Nicolo asked him, point-blank, what was going on.

Dante told them about his girl.

And the three of them, Nicolo and Raffaele and Falco, looked at each other, looked at him and said, was he out of his freaking mind? If he'd used protection, how could she have gotten knocked up?

She had to be lying.

He went after Falco because he'd said it first. When Rafe and Nick repeated it, he went after them, too. Falco grabbed him in an arm lock.

"I love her, dammit," Dante said. "You hear me? I love her and she loves me."

"She loves your money, dude," Nicolo had said, and for the first time in days Dante had laughed.

"What money?"

Falco let go of him. And Rafe pointed out that the girl didn't know he wasn't loaded. That even way back then, all four Orsini brothers had thumbed their noses at their old man's money and power and everything that went with it.

"Ask around," Falco, the oldest of them, said bluntly. "Find out how many other guys she's been with."

Dante lunged for him again. Nick and Rafe held him back.

"Use your head," Nick snapped, "not that divining rod in your pants."

Rafe nodded in agreement. "And tell her you want a paternity test."

"She wouldn't lie to me," Dante protested. "She loves me."

"Tell her you want the damned test," Rafe growled. "Or we'll tell her for you."

He knew Rafe meant it. So, with a dozen apologies, he'd suggested the test.

Teresa's tears had given way to fury. She'd called him every name in the book and he'd never heard from her again. Yeah, she'd broken his heart but she'd also taught him a lesson that still came back to haunt him when he least expected it.

Like that ridiculous dream.

Dante took a couple of deep breaths, sank back against the pillows and folded his arms behind his head.

Marriage? A wife? Kids? No way. After years of trying to decide what to do with his life, of coming close to losing it a couple of times in places no sane man should have been, he'd finally sorted things out. Now he had everything a man could possibly want: this penthouse, with the morning sun pouring through the skylight above his bed. A cherry-red Ferrari. A private jet.

And women.

A wicked grin lit his hard, handsome face.

More women, sometimes, than a guy could handle and all of them beautiful, sexy and not foolish enough to think they could con him into anything more permanent than a relationship—and, God, he hated that word—a relationship of a few months duration.

He was between women right now.

Taking a breather, Falco had said wryly. True. And enjoying every minute of it. Like the blonde at that charity thing last week. He'd gone to what should have been a dull cocktail party. Save the City, Save the World, Save the Squirrels, who knew what? Orsini Brothers Investments had bought four tickets, but only one of the brothers had to show his face.

As Rafe had so elegantly put it, it was Dante's turn in the barrel.

So he'd showered and changed in his private bathroom at the office, taxied to the Waldorf figuring on a few polite handshakes and a glass of not-very-good wine—the wine was never very good at these things even if it cost five thousand bucks to buy a ticket.

And felt someone watching him.

It was the blonde, and she was spectacular. Long legs. Lots of shiny hair. A slow, sexy smile and enough cleavage to get lost in.

He'd made his way through the crowd, introduced himself. A few minutes of conversation and the lady got to the point.

"It's so noisy here," she'd purred and he'd said, yeah, it was and why didn't he take her somewhere quiet, where they could talk?

But what happened in the taxi the doorman hailed had nothing to do with talk. Carin or Carla or whatever her name was had been all over him. By the time they got to her apartment, they were both so hot they'd barely made it through the door....

Dante threw back the blankets, rose from the bed and made his way to the bathroom. He had her cell number but he wouldn't use it tonight. Tonight he had a date with a cute redhead he'd met last week. As for that dream...

Ridiculous.

All that had happened almost fifteen years ago. He knew now he'd never loved the girl who'd claimed he'd made her pregnant, though he did owe her a thank-you for teaching him an important life lesson.

When you took a woman to bed, it was your trousers you left on the floor, not your brain.

Dante tilted his head back, closed his pale-blue eyes, let the water sluice the shampoo from his dark-as-midnight hair.

No woman, no matter how beautiful, was worth any deeper involvement than the kind that took place between the sheets.

Without warning a memory shot into his head. A woman. Eyes the color of rich coffee. Hair so many shades of gold the sun seemed trapped there. A soft, rosy mouth that tasted of honey...

Scowling, he shot out his hand, turned off the water and reached for a towel. What the hell was the matter with him this morning? First the insane dream. Now this.

Gabriella Reyes—amazing how he could remember her name and not the name of a woman he'd been with last night, especially since it was a year since he'd seen Gabriella.

One year and two months. And, yeah, okay, twenty-four days...

Dante snorted.

That was what came of having a thing for numbers, he thought as he dumped the towel on the marble vanity. It made him good at what he did at Orsini's but it also made the damnedest nonsense stick in his head.

He dressed quickly in a beat-up New York University T-shirt, the sleeves long since torn out, and a pair of equally disreputable NYU gym shorts, and went down the circular staircase to the lower level of his penthouse, hurrying past the big, high-ceilinged rooms until he reached his gym. It wasn't an elaborate setup. He had only a Nautilus, some free weights, an old treadmill. He only used the stuff when the weather was bad enough to keep him from running in Central Park, but this morning, despite the sunshine, he knew he needed more than a five-mile run if he was going to sweat a couple of old ghosts out of his system. It was a Saturday; he could afford the extra time.

When he was done, he spent a couple of hours online looking at auction sites that dealt in vintage Ferraris, checking to see if there was anything out there that came close to the 1958 Ferrari 250GT Berlinetta "Tour de France" he'd been searching for. There'd been word one had been coming on the market about a year ago in Gstaad; he'd thought about flying over to check it out, but something—he couldn't recall what—had come up just then...

His hands stilled on the keyboard.

Gabriella Reyes. That was what had come up. He'd met her and everything else had flown straight out of his head.

"Dammit," Dante said tightly. That was twice today he'd thought about the woman, and it made no sense. She was history.

Okay. Enough sitting around. He closed his computer,

changed into another pair of shorts and a T-shirt and went out for a run.

Getting all those endorphins pumping did it. He came home feeling good and felt even better when Rafe phoned to say he'd just put away the French bank deal they'd been after. He'd already called Falco and Nick. How about meeting for a couple of drinks to celebrate at their favorite hangout, The Bar down in Chelsea?

By the time the brothers parted, it was hard to remember the day had started badly, but his good mood evaporated when his mother called. Dante loved her with all his heart and even her usual questions—was he keeping good hours? Was he eating properly? Had he found a nice Italian girl to bring to dinner?—even those things couldn't dim his pleasure at hearing her voice.

The message she delivered from his father did.

"Dante, *mio figlio,* Papa wishes you and Raffaele to come for breakfast tomorrow."

He knew what that meant. His father was in a strange mood lately, talking of age and death as if the grim reaper was knocking at the door. This would be another endless litany about attorneys and accountants and bank vaults…as if his sons would touch a dollar of his after he was gone.

His mother knew how he felt. How all her sons felt. Only she and their sisters, Anna and Isabella, persisted in believing the fiction that the old man was a legitimate businessman instead of the *don* he was.

"Dante?" Sofia's tone lightened. "I will make you that pesto frittata you adore. *Si?*"

Dante rolled his eyes. He despised the sight, the smell, the taste of pesto but how could a man ever say such a thing to his mother without hurting her feelings? Which, he thought grimly, was exactly why Cesare sent these invitations through his wife.

So he sighed and said yes, sure, he'd be there.

"With Raffaele. Eight o'clock. You will call him, *si?*"

That, at least, made him grin. "Absolutely, Mama. I know Rafe will be delighted."

All of which was why Sunday morning, when the rest of Manhattan was undoubtedly still asleep, Dante sauntered into the Orsini town house in what had once been Little Italy but was now an increasingly fashionable part of Greenwich Village.

Rafe had arrived before him.

Sofia had already seated him at the big kitchen table where they'd had so many meals *a famiglia*. The table groaned under the weight of endless platters of food, and Rafe, looking not too bad for a man who'd spent last night partying with Dante, the redhead and a blonde Red had come up with after Dante had called and told her his brother needed something to cheer him up—considering all that, Rafe looked pretty good.

Rafe looked up, met Dante's eyes and grunted something Dante figured was "good morning."

Dante grunted back.

He'd danced the night away with Red, first at a club in the meatpacking district, then in her bed. It had been a long night, a great night, lots of laughter, lots of sex…lots and lots of sex during which his body had done its thing but his head had been elsewhere. He'd awakened in his own bed—he made it a point never to spend the night in a woman's bed—with a headache, a bad attitude and no desire whatsoever for conversation or his old man.

Or for the frittata his mother placed in front of him.

"Mangia," she said.

It was an order, not a suggestion. He shuddered slightly—

food was not supposed to be green—and picked up his fork.

The brothers were on their second cups of espresso when Cesare's capo, Felipe, stepped into the room.

"Your father will see you now."

Dante and Rafe rose to their feet. Felipe shook his head. "No, not together. One at a time. Raffaele, you are first."

Rafe smiled tightly and muttered something about the privileges of popes and kings. Dante grinned and told him to have fun.

When he looked back at his plate, there was another frittata on it.

He ate it, got it down with another cup of coffee, then fended off his mother's offerings. Some cheese? Some biscotti? She had that round wheel of bread he liked, from Celini's.

Dante assured her he was not hungry, surreptitiously checked his watch and grew more and more annoyed. After forty minutes he shoved back his chair and got to his feet.

"Mama, I'm afraid I have things to do. Please tell my father that—"

The capo appeared in the doorway. "Your father will see you now."

"So well trained," Dante said pleasantly. "Just like a nice little lap dog."

His father's second in command said nothing, but the look in his eyes was easy to read. Dante showed his teeth in a grin.

"Same to you, too, pal," he said as he pushed past him to the old man's study.

The room was just the way it had always been. Big. Dark. Furnished in impeccably poor taste with paintings of saints and madonnas and God-only-knew-who on the walls. Heavy drapes were pulled across the French doors and windows that led to the garden.

Cesare, seated in a thronelike chair behind his mahogany desk, gestured for Felipe to leave them.

"And close the door," he said, his voice hoarsened by decades' worth of cigars.

Dante sat in a chair across from his father, long legs extended and crossed at the ankles, arms folded. He had dressed in a long-sleeved navy sweater and faded jeans; on his feet were scuffed, well-worn sneakers. His father had never approved of such clothes—one reason, of course, that Dante did.

"Dante."

"Father."

"Thank you for coming."

"You summoned me. What do you want?"

Cesare sighed, shook his head and folded his perfectly manicured hands on the desk.

"'How are you feeling, Father? What is new in your life, Father? Have you done anything interesting lately?'" His bushy eyebrows rose. "Are you incapable of making polite conversation?"

"I know how you're feeling. Hale and hearty, despite your conviction you're approaching death's door, just as I know whatever might be new in your life is best left unmentioned." Dante smiled coldly. "And if you've done anything interesting lately, perhaps you should entertain the Feds by telling it to them, not to me."

Cesare chuckled. "You have a good sense of humor, my son."

"But not much tolerance for BS so let's get to it. What do you want? Is this another session of 'I am dying and you must know certain things'? Because if it is—"

"It isn't."

"Straight and to the point." Dante nodded. "I'm impressed. As impressed as I can ever be, by the likes of you."

Cesare flushed. "Insults from two sons, all in one morning. It is I who am impressed."

Dante grinned. "I gather your conversation with Rafe was so pleasant he decided to leave through the garden rather than spend an extra minute under your roof."

"Dante. Do you think you might grant me time to speak?"

Well, well. A new approach. No barking. No commands. Instead, a tone that bordered on civility. Not that it changed anything, but Dante was, he had to admit, curious.

"Sure," he said politely, checked his watch then met the old man's eyes. "How's five minutes sound?"

A muscle knotted in Cesare's jaw but he kept silent, opened a desk drawer, took out a manila folder and slid it toward his son.

"You are a successful investor, are you not, *mio figlio?* Take a look and tell me what you think."

Damn, another surprise. That was as close as his father had ever come to giving him a compliment. Clever, too. The old man surely knew he couldn't resist opening the folder after that.

The sheaf of papers inside was thick. The top sheet, labeled *Overview* surprised him.

"This is about a ranch," he said, glancing up.

"Not just a ranch, Dante. It is about Viera y Filho. Viera and Son. The name of an enormous *fazenda* in Brazil."

Dante's eyes narrowed. "Brazil?"

"*Si.*" His father's mouth twitched. "You have heard of the place, I assume?"

"Very amusing."

"The ranch covers tens of thousands of acres."

"And?"

"And," Cesare said with a casual shrug, "I wish to purchase it."

Dante stared at his father. Cesare owned a sanitation company. A construction company. Real estate. But a ranch?

"What the hell for?"

"It is, according to those documents, a good investment."

"So is the Empire State Building."

"I know the owner," Cesare said, ignoring the remark. "Juan Viera. Well, I did, years ago. We, ah, we had some business dealings together."

Dante laughed. "I'll bet."

"He came to me for a loan. I turned him down."

"So?"

"So, he is ill. And I feel guilty. I should have—" Cesare's eyes went flat. "You find this amusing?"

"You? Feeling guilt? Come on, Father. This is me, not Isabella or Anna. You don't know the meaning of the word."

"Viera is dying. His only son, Arturo, will inherit the property. The boy is unfit. The ranch has been in the Viera family for two centuries, but Arturo will lose it, one way or another, before Viera is cold in the ground."

"Let me get this straight. You expect me to believe your motives are purely altruistic? That you want to buy this ranch to save it?"

"I know you do not think highly of me—"

Dante laughed.

"Perhaps I have done some things I regret. Don't look so shocked, *mio figlio*. A man nearing the end of his life is entitled to begin thinking about the disposition of his immortal soul."

Dante put the folder on the desk. This was turning into one hell of a strange day.

"I ask only that you fly to Brazil, look things over and, if you deem it appropriate, make an offer on the ranch."

"The market's going to hell in a hand basket and you expect me to set aside my work, fly to South America and make an enemy of yours an offer he cannot refuse?"

"Very amusing. And very incorrect. Viera is not my enemy."

"Whatever. The point is, I am busy. I have no time to stomp around in cow manure just so you can assuage a guilty conscience."

"This is a far simpler thing than I asked of your brother."

"Yeah, well, whatever you asked him, I'll bet he told you what I'm going to tell you." Dante shot to his feet. "You can take your so-called conscience and—"

"Have you ever been to Brazil, Dante? Do you know anything about it?"

Dante's jaw tightened. The only thing he knew about Brazil was that it was Gabriella Reyes's birthplace, and what the hell did she have to do with anything?

"I've been to Sao Paulo," he said coldly. "On business."

"Business. For that company of yours."

"It's called Orsini Investments," Dante said, even more coldly.

"It is said you are excellent at negotiating."

"So?"

His father shrugged. "Why ask a stranger for help when one's own son is considered the best?"

A compliment? Pure bull, sure, but, dammit, it hit its mark. Why not admit that?

"Well," Cesare said, on a dramatic sigh, "if you will not do this thing…"

Dante looked at his father. "I can only spare a couple of days."

His father smiled. "That will surely be enough. And, who knows? You might even learn something new."

"About?"

Cesare smiled again. "About negotiating, *mio figlio*. About negotiating."

A world away, more than five thousand miles southwest of New York, Gabriella Reyes sat on the veranda of the big house in which she'd grown up.

Back then the house, the veranda, the *fazenda* itself had been magnificent.

Not anymore. Everything was different now.

So was she.

As a child on this ranch, she'd been scrawny, all legs and pigtails. Shy to the point of being tongue-tied. Her father had hated that about her; the truth was, she couldn't think of anything about herself that he hadn't hated.

This place, the verandah, had been her sanctuary. Hers and her brother's. Arturo had been even less favored by their father than she had been.

Arturo had left the ranch the day he turned eighteen. She had missed him terribly but she'd understood, he'd had to leave this place to survive.

At eighteen, Gabriella had suddenly blossomed. The ugly ducking had become a swan. She hadn't seen it but others did, including a North American who had seen her on a street in Bonito, doubled back and handed her his business card. A week later she'd flown to New York and landed her first modeling assignment. She'd loved her work...

And she'd met a man.

She'd been happy, at least for a little while.

Now, she was back at Viera y Filho. Her father was dead. So was her brother. The man was gone from her life. She was alone in this sad, silent house, but then, one way or another, she had always been alone.

Even when she had been Dante Orsini's lover.

Perhaps never as much as when she had been Dante's lover, if she had ever really been that. She had warmed his bed but not his heart, and why was she wasting time thinking of him? There was no point in it, no reason, no logic—

"Senhorita?"

Gabriella looked up into the worried face of the *ama* who had all but raised her. *"Sim, Yara?"*

"Ele chama lhe."

Gabriella shot to her feet and hurried into the house. He was calling for her! How could she have forgotten, even for a moment?

She was not alone. Not anymore.

CHAPTER TWO

HE FLEW to Brazil by commercial jet. Falco was using the Orsini plane.

Based on the way they were dressed, he figured that most of the other passengers in the first-class cabin were going to Campo Grande on vacation. The city was near something called the Pantanal. His travel agent had started gushing about the area's trails, the canoeing, the amazing variety of wildlife.

Dante had cut her short.

"Just book me into a decent hotel and arrange for a rental car," he'd said curtly.

He was most assuredly not heading to South America for pleasure.

This was strictly business. His father's business, and that he'd let Cesare push the right buttons ticked him off no end.

"Mr. Orsini," the flight attendant said pleasantly, "may I get you something?"

Somebody to examine my head, Dante thought grimly.

"Sir? Something to drink?"

He asked for red wine; she launched into a listing of the choices available and he stopped himself from snarling at her the way he'd snarled at the travel agent.

"Your choice," he said, before she could ask him any-thing else.

Then he opened his briefcase and read through the papers his father had given him.

They didn't tell him very much that he didn't already know. The Viera ranch ran thousands of head of cattle as well as a relatively small number of horses. It had been owned by the same family for generations.

A vellum business card bore the name, phone number and address of Juan Viera's lawyer. A note in Cesare's handwriting was scrawled on the back:

"Deal through him, not through the Vieras."

Fine.

He'd call the man first thing, maybe even tonight. Brazilians kept late hours; the times he'd been in Sao Paulo on business, dinner never started much before 10 p.m. Whenever he called the lawyer, he would request an im-mediate meeting. He'd explain the purpose of his visit and make an offer for the ranch.

How long could that take? Maybe not even the two days he'd allocated for it.

He felt his mood lighten. With luck, he might be heading back to New York in no time.

It was midevening when he stepped off the plane.

Thanks to the time change, he'd lost two hours. Too late to phone Viera's attorney and maybe that was just as well. All he wanted to do after the seemingly endless flight was pick up a car, get to his hotel, shower and eat something prepared by a human being instead of an airline catering service's assembly line.

The hotel, in the town of Bonito, maybe twenty minutes from the Campo Grande Airport, met the requirements he'd laid out to his travel agent. It was comfortable and quiet, as was his suite. He showered, changed into a pale blue cotton shirt and faded jeans. Room service sent up a rare steak, green salad and a pot of coffee, and Dante settled down to leaf through the documents again.

Maybe he'd missed something the first time.

Ten minutes later he tossed the papers aside. No. He hadn't missed anything. What he'd hoped to see was something about the *filho* of Viera y Filho. Why Cesare was so convinced that the son's stewardship would lead to disaster. A hint as to why his father should give a damn.

But there was nothing.

Dante took a bottle of beer from the minibar, opened it and stepped onto a small balcony that overlooked a moonlit pool. He was exhausted but he knew he wouldn't sleep. The long flight, the time change, the fact that he was still angry at being here...

If a man carved time out of a busy week to fly more than 5,000 miles, it should be for a better reason than running an errand he didn't understand for a father he didn't respect.

Like conducting business for Orsini Brothers. Or kicking back and enjoying a vacation.

Or locating Gabriella.

Dante scowled, lifted the bottle of beer and took a long swallow.

Where had that come from? Why would he want to locate her? For starters, Brazil was an enormous country. He had no idea what part she was from, no certainty she'd returned there. Rafe's girlfriend, Miss Germany 2000-something-or-other, Rafe's *former* girlfriend, a model the same as Gabriella, had once said that was what she'd heard.

Not that he'd asked, Dante thought quickly.

He'd just sort of wondered, out loud, if Rafe's ex had known her.

Dammit, why was he even thinking about Gabriella? The affair had been fun while it lasted. A couple of months, that was all, and then she'd slipped out of his life or maybe he'd slipped out of hers….

Okay. So it hadn't been quite like that.

He'd gone away on business, a trip Nick was supposed to make but Nick had had other things going on and Dante had offered to go in his place.

"You sure?" Nick had said. "Because I can just postpone this for a week…"

"No," Dante had said, "no, that's fine. I can use a break in routine."

So he'd flown to Rome or maybe it was Paris, and he hadn't said anything about leaving to Gabriella because why would he? They were dating, that was all. Dating exclusively because that was how he did things, one woman at a time while it lasted, but dating was all it was.

While he was away it had hit him that the thing with Gabriella had pretty much run its course. He'd gone to Tiffany's as soon as he got back, bought a pair of diamond earrings, phoned her, arranged to meet her at Perse for dinner.

He'd been uncommonly nervous through the meal. Ridiculous, when he'd been through moments like this many times before. Finally, over coffee, he'd taken her hand.

"Gabriella. I have something to tell you."

"And I…I have something to tell you, too."

Her voice had been a whisper. Her cheeks had been flushed. Hell. She was going to tell him she'd fallen in love with him. He'd lived this scene before; he knew the warning signs. So he'd moved fast, put the little box that held the earrings on the table between them and said, quickly, how fond he was of her but how busy things had suddenly become at work, how he wished her the best of luck and if she ever needed him for anything...

She hadn't said a word.

The flush had left her cheeks. In fact, she'd gone white. Then she'd pushed back her chair and walked out of the restaurant, leaving the earrings, leaving him, just walked, head up, spine straight, never once looked back.

Dante tossed back the last of the beer, exchanged his jeans for shorts and went out for a run. When he returned an hour later, he tumbled into bed and slept, dream free, until the wake-up call from the front desk awakened him the next morning.

Eduardo de Souza, the Viera attorney, sounded pleasant enough.

Dante explained he was the son of an old acquaintance of Juan Viera and asked if they could meet as soon as possible.

"Ah," de Souza said, on a long sigh. "And your father knows what has happened?"

That Viera was dying? That the man's son was about to inherit the Viera ranch?

"Yes," Dante said, "he does. That's why I'm here, *senhor.*" He paused, unsure of how the lawyer would react. "My father wishes to buy the place from him."

Silence. Then de Souza, sounding puzzled, said, "From whom?"

"From Viera. From the estate. Look, *senhor,* if we could meet to discuss this..."

"Indeed. I can see we have much to discuss...but little time in which to do it. I am, in fact, on my way to the Viera *fazenda* right now. Can you meet me there?"

De Souza gave him directions, told him to watch for a turnoff about thirty miles from town.

"The sign is gone, I am afraid, but you will know you are in the right place because it will be the only turnoff for miles in any direction. Just drive through the gate. It is perhaps one mile from there to the house."

Dante found the turnoff without any difficulty. The gate was open, the gravel road ahead pockmarked with holes. After about a mile, a house and half a dozen outbuildings came into view. A corral stood off to one side of the clearing.

Dante frowned. The buildings, including the house, gave off a general sense of neglect. The corral enclosed only weeds. There were some vehicles in the clearing: a few well-used pickups, cars with mud caked on their wheels, and an enormous SUV, all gleaming black paint and shiny chrome. Stupid to dislike a vehicle, Dante knew, but he disliked this thing on sight.

Slowly he stepped from his car. This was a successful ranch? Maybe he'd taken the wrong road...

"*Senhor* Orsini?"

A short, stout man was hurrying down the steps, patting his sweating face with a handkerchief.

"*Senhor* de Souza?" Dante extended his hand. "It's good to meet you, sir."

"I tried to delay things, *senhor,* but there was some impatience. You understand."

Delay what? Dante started to ask, but the lawyer clutched his elbow and hurried him into the house. Men stood in little clusters, arms folded. One man, huge in girth and height, dressed like a movie villain in black and puffing on a cigar that filled the room with its stink, stood alone. Dante pegged him instantly as the owner of the SUV. A wide staircase rose toward the second floor; in front of it stood a guy in a shiny suit, rattling away in indecipherable

Brazilian Portuguese. Every now and then, one of the spectators grunted in response.

Dante frowned. "What's going on here?"

"Why, the auction, of course," de Souza whispered. "Of the ranch. By the bank." An expressive shrug. "You know."

No, Dante thought furiously, he did not know. His father had sent him into a situation without giving him any of the necessary facts. He grabbed the lawyer's arm, dragged him into a corner.

"Juan Viera is selling the place?"

The little man's eyebrows lifted. "Juan Viera is dead, *senhor.*"

Dead? Dante took a breath. "His son, then? Arturo is selling it?"

"Arturo is dead, too. Is that not why you are here? To bid on Viera y Filho?"

"Well, yeah, but I had no idea that—"

"You must be prepared to bid strongly, *senhor.*"

Hell. This was not a way to do business.

"What's the place worth?"

The lawyer quoted a figure in Brazilian *reals,* quickly amended it to its U.S. dollar equivalent.

"That's it? Fifty thousand is all?"

"That will cover the money owed the bank." De Souza hesitated. "But if *you* bid, you will have to go much higher." His voice fell to a whisper. "There is another interested party, you see."

Dante had been to auctions before. He'd bought a couple of paintings at Sotheby's. There was often another interested party but Sotheby's hadn't been like this. There was a sense of something not just competitive but raw in the air.

"Okay. What's the bid up to?"

The lawyer listened. "Twenty thousand *reals*. Half what the bank wants."

Dante nodded. This wasn't his money, it was his old man's. Spend what you must, Cesare had ended up telling him, up to half a million bucks. That gave him significant leeway—and the sooner this was over, the sooner he could leave.

"Bid one hundred thousand."

The lawyer cleared his throat. Called out the amount in *reals*. The room fell silent. Everyone looked first at Dante, then at the big guy in black who slowly turned and looked at him, too. Dante held the man's gaze until he shifted the cigar from one side of his mouth to the other and showed all his teeth in what no one in his right mind would ever call a smile.

"Two hundred thousand dollars, U.S.," the man said, in lightly accented English.

There were audible gasps from the others.

What was this? A contest over what looked like a place that would suck in tens, maybe hundreds of thousands to put right? Maybe Cesare was nuts, Dante thought, but he wasn't, and hadn't his father said he was handing this off to him because of his business expertise?

Dante shrugged. "You want it that bad," he started to say…

And then a voice as soft as the petal of a rose said his name and he knew, God, he knew who it was even before he turned to the stairs and saw her.

Gabriella's heart was pounding.

It was Dante. But it couldn't be. He was a bitter memory from another time, another place…

"Gabriella?"

Deus, he was real!

Almost a year and a half had gone by and yet everything about him was familiar. His broad shoulders and long, leanly muscled body. The hard planes and angles of his face. His eyes, the palest shade of blue.

And his mouth. Firm and sensual, and even now she remembered the feel of it against hers.

He was moving toward her. She shook her head, stepped back. She knew she could not let him touch her. If he did, she might crumple. All the nights she'd thought of him. Willed herself *not* to think of him. Told herself she hated him, that she hoped and prayed she would never see him again…

True, all of it.

And yet, standing in the shadows of the second-floor landing, listening as her fate was decided by a group of faceless men, she'd heard his voice and reacted with the predictability of Pavlov's dog, her heart racing, her lips readying to curve in a smile.

She drew a deep, unsteady breath.

Those days were gone. She had no reason to smile at this man. She felt nothing for him. Not even hatred. The sight of him had stunned her, that was all…

Unless…unless he had come for her. In the darkest hours of the darkest nights, even despising him, she had wept for him. For his touch. And sometimes…sometimes, she had dared to dream that he had discovered her secret, that he was coming to her, coming for her…

"What are you doing here?" he said.

His bewildered question shattered the last of those ridiculous dreams. Reality rushed in and with it, the cold knowledge that she had to get rid of him as quickly as possible. Her heart was racing again, this time with trepidation, but the recent changes in her life had brought back the ingrained habits of childhood, and she drew herself up and met his confusion with calm resolution.

"I think a far better question is, what are *you* doing here?"

He looked surprised. Well, why wouldn't he? He was a man who never had to answer to anyone.

"I'm here on business."

"What kind of business would bring you to the end of the earth?"

"I came to buy this ranch."

She felt the color leave her face.

"Viera y Filho," he said impatiently, "and you still haven't answered *my* question."

A sigh swept through the room, followed by the sound of a man's unpleasant laughter. She saw Dante turn toward Andre Ferrantes and she felt a rush of panic. Who knew what he would say?

"Something about this amuses you?" Dante said coldly.

Ferrantes smiled. "Everything about this amuses me, *senhor*, including this touching scene of reunion." Ferrantes cocked his head. "I only wonder…how well do you know the *senhorita?*"

"Dante," Gabriella said quickly, "listen to me…"

Ferrantes stepped forward, elbowing another man aside. "I ask," he said softly, "because I know her well." Gabriella gasped as he wrapped a thick arm around her waist and tugged her to his side. "Intimately, one might say. Isn't that correct, Gabriella?"

Dante's eyes went cold and flat. They locked on Ferrantes's face even as he directed his question to her.

"What is he talking about?"

She had heard him use that tone before, not long after they'd met. They'd been strolling along a street in Soho. It was late, after midnight, and they'd heard a thin cry down a dark alley, the thump of something hitting the ground.

"Stay here," Dante had told her.

It had been a command, not a request, and she'd obeyed it instinctively, standing where he'd left her, hearing scuffling sounds and then thuds until she'd said to hell with obedience. She'd run toward the alley just as Dante had reappeared with an old man shuffling beside him. A street person, from the looks of him, saying "Thank you, sir," over and over, and then she'd looked at Dante, saw that his suit coat was torn, his jaw was already swelling...saw the look in his eyes that said he had done what he'd had to do...

And had enjoyed it.

"Gabriella, what is he talking about? Answer me!"

She opened her mouth. Shut it again. What could she possibly tell him? Not the truth. Never that. Never, ever that!

"Perhaps I can help, *senhor*." It was the lawyer, looking from one man to the other and smiling nervously. "Obviously, you and the *senhorita* have met before. In the States, I assume."

"*Senhor* de Souza," Gabriella said, "I beg you—"

"You could say that," Dante growled, his eyes never leaving the big man who still stood with his arm around Gabriella. Her face was as white as paper. She was trembling. Why didn't she step away from the greasy son of a bitch? Why didn't she call him a liar? No way would she have given herself to someone like this.

"In that case," the lawyer said, "you probably knew her as Gabriella Reyes."

Dante folded his arms over his chest. "Of course I know her as—"

"Her true name, her full name, is Gabriella Reyes

Viera." De Souza paused. "She is the daughter of Juan Viera."

Dante looked at him. "I thought Viera had only one child. A son."

"He had a son and a daughter." De Souza paused, delicately cleared his throat. "Ah, perhaps—perhaps we should discuss this in private, *Senhor* Orsini, yes?"

"Indeed you should," Ferrantes snarled. "There is an auction taking place here, *advogado,* or have you forgotten?"

"Let me get this straight," Dante said, ignoring him, his attention only on the attorney. "The ranch, which should be Gabriella's, will be sold to the highest bidder?"

"To me," Ferrantes looked down at Gabriella. The meaty hand that rested at her waist rose slowly, deliberately, until it lay just beneath her breast. "*Everything* will be sold to me. So you see, American, you are wrong. There is no business here for you, whatsoever."

Dante looked at him. Looked at Gabriella. Something was very wrong here. He had no idea what it was, no time to find out. He could only act on instinct, as he had done so many times in his life.

He took a deep breath, looked at the auctioneer. "What was the last bid?"

The auctioneer swallowed. "*Senhor* Ferrantes bid two hundred thousand United States dollars."

Dante nodded. "Four hundred thousand."

The crowd gasped. Ferrantes narrowed his eyes. "Six."

Dante looked at Gabriella. What had happened to her? She was as beautiful as in the past, but she had lost weight. Her eyes were enormous in the weary planes of her face. And though she was tolerating Ferrantes's touch, he could almost see her drawing into herself as if she could somehow stand within the man's embrace and yet remain apart from it.

"Gabriella," he said quietly. "I can buy this place for you."

The crowd stirred. Ferrantes's face darkened, but Dante had eyes only for the woman who had once been his lover.

"No strings," he said. "I'll buy it, sign it over to you and that'll be the end of it."

She stared at him. He could see her weighing her choices but, dammit, what was there to weigh?

"Gabriella," he said, urgency in his tone, "tell me what you want."

Ferrantes pushed Gabriella aside, took a menacing step forward. "You think you can walk in here and do anything you want, American?"

Dante ignored him. "Talk to me, Gabriella."

She almost laughed. Talk? It was too late for that. They should have talked that terrible day when her life had changed forever. She had been so alone, so frightened, so in need of her lover's strength and comfort. She'd phoned his office, found out he was away. He had not told her that. She saw it as a bad sign, but when he called the next evening and said he was back and wanted to see her, her heart had lifted. And that night, when he said he had something to tell her, she'd been sure fate had answered her plea, that he was going to say that he had gone away not to put distance between them but to think about her and now he knew, knew what he felt...

But what he had felt was that he was tired of her.

She would never forget the small blue box. The exquisite, obscenely expensive earrings. And his oh-so-polite little speech including that guilt-driven assurance that if she ever needed anything, she had only to ask.

The pain of his rejection had been momentarily dulled

by his sheer arrogance. She could not have imagined ever wanting anything from him.

But the world and her life had changed.

"The *fazenda* is mine," Ferrantes growled, "as is the woman."

Gabriella dragged a steadying breath into her lungs. "*Sim*. Please. Buy…buy the *fazenda* for me." Her words were rushed and desperate. "I will pay you back. It will take time but I'll repay every dollar."

Dante never hesitated.

"Five million dollars," he called out. "Five million, U.S."

The crowd gasped. Ferrantes cursed. The auctioneer swung his gavel.

And Dante took Gabriella in his arms and kissed her.

CHAPTER THREE

DANTE'S kiss was the last thing Gabriella expected.

The last thing she wanted.

Once, his kisses had meant everything. Tender, they'd been soft enough to bring her to the verge of tears; passionate, they'd made her dizzy and hungry for more.

And it hadn't been only his kisses that meant everything. It was the man.

Deep inside, she'd known it had not been the same for him. She'd never been foolish enough to think it was. He was rich, powerful, incredibly good-looking. Many of the models she knew dated such men. She never had...

Until him.

His initial interest had been flattering. Exciting. She had thought, *Why not?* She'd promised herself dating him would be nothing serious.

And then, despite everything, she had fallen in love with him. Deeply, desperately in love.

Dante had been magic.

But the magic was gone, lost in the cold reality of the past year. Completely gone, she told herself frantically, when she saw the sudden darkening of his eyes, the tightening of skin over bone, the all-too-familiar signs that said he was going to take her in his arms.

"Don't," she said, slapping her hands against his chest, but he was not listening, he was not listening…

"Gabriella," he murmured, saying her name softly as he used to when they made love. His arms tightened around her, he drew her against him…

And kissed her.

The room spun. The crowd disappeared. All that mattered was the sweetness of his kiss, the hardness of his body, the strength of his arms. Her foolish, desperate heart began to race.

"Dante," she whispered. The hands that had tried to push him away rose and slid up his chest, skimmed the steady beat of his heart and curved around his neck. She rose on her toes, leaned into him, parted her lips to his just as she'd done in the past.

She felt him shudder with desire at her touch.

He wanted her, still.

Wanted her as if nothing had ever separated them.

The realization shot through her like a drug, and when he groaned, thrust one hand into her hair, slid the other to the base of her spine and angled his lips over hers, his kiss going from sweet to passionate as if they were alone, alone in that perfect world his lovemaking had always created, a world in which he had never abandoned her…

A meaty hand clamped down on her shoulder, fingers biting hard into her flesh.

"Pirhana!"

The foul Portuguese curse word was followed by a stream of profanities. Her eyes flew open as Ferrantes yanked her out of Dante's arms, a stream of words even worse than *whore* flying from his lips.

Dante shot into action, grabbed Ferrantes's arm, twisted and jerked it high behind the man's back. Ferrantes hissed with fury and pain.

"I will kill you, Orsini," he said, spittle flying from his lips.

"Dante," Gabriella said desperately, "Dante, please. He'll hurt you!"

Dante pushed her behind him and brought his lips close to Ferrantes's ear.

"Touch her again," he snarled, "and I promise, you bastard, I'll be the one doing the killing!"

"She is a witch! She makes a fool of you. That you do not see it— Ahh!"

The big man yelped; his face contorted with pain as Dante forced his arm even higher.

"Listen to me, Ferrantes. You are not to speak to her. You are not to speak of her. You are not to so much as look at her or so help me God, you're a dead man!"

Dante was dimly aware of the room emptying, men rushing for the door, footsteps hurrying across the veranda, truck and car engines roaring to life outside, but he never took his eyes from Ferrantes.

"You hear me? You're to keep away from her. You got that?"

The big man's breathing was heavy. At last he gave a quick jerk of his head in assent.

Dante let go, took a step back, and Ferrantes spun around and swung at him. His hand was the size of a ham but there had been many things to learn in the wilds of Alaska, including how to defend yourself in some of the roughest bars in the world. Dante danced back; Ferrantes's fist sailed harmlessly by his face and when the big man came at him again he grunted, balled his own fist and jabbed it into the man's solar plexus with the force of a piston.

Ferrantes went down like a felled tree.

Dante stood over him for a long moment. Then he looked up, saw de Souza, saw the auctioneer…

But Gabriella was gone.

De Souza was staring at the motionless hulk on the floor as if it were a rodent. Dante grabbed him by the shoulders.

"Where is she?" he demanded.

De Souza gulped, looked from Ferrantes to Dante. "You have made a bad enemy, *senhor*."

"Answer the question, man. Where is Gabriella?"

The *advogado* shrugged. "She is gone."

"I can see that for myself. Where?"

De Souza licked his lips. "Listen to me, *Senhor* Orsini. This situation is—how do you say—more complicated than it might at first seem."

Dante barked a laugh. "You think?" His eyes fixed on the lawyer's. "Where did she go?" he demanded. "Upstairs?"

"Not there," de Souza said quickly. He gave another expressive shrug. "She fled with the others."

Dante ran from the house. Only three vehicles remained in the clearing: his, a gold Caddy he figured was the lawyer's and the big, ugly black SUV that surely belonged to Ferrantes.

He sagged against the veranda railing.

Gabriella was gone.

And maybe that was just as well.

He'd come here to buy this place for his father. Instead, he'd bought it for a woman who had once meant something to him but no longer did. Yes, he'd kissed her. And, yes, that one kiss had damned near consumed him, but so what?

He was a normal, healthy male. She was a beautiful woman. They had a shared history. But that was it.

He looked around him at the weed-choked corral, the

dilapidated outbuildings. He'd dropped five million bucks on this place—his money, not Cesare's—but so what? The truth was he had a lot of money. An obscene amount of money, and he'd made every penny on his own. Losing five million dollars was nothing. And Gabriella didn't owe him anything. Hadn't he promised her there would be no strings? Hadn't buying the *fazenda* for her been his idea?

A muscle in Dante's jaw began to tick.

It had been his idea…hadn't it?

Yes. It damned well had. Still, he had the right to a couple of minutes of conversation. Okay, questions, not conversation, but he was entitled to ask them. Why had she returned to Brazil? Why did she want this rundown disaster? Why did it belong to the bank?

Most of all, why would an ugly SOB like Ferrantes act as if he had a claim on her?

The muscle ticked again.

And then there was the biggest question of all. Why had she melted in his arms when he'd kissed her? Hell, why had he kissed her in the first place? Forget the history thing. He was a man who never looked back—

"Yo, American!" Ferrantes stepped out of the house. He was grinning, even though his gut had to be aching. "You throw a good punch, for a Yankee."

Dante's lips drew back from his teeth. "My pleasure."

The other man chuckled. "The pleasure is all mine, Orsini. Your blow gave me the chance to think. That two intelligent men would have fought over such a woman…"

Dante narrowed his eyes. "Didn't you learn anything?" he said, his tone soft and dangerous. "I told you to watch your mouth!"

The big man lifted his hands in mock surrender. "Trust me, *meu amigo*. The woman is all yours." A sly smirk lifted one corner of his mouth. "But I must be honest. You saved me from wasting a lot of money."

Dante folded his arms. "Glad to have been of service."

"And from wasting the rest of my life."

What in hell was the man talking about?

"So, *senhor,* now I owe you a favor." Ferrantes made a show of looking around, then lowered his voice. "Before you get in too deep, ask the lady a question."

"Listen, pal, when I need advice from you—"

"Or ask the *advogado.* Perhaps he will tell you what you need to know about his charming client."

A coldness danced along Dante's spine. *Don't fall for it,* he told himself, but it was impossible to ignore the bait.

"What in hell are you talking about?"

All pretence at camaraderie vanished from Andre Ferrantes's ugly face.

"Ask de Souza whose bed your Gabriella has been sleeping in," he said coldly, "until you showed up and she decided it might be more profitable to sleep in yours."

He'd wanted to go for Ferrantes's throat, but pride held him back.

Why give the man even a small victory? Dante thought hours later, as he sped along a narrow road that led deeper and deeper into a verdant wilderness.

Bad enough she'd played him for a fool in front of everybody, including the lawyer, who'd known her game all along, and the auctioneer, who was probably still celebrating the haul he'd made. Bad enough, too, that every man in that room knew she'd slept with Ferrantes.

Not that he gave a damn that she'd been with someone else—he had no claims on her anymore—but Ferrantes? She'd wanted the ranch badly enough to lie beneath a pig like that? Open herself to him, take him deep inside her, beg him to touch her, taste her, take her...

Dante's hands tightened on the steering wheel.

She'd done all the things with Ferrantes she had once done with him—and then he'd come along and she'd seen an easy way to put the bastard out of her life.

His mouth twisted.

What a piece of work she was! The earrings he'd bought her had been worth a small fortune but she'd made it seem as if she were too good to accept such an expensive gift from a lover. A former lover, okay, but that wasn't the point.

Apparently, accepting a ranch was different.

The car hit a pothole and swerved to the right. Dante cursed and fought the wheel, brought the car back on the road.

No wonder Ferrantes had stood there with that slab of beef he called an arm wrapped around Gabriella's waist. No wonder he'd objected when Dante kissed her. Gone crazy when she'd kissed him back.

Except, she hadn't.

He knew that now. It had all been a carefully calculated performance. The lady had seen her chance to get possession of those useless acres without continuing to spread her legs for Ferrantes.

An image, so hot and erotic it all but obliterated his vision, filled Dante's mind.

"Dammit," he snarled, and pushed the gas pedal the last inch to the floor.

The car rocketed ahead.

What an idiot he'd been! Falling for her act. Behaving precisely as she'd intended so that now he owned a useless piece of dirt in the middle of nowhere, every stinking weed, every collapsing outbuilding all his. He'd written a check for the auctioneer, ignored the man's outstretched hand, brushed past the lawyer without a word because they'd both known what was happening. They could have told him. Warned him.

Warned him?

The auctioneer's job was to sell the ranch. The lawyer's was to protect his client. Besides, de Souza had tried. *There is more to this than you know,* Senhor, he'd said. Something like that and Dante had chosen to ignore—

Something raced across the road, came to a dead stop, glared at him through eyes that were a shocking red against the dark onset of night. Dante stood on the brakes, fought to control the steering. The car swerved, spun; the tires squealed as if in pain. A wall of thick trees reared up ahead and he cursed, hung on to the steering wheel...

The car came to a shuddering halt.

The sound of the engine died. Silence and the night closed in as he sat behind the wheel breathing hard, hands shaking.

The car had done a one-eighty, ending up pointing in the direction from which he'd come.

He looked in the rearview mirror. The road behind him, what had moments ago been the road *ahead* of him, was empty. The animal—a big cat, he was almost certain—was gone.

His heart was still pounding. He took half a dozen breaths, sat back until his hands were steady again.

All this crap, reliving the stupid things he'd done almost as soon as he'd stepped off the plane at Campo Grande, was not getting him anywhere. What was done, was done. It was something he had learned to live by, how he had gone from almost flunking out of high school to doing okay in college and then putting in those years in Alaska before finally admitting that success in life wasn't such a bad thing, after all.

Besides, he was the one who'd get the last laugh.

Sure, he'd been conned into dropping a big chunk of change buying property he didn't want for a woman who meant nothing to him, but this wasn't over. As he'd walked past de Souza, the lawyer had put out his hand.

"*Senhor* Orsini?" he'd said politely. "I will expect your phone call."

Dante had looked at him blankly. De Souza had cleared his throat.

"To make an appointment to come to my office, yes? To transfer ownership of Viera y Filho to *Senhorita* Reyes."

"Yeah," he'd said brusquely, as he'd brushed by the man.

Now, Dante smiled.

Why would he transfer the deed to Gabriella?

She'd wasted her time. No way would he give her the ranch. He'd sell it to the first buyer that wanted it. Or let it go on rotting until every last sign of it had been swallowed up by the surrounding scrub. He would do whatever it took to keep her from profiting from what she'd done to him.

Still smiling, he turned the key. The engine coughed, then caught, and he headed for Bonito.

The drive, even the near accident, had done him some good. Cleared his head. He felt a thousand times better, calm and in control, and that was important.

He was a man who prided himself on being in control.

Goodbye and good riddance to this place, this cast of characters. He was going home.

By the time he reached the main road, he was whistling. He felt good. He'd get to the hotel, shower, change, phone down for room service—or no, why do that? The travel agent had faxed him a list of restaurants and bars. This was

Brazil and even in a town that specialized in eco-friendly tours, there was sure to be a hot night scene, and Brazilian women were spectacularly beautiful.

A little rest and relaxation was what he needed.

He didn't just feel good, he felt great…

Until he approached the road that led to the Viera y Filho *fazenda* and saw distant lights blazing like the fires of hell against the black night sky at the end of that road.

His good mood disappeared.

Lights. There was someone in the house. And he knew, instinctively, that someone was Gabriella. De Souza had deliberately misled him. Gabriella hadn't gone out the door, she'd gone up the stairs.

The rage he'd fought for so many hours reached out, all but consumed him. To hell with heading back to the States without confronting her. No matter what he told himself, he'd be leaving with his tail between his legs.

No way, he thought grimly. Not him.

Dante made a sharp left and headed for Gabriella.

CHAPTER FOUR

GABRIELLA came slowly down the stairs, exhausted at the end of the long day.

At least the house was quiet. Yara had left; she had her own responsibilities.

Just as well. Gabriella wanted to be alone. There were memories in this house, some bad but a few that were good; she could, at least, gather them to her tonight.

She went from room to room, switching on the lights. She'd been up since before dawn. There was nothing she could do to restore the property from the years of neglect it had suffered, but she'd done what she could inside the house, cleaning and polishing as if for company, ridiculous when the only people who had been coming were those who had wanted to take it from her.

The bank's representative. The auctioneer. Her attorney, who kept patting her on the shoulder and saying how sorry he was, yet never finding a single way to help her.

And Andre Ferrantes.

She shuddered.

Just thinking of Ferrantes sent a chill through her. He'd turned up, too. No surprise there. He'd sniffed after her like a wolf on a blood trail ever since she'd returned to the *fazenda.* Lots of sympathetic words. Lots of tsk-tsking. Lots of deep sighs.

But none of those things ever disguised the avaricious glint in his tiny eyes or the way he ran his tongue over his fleshy wet lips when he looked at her.

Today he'd finally made his move. Put his thick arm around her, his way of announcing his intentions to the world, that when he bought the ranch, she would be part of the furnishings.

Never, she thought grimly, plucking a throw pillow from the sofa and all but beating it into shape. No matter how badly she wanted this land, this house, no matter what the reasons, she'd sooner live on the streets than be in Ferrantes's debt or, even worse, his bed.

The thought was enough to make her feel ill.

And then, the miracle. The second miracle, because the first had been hearing Dante's voice, discovering him in the room, tall and imposing, hard-faced and intent. For an instant she'd imagined he'd come for her. Searched for her, found her, wanted her again.

Gabriella wrapped her arms around the pillow and shut her eyes.

Stupid thoughts, all of them.

He was here, that was all. She still didn't know why he'd come; she only knew it had nothing to do with her. But his coming had still saved her. He'd bought the *fazenda.* For her. At least, that was what he'd said.

So far, that had not happened.

He had not gone to the *advogado's* office to sign the documents de Souza said he would have to sign for the transfer of ownership. Instead he had vanished.

The lawyer had no idea where.

"Perhaps he returned to New York," de Souza told her, shrugging his shoulders. "I do not know, *Senhorita.* I have not heard from him. I know only that he spoke with *Senhor* Ferrantes after their, ah, their disagreement."

Gabriella tossed the pillow aside.

Disagreement? She almost laughed. Was that what you called it when two men went at each other with blood in their eyes? She had fled then, terrified of the consequences, of Ferrantes winning the fight...

Of the noise of it traveling up the stairs.

So she'd gone up to the rooms that were hers, stayed there until de Souza called her name. Everyone was gone, he'd told her, including the *senhor* from the United States.

"How did—how did the fight end?" she'd asked in a shaky voice.

"*Senhor* Orsini won," the lawyer had replied with a little smile. Then his expression had sobered. "But he and Ferrantes had a private talk after. When it was done, the *senhor* drove away very fast."

Without arranging to sign transfer papers. Without doing anything to fulfill that "no strings" promise.

Why? The question plagued her through the ensuing hours. She'd come at it from a dozen different angles but she still had no answer, only the nagging worry that though Dante's initial intent had been decent, his machismo had gotten in the way.

That kiss.

The way he'd held her. Plundered her mouth. As if no time had passed since they'd been lovers. As if he still owned her. Not that he ever had, but that was the way he'd acted when they were together, as if she belonged to him even though she'd known he had no wish to belong to her.

Had it all been an act for Ferrantes? The kiss? The outrageous bid? The promise? The questions were endless, but the one that mattered most was the one she'd posed to de Souza.

"What do we do now?" she'd said.

That had earned her another little smile.

"We wait to hear from *Senhor* Orsini, of course." The smile had turned sly. "It is good to have such a powerful man as a friend, yes?"

The way he'd said "friend" had made her want to slap his face.

But she hadn't.

She knew how things looked. Dante had kissed her and she had responded, but so what? It was a simple matter of hormones and he was an expert at making her hormones respond. Besides, he'd caught her by surprise. She had never expected to see him again, never wanted to see him again. He meant nothing to her; he never had. It had taken her a while to figure that out—his easy disposal of her had wounded her pride, that was all.

She was over him. Completely over him, and—

What was that?

Gabriella threw up her hand. Lights blazing through the front windows from a fast-moving vehicle all but blinded her.

Her heart began to gallop.

"Ferrantes," she whispered. It had to be him, hot with fury. Dante had made a fool of him in front of everyone, and, he would surely think, so had she.

Tires squealed. A car door slammed. Footsteps pounded up the steps to the veranda and a hand stabbed at the doorbell, over and over and over.

Her mind raced.

What should she do? Phone the *policia?* The nearest station was miles away. Besides, would they give a damn? Ferrantes was of this place. She was not. Not anymore. Her father had seen to that. He'd told endless lies about her, turned her into an outsider...

The bell was still ringing and now the sound of a fist pounding on the door added to the din. She could not let this continue. It was too much, far too much, and she gave one last frantic look up the stairs before she took a deep breath, went to the door and flung it open.

But it wasn't Ferrantes filling the night with his presence.

It was Dante. And even as her traitorous heart lifted at the sight of him, the expression on his face made the breath catch in her throat.

Dante saw a rush of emotions flash across Gabriella's face.

Surprise. Shock. Fear. And, just before that, something he couldn't identify. Not that it mattered. Whatever she felt was meaningless compared to his rage.

She was good, though. He could almost see her clamp the lid on all the things she'd felt on seeing him again.

"Dante," she said, as politely as a capable hostess greeting a not-so-welcome drop-in guest. "I didn't expect to see you tonight."

"I'll bet you didn't."

"In fact, I thought—*Senhor* de Souza and I both thought—you'd gone back to New York."

"Without signing over the deed?"

She could almost see the sneer on his face. *Don't react to it,* she told herself, and forced a calm response.

"I only meant—"

"Trust me, sweetheart. I know exactly what you meant." He smiled; he could feel the pressure of his lips drawing back from his teeth. "Aren't you going to ask me in?"

She hesitated. He couldn't blame her. She was far from stupid.

"Actually, it's rather late."

"It's the shank of the evening. Back home, you and I would be heading out for a late supper right about now."

She flushed. "That was a long time ago."

"Supper," he said, as if she hadn't spoken, "and then maybe a stop at one of those little clubs way downtown that you liked so much."

"You liked them," she said stiffly, "I preferred simpler places."

He felt a stir of anticipation in his blood. Her accent had just thickened. She had only the slightest accent. She'd told him once, in a rare moment when they'd talked about their lives, that she'd been tutored in English from childhood—but her accent always grew more pronounced when she was trying to contain her emotions.

In bed, for example.

When they'd been making love. Her whispered words would take on the soft sounds of her native tongue. Sometimes she'd say things to him in Portuguese. Things he had not understood but his body, his mouth, his hands had known their meaning.

He looked down at her, his muscles tense.

"But you liked what we did when we went back to your apartment or mine," he said, his voice low and rough. "What we did in bed."

Her color deepened. Or maybe the rest of her face turned pale. He didn't give a damn. If she thought she was going to control the situation the way she'd controlled it this morning, she was in for a hell of a surprise.

She took a deep breath that lifted her breasts. They seemed larger than in the past. Fuller. But then, he hadn't seen her breasts in a very long time.

Too long, he thought, and a surge of hot lust rolled deep in his belly.

Lust? For a woman with no makeup on her face? A

woman wearing a loose cotton top over baggy jeans? Hell, she looked beautiful anyway, though he had never seen her dressed like this before. She'd always worn chic designer clothes when they were together. Her own clothes, though he'd often tried to buy things for her.

"I prefer to pay for my own things," she'd always said with a polite smile. She'd used that same line when he tried to buy her any but the simplest of gifts.

She didn't need convincing anymore, he thought coldly. She hadn't blinked an eye at his dropping five million bucks on her this morning.

"Whatever we did in New York is over, *senhor.*"

"Such formality, sweetheart. After all we've been to each other?"

"The past," she said stiffly, ignoring his remark, "has no bearing on this matter."

"But it does," he said softly. "After all, I bought this house today."

She nodded, folded her arms over her breasts. "Yes. And…and it was a very kind thing for you to—"

"Based on the way you looked at your boyfriend, I have to assume you were glad I did."

"*Sim.* I was. But Ferrantes is not—"

"Your lover." He shrugged his shoulders. "Whatever you want to call him."

He watched the tip of her tongue peep out, watched it sweep across her lips and hated himself for the way it made him feel, hated her for doing it. It was deliberate; everything she'd done from the second she'd set eyes on him this morning had been deliberate.

"Must have been hell, a woman as fastidious as you, sleeping with a man like—"

She slapped him. Her hand moved so fast he never really saw the blow coming. The best he could do was jerk back, grab her wrist, twist it behind her as he tugged her toward him.

"What's the matter, baby? Does the truth hurt?"

"Get out," she hissed. "Get out of my house!"

"This isn't your house. Not anymore."

Tears filled her eyes. Angry tears, phony tears. One of the two. He knew damned well they couldn't be any other kind.

"I bought it. Just as you assumed I would."

She looked at him as if he'd lost his mind. "Assumed?" A choked laugh burst from her throat. "I didn't even know you were in Brazil! Come to think of it, why *are* you in my country?"

"Don't flatter yourself, sweetheart. I didn't come looking for you."

She knew that. Still, hearing it hurt. It was time to hurt him back.

"I came on business. Family business."

"Ah, yes," she said, tossing her head. "The famous *famiglia* Orsini. How could I have forgotten?"

She gasped as his hold on her tightened. In the few months they'd been together, they had never discussed his family, his father's underworld connections. She'd have known about it, of course. That the Orsini brothers were sons of Cesare Orsini was favorite gossip-column fodder.

"What's that supposed to mean?"

"Only that perhaps the apple doesn't fall far from the tree. Dammit, you're hurting me!"

She was twisting against his hand, trying to get free, but each jerk of her body only brought her more closely against him.

It was agony.

Exquisite agony.

The soft brush of her breasts against the hardness of his

chest. The whisper of her belly against his. The feel of her thighs rubbing lightly over his. Just the sight of her, all that sun-streaked hair tumbling around her face, that lush mouth, the eyes deep enough for a man to get lost in.

Memories swept through him.

The feel of her, moving beneath him.

The scent of her, when he brought her to climax.

The taste of her mouth, her skin, her clitoris.

Desire, wild, hot and dangerous, took fire. It thickened his blood, ignited nerve endings, brought him to full, rampant arousal. Maybe she was right. Maybe the apple didn't fall far from the tree. Go back a couple of generations, to the land of his ancestors, a woman would not have dared make a fool of an Orsini as this woman had done this morning.

On a low growl, Dante clasped Gabriella's shoulders, lifted her to him and claimed her mouth.

She fought. It didn't matter. Kissing her, subduing her, taking her was everything.

This morning she had told him what she wanted. Now, it was his turn to tell her what he wanted.

Her. Her, in his bed, again. For as long as he chose to keep her there. He'd never wanted another man's leavings but this—this was different.

He would wipe Ferrantes's possession away. Replace it with his own demands. His own pleasure. Her pleasure, too, because that would happen, she would soften under his touch as she had earlier today, she would moan against his lips, run her hands up his chest, press herself to him, yes, as she was doing now, moving her hips against his, making those sexy little whimpers that could raise the temperature a hundred degrees.

He groaned her name. Slid his hands under her bulky shirt. Cupped her breasts and groaned again at the feel of them in his hands, all warm, sweet silky flesh straining against her bra, filling his palms, the nipples lifting to the caressing sweep of his thumbs.

"Gabriella," he said, his voice urgent, and she wound her arms around his neck, sucked his tongue into the heat of her mouth...

Merda! What in hell was he doing?

Cursing, he pushed her from him. She stumbled back, shoulders hitting the wall, eyes flying open and fixing on his. She looked shocked, on the verge of tears, but he wasn't fooled. He was letting her do it all over again, blinding him to reality, using sex to turn his body on and his brain off as if she were a sorceress and he a fool she could enchant.

But he wasn't.

"Nice," he said, as if he'd been in control all the time. "Very nice. We're going to get along just fine."

"Get out," she said, her voice trembling.

"Come on, sweetheart. Don't take it so hard. And, what the hell, it'll be easier with me than it was with Ferrantes, we both know that."

She swung at him again but he was ready this time. He caught her hand, dragged her against him.

"You said—you said you would give my home to me. No strings, you said."

"That was before I knew you'd already made a deal with good old Andre."

She spat a word at him and he laughed. Turned out, some obscenities sounded pretty much the same whether they were said in the Sicilian of his youth or the Portuguese of hers.

"You think this is amusing?"

Dante lowered his head until his eyes were almost even with hers.

"What I think," he said in a cold whisper, "is that you get to have a choice."

"What is that supposed to mean?"

"It means I'll sell the place to Ferrantes in the blink of an eye."

"He wouldn't pay five million dollars."

"My accountant keeps telling me I can use a couple more nonperforming assets."

Her mouth trembled. Her eyes filled. It was hard not to feel sorry for her. Hard—but not impossible.

"I hate you, Dante Orsini!"

"I guess the question is, who do you hate more? Me or Ferrantes? Of course, you can always turn us both down. Pack up, move out—"

A thin cry drifted into the room. Gabriella stiffened, jerked back in his arms.

"What's that?"

"A...a fox," she said quickly.

She was lying. He could see it in her face. The cry came again. Dante narrowed his eyes.

"A fox in the house?"

"A monkey, then," Gabriella said, rushing the words together. "Sometimes they get into the attic."

The hell it was. You didn't have to grow up in the country to know whatever was making that sound was not a monkey or a fox. Dante thrust her aside and started for the stairs. She ran in front of him and held out her hands.

"Get out of my way," he growled.

"Dante. Please. Just leave. I'll pack tonight. I'll be out by morning. I promise—"

He lifted her as if she were a feather, set her aside, took the stairs two at a time, following what were now steady sobs down a long hall, through an open door, into a softly lit room...

And saw a crib, a blue blanket, a blue teddy bear…

And a baby, kicking its arms and legs and sobbing its heart out.

Dante stopped on a dime. Gabriella rushed past him and lifted the child into her arms. *Say something,* Dante thought furiously…but no words would come. He didn't seem capable of anything besides looking at her and at the baby.

"Meu querido," she crooned, "dearest one, don't cry!"

The baby's cries changed to sad little hiccups; Gabriella held the small body against her so that the baby's face was against her shoulder. A pair of eyes—pale-blue eyes fringed by long, dark lashes—peered at Dante.

The room filled with silence. After a very long time, Dante cleared his throat.

"Yours?" It was not a brilliant comment but it was all he could think of saying.

Gabriella looked at him. He could read nothing in her face.

"I said, is the child—"

"I heard your question." Her eyes were bright with what he could only assume was defiance. "Yes. The child is mine."

He felt as if someone had dropped a weight onto his heart.

"Yours," he said thickly. "And Ferrantes's."

Gabriella made a choked sound, neither a laugh or a sob, then lowered her face to the baby's. Dante stared at her. At the child. He knew he should say something…or maybe he should just smash his fist through the wall.

He did neither. If life lesson number one was that what was over was over, number two was the importance of maintaining self-control.

Dante turned and walked out.

CHAPTER FIVE

HE DROVE like a man possessed by demons, a hot fist of rage twisting in his belly.

That Gabriella should have slept with a pig like Ferrantes, that she'd carried his child in her womb…

Dante slammed the heel of his hand against the steering wheel.

"Come on," he muttered, "come on, dammit!" Couldn't this freaking car go any faster? He couldn't wait to get back to the hotel, toss his stuff in his suitcase and get the hell out of Brazil.

He had to phone his old man eventually, but what would he tell him? That he'd gotten it all wrong, there was no dissolute Viera son inheriting the ranch…

Only a dissolute daughter.

A woman who'd warmed his bed every night for, what, a few weeks? Okay. For three months. He'd taken her the first night they'd gone out, in an explosion of mutual passion like nothing he'd ever known before, taken her night after night, and the intensity of that passion had never diminished, not even when it had begun a subtle change to something he hadn't been able to define except to know that it made him uncomfortable.

Was that the reason he'd ended their affair?

Not that it mattered. There were more important things to consider.

Like what in hell he was going to do with a ranch.

He'd bought it for a woman who'd never existed, a woman who'd walked away from him and never looked back, who'd gone from his arms to another's without missing a beat, and who gave a damn? God knew, he hadn't been celibate these past months. There'd been a parade of women in and out of his life. So what if there'd been a parade of men in and out of hers?

What mattered now was that he was stuck with five million bucks' worth of absolutely nothing.

He'd been scammed, and scammed good—and now he was the unfortunate owner of a place he didn't want, all his until he could unload it.

Note to self, Dante thought grimly. Phone de Souza. Instruct him to sell the *fazenda* and never mind the price. Forget how much money he'd lose on the deal. Just find a buyer, he'd say. Any buyer and, yeah, that included Ferrantes. In fact, selling the ranch to Ferrantes was a great idea.

Until he'd shown up, Gabriella had been more than willing to pay the price Ferrantes demanded. She could damned well go on paying it now.

He wasn't the Sir Galahad type. Sir Stupid, was more like it, a Don Quixote tilting at windmills. Well, that was over. Yeah, definitely, let Ferrantes buy the damned ranch. It was what Gabriella deserved, the perfect payback. Let her spend the next hundred years in the pig's bed. It didn't matter to him. She was just someone he'd been with for a while.

Nothing special. Just like seeing her with another man's kid was nothing special...

A kid with a solemn expression and pale-blue eyes.

Dante cursed and pulled onto the shoulder of the road, put the engine in neutral and sat gripping the steering wheel hard enough to turn his knuckles white.

You could put what he knew about kids in a teacup and have room left. Why would he know anything about them? His brothers, his sisters, were all unmarried. If the guys he played touch football with Sundays in Central Park had kids, he never saw them. Children were aliens from a planet he'd never had any interest in inhabiting.

The only children he ever saw were being pushed through the park in strollers. And, yeah, there were people with kids living in his condo building, now that he thought about it. Like a woman he'd met in the lobby a couple of weeks ago. He'd been heading out, so had she, both of them waiting for taxis in a driving rainstorm, except she'd had a pink-swathed bundle in her arms.

"Nasty weather," he'd said, because she'd kept looking at him as if she expected him to make conversation.

"Uh-huh," she'd replied, but she'd seemed to be waiting for something more. Finally he'd caught on.

"Cute," he'd said, nodding at the bundle. It wasn't. Not particularly. It was just a baby, but evidently he'd said the right thing because the mom beamed.

"Isn't she?" she'd said, and then she'd added, proudly, as if the information rated applause, "She's four months old today."

Four months.

And about the same size as the baby he'd just seen. The difference was that Gabriella's kid had those blue eyes, that solemn I'm-an-adult-in-miniature look he'd seen before....

The realization almost stole his breath away.

He saw those eyes, that expression in the mirror each morning when he shaved.

"No," he said aloud. "No! Impossible."

But it was adding up. The eyes. The expression. The dark hair. Figure the child's age at four months, add on nine more… His head did the calculations no single, unattached, contented male wanted to do and reached an inescapable possibility.

Gabriella might have become pregnant in New York. And if she had…

Dante sat back. No. He couldn't go there. All those years ago, Teresa D'Angelo's monumental lie. He'd never had sex with her, with any woman without using a condom.

Gabriella could be lying, too.

Except she hadn't lied. She hadn't said the child was his. And she'd have told him. "Dante," she'd have said, "I'm pregnant with your baby." Teresa damned well had. There were times he could still hear her voice whining that he had to marry her.

Surely, Gabriella, any woman, would have made the same demand.

Which meant, he thought, on a relieved rush of exhaled breath, which meant the kid was not his. Forget the eye color. The face. The time frame. Babies were babies. They all looked alike…

"Merda," he hissed, and he turned the key, put the car in gear, and drove back to the *fazenda* for the second time that night.

Daniel had finally fallen asleep.

He'd fussed for the last half hour. Unusual for him. He was generally an easy baby to deal with. He ate, he slept, he kicked his tiny legs, pumped his arms and grinned. The grin, especially, was a delight because his usual expression was thoughtful, almost solemn, so that when he grinned, his whole face lit.

Just like his—

Gabriella blinked. No. She was not going there. It had taken her weeks and weeks not to look at her son and see the man who'd once been her lover. She was not going to permit the events of one day to start her on that path again.

Carefully she lowered her baby into his crib, drew a light blanket to his chin, then bent and kissed his forehead, inhaling his sweet, baby scent. Her lips curved in a smile. *Deus,* how she adored her little boy. She'd been terrified when she'd realized she was carrying him. Now he was the focal point of her life.

Everything she did, she did for him.

It was why she'd wanted to save the *fazenda.*

Sighing, she turned out the light, went to her own room and undressed.

If only she could have done it. For Daniel. For his connection to a place that was in the Viera blood. And for the memory of her brother. She had loved Arturo with all her heart, just as he had loved her. No one else ever had, surely not Dante. She'd been his plaything. His toy.

And she had let him hurt her for the last time today.

Gabriella turned on the shower and stepped under the spray.

Dante was history. Her son was the future. She had to plan what she would do next, now that the ranch was truly gone. She'd harbored hope until the last minute, even though she'd known, in her heart, that the small amount of money she still possessed would not be sufficient to save it. The amount owed on it was too big. Her father had mortgaged and remortgaged the *fazenda* so often she'd lost count, frittering the money away on women, horses and cards. By the time Arturo had inherited it, the bank stood ready to foreclose.

And then, despite the doctors, the treatments, virtually all her savings from modeling, he had died.

The bank had moved in for the kill. She'd made her pathetic financial offer, they'd turned it down, and Ferrantes had come sniffing at her heels. She'd told him what he could do with his disgusting suggestions. He'd laughed and said she would change her mind after the auction. She told him she would never do that; in fact, she had not even intended to go to the auction—why break her heart even more by seeing a pig such as him take what should have been her son's inheritance?

Then she'd heard Dante's voice.

She could not have kept from going to him any more than the big, beautiful hawk moths could keep from beating themselves to death against the lit windows of the house at night.

Why had she believed he'd buy the *fazenda* for her? Worse, why had she let him kiss her? To let that happen… to give in to the kiss, to respond like a wanton to the feel of his arms, the heat of his body, the never-forgotten taste of his mouth and then to have him show how little he thought of her by believing she would have slept with Ferrantes…

That she would have slept with any man after having been with him and, *Deus,* she hated him for that, for leaving his mark on her lips, her skin, her stupid heart.

Gabriella froze.

Someone was ringing the doorbell. Banging on the door. She could hear it all the way up here, even with the water running. It would wake Daniel, but how could she let Ferrantes in?

Because, this time it would be him.

She didn't take the time to towel off. Instead, she flung on her robe, tied the sash and ran downstairs. Her heart was racing. She needed a weapon. Her father had kept guns but she didn't know where they'd be. Arturo, who'd despised killing things, had probably disposed of them.

"Gabriella! Open this door."

She blinked. Dante? Why had he returned? It couldn't be him. But when she turned on the outside lights and peered out the window, it was his rental car she saw parked before the house, not Ferrantes's obscenely extravagant SUV.

What did he want now? There was only one way to find out. She took a steadying breath and cracked the door an inch.

"I don't know why you came back," she said, or started to say. But just as he'd done a little while ago, Dante brushed past her as if she were nothing. His easy arrogance was infuriating.

A good thing, because it swept away the sudden ache in her heart the unexpected sight of him provoked.

"Excuse me," she said coldly, "but I did not invite you in. It is very late, and—"

He swung toward her, eyes bright and hard as diamonds.

"Yes," he said coldly, "it is definitely very late."

His gaze swept over her, lingering on the rise of her breasts, the length of her thighs. She thought of how the thin cotton robe must be clinging to her damp body and she flushed and folded her arms.

His smile was thin and dangerous. "Dressed for company?" he said softly.

She could feel her color deepen. "Dressed for bed," she said coolly. "My days have an early start."

His smile vanished.

"Taking care of a kid must cut down on your social life."

Her chin lifted. "What do you want?"

"It's hard to imagine a city girl like you enjoying this kind of life."

"That only shows how little you know about me."

A muscle jumped in his cheek. What was she talking about? He knew a lot about her. She preferred white wine. She didn't eat red meat. She wore clothes by big-time designers.

Those things constituted knowing a woman, didn't they? Sure they did. It meant he knew what restaurants she preferred, what to choose on a menu, what to tell his PA to buy her whenever he decided it was time to give a woman a gift.

"Dante. I asked you a question. Why did you come back? We said all we had to say an hour ago."

He dragged his thoughts together. She was wrong; they hadn't said all there was to say an hour ago and he damned well wasn't leaving this time until they had.

"That's just the point," he said slowly. "I'm not sure we did."

"What are you talking about?"

"You never answered the one question that matters."

She kept her eyes on his, but her face lost a little color. "What question?"

"Gabriella. No games." He took a step toward her; his eyes grew suddenly dark. "Is the child his?" He paused. "Or is it mine?"

His words hit her with an almost physical force. When she'd first realized she was pregnant, she'd imagined this scene endless times.

It had never ended well.

That was the reason she hadn't fallen apart that terrible night Dante had taken her to dinner and told her he didn't want her anymore, just seconds before she'd been about to tell him she was carrying his child.

He had not wanted her then. He did not want her now. So, why was he asking the question?

Better still, how should she answer it?

He came closer, close enough so she had to tilt her head back to look at him.

"It's a simple question, Gabriella. Whose kid is it?"

Her heart was pounding. His voice was hard. So was his face. Hard and threatening. What did he want? If only she knew.

His hands closed on her wrists.

"Answer the question."

Why should she tell him now? She'd gone through the worst alone. Pregnant. No longer able to model. Coming home because she had no other choice, coming home to her father's cold derision, to the illness and death of first him and then her brother.

Gabriella tossed her head, searched and found the you're-boring-me look she'd perfected for her stints on the runways of Paris, Milan and New York.

"Why ask when you already supplied the answer?"

His hands gripped her harder. She could sense the tightly controlled anger all but pouring off him.

"Answering a question with a question is a load of bull and you know it," he said grimly. "One more time. Who does the kid belong to?"

"The 'kid,' as you so charmingly put it, belongs to me. That's all you need to know. Now, get out!"

She gasped as he put a little twist on her wrists, lifted her to her toes. "Get out?" he said very softly, and flashed another of those thin, dangerous smiles. "Aren't you for-getting something, baby? This isn't your house. It's mine."

Her heart gave a thump so loud she was amazed he didn't seem to hear it.

"The *advogado*—*Senhor* de Souza said I did not have to vacate for forty-eight hours."

"You'll vacate when I say so." His mouth twisted. "You want those forty-eight hours? Tell me what I want to know."

Gabriella jerked against his grasp; he slid his hands to her shoulders, cupped them hard enough so she could feel the imprint of his fingers.

"It is none of your business."

"How old is the kid?"

"Four months. You see? I have given you an answer. Now, get—"

"Four months. And you left me a year ago."

"*I* left *you?*" She laughed. "You left me, Dante. You…you discarded me like…like a toy you'd tired of."

His mouth twisted. "I never thought of you as a toy."

"'It's been fun, Gabriella,'" she said, in uncanny imitation of his message if not his exact words, "'but it's time I moved on. There are so many women out there—'"

"I never said that," he shot back, but he could feel the color rising in his face.

"It was what you meant."

She tossed her head; her damp curls flew about her face in wild abandon.

God, she was so beautiful!

Her robe was made of cotton. It was not fashionable. It looked old, a little worn, but she made it look regal. The thin fabric clung to her body like silk, outlining her breasts, cupping them as his hands had once had the right to do. Her nipples poked against the cotton. He remembered their shape, their size, their color.

Their taste.

Sweet. Incredibly sweet. How he had loved to lick them. Suck them. Bite gently on them while she buried her hands in his hair and sobbed his name. He'd feast on her breasts until she trembled in his arms and then he'd slide his hand down, down, down until he cupped her, felt her heat, felt her body weep with need for his.

His erection was swift and almost painful. He let go of her, turned his back, strode across the room while he fought for control, furious with himself for losing it, with her for making him lose it. Seconds passed. At last he swung toward her again.

"How long do you think it will take me to get answers, Gabriella? An hour? A day? One call to my lawyer and he'll set the wheels in motion. I'll know where the kid was born—"

"Stop talking about him that way! He has a name. Daniel."

"And on his birth certificate? What's his surname?"

"Reyes," she said, lying, hating herself for the instant of weak sentimentality that had made her list Dante Orsini as her son's father.

"Fine." Dante took his mobile phone from his pocket and flipped it open.

"What are you doing?"

"Calling my attorney. You want to do this the hard way, we will. But I promise you, you're only making me even more angry than I already am." His lips twisted. "And that's not what you want. I promise you it isn't."

He was right. She knew that. He would be a formidable enemy. Besides, what would it matter if she told him the truth? Nothing. Absolutely nothing. Nothing was what she wanted from him. She had reached that decision the night he'd cast her aside.

Really, what was she protecting but her pride?

And yet…and yet he was a powerful man. A complex man. That he had returned to ask her about the baby proved it. If she admitted he was Daniel's father, anything was possible.

"Gabriella." His voice was soft but his eyes were ice. "What's it going to be? Do we do this my way—or the hard way?"

He watched her face, saw the play of emotions across it. She was shivering, from the cool of the night or from anger. He didn't give a damn. And if it was all he could do to keep from hauling her into his arms again and kissing her until she sighed his name and trembled not with cold or rage but with need, what did that prove except that she was a woman, an incredibly beautiful woman he'd never stopped wanting and—dammit, what did *that* have to do with anything?

"For the last time," he said sharply. "Is Daniel mine?"

Perhaps it was exhaustion. Perhaps it was acceptance of the inevitable. Or perhaps, Gabriella thought, perhaps it was hearing her son's name on the lips of the man who had planted his seed deep in her womb thirteen long months ago.

Whatever the reason, she knew it was time to stop fighting.

"Yes," she said wearily, "he is. So what?"

Of all the night's questions, that was the only one that mattered. And Dante knew, in that instant, his world would never be the same again.

CHAPTER SIX

GABRIELLA had promised herself she would not tell Dante that her baby was his—but that was when telling him would have meant seeking him out after Daniel's birth, and what would she have said then?

"Hello, Dante, how have you been and, by the way, here's your son?"

Logic had kept her from something so foolish. Dante didn't want her; why would he want to know she'd had his child?

But this—this was different.

Fate, circumstance, whatever, had brought him back into her life. He had seen her little boy, asked her a direct question. How could she lie to him?

Now, waiting for him to react, she realized that she *should* have lied.

He looked as if he'd been struck dumb.

If this were an old movie, if she was Meg Ryan and he was Tom Hanks, he'd have gone from shock to joy in a heartbeat. But this wasn't a movie. More to the point, this was Dante Orsini, the man who lost interest in a woman after a couple of months. She'd known his reputation—and she'd wanted him anyway. The part of her that yearned to be a sophisticate had said she could handle an affair like that.

Wrong. Agonizingly wrong. She had not been able to handle it, especially when he'd cut her from his life as if she'd never been part of it. How on earth could she have told him she'd had his child after that?

But she *had* told him now, only after he'd bullied her into submission.

No, she thought, watching him, no, this was not a movie. It was real life. And Dante's face said it all.

Shock. Disbelief. Horror. His color had drained away until the same pale-blue eyes she saw in her baby's face glittered like pools of winter ice in his.

She took a steadying breath. She wasn't feeling very well. The auction. Ferrantes. Dante turning up and now this. Her head ached. The truth was, everything ached. Maybe she was coming down with something or maybe she was simply reacting to the endless, awful day. Whatever the reason, she wanted Dante out of here. She was not up to trying to explain anything to him or to hearing him deny that Daniel was his.

But, strange as it might seem, she could understand it.

She'd been in denial, too. Complete denial. She hadn't even admitted the possibility she might be pregnant when she had missed her period. Her cycle had never been regular so she hadn't thought anything about being late. She had no morning queasiness. No tenderness in her breasts. And then one night, alone in her bed because Dante was away on business, it had simply hit her.

Maybe she was pregnant.

She'd thrown on some clothes, rushed to the all-night pharmacy on the next block, bought a home pregnancy test kit, took it home, peed on the little stick…

Two hours and six test kits later, she'd slumped to the

cold tile bathroom floor in horror. So, yes, she could see that Dante might react with shock....

"—be mine, Gabriella?"

She blinked, looked at him. His color was back. So was his arrogance. It was in his voice, in the way he was looking at her, even in the way he held himself. Aloof, removed, apart. Once, she'd found that lord-of-the-universe attitude sexy. Not anymore. She was no longer the foolish, impressionable woman who'd fallen for the great Dante Orsini.

"Did you hear me? I said, how could the child be mine?"

She felt the throbbing in her temples increase in tempo. The cold question hurt. She would not let him know that, of course. He had hurt her enough the night he'd handed her those damnable earrings.

"The usual way," she said with deliberate sarcasm. "Or did you not take Sex Ed 101?"

"This isn't the least bit amusing," he said coldly. "I used condoms. Always."

Yes, he had. Sometimes, she'd done it for him. They'd both liked that. She could remember, with heart-stopping clarity, the silk-over-steel feel of him against her palms. The feel of his hand in her hair, cupping the back of her head as she bent to him.

"Gabriella." His voice was frigid. "Did you hear what I said? You know damned well that I always used protection."

This was more than denial. He was accusing her of lying. She wanted to ball up her fist and hit him. What kind of woman did he think she was? Did he think she would make up a story such as this?

"What I know," she said, "is that I became pregnant despite your 'protection.'"

His mouth thinned. "If a condom had failed, I'd have known it."

Oh, how she wanted to slap that superior-to-thou expression off his face!

"Of course," she said with a bitter smile. "You are, after all, the man who knows everything."

"I know that it would be difficult for anyone to see how I could have impregnated you."

He sounded as if he were describing a laboratory experiment instead of the coming together of a man and a woman. Didn't he remember how sex had been between them? She did. She could remember it all. Dante, between her thighs. His mouth drinking from hers. The feel of him, slowly entering her. The scent of his skin, the essence of their shared passion....

Deus, what was the matter with her? Why had she told him Daniel was his? This discussion was without purpose. The only interest he would possibly have in her baby was in convincing himself the baby was not his.

And that was fine, she thought, and moved briskly to the door, wrapped her hand around the knob and yanked it open.

"We are done here, Dante."

"Done?" He laughed. "We haven't even started. I want answers."

"You have your answer. You asked whose child Daniel was. I told you. You denied it. We have nothing more to say to each other."

He reached out his hand, slapped the door closed and stepped closer to her. He could feel his adrenaline pumping. Did she really think she could toss him out? Never mind that he owned this house. How about the bombshell she'd just dropped on him? Telling him the kid upstairs was his....

You asked, a sly voice inside him whispered.

Yes. He'd asked. And she'd answered. He had every

right to follow up with questions—or did she assume he'd accept her fantastic claim just because she'd made it?

A man only did something that stupid once in a lifetime. He'd done a lot of growing up since the incident with Teresa D'Angelo.

"Let's assume the kid is mine."

Bile rose in her throat. "Go away," she said, her voice shaking. "Forget this conversation ever took place."

"Which is it? Are you claiming he's mine or that he isn't?"

It was too late to lie. "He is yours," she said wearily, "but only by biological accident."

"Did you know you were pregnant with the kid the night we broke up?"

"I told you," she said, her eyes suspiciously bright, "he has a name. Daniel."

"Fine. Great. Did you know you were carrying Daniel when we broke up?"

"The night you said I'd worn out my welcome, you mean?"

"Dammit, answer the question. Did you know?"

"What if I did?"

"Didn't it occur to you to tell me?"

Her eyes brightened with anger. "When? Before the earrings or after?"

He felt his face heat. She made it sound as if he'd been trying to buy her off, as if this whole damned thing was his fault.

"I gave you a gift because I...I wanted you to know you'd meant something to me."

Her hand flew through the air, connected, hard, with his cheek. He caught her wrist, dragged her arm behind her back. He knew he wasn't being gentle. She winced, rose to her toes but he didn't give a damn.

"Do not," he snarled, "do not, whatever you do, try to make it my fault you didn't inform me of this—of this situation!"

"Is that what it was?" Her voice shook. "Because I'd describe it differently. I was pregnant. Pregnant with your child. And you were dumping me and tossing me a...a bauble when all I'd ever wanted from you was...was—" She tried to jerk away but his hand only tightened on her. "Let go of me, Dante. Do us both a favor and just go away."

She was trembling.

She had trembled that night, too. He had noticed it but he'd told himself it meant nothing, that she'd get over it. She was an adult; she was a model, dammit. She'd dated a lot of men.

Hadn't she?

She'd seemed so innocent in his bed. As if everything they did, everything he did, was new to her. And that night, after he'd told her it was over, there'd been something in her eyes, a quick flash he'd chosen not to think about.

It was there now.

Was it a flash of pain?

His throat tightened.

He knew how to soothe that pain. He could gather her in his arms. Hold her against his heart. Kiss her. Caress her. Tell her that he'd never stopped thinking of her. That he'd missed her. That he still wanted her.

Merda!

What in hell was he thinking? How could she still have this effect on him? It was why he'd stopped seeing her, not because the affair had gone on too long but because he'd felt her getting inside him, getting to him. Well, it wasn't going to happen again, especially now. The last thing he needed was to react to her, feel that tug of lust low in his belly that he'd always felt when he was with her.

For all he knew, she was counting on it.

Some tears, a kiss, and he'd bought her the *fazenda*. Now this fantastic story, a few tears, another kiss and he would say, sure, the kid was his and how much would she need to keep it and herself in the style to which she so obviously wanted to grow accustomed?

Was the boy his? That was the question of the century. If the answer was yes, he'd do whatever had to be done, but he wasn't about to accept a woman's word as proof. Been there, done that, he thought grimly, and he let go of Gabriella's wrist and stepped back.

"I want proof."

"You don't need proof. I want nothing from you."

"Like you didn't want the *fazenda* when you climbed all over me this morning? Come on, baby. Let's not play games. I want proof of the kid's—of Daniel's parentage. When was he born? Where? Is my name on his birth certificate?"

Tears were streaming down her face. If this was a performance, it was a damned good one.

"Get out," she hissed. "Get out of my life! I did not ask you for anything when I carried my baby. I am not asking you for anything now. I *never* wanted anything from you, Dante! Not your money, not your fancy gifts—"

"But you wanted this," he growled, and he gave up fighting what he wanted, what he always wanted when he was near her. He swept his arms around her, bent his head and captured her mouth with his, kissing her hard, kissing her without mercy, forcing her lips apart, his tongue penetrating her, demanding the response she had always, always given him.

But she gave him nothing tonight. She stood motionless within his embrace. Slowly he raised his head. Her eyes were open, dark and empty and filled with pain.

"I beg you," she whispered. "If you ever cared for me at all, please, go away."

He stared at her. Of course he had cared for her. The truth was, he'd cared for her too much. He wanted to tell her that, to kiss her again, to hold her close and change her unhappy tears to soft, sweet sighs…

He stepped back.

What the hell had he been thinking?

The fact of it was, he *hadn't* been thinking.

He had to get out of here. Talk to his lawyer. His brothers. Arrange for tests and if the tests came up positive, figure out how to handle all of this.

He went out of the house without so much as a backward look.

One thing was certain, he told himself as he drove away.

This time, he would not turn around and go back. He was done with Gabriella. With Brazil.

There was nothing, absolutely nothing here for him.

All he could think of was getting home.

To hell with waiting for morning, he thought grimly as he strode into the lobby of his hotel. It was very late and the concierge was dozing behind his desk, but who gave a damn?

Dante woke him. Told him he wanted to rent a plane and a pilot. The concierge yawned. Dante spoke sharply. Pulled out his checkbook, said he wanted that plane, wanted it now.

A couple of calls, and it was done.

He was airborne an hour later. The plane was handsome, the pilot was efficient, the sky was shot through with moonlight and stars.

And Dante…Dante was in a mess.

He was a man who had never shirked responsibility.

Wasn't that how he'd ended up in Bonito in the first place? Because Cesare had somehow transferred responsibility for righting some long-ago wrong to him? Yes, Cesare had gotten the details wrong. There was no dying man, no successful ranch about to be dropped into the hands of a son incapable of running it. There was, instead, a ranch he'd somehow ended up owning.

Like it or not, the *fazenda* was his, not his father's.

A muscle knotted in his jaw.

And there was more.

There was a woman, alone and penniless. A baby she said was his.

Dante groaned and closed his eyes.

A mess, indeed.

What he'd said was true. He always used a condom even though, okay, there'd been times with Gabriella—and only with Gabriella—that he'd wanted to make love without that thin layer of latex sheathing him. The need to feel the slide of his erect penis against the warm silk walls of her had driven him half-crazy. He'd wanted to know that nothing, absolutely nothing separated him from her, that she was his in a way he'd never wanted another woman to be his.

"Dammit," he growled, shifting his weight in the leather seat.

Thinking X-rated thoughts gave a man's body a predictable reaction. And turning himself on was not what this was all about.

Besides, he would never have done such a stupid thing as have unprotected sex.

He enjoyed risk. Back-country skiing with the ever-present danger of avalanche. White-water kayaking. Skydiving. Letting his money and his reputation ride on financial deals that made other men blanch. He was into all that.

But sex without protection? That wasn't risk, it was suicide unless you were ready to marry, settle down, have kids. He wasn't. For all he knew, he would never be ready. He knew what women were like. They schemed. They plotted. They wanted wealthy husbands and they weren't above doing whatever it took to get them.

So, no sex without protection.

Still, accidents happened.

If you didn't leave a woman's body quickly enough, after you ejaculated, if you didn't get out and get that rubber off, there could be a problem. He'd always done it right. That one explosive moment, the sense of welcome release and then a kiss, because he knew after-play was important to a woman, a light caress, and he withdrew, headed for the john, took care of things. No wham, bam, thank you, ma'am, but no lingering so long that a rubber could leak, either.

Except…except, toward the end of things with Gabriella, he hadn't always followed those rules.

There'd been times the thought of withdrawing from all that heat, that sweet warmth, had seemed impossible. Times he'd stayed deep inside her, holding her, kissing her, not wanting to leave her even after he'd come.

How protective was a condom then?

Not very, he thought glumly. And whose fault was that, if not his own?

And, damn, even now, his body stirred at the memory.

Okay. Enough of that. The sex had been fantastic. The truth was, he'd never had better sex before or since, but that had nothing to do with this situation. And, yeah, it *was* a situation, even if she found the word offensive. And the only way to deal with it was head-on.

He took out his phone, flipped it open. Brought up his contact list. Paused, his finger above his attorney's name. Thought about the tests the guy would recommend, the time they'd take to run. Thought about Gabriella, alone with a baby in that big, falling-down house and Ferrantes salivating all over her.

Dante muttered a couple of ripe obscenities, put the phone away, rose to his feet and walked to the front of the plane. The flight attendant looked up as he made his way past her, gave him a surprised smile.

"Ah, *senhor,* you wish something? You had only to press the call button."

He ignored her, rapped sharply on the cockpit door, then opened it.

"Captain."

The pilot and copilot turned and looked at him. He saw confusion, then concern on their faces and silently called himself a fool. One did not enter an airplane cockpit, even on a chartered plane, so precipitously in today's world. That he had done so only gave proof to what he already knew: he had not settled things in Brazil, and until he did, he would not be in any condition to move on with his own life.

"Captain," he said quickly, offering what he hoped was a reassuring smile, "forgive me for intruding but I wish to change our destination."

His words only made the men look more alarmed.

"I wish to return to Bonito," he said, even more quickly. "My apologies for the inconvenience and, of course, I will pay for the flight as arranged, plus an additional amount for the change in plans."

The pilot got straight to the point.

"Because?" he said, and waited.

What was the answer that would be best understood? "A woman," Dante said briskly.

The pilot and copilot both grinned. "Ah. In that case...*no problema, Senhor* Orsini. We will be back on the ground in no time."

Dante nodded. "Excellent."

And it was excellent. He'd return to Brazil, do everything that had to be done. He'd promised Gabriella the deed to the *fazenda* and she could have it. As for the rest...DNA tests. Blood tests. Sure, but who was he kidding? The child was his. The blue eyes. The dark hair. Besides, he knew Gabriella. She wouldn't lie to him. There wasn't a deceitful bone in her body.

Her lush, beautiful body— And what did that matter?

She was out of his life. That was what he'd wanted the night he broke up with her; it was what he wanted now. But he'd do the right thing. Give her the ranch. Set up a trust fund for the kid. Another for her. And that would be the end of it.

The absolute, complete end.

Then he'd get on with his life.

CHAPTER SEVEN

HE DIDN'T go to the *fazenda* or the hotel.

What would be the point?

He didn't need to see Gabriella and he certainly didn't need a room. His stay in Bonito would be brief, a couple of hours at most. All he had to do was meet with de Souza, set things up, then turn around and head home.

He arranged for the pilot and plane to remain on call, phoned to arrange for another rental vehicle, then phoned the *advogado,* who sounded astonished to hear that he was in Bonito.

"I thought you had returned to New York, *Senhor* Orsini."

"You thought wrong. I wish to see you this morning, *senhor.*"

De Souza hesitated. "That is not much notice. Let me put you through to my secretary. She can check my appointment schedule—"

"I'll be at your office in half an hour," Dante said, and ended the call.

He grabbed a cup of coffee on his way to the car rental counter. His stomach growled as he sipped the hot liquid, reminding him that he hadn't eaten in a while. First things first. The meeting with the lawyer. Get the legal details out of the way. Then there'd be time for everything else.

For getting his life on track.

De Souza sprang to his feet when Dante stepped into his office. Did the *senhor* want anything to drink? Coffee? Water? It was early but perhaps a *capirihana?* Dante thanked him, said he wanted nothing and wondered at the drops of sweat on the lawyer's shiny brow. It was a hot day but not in here; if anything, the AC was set to an uncomfortable low. When he shook de Souza's extended hand, it was like shaking hands with a chunk of ice.

The man was nervous, but why?

"Sit down, please, *Senhor* Orsini. This is an unexpected pleasure, but I am afraid my time is limited. Had you called last evening—"

"My time is limited, as well," Dante said briskly. He took the chair in front of the lawyer's desk and opened the black leather briefcase he'd brought with him. "So let's get straight to business. I want the deed to Viera y Filho transferred to *Senhorita* Reyes immediately. What will you require from me?"

The attorney took a pristine white handkerchief from his breast pocket and delicately mopped his brow.

"A transfer," he said. "But when you left without making those arrangements, I assumed—"

"I signed some papers after the auction yesterday." Dante took the papers from the briefcase and slid them across the desk. "They're in Portuguese, of course, but I've seen enough such documents to assume the blank lines on the last page are where I'd sign to transfer ownership."

De Souza barely glanced at the papers.

"Actually…actually, it's a bit more complicated than

that, *senhor.* The documents you signed should have been accompanied by a check."

"They were accompanied by a check." The *advogado* was shaking his head. Dante frowned. "What?"

"The check must be a—what do you call it? A check authorized by a bank."

"A cashier's check? I understand that, but I didn't have one with me. I had no way of knowing the auction was taking place yesterday morning and I definitely had no idea how much I would bid, but the auctioneer said— Dammit, de Souza, why do you keep shaking your head? Is there a problem? Fine. I'll call my bank. They can wire the funds here, to you or to the bank, or—" Dante narrowed his eyes until they were an icy blue glimmer. "Now what?"

"Twenty-four hours have passed, *Senhor* Orsini." De Souza gave an expressive shrug. "You have forfeited your option to the property."

"That's ridiculous!"

"It is in the contract you signed."

"Well, what happens now? Do I contact the auctioneer? The bank? Surely we don't have to go through that bidding process all over again?"

"There will be no bidding process, *senhor.*"

"Well, that's something." Dante took his cell phone from his pocket. "I'll contact my bank in New York while you contact the bank—"

"The property has already been purchased."

Dante felt his body stiffen. He had participated in enough tough business deals to sense that the statement was not a negotiating tactic.

"Purchased," he said softly.

"Sim."

"By whom?" Dante asked, though he was sure he knew the answer.

De Souza looked at him and flushed.

"Understand, please, I am simply the legal tool of the bank in the transaction."

Dante rose slowly from the chair. "Answer the question. Who bought it?"

The lawyer swallowed hard. "*Senhor* Ferrantes."

Dante wanted to haul de Souza to his feet.

"You were supposed to be working for Gabriclla," he growled, "but you were working for Ferrantes all along."

"You must understand. *Senhor* Ferrantes is an important member of our community."

Dante reached across the desk, took some small satisfaction as the lawyer shrank back in his chair. He scooped up the documents, stuffed them into the briefcase and stalked out the door. Out in the street again, he drew a deep breath as he took out his cell phone and called his own attorney. Sam was a senior partner at one of New York's most respected law firms; Dante used his private number and Sam answered on the second ring.

"Dante," he said pleasantly, "good to hear from—"

"Sam. I have a problem."

"Tell me," Sam said.

Dante gave him all the details. Well, almost all. He didn't mention that he'd had a prior relationship with Gabriella Reyes. He damned well didn't say that there was a strong possibility he had a son. What he explained, in concise terms, was that he was in Brazil, that he'd bid on a property and paid for it with a check that been deemed unacceptable twenty-four hours after the fact, and that the property in question had now been sold to someone else.

But he and his lawyer had gone to school together. Sam knew him well. Too well. There was a silence after Dante finished talking. Then Sam cleared his throat.

"What else?" he said. "Come on, man. I know there's

more to this than you're saying. You want me to give you an opinion that has teeth, I need to hear the rest."

So Dante told him. About Gabriella. That he and she had once been—that they had been involved. That she had a child. That it was his.

"You mean," Sam said coolly, "she says it's yours."

A muscled knotted in Dante's jaw. "Yes."

"And you want to believe her."

"Yes. No. Dammit, she's not a liar—"

Sam interrupted. Asked him if the word *option* had ever been mentioned in the sale of the ranch, asked him for the name and phone number of the bank that had foreclosed on it, then said he'd get back to him in ten minutes.

The line went dead.

Dante stood in the heat of the Brazilian sun, impatience and anger humming through him. He wanted to go back into de Souza's office, drag the man to his feet and show him what happened to those who sold out to the devil. Better still, he wanted to find Ferrantes and beat the crap out of him.

Logic prevailed.

He was in a strange country. His best bet was to let his lawyer find the appropriate legal solution, which he was doing right now. Ten minutes wasn't that long to wait.

There was a café next door. He went inside, ordered coffee, sat at a small table and drank the coffee while he waited, eyes glued to his watch. Was the damned thing working? The minute hand seemed not to move. And then his phone rang and he flipped it open.

"Dante," Sam said.

"Well?"

"The easy stuff first. Don't make any legal commitments to the woman. Be pleasant, stay calm, but—I hate to use the word—keep your options open until we do some tests. Okay?"

It was solid legal advice. "Okay. What about the property issue?"

"The property." Sam exhaled noisily. "You want it in legalese or words of one syllable?"

A muscle flexed in Dante's jaw. It didn't take a genius to know that Sam had not asked him a question meant to raise his hopes.

"Just tell me the bottom line."

"The bottom line, dude, is that you're screwed."

"Screwed how? You mean, the bidding process has to begin all over again?"

"I mean," Sam said carefully, "you bought an option to purchase the property and the option expired twenty-four hours from the moment you signed it. In other words, you have no further legal rights to it."

Dante sprang to his feet. The other customers in the café shot him wary looks. He ignored them, tossed his coffee cup in the trash and stormed outside.

"I made the winning bid," he said sharply. "The bank accepted it."

"The auctioneer accepted it."

"As the bank's rightful agent. Listen here, Sam—"

"The guy who bought the property after the twenty-four hours were up is a national."

"The twenty-four-hour thing is bull!"

"Maybe. But you're not on a level playing field, Dante. You're not in the U.S. of A., you're in another country. Is what they've done legal?" Sam Cohen's lift of the shoulders all but came through the phone. "Probably, but who knows? The only certainty is that you'd need a Brazilian attorney to walk you through this. I can get a name, fly down, meet with you and whatever guy is recommended, but—"

"There's no time for all that," Dante said grimly.

"Yeah. I figured as much. And, to be blunt, I can't guarantee how it would work out. My best advice? Find yourself another ranch, man. Hey, you're in Brazil. How tough could that be?"

Dante laughed. Even to his own ears, it was not a happy sound. He thanked his lawyer, disconnected and headed for his car.

Somehow the *fazenda* looked worse today than yesterday.

The potholes in the road seemed more numerous, the weeds higher, the house and outbuildings more forlorn. Dante parked, walked up the steps to the door and rang the bell. He could hear it echoing through the rooms.

He rang it again. And again. Finally the door swung open. A white-haired woman in a shapeless flowered dress scowled at him. She barked a question he figured was either what do you want or who are you? So he told her his name and said he wanted to see *Senhorita* Reyes.

The woman stood immobile. He started to repeat what he'd said when he heard Gabriella's voice. He brushed past the woman, who hurried after him, and followed the sound to what seemed to be a library although, like everything else here, it had seen better times.

Gabriella's back was to him as she squatted beside a cardboard box half-filled with books. She wore jeans and a T-shirt; the shirt had ridden up and he could see the ridge of her spine. Her hair was pulled back and secured with one of those things that looked like a rubber band but wasn't. Her feet were bare and dusty.

She was, in other words, a mess.

And she was beautiful. So beautiful, she made his heart ache.

"Yara," she said, without looking around, "*quem está aí?* Is it the man with the truck? If it is—"

"Hello, Gabriella."

Gabriella sprang to her feet so quickly that she kicked over a stack of books piled on the floor. That voice. She had never expected to hear it again. Never wanted to hear it again—and yet, the sound of it made her heartbeat quicken. And when she turned and saw Dante, the joy that swept through her was indescribable.

The intensity of it shocked her. Joy? For what? This man meant nothing to her. She meant nothing to him. She put her hand to her temple, where last night's headache had taken up what felt like permanent residence.

She was coming down with something, and was that not perfect timing?

This was even worse timing. That Dante should turn up again...

And why was he looking at her that way? As if she were a...a specimen in a zoo. She was a mess; she knew it. She'd dressed for the work of the day. A torn shirt. Ragged jeans. In New York, she had dressed for him, she had done everything for him because she had been fool enough to think she mattered to him.

But she never had.

She'd just been another of the endless string of shadow women who moved through his life, and if she'd lasted a little longer than most, so what? It had all come to nothing in the end.

Dante had never known the real her.

But she knew the real Dante Orsini. The man who had it all, who never looked back, who believed commitment to a relationship didn't involve anything deeper than temporary exclusivity and pricey gifts, although there had been times like that one weekend, that lovely, glorious weekend…

"What are you doing?"

He was looking from her to the box of dusty books, scowling as if he'd discovered something unpleasant on his shoe. It made her angry. Everything about him made her angry, especially after last night. To think she'd been fool enough to believe he'd really wanted to help her…

She blew an errant curl off her forehead.

"I have a better question," she said coldly. "What are *you* doing here?"

He flashed a quick smile. "Such a warm greeting."

Gabriella narrowed her eyes. "My lawyer told me you went back to New York."

"Your lawyer," he said, his mouth twisting. "Is that what you think that double-dealing bastard is?"

"Answer my question. Why didn't you return to the States?"

"I started to." He moved slowly toward her. "But I thought things over and I realized…I decided to come back and try to sort things out."

"There's nothing to sort out. Not anymore." Her chin rose. "*Senhor* de Souza explained everything to me. You chose not to buy the *fazenda* after all, and Ferrantes—"

"De Souza's a liar!"

"Is he?" Her chin rose. "Then why is Ferrantes the new owner of Viera y Filho?"

"He's the new owner because your wonderful attorney sold you out! He and Ferrantes and the bank sneaked a joker into the deck. I didn't know a damned thing about it until I saw de Souza an hour ago."

She gave a weary shrug. "It does not matter. You had already decided not to give the ranch to me. You made that clear. And that was for the best. It was a mistake for me to have asked such a thing of you."

"It wasn't a mistake, dammit! You had every right to ask. You and I were—we were close, once."

"No," she said stiffly, "we were not close. We were a man and a woman who came together in bed. Nothing more."

She was right. That was how it had been, how he had wanted it. Then why did hearing those words make him so angry? Like it or not, there'd been more between them than sex. Like the weekend they'd gone away to his house in Connecticut, the one Nick had dragged him north to look at and he'd ended up buying instead of Nick. He'd planned two long days and nights of making love, but the house hadn't cooperated. It had been built in the 1600s, and that weekend every piece of it decided to admit its age. You turned a faucet, the indoor plumbing—installed in the 1800s—coughed once and that was it. You turned on the furnace, vintage early 1900s, and nothing happened. The refrigerator—a handsome 1950s antique—groaned and died. And then there was the final insult: a storm sprang up and rain found a hole in the roof, right over their bed.

So, no. There had not been two days and nights of endless sex...but they'd had a wonderful time, anyway.

He'd turned up an old Scrabble set and she'd beaten him, three games running. She'd beaten him at gin, too, and at checkers, and he'd sighed and hung his head and talked her into one more game of everything, Scrabble and gin and checkers, winner take all, and when he won each and every time, she accused him of letting her win the first time around and he grinned, pulled her into his arms and said the "all" he wanted was her, naked in front of the fireplace....

Dammit, what did old memories have to do with

anything? He'd come here to do exactly what he'd said. To sort things out, nothing more.

"There's no sense debating our relationship," he said gruffly.

"I agree. So if that is what you came here to do—"

"It isn't. I was on my way home and then I began to think about things."

"What things?"

Dante looked at the woman who'd let him into the house. She stood, arms folded over her ample bosom, glaring at him as if he were here to steal the family silver.

"Do me a favor, okay? Ask your guard dog to step out of the room."

Gabriella laughed. Yara, a native of the Pantanal, *did* look as if she was standing guard. She'd stood that same way early this morning, when Ferrantes had come by, unannounced, with his ugly news.

Dante, for all his faults, was not Andre. He had hurt her heart once, he had even managed to hurt it again yesterday, but he would never hurt her physically.

She told that to Yara. "You can leave us alone," she said, in a rapid burst of Portuguese. "This man will not hurt me."

Yara's bushy eyebrows drew together. "What you mean is that he will not strike you."

Gabriella smiled at the old woman's wisdom.

"No. He will not."

"But he will hurt you in other ways."

Gabriella shook her head. "He no longer has that kind of power over me."

Yara made a sound that made it clear she did not believe that. Still, she threw Dante one last meaningful look and left the room. Gabriella wiped her dusty hands on her jeans and looked at Dante.

"Now," she said, "tell me why you have come here."

Dante took a deep breath. Where to start? He thought of all the tough business meetings he'd survived, of how there was always the right thing to say and the right way to say it, knew that this was going to be more difficult than any of those, and that the only way to handle it was head-on.

"I came back because of the boy. Daniel."

Gabriella raised an eyebrow. "This time he has a name?"

"To tell you that…that I accept responsibility for him."

"He has a name—and you've had a change in attitude. How interesting."

"Dammit, you're not making this easy…"

"Did you expect that I would? Get to the point, please. I have much to do."

Dante took another deep breath. "I had time to think. And I realized that I want to do the right thing for him. For you both. If he's my son—"

"If?" she said coldly. "*If* he is your son?"

"Gabriella, you know what I mean."

"No. I do not. Why don't you explain it to me?"

"Try looking at this from my vantage point. You walked out. I didn't hear a word from you, and all of a sudden here's this child—"

She moved quickly, covering the distance between them before he could think, and lifted her furious face to his.

"You keep saying that I walked out. I did not. *You* did the walking, *senhor*. And no, you did not hear a word from me. Why would you? What could we have said that had not already been said by you that night you sent me away?"

"All right." His mouth thinned. "Have it your way. This has to do with the baby. With Daniel. If he's mine—"

"Stop saying that! Do you think I would lie about such a thing? That I would have slept with another man after—"

"Would you?" Dante's voice was rough. "Would you

have slept with another man after you'd been with me?" He moved forward quickly, framed her face with his hands, forced her to look up at him. "Because I don't want to think of you that way, Gabriella, I don't want to think of you in someone else's bed with your hands on him the way they used to be on me, your mouth on his, your skin hot against his."

"Damn you, Dante," she said in a shaky whisper, "damn you, damn you, damn—"

He kissed her.

Kissed her hard, with anger, forcing her lips to part to the thrust of his tongue, and when she cried out against his mouth he groaned, his kiss gentled and he gathered her against him, ignoring the way her hands rose to flatten against his chest and push him away. He kept kissing her, slanting his mouth over hers again and again as if he would consume her sweet taste, and at last she gave that little moan of surrender he had always loved, rose to him, wound her arms around his neck and kissed him back.

But her acquiescence didn't last. A heartbeat later she tore her mouth from his.

"Please. If you ever cared for me, let me go."

He didn't want to. He wanted to hold her forever, which was crazy. He was here for the child, not for any other reason. So he took a steadying breath, dropped his hands to his sides and stepped back.

"Tell me about Ferrantes."

Her eyes flashed.

"No," he said quickly, "I don't mean— Tell me what's happening. De Souza says he's bought this place. Has he contacted you?"

Gabriella shivered and wrapped her arms around herself.

"*Sim*. He was here this morning." She touched the tip

of her tongue to her lips. "He gave me—he gave me an… an— I do not know what you call it. A decision I must make."

"An ultimatum?"

"Yes. Either he gets what he wants," she said, so softly Dante had to bend his head to hear her, "or he will sell Viera y Filho to the rancher who owns the adjoining 50,000 hectares."

Dante nodded. "And what he wants," he said tonelessly, "is you."

She looked up, eyes bright with determination. "I told him what he could do with his ultimatum. And he told me—"

"He told you…?"

She shrugged, turned away, began taking books from the shelves. "He said it was my choice, that I could do as he demanded or I had until this evening to leave this place."

A string of Sicilian profanities, learned on the streets of his childhood, fell from Dante's lips. "He can't do that."

Gabriella swung toward him. "Of course he can!"

She was right. Ferrantes could do any damned thing he wanted, or so it seemed.

"But where will you go?"

Another shrug, her face once more averted. "Yara can take us in for a few weeks."

"Yara. The guard dog?"

"She is a good woman. She all but raised me."

"She has a house you can share?"

Gabriella thought of Yara's house. Small. Very small. Smaller still, these last months since Yara's daughter, son-in-law and their three small children had come to live with her and her husband.

"Yes."

It was the least certain "yes" Dante had ever heard. He stepped in front of Gabriella, took a book from her hands, set it aside and clasped her shoulders.

"To hell with that."

Her eyes, filled with defiance, met his.

"I will do what I must."

"There's no room at Yara's for you and the baby," he said flatly, "is there?"

"I will do what I must," she said again.

He nodded. She would. She had done what she had to do all these months, returning to Brazil to have her child, living out here in the middle of nowhere with nothing but the barren land for company.

"Is your clothing packed?"

Her eyebrows rose. "Why?"

"Dammit, just answer the question. I can hire someone to pack this stuff, whatever you don't want to leave behind."

"I am perfectly capable of doing it myself."

He took a deep breath. "I'm taking you with me. To New York."

She stared at him as if he'd lost his sanity. "Why would you do that? Why would I *permit* you to do that?"

"Because I say so."

She looked up into his eyes. He meant every word; she knew it. The blood of his ancestors flowed within him. He was a man who would not tolerate any obstacles once he had decided he wanted something.

There had been times he'd been like that in bed.

The tender Dante, the sweet lover she'd adored, would vanish. His lovemaking would turn hot and hungry. He'd clasp her wrists, hold her arms above her head, say things, tell her things while he was deep inside her, while his body moved within hers, and at those moments she would come and come and come...

"I do not take orders from you," she said, forcing the un-welcome memories away.

A muscle knotted in his jaw. "Listen to me, I can't leave you here alone, and I can't stay with you. You must come with me. You and the baby."

"The baby." Her voice broke. "The baby you still think does not belong to you."

He knew what she wanted him to say, but he couldn't bring himself to say it. "There's no other solution."

She shook her head. "It is all happening too fast," she whispered. "Much, much too fast. I need time to think. To plan."

She was right about everything happening fast. He'd come back to Brazil to make careful arrangements. Give her the *fazenda*, arrange for paternity tests, set up funds for her and the child, do all the right things but do them logically and slowly.

Taking her with him flew in the face of all that.

His plan had turned into no plan at all, certainly not one Sam or any other good attorney would advise, much less approve.

And yet, what else could he do? Leave her to the not so tender mercies of Ferrantes?

"It *is* quick," he said, because what good would it be to lie? He framed her face with his hands and slowly raised it to his. "We'll work out the details later. And it will all work out. You'll see."

She hesitated. He could almost see her weighing his words.

"Dante," she said, "I do not think—"

"Good," he said softly. "Don't think. Just trust me. Say you'll come with me."

She wanted to trust him. At least, her heart did. Her head said something else…but then he bent to her and kissed her and, like a fool, she agreed.

CHAPTER EIGHT

DANTE stood on the wraparound terrace of his two-story Central Park West penthouse, a cup of rapidly cooling coffee in his hand.

Was it possible he'd been away from New York for only two days?

It felt more like weeks.

Either autumn had suddenly overtaken the park or he simply hadn't noticed it, now that the leaves of the maples, oaks and sycamores far below were turning rich shades of crimson, brown and gold. Up here the mums and asters and who-knew-what-else his sister Isabella had planted in big redwood tubs had burst into vivid bloom.

Izzy would be thrilled.

She'd planted them last spring. Even when she was a kid, she'd loved to dig around in the dirt. Cesare would spend hours in the fenced-in yard behind the house in the Village, planting, then feeding and watering his annual crop of tomatoes. Izzy would accompany him, down on all fours tending the scraggly daisies that seemed the only flowers hardy enough to survive the Manhattan air. Now, all grown up, she'd taken one look at Dante's terrace after he'd bought the penthouse, gotten a dreamy look and said she could just imagine how perfect some plantings would be here, and here, and here....

So he'd let her poke and plant, he'd teased her like crazy and the result had been a summer of roses and daffs and other stuff, and now here came autumn.

His first reaction, seeing the blaze of color this morning, was to grab the phone, call her and say, "Hey, Iz, so maybe playing in the dirt isn't such a bad thing."

"It's called gardening, you idiot," Iz would say, and laugh.

Except, he couldn't tell her.

She'd want to come by, and how could he let that happen because if she did stop over, if any of his family did, how in hell would he explain the woman and baby living in the guest suite? Would he say, "Hi, good to see you and by the way, this is Gabriella—no, I don't think I ever introduced you to her before, Mama, and oh, by the way, this is her baby who might, emphasis on the 'might,' also be mine and yeah, that 'might' is important because somehow or other, I blew straight past the whole DNA/blood-test/paternity-test thing..."

Right. That would work out just fine. His mother would pass out, his sisters would shriek, his brothers would tell him he was an idiot, and his father would laugh and say that obviously, the trip to Brazil had not taught him anything about negotiating.

Dante took a long breath.

Maybe the problem was he'd come up against someone who was a hell of a lot better at negotiating than he'd ever been.

He raised the coffee cup and drank. Maybe caffeine would help. God knew, something had to. What in hell had he been thinking yesterday? Better still, had he really convinced Gabriella to come north…or had she played her role so well that she'd convinced him to ask her to do it?

At this point he honestly didn't know.

The only certainty was that yesterday's brilliant plan was clearly today's potential disaster. Either he'd been manipulated big-time or he'd lost his sanity. However he looked at it, the truth was that he didn't have any idea how he could have thought bringing her and the kid home with him would be a good idea.

How could it be?

The only positive thing was that nobody knew about this mess. And he had to keep it that way until it was resolved. Not easy, considering the presence of the woman and child sleeping in the guest suite, but if he moved fast, he could do it. Nobody even knew he was back. His office didn't expect him for a couple more days. Neither did his brothers. He'd given his housekeeper a few days off because he hadn't known exactly how long he'd be gone; he'd told his driver the same thing. The night doorman had been on duty, ditto the concierge, but why would anybody question them?

At least he had some breathing room.

As for why he'd acted so foolishly…he had no ready answer. Maybe he'd been punchy from lack of sleep. From all the flying back and forth. From the shock of seeing Gabriella again. From looking at a baby and being told it was his.

Dante slugged down more of the coffee and shuddered. It was cold, oily and acrid but he drank it with grim determination. He'd brewed the pot hours ago, knowing he needed the jolt, trying to come up with a plan. Gabriella, thanks for small favors, was still sleeping. She and the baby. At least, he assumed they were because there hadn't been a sound from the guest suite. He'd taken her there as soon as they'd stepped from his private elevator and there hadn't been a whisper from it since.

Not that they'd exchanged so much as a word during the flight home.

"There's a small room in the rear of the plane, *senhor,*" the attendant had told him in hushed terms when she saw Gabriella board with a swaddled infant in her arms. "The lady might find it more comfortable."

That was where Gabriella had spent the entire flight, curled up on a sofa in that room, the kid asleep in a contraption that looked more like the kind of pack frame he'd used hiking in Alaska than a thing meant for carrying a kid but, hey, what did he know about babies?

Nada, he thought grimly, *niente,* zip. He didn't have one fact in his head about babies beyond that they were small. And that was how he'd always liked it. He'd never been one of those guys who got off thinking about someday having children. Truth was, he always had to fake it when somebody showed him baby pictures. You had to say something, he understood that, and his standard response was "Cute," accompanied by a big smile, the same as he'd done that day in the lobby.

Was it his fault children, especially babies, looked pretty much alike? Or that they didn't much interest him at this point in his life? Someday, maybe, but surely not yet.

Which led to the distinct possibility that he might have moved too quickly in this entire situation, and yes, that was absolutely the word for it even though he knew better than to use it again with Gabriella.

Simply put, he'd made an enormous mistake.

The plan he'd started with—sitting down with Sam Cohen, arranging for paternity tests and, if they panned out, establishing the necessary trust funds—had been the right one. So what if the bank had sold Viera y Filho to

Ferrantes? A ranch, as Sam had so reasonably pointed out, was just a ranch. He could have found another place for Gabriella, left her there while he flew home and arranged all the rest. She'd have been safe from Ferrantes, safe from poverty...

And five thousand miles from him.

A muscle knotted in his jaw.

A little distance between them would have had nothing to do with his Doing The Right Thing. There was no reason for her to be here where he could see her face. Smell the unique delicacy of her perfume. Know that she'd spent the night just down the hall from his bedroom...

"Dammit," he muttered, and strode from the terrace into the living room.

That was precisely the kind of crap that had brought him to this point. How could a man cling to reason when a woman who had once shared his bed sighed as he kissed her? How could he think straight when she returned his kisses as if she'd been aching for them? That had always been one of the things that had gotten to him about her, the way she'd made him feel as if he was the only man who'd ever mattered. That he was important to her.

That she'd been becoming important to him.

Dante snorted as he dumped the rest of the coffee into the kitchen sink.

Why think about all this stuff again, especially since it was ridiculous? She was beautiful and bright; they'd had fun together and she was amazing in bed. End of story.

That she could still affect him, still push the right buttons, was not good. Dante narrowed his eyes.

Responding to his kisses even as she faced him with apparent defiance, holding herself aloof even as she trembled in his arms, insisting she wanted nothing from him after saying her son was his...

Just look where that had landed him.

He'd left here a couple of days ago to deal with a problem of his father's. Instead, he'd found himself facing a problem of his own—a potentially life-changing problem he had to confront head-on. He dealt with problems every day of his life. It was how he'd helped make Orsini's into a world-class investment firm that remained respected and rock solid even in the current economic nightmare.

He'd aced Financial Analysis 101. So, how come he'd made such a muck-up of Real-Life Analysis, Grade School Level?

It was time to start making some intelligent moves, starting with settling Gabriella and the kid elsewhere. The real estate agent who'd got him this place understood his tastes, his needs; the guy's firm was a high-end operation that understood the importance of discretion. That would be step one. Find her a place to live. Someplace within hailing distance but not where anyone would stumble over her.

He thought about that for a moment. To someone not familiar with the circumstances, a set-up like that would look as if he were trying to deny the ramifications of the situation.

Ridiculous.

He was just doing what he should have done in the first place. Behaving intelligently. Sam Cohen would surely agree. Not that he'd involve him until he had the move in motion, otherwise he'd have to admit Sam had an ass for a client.

Dante smiled thinly. He'd call Sam later today, set up an appointment, arrange for the necessary tests, for temporary financial support, long-term if that proved necessary because hadn't he finally faced the fact that anything was possible?

For no discernible reason, an image of Gabriella flashed before him.

Her wide eyes. Her lovely mouth. Her smile. And, though it wasn't something one could see, her honesty all the time they'd been together, starting the first time he'd phoned.

"It's Dante Orsini," he'd said, and then, because the need to see her had been near all consuming, he'd skipped the niceties and gone straight to the point. "I'll be there at eight, to take you to dinner."

"Did I miss something?" she'd said, with a little laugh. "When, exactly, did you ask me out?"

"I didn't," he'd replied bluntly. "Why would I ask you for something we both want?"

He'd heard the catch of her breath. And then she'd said, "Yes." Just that one word, that "yes," delivered in such a low, sexy voice that it had filled him with heat.

She was into honesty from the small things to the big ones. She'd told him she was a Jets fan when he said he was into the Giants. He'd mentioned his preference for the Giants to an endless stream of women and every last one had quickly said wasn't that nice because she loved them, too, and that included the ones who probably couldn't tell a football from a volley ball.

She ate with gusto, packing away a loaded-with-everything hot dog at a Yankees game, warning him she knew no bounds when it came to lobster and proving it by finishing every bite at The Boathouse, ending with butter on her chin that he'd just had to kiss away.

She was upfront about everything.

Especially in bed.

Her passion, her arousal, her eagerness when he touched her, when he tasted her breasts, when he put his mouth on that perfect bud between her thighs, all of it so real, so sweet, so amazing it shook his world.

And when she responded, when she caressed him, put her hands and mouth on him…

"Dammit," he growled.

None of that meant he should believe this child was his without proof, he thought coldly.

First things first. Shower. Phone that real estate agent. And then tap politely at Gabriella's door, tell her he'd been thinking things over and that he'd come up with a workable plan.

He felt better already.

Showered, shaved, dressed in faded jeans and a navy T-shirt, Dante headed for the kitchen.

He'd lost track not only of days but of hours. All that going back and forth had confused his internal clock. Was it time for breakfast? Lunch? Dinner? He didn't know and didn't much care. He was hungry, was all he knew; his stomach was growling. He'd had a sandwich on the plane but that seemed a long time ago. Gabriella hadn't eaten at all. During the flight, the attendant had said she'd checked and both Gabriella and the baby were sleeping. He'd thought about going back there, just to see how things were, but if Gabriella was asleep…

Okay. So maybe the truth was, he hadn't been ready to talk to her. Not then.

But he was ready now.

So, he'd cook something for the two of them.

He frowned as he opened the fridge. The shelves were pretty empty except for the requisite things. Eggs. Bread. Butter. A container of light cream that passed the sniff test. An unopened quart of milk. There was a wedge of cheddar in the cheese keeper on the door. He wasn't the world's best cook but he could put together a cheese omelet, make some toast, a pot of coffee. As for the baby…

What did babies that small eat? Formula? Little jars of vile-looking, strange-colored food? Not that it would be his problem. Gabriella had filled a big carry-on with what she'd called baby stuff. She surely had food for the kid inside it.

He took out the eggs, the milk, the butter, the cheese—

And hesitated.

Come to think of it, how come it was so quiet? He'd been up and pacing around for hours. He figured Gabriella was exhausted, but still, what about the kid? When his sister Anna was a baby, she'd cried nonstop.

For no good reason the skin on the back of his neck prickled. He shut the refrigerator door and headed up the stairs.

Nothing. No sounds at all drifting down the wide hall.

He paused at the guest suite. "Gabriella?" He moved closer to the door. Tapped at it. "Gabriella?" No answer. "Gabriella," he said loudly, and then he said to hell with it, turned the knob and stepped inside.

The curtains in the sitting room were drawn. Beyond, the bedroom door stood open. He walked toward it.

The baby lay on the bed, surrounded by pillows. He was on his belly, his rump up in the air, head to the side and part of his fist jammed into his mouth. He was sound asleep and… Dante frowned. Hell. The kid was that all-purpose word. Cute. A cliché but accurate. The kid was so small, the bed so big…

Dante cleared his throat. He hadn't come up here to look at babies, he'd come to check on Gabriella. Obviously, she was in the bathroom.

Oh, hell.

The bathroom door was shut but the sound of someone

being sick traveled straight through it. "Gabriella?" he said, hurrying to the door. "Are you sick?"

"Dante." Her voice was weak. Frighteningly weak. "Don't come in. I have a bug. The flu—"

He could almost feel the blood draining from his face. He wasn't good at this, either. Somebody throwing up...

Gabriella groaned. Retched. He didn't think, didn't hesitate; he flung the door open and stepped into the room. His Gabriella was hunched over the toilet, her hair streaming down her back, her body trembling. He cursed, ran to her and clasped her shoulders from behind.

"Sweetheart. Why didn't you ask me to help you? I'll get a doctor—"

"Go away. I don't need—"

She retched again. His hands tightened on her. He could feel her shaking; she was wearing a nightgown and she was soaked straight through with sweat. His heart turned over.

"Gaby. Honey, what can I do to help?"

What could he do? If she hadn't felt as if she were dying, Gabriella would have laughed. What he could do was disappear. This was not what a woman wanted, to have a man see her like this. Sweaty, disheveled—and throwing up everything, starting at her toes.

Pain fisted in her belly and she bent over and gave herself up to the spasm. By the time it ended, she was swaying on her feet. Dante cursed softly, drew her gently back against him. *Go away,* she thought desperately, *just go away.*

But his body felt so good against hers. Strong. Hard. Comforting. Shivering, icy cold, she let his warmth seep into her.

"Gaby?"

His voice was filled with alarm. She wanted to reassure

him that she'd be okay, that she'd come down with whatever had sickened Yara the week before, but it happened again, the wave of agonizing nausea, and she gagged, leaned forward and vomited.

When she straightened up this time, she knew the spasms were over.

"I'm okay now," she said weakly.

She reached out to flush the toilet but Dante did it instead. She felt her face fill with heat. *Deus,* the embarrassment of it! That he should see her like this, desperate and all but helpless when she prided herself on her independence, when it was, she knew, one of the things that had drawn him to her.

Not that she cared about that anymore; it didn't matter if he was drawn to her or not. Still, it was—it was—

"Here," he said gently.

He brought a cup of water to her lips. She wanted to tell him she didn't need his help, but that would have been a lie. Instead, she sipped the cool liquid, rinsed her mouth, spat it out. She did it twice and then he eased her onto the closed toilet and washed her face with a soft, damp washcloth.

"Better?"

She nodded. "Yes. Thank you. But really, you can go now. I'll be—"

"Do not," he said quietly, "tell me what I can do, Gabriella." He bent, lifted her in his arms and carried her into the bedroom. "I know exactly what I can do. What I'm going to do. And it starts with putting you to bed and calling the doctor, whether you like it or not."

"No. I do not need—"

She followed his gaze to the bed, sighing with relief when she saw that Daniel had slept through it all.

Dante headed for the door.

"Where are you taking me?"

"Don't worry. I'll come back for the baby after I get you settled."

"But—"

Arguing was pointless. She knew that. Once Dante made up his mind to do something, nothing would deter him. She had no choice but to loop her arms around his neck and give in as he carried her down the corridor. When he shouldered open a door and she saw that he had brought her to his bedroom, sick as she was it sent a little thrill of recognition through her. She had not been here in a very, very long time but it looked the same. Big, masculine. A perfect reflection of the man who had once been her lover.

He carried her to the bed. His bed. As he eased her back against the pillows, she thought of how many times he had done that in the months they'd been together.

"Dante. Wait…"

Too late. He was gone, returning seconds later with Daniel in his arms. Her heart skipped a beat. Her son, in his father's powerful arms. The sight made her throat tighten. He gave Daniel to her while he arranged a pair of big, upholstered chairs so they faced each other, their soft, high arms forming the walls of an improvised crib. Then he took the still-sleeping baby from her, laid him gently in the improvised crib and covered him with a cashmere throw.

"Okay?" he said softly, looking at her.

Gabriella smiled. "Perfect. Thank you."

He nodded. His gaze swept over her; his dark eyebrows drew together. "You're soaked."

She looked down at herself. Her cotton nightgown, plastered to her skin with sweat, She flushed, slipped under the duvet and drew it to her chin. The bed smelled of Dante:

masculine, clean...wonderful. She looked up, ready to tell him she couldn't stay here but he was gone again. Of course. She felt her color deepen. He had done all she could possibly expect and more, held her while she was violently ill, taken care of the baby...

"Sit up."

She raised her head in surprise. His voice was gentle; he had a bowl of water, a towel and one of his T-shirts in his hands.

"Dante. Really—"

"Gabriella," he said softly, "really. Just relax, sweetheart, and let me take care of you."

No, she thought, no, she could not do that. Not even for these precious moments. She could not permit herself to fall under his spell again; it would break her, if she did. He was kind, he was generous, he was the most gorgeous man she had ever known, but there could never be more to it than that.

The cloth stroked lightly over her face. It felt wonderful. His nearness to her felt wonderful. Sighing, she closed her eyes and gave in. Let him bathe her face, her throat. Let him push aside the straps of her damp nightgown, run the warm cloth lightly over her shoulders, her arms...

The upper slope of her breasts.

His hand slowed. His breath quickened. So did hers. Her eyes flew open. Her lover's face was all harsh planes and angles, his pale-blue eyes blazed with flame.

"Gaby," he said hoarsely.

He had never called her that until today. There was something incredibly intimate in it. And when his hand paused, cupped her breast, she cried out at the pleasure of his touch. She was going to die from this. From wanting him. Needing him. Aching for him.

He said her name again, brushed his thumb across her

nipple, erect under the nightgown. He bent toward her, closer and closer—

A thin wail broke the silence. It was Daniel. Her son's cry grew stronger.

"The baby," she whispered.

Dante drew back. His hand fell away from her; he was all business now.

"Lift your arms," he said briskly, and when she did, he pulled the nightgown over her head, his gaze never dropping below her arms and face, and replaced the gown with the T-shirt. By the time she'd finished easing it down her body under cover of the duvet, he was leaning over her with the baby in his arms.

She reached for her son. Daniel was kicking and crying as if he had not nursed at her breasts only three hours ago. She smiled at her little boy, tugged down the loose neckline of the T-shirt and brought him to her breast. She did it without thinking; she had nursed him from the day of his birth, completely unselfconsciously...

But not in front of the man who had given her baby to her.

Dante made a soft sound. A groan. She looked up. His gaze was fixed on the baby, on his small hand against her breast, his small mouth at her nipple. A sensation so powerful it made her tremble swept through her. She whispered Dante's name. His eyes met hers; he groaned again, bent to her, cupped her face and took her mouth in a hot, hungry kiss.

And then he was gone.

CHAPTER NINE

THE baby nursed until Gabriella was certain she could almost feel his little tummy rounding under her hand. She shifted him to her shoulder, gently patted his back and was rewarded with a contented burp.

"That's my boy," she said softly. He gave her a happy grin and she laughed and played a round of I-See with him, forgetting everything for a few happy minutes. Her aching head and bones, her unsettled stomach…

Her unsettled life.

Daniel seemed to sense her change in mood. His dark, winged brows drew together. His sculpted lips turned down. His features were such a perfect duplication of Dante's…

Gabriella swallowed hard. "It's all right, *bebé,*" she crooned. "Mama loves you. She'll always love you." She touched the tip of her finger to his nose. "We'll be fine, you and I. Just wait and see."

The baby's expression softened. He smiled. Yawned. Yawned again, and Gabriella scooted down in the big bed, holding him securely in the curve of her arm. In a few seconds he was fast asleep. The flight, the change in routine, had tired him.

She looked at the thick, dark lashes that lay against his

cheeks, noting again that he was the very image of his father. When her boy grew up, he and Dante would be mirror images.

Mirror images no one would see.

Dante had made it sound as if she and Daniel were to be part of his life, but she knew better. It wasn't that he'd lied but that he'd spoken under stress. He was, at heart, a decent man and he'd reacted with gallantry to her circumstances.

Reality had come after they'd boarded the plane. It had not been difficult to see. He had become distant. When the flight attendant suggested she and Daniel might be more comfortable in the small private room at the rear, Dante had said that was an excellent idea. It was, in a way. It had meant she could nurse the baby, change him, rock him to sleep in her arms without any distractions, but still…

Foolishly enough, she'd thought Dante might at least spend some time with her and the baby, but he had not entered the little room, not even once. It wasn't as if he'd forgotten their presence. He'd sent the attendant to her, several times.

Was everything all right? the woman had inquired politely. Did the *senhorita* need anything? If so, she had only to press the call button.

What Gabriella needed could not be gotten by pressing the call button. She hadn't said that, of course, she'd simply smiled politely and said she would be sure to do that. Then she'd fed the baby, put him into a fresh diaper, curled up on the sofa with him and fallen into a deep, dreamless sleep.

To her surprise, she'd slept for hours. She knew she was tired but it was as if only now, miles above the earth and from the *fazenda,* her mind and body were ready to admit she was not just tired but exhausted.

So much had happened during the past months! She had first tended to her father, then to her brother. Her father, true to form, had seemed to expect everything she'd done for him until his last breath; her brother, also true to form, had worried she was doing too much.

"You are with child," he'd said. "You must worry about a new life, Gabriella, not a worn-out one like mine."

Remembering those months before Arturo's death was bittersweet. They had been as close as when they'd been children—but all the while, she'd known she could not save him.

And she'd been pregnant. An easy pregnancy, thankfully, but still, she was exhausted all the time, going without sleep, worrying over the increasing awareness that her father had gambled away everything, that there was no money left in his accounts or, eventually, in hers. Looking back, it seemed as if she had done nothing but worry.

Then Dante had appeared.

For a little while, at least, she could lift her head, take a breath, make plans. Yes, he'd obviously realized what a burden he'd undertaken, but once she was in New York, things would be better. She'd lost the *fazenda* and that broke her heart, but perhaps the cold truth was that she'd be better off in Manhattan. She knew it better than she knew Bonito. She had friends in the city, contacts, her old agent. She could find a small apartment, get some modeling assignments, start to regain her feet.

She had thought about all those things during the flight, but by the time the plane landed she was sick. Whatever bug she'd been fighting had finally won. Everything ached; her belly felt as if someone had jabbed it with a hot poker.

She hid it from Dante. Not that he'd have abandoned her if he learned she was ill—she knew that. But the last thing she'd wanted was to be more of a burden than she already was. She would never have let him know she was sick if he hadn't stumbled across the information by accident.

But she would get better. She would not overstay her welcome. A few days. A week, at most, and she would move on.

She had to, she thought now, as the baby slept beside her. Oh, yes, she had to move on. And quickly, before her foolish heart led her into trouble. Into temptation. Look at what had happened a little while ago. That kiss. The whisper of Dante's fingers against her breast. She'd felt her body come alive, reminding her that she was not only a mother, she was a woman.

Yara had said she would be free of such urges for a very long time but clearly, her old *ama* was wrong. Those urges, those needs, were still there. They were there for Dante, only for Dante.

A light knock sounded at the closed door. Gabriella drew the duvet higher.

"Yes?"

"Is it okay to come in?"

It wasn't, not while her heart was pounding like this.

"*Sim.* Yes, of course."

Dante had a tray in his hands. There were things arranged on it. A carafe of iced water. A glass. A teapot, cup and saucer. A box of tissues. And a small brass bell.

"In case you're thirsty," he said briskly, making room on the teak night table. "And a bell, if you should need me."

"A bell," she said, as if she'd never heard the word before. Why wouldn't he look at her? Moments ago he had kissed her as if he would never get enough of kissing her and now...

"One of my sisters, Anna, brought it back from somewhere. Thailand. Katmandu. Wherever aging hippies go to die." He did look at her then, flashed a quick smile. "Not that Anna's an aging anything. I keep telling her she was born a few decades too late."

"Anna," Gabriella said, and it truly was a word she'd never heard before. In the months they'd been together, she'd met his brothers once, purely by chance, but Dante had never talked about his family. Of course, neither had she. "It's…it's a lovely name."

"Old-fashioned, Anna says, but…"

But what? Dante thought. Why was he talking about his sister? Was it because it was safer than doing what he really wanted to do, reaching for Gabriella, drawing her into his arms and kissing her until she wrapped her arms around his neck and begged him to finish what they had started a little while ago? No way. She was sick. He couldn't take advantage of her and besides, it would only complicate things—as if they weren't complicated enough.

He moved the pitcher of water, the glass, the teapot, did a handful of absolutely unnecessary things and then he stepped back.

"Okay," he said brightly. "As I said, if you need anything…"

"Thank you."

"Do you feel better?"

"I'm fine."

The hell she was. Her face was almost the same shade of ivory as the pillow. The baby, at least, looked okay. He was sleeping, lashes dusting his cheeks, mouth pursed in a small bow.

Cute.

Dante frowned. Wrong. The baby didn't look cute as much as he looked, well, like a miniature of a familiar face. A very familiar face…

He swallowed hard. Turned his gaze on Gabriella.

"Yeah. Well, we'll see what the doctor has to say."

"Dante. I don't need a—"

"Yes. You do."

"I don't. Honestly, Dante—"

"Honestly, Gabriella," he said, and then, because he damned well had to do it, he bent and kissed her, very lightly, on the mouth. "Ring the bell if you need me," he said, and then he was gone.

Gabriella glared at the closed door. Damn the man! Did he think he could give her orders? Kiss her into obedience? He had not changed at all. He still acted as if he owned the world.

She had hated that about him.

She had adored that about him.

Until he'd come into her life, she'd never known you could be furious at a man and crazy about him at the same time, but how could anyone hold Dante's macho arrogance against him? It was part of him and it was incredibly sexy. He'd shown it the first time he phoned to ask her out, except he hadn't "asked" her anything. He'd said hello, reminded her they'd met at a party a few nights before, and then he'd told her he'd be by at eight to take her to dinner.

"Did I miss something?" she'd said, even though she'd been hoping he would call. "I mean, exactly when did you ask me out?"

"Why should I ask you for something we both want?" he'd said in a low, husky voice.

Being sure of himself was part of who Dante Orsini was.

The trouble was, he was sure of her, too. Sure that she was mesmerized by him. And she had been. For all her air of cool sophistication, she'd been his from the start.

"I don't want you seeing anyone but me," he'd said, that very first night. She'd been in his arms by then. In his bed. In this bed. And he'd been deep, deep inside her. "You belong to me," he'd added, his voice rough. "You're mine. Do you understand that?"

Yes, she'd said, yes, yes, yes.

Gabriella blinked back the sudden threat of tears. Ridiculous. It had been fun. She had been faithful. So had Dante. He was, after all, a moral man. It was just that his interest in a woman never lasted all that long.

As for what seemed to be happening now...it meant nothing. He was a virile male in his prime. And she—she was a woman who had not had sex in quite a while.

All right.

She had not had sex since the night before he'd gone away on business.

The baby gave a little cry in his sleep. Gabriella drew him closer. She would get them out of here as fast as she could. A few phone calls would start the process. Then she'd thank Dante for all his help and say goodbye.

Another knock at the door.

Dante again. This time with a physician in tow. He introduced them, then left the room. If the doctor was surprised at finding a woman and an infant in Dante Orsini's bed, he gave no sign, simply examined her and then Daniel, who reacted to the insult to his small person with ear-splitting wails of protest.

The doctor packed away his stethoscope.

"You have a virus."

"I could have told you that," Gabriella said grumpily.

"The baby's fine," he said, ignoring her bad manners. "Has he ever had formula?"

"Yes, but why? Will it be dangerous for me to nurse him while I'm sick?"

"Not dangerous. Tiring. You need to rest. And to drink plenty of fluids. Let Mr. Orsini take care of things while you concentrate on getting better."

The doctor left. Dante reappeared. The ease with which he had taken over, making decisions for her, was, for some reason, infuriating. When he held out his hand and showed her the two capsules in his palm, she shook her head.

"No."

"No, what?"

"No, I'm not taking those things. Your doctor should know better than to prescribe antibiotics for a virus."

Dante rolled his eyes. "They're Tylenol."

Of course they were. And they'd help ease the ache in her bones, in her head. Another decision she'd let Dante make…and what did it matter? It was only temporary.

She took the capsules. Drank some water.

"More," Dante ordered.

She glowered at him but she finished what was in the glass.

"Thank you," Dante said, straight-faced. He took the glass, put it on the night table. Then he scooped the baby from the improvised crib where the doctor had put him.

"What are you doing?"

"Lie back. Close your eyes. Get some rest."

"Listen here, Dante, I am not yours to command. I am not a child—"

"Listen here, Gabriella," he said, spoiling it by flashing a grin that made her want to grin in return. She didn't, of course, and he swooped in to press a quick, soft kiss to her parted lips.

"You'll catch the flu," she said, because she had to say something or run the danger of kissing him back.

He touched the tip of his finger to her nose. "Time to take a nap."

"But Daniel…"

"Daniel and I will do just fine."

Hearing her son's name slip so softly and simply from

Dante's lips did something to her, something that left her knowing she dared not reply for danger of doing something stupid...like weeping. Instead she watched Dante stroll from the room, the baby pressed to his shoulder, her son's pale eyes filled with curiosity.

All right. She'd lie here for a few minutes. Then she'd go rescue the baby from a man who knew nothing about babies.

She awoke and knew that hours must have gone by.

Experimentally she stretched her limbs. She hurt a little but nowhere near as much as before.

Cautiously she sat up. Got to her feet. Her legs felt a little like undercooked pasta, but nothing major seemed wrong except that she needed to pee, desperately, and there wasn't a way in the world she was going to ring for Dante and ask him to help her with that.

She made it to the bathroom, sank down on the toilet, sighed with relief as she emptied her bladder. She flushed, gave the huge walk-in shower a longing glance but decided not to push her luck. Instead she washed her hands and face, used Dante's brush on her hair, automatically opened the drawer that had always held a couple of packaged toothbrushes, tried not to think of how many women had opened this same drawer in the past months, unwrapped a brush and cleaned her teeth.

She looked in the mirror.

Not great but it would have to do.

Dante's soft terry robe hung, as it always had, behind the door. She put it on over the T-shirt, paused in the bedroom to get a pair of panties and set out in search of her baby.

The enormous two-story penthouse was quiet. What

time was it? It was light outside, but barely. Was it night or was it day? Amazing, how she'd lost track of the hours.

She went down the wide, curved staircase, a cautious hand on the carved banister. Her legs had gone from feeling like undercooked spaghetti to spaghetti *al dente*. A good sign, surely...

Was that a sound? A voice? She paused at the foot of the stairs.

Yes. There was bright light at the end of the wide corridor she knew led to Dante's big, if rarely used, showplace of a kitchen. Slowly she made her way there, her bare feet soundless against the cool marble floor—and stopped at the entrance, eyes widening.

The voice she'd heard was Dante's. Barefoot the same as she, wearing jeans and a T-shirt that clung to his muscled torso, he sat in a high-backed swivel stool at the granite counter, Daniel in the curve of his arm.

The baby was staring up at him and sucking contentedly at a bottle of formula.

The two of them looked as if they'd been doing this kind of thing forever.

"Hey, buddy," Dante said, "you're doing a great job. That's the way. Drink it all down. I know it isn't what you're used to but it's good for you just the same. It'll put hair on your chest, you'll see."

Gabriella's eyes filled with tears. She leaned back against the wall, determined not to let Dante see her until she got herself under control. Seeing her lover—her once-upon-a-time lover—and her son like this was almost more than she could bear.

And yet she knew better than to read anything into the scene.

Dante was an intelligent, capable man. Faced with a problem, he would always attempt to solve it: she was sick; the baby needed to be cared for; he'd taken charge. He was good at that. Still, it was hard to see the two of them together without feeling almost indescribable joy.

"Okay, pal. What happens next?"

The baby gave an enormous burp. Dante laughed. "Well, that answers that question." Another huge burp. Dante grinned. "That good, huh? Hey, I'm a steak-and-potatoes guy myself but whatever floats your boat works for me. So, okay. Your belly's full. You don't look the least bit sleepy. You need a trip to the john? I'll bet you do. Well, let's give it a try—"

Gabriella took a breath and stepped briskly into the kitchen. Dante turned toward her, eyebrows lifting.

"Hey."

"Hey, yourself." She smiled. "Thank you for feeding the baby."

"Nothing to it," he said with just a touch of macho pride. "The doctor recommended this brand of formula and I had the pharmacy send up a case." He frowned. "But what are you doing out of bed? You were supposed to ring the bell if you needed me."

She held out her arms for the baby, who gave her a loopy grin.

"I know. But I thought a little exercise might do me good." The baby kicked its arms and legs. Gabriella smiled as she reached for him. "Besides," she said softly, "I missed you."

Fool that he was, Dante at first thought she was talking to him. She wasn't, of course, she was talking to Daniel. He realized it just in time to stop from saying that he had missed her, too.

But, dammit, he had.

It was a long time since she'd been here.

He'd always loved it when she'd stayed the night. It

hadn't happened often. She'd almost always refused to do it and he—well, he'd never been big on having women spend the night in his bed. It led to too many expectations.

But he'd loved having Gabriella stay here. Being able to reach for her, not just during the dark hours of night but in that quiet time just before dawn. Seeing her, first thing in the morning, looking the way she looked now, warm and tousled, wrapped in his robe, her hair brushed into a cloud of gold and chestnut, no makeup, no what Falco had dubbed the "*Five A.M. face*" women obviously put on while a guy was still sleeping.

The fact was, it was more than a year and he'd never had another woman here overnight. He hadn't wanted to, hadn't wanted anybody else in his bed or in his life for more than an evening.

Hell, he thought, and cleared his throat.

"Okay," he said brightly. "It's bathroom time. Hand the kid over."

Gabriella laughed. "He can't do 'bathroom time.' He's only a baby."

Dante gave her a look, then lifted the baby from her arms.

"She thinks I don't know that," he said to Daniel, who stared at him with solemnity. "Should we show her how wrong she is?"

"Dante, honestly—"

"She likes that word," he told the baby. "That word, 'honestly.' What she means when she says it is, 'Honestly, you men. You think you know everything.'" While he spoke, he was moving out of the kitchen, down the hall, to the stairs, the baby now making happy sounds, little trills of laughter. "Can you do the stairs?"

It took Gabriella a second to realize he meant her.

"Yes. Of course I can. But what…"

"No. Come to think of it, I don't trust you on the stairs. Not yet. So, you stay right there. I'll come back for you."

"Dante. Honestly—"

"Two 'honestlys' in one conversation." Dante shook his head, turned back to her and brushed his mouth lightly over hers. "Amazing."

She couldn't help laughing, even though she didn't want to. "No. I mean, honestly—"

He kissed her again, his lips lingering on hers, the baby between them cooing at this new, delightful game. When he drew back, he ran his hand along her cheek.

"That's the penalty," he said softly. "A kiss, each time you use that word. Now, stay put. Okay?"

She nodded. It was all she could manage.

He went up the stairs quickly, came down just as quickly but without the baby. She waited for a wail of protest and heard, instead, her son's contented gurgles.

Dante swept her into his arms. It felt—it felt wonderful. Hours ago he'd carried her up these same steps but she'd been too sick to enjoy it. Now she was aware of everything it entailed. The steady beat of his heart. The solid feel of his chest. The light pressure of his hand at the side of her breast. The clean, soap-and-water scent of his skin and hair.

The sweet pull of desire in her breasts and belly.

"You've lost weight."

His voice was gruff. She nodded.

"Maybe a little."

"What for? You were perfect, just the way you were."

Perfect. The word seemed to shimmer with light.

"I…it wasn't deliberate. I…I had a lot of things to do, when I got back to the *fazenda*."

"The baby." His tone grew even more gruff. "I'm sorry you had to go through that alone."

She thought of telling him that she had not been entirely alone, that her brother had been there for her, at least at the beginning. But that would only lead to questions. Dante didn't know anything about her brother; they'd always kept their talk impersonal. Intimate, yes. Dante had whispered things to her in bed. Things that had made her tremble with desire. With need. With…with what she felt for him.

"Here we go," he said, as he carried her through a door, not to his room but to one just across from it.

Gabriella's mouth fell open.

This was a baby's room.

Not in decor. The walls were cream; there were white-and-black vertical blinds at the windows, a black-and-white Scandinavian area rug underfoot. But it was furnished for a small child.

Winnie the Pooh smiled from atop a bird's-eye maple dresser, side by side with a baby monitor. A teddy bear with button eyes sat in the seat of a baby swing. A changing table stood against one wall, a big maple rocker against another. Facing her was surely the most beautiful crib in the whole world, also made of maple, fitted with sheets patterned with kittens and puppies. A mobile of rocket ships and suited spacemen amid stars, moons and planets hung over it.

Her son lay on his back in the crib, arms and legs going like mad, eyes fixed to the mobile, his face a portrait of delight.

"I didn't know what you'd like," Dante said. "So I just ordered some stuff."

She looked up at him. His mouth was a whisper away. *Say something,* her brain shrieked, but she couldn't come up with a single word.

Dante cleared his throat.

"Look, there's no problem with sending it all back. You know, if it's not what you wanted—"

"Oh, Dante! It's wonderful!"

His face cleared. "You think?"

"It's just that—" she hesitated "—we can't impose on you this way. I mean, I know how busy you are. Orsini Investments. Your family. The last thing you need is…is someone from the past cluttering up your life, your home—"

He silenced her the only way he could.

He kissed her. And kissed her. And when she kissed him back and sighed his name in the way that had always sent spirals of desire straight down to his toes, he knew that everything he had done—bringing her here, sweeping aside his plans to find her an apartment and instead settling her into his home, was right.

The idea had come to him while the doctor was with her. Gabriella was sick; she had the baby to care for. No way could he let her be on her own just yet. She'd simply have to stay with him for a couple of days. Just a temporary arrangement, of course, but even so, the baby would need things…

Except that now, looking down at the woman in his arms, he knew those were all pathetic rationalizations.

"I want you here," he said softly, when he finally ended the kiss. "Here. With me. You and the boy—you and Daniel belong here."

"Dante." Her voice shook. "Please. Don't say that and not mean it."

"We'll take things one step at a time."

It wasn't quite the answer her heart wanted but it was an honest answer. How could she fault him for that? she thought, and she nodded and said, very softly, "Okay."

He leaned his forehead against hers. "Starting with that bathroom stuff you were positive I couldn't handle."

She smiled into his eyes. "Somehow, I can't picture you changing a diaper."

"Who says? Put your money where your mouth is."

Her smile became a grin. "A buck says you can't."

"You're on."

She lost the bet.

Dante could do everything. Run a powerful corporation? Sure. Make every man in a room defer to him? That, too. Be the man all the women in the world wanted? Easy.

She'd known all that from experience.

What she'd never known until now was that he could diaper a baby as if he'd done it all his life. Take care of her. Brew her a cup of tea. Stand over her until she gave up and downed another couple of Tylenol. Whip up a meal— though as he pointed out, heating a can of chicken broth for her, taking a steak from the freezer and broiling it for himself wasn't exactly gourmet cooking. But it was much, much more than she'd ever seen him do in the past. Back then he'd been a whiz at making restaurant reservations and, once or twice, phoning down for Chinese take-out.

Dante Orsini, doing kitchen duty?

Never…until tonight.

Hours later she and Daniel were both yawning. Dante offered to give the baby a bottle but she said no, she'd nurse him. "Are you sure?" Dante said and she nodded and decided that telling him she really had to do it, that her breasts would be swollen and heavy unless she did, was more than she wanted to discuss. It was too private, too intimate…

Too much.

She nursed Daniel, sitting in the beautiful rocking chair in his room while Dante cleaned up the kitchen. When she was done, they bathed the baby together. Dante said he felt too clumsy to do it, but he took over halfway through, laughing when Daniel splashed water all over him, wrapping the baby in a big bath towel, then diapering him and dressing him in a blue onesie.

Dante lowered him gently into his crib. Gabriella kissed her son's head. Dante stroked his dark hair.

"Good night, pal," he said softly.

Out in the hall, for the first time all day, they were alone. The penthouse seemed wrapped in silence. Their eyes met. She felt the heat rise in her face. He took a step toward her. She took a quick step back.

"No. We can't." Her voice was breathless. "It would—it would only complicate things."

He nodded. Hadn't he already reached that same conclusion?

It was her turn to nod. "So…so, good night."

"Good night, sweetheart," he whispered. And then he reached for her and she went into his arms.

CHAPTER TEN

SHE went into his arms as if she had never left them.

A dozen thoughts raced through his head.

He wanted to tell her how he had missed her. How it felt to hold her again. But the need to kiss her, taste her, the need to possess her, make her his again had a hot urgency that drove away reason.

It was the same for her.

He could tell by the little sounds she made, the way she clung to his neck. By the motion of her body against his; that long, elegant body he had, yes, never forgotten.

And her mouth.

Sweet. Soft. Giving. A man could lose himself, just taking her mouth again and again, but it wasn't enough, not now, not after all these endless months. He drew her away from the door, backed her against the wall, tore open her robe and swept his hands over her silken skin. Her hands were on him, too, at his jeans, undoing the closure, unzipping him, and he groaned as she closed her hand around him and said his name in a broken whisper that almost drove him to his knees.

"Yes," he said, "yes, sweetheart."

He hooked his fingers in her panties. Eased them down. He knelt; she put a hand on his head to steady herself as she stepped free of the scrap of silk. He clasped her ankle. Rose to his feet, his hand moving up and up her leg. His touch was warm and possessive and it made her tremble.

"Open for me," he said in a strangled voice, and when she did, he put his hand between her thighs.

A cry burst from her throat. She was wet and hot for him, only for him, and he couldn't wait. Not anymore. He had wanted this without knowing it, waited for this for more than a year, and if he didn't have her now, he'd be lost forever.

He reversed their positions so that the wall was at his back. And as she sobbed his name, he lifted her, brought her down onto his rigid length. Her arms tightened around his neck, her legs wrapped around his waist. She buried her face against his throat and he could feel the heat of her breath, hear her breathy moans of ecstasy.

Too fast, his fevered brain told him, *dammit, too fast....*

She cried out. Sank her teeth into his flesh. And as she convulsed around him, Dante drove deep, rode her even harder, and flew off the edge of the world.

They stayed that way for long minutes, breathing hard, letting the aftermath of their passion ease. Then Gabriella gave a soft laugh. He remembered that laugh, low and delicious and earthy.

"What?" he said, his lips curving in a smile against her forehead.

"All those years of yoga that I took..." Another husky laugh. "Turns out they were worth it."

He grinned, let her down slowly. She looked up at him and she was so beautiful...the tightness in his chest almost overwhelmed him.

"Gabriella."

"Mmm?"

He shook his head. "Nothing," he said quietly, "just…" He bent his head and kissed her. Then he lifted her in his arms and carried her to his bed. She lay with her head on his shoulder, her hand playing with the dark curls on his chest.

"What are you thinking?"

Gently he stroked a tousled mass of golden curls from her cheek.

"That I've missed you."

She turned her face, pressed a kiss to his skin. "Me, too."

In truth he was thinking far more than that. He was thinking that a man went through life certain he knew what he needed to be happy. Success in his work. The love of his family. Friends who stood by him. Things that seemed simple and attainable.

It wasn't enough.

He needed this.

Gabriella, in his arms. Winding her arms around his neck as he gathered her closer, returning his kisses as if nothing in the world mattered but him.

He gathered her closer. How had he lived without her?

Without warning, a thought raced through him like a gust of cold air. *This could be dangerous.* There was so much to discuss, to work through. But then Gabriella sighed, kissed his throat and he knew that nothing mattered but her.

The swift tide of desire rose inside him again.

Kissing her, he rolled her onto her back, caught her hands in his and laced their fingers together. He drew back a little, just far enough to see her.

She was exquisite.

Her hair was a tangled mass of gleaming golds, her eyes were wide and luminous, her lips were softly swollen from his kisses. Everything had happened so quickly that

she was still wearing his robe and, under it, his T-shirt. He
bent his head, kissed her throat, the pulse racing wildly in
its hollow. His tongue dipped into her mouth, capturing the
honeyed sweetness he had never forgotten.

"Gabriella."

His voice was thick, his breathing ragged. He ached, not
only to make love to her again but to see all of her. Gently
he eased the robe from her shoulders and slid his hands
under the hem of the shirt. Her skin felt like silk; the scent
of her arousal made his blood pound even harder.

The back of his hand brushed against the soft curls
between her thighs. She moaned; the sound inflamed him.
Watching her face, he parted her labia with the tips of his
fingers. Her head fell back, her lashes drooped over her
eyes.

"Do you like it when I do this?" The words were thick,
raw with need. "Gabriella? When I touch you here?"

"Yes," she sobbed, "yes, yes…"

His finger stroked her clitoris. It was the most perfect
flower imaginable. He loved the feel of it, the desperate
little sounds she made when he caressed it. But it wasn't
enough. He wanted to kiss her belly, her breasts.

"Sweetheart," he whispered. "Sit up. Let me get this
damned shirt out of the way…"

"Dante…"

"Just lift your arms and I'll—"

"Don't!" She caught his wrists, her eyes pleading with
his. "Don't," she said unsteadily. "Please."

"What is it? What did I do? Gaby. Baby…" Hell! What
a fool he was. He exhaled sharply, gathered her in his arms,
kissed her temples, her eyelids, her mouth. "Forgive me. I
should have realized. It's too much. You're sick…."

"No. Oh, no. I'm fine."

Even worse. Dante cursed himself for being a fool.

She'd had a baby only four months ago. He should have thought, should have asked.

"It's…it's—"

"The baby. Daniel. I understand. Just tell me I didn't hurt you because if I did, God, if I did—"

She put her fingers against his lips.

"No. It isn't that." She took a deep breath. "It's…it's that I've changed." She hesitated. "My breasts. My body." The tip of her tongue swiped lightly over her lips. "Maybe…maybe if you just leave the shirt—"

He silenced her with a kiss. "I want to see you," he whispered.

Gabriella shook her head. "My breasts aren't the way they used to be. And…and there are stretch marks on my belly."

He kissed her again, framing her face with his hands, then gently stroked her hair back from her face.

"You are the most beautiful woman in the world, sweetheart."

"No. I'm not. Having a baby changes things."

"Yes. It makes you a woman. My woman."

She offered a tremulous smile. "I know I must sound silly. But I don't want to disappoint you. I couldn't stand it if—"

"Gaby. How could you ever do that?" His mouth twisted. "I'm the one, not you. I disappointed you. I hurt you. I left you alone to face the hardest days in your life and—"

"You didn't know."

"But I do now. And I want to see you. Please…"

He waited, wondering how he would survive it if she refused him, knowing he would never force her to do anything even if it meant he had to spend the next twenty-four hours under a cold shower.

She took a breath. Nodded. And let go of his wrists.

Even more slowly, he drew the cotton T up, eased it carefully over her head. He could feel her trembling and he wanted to gather her in his arms, rock her against him, tell her she would always be perfect in his eyes whether she thought so or not.

He tossed the shirt aside. Her hands flew to her breasts. Dante shook his head and drew them away. He looked at her, and the breath caught in his throat.

She was more than beautiful, she was heart-stoppingly lovely.

Her breasts were fuller and all the more feminine for it. Her nipples, a pale pink that had always reminded him of summer roses, were a duskier shade than in the past.

His eyes moved down her body. The elegant indentation of her waist. Her belly, not flat but delicately convex and faintly, all but invisibly, striped with silver.

Yes, her body was changed. His seed, his son, had changed it. She was the essence of femininity.

And she was his.

Pride, primitive and male, the same emotions that must have driven the earliest man when he first emerged from his cave, swept through him. *Mine,* he thought, and he reached for her and brought her close against his heart within his encircling arms.

"Gabriella. You are exquisite."

"You don't have to say—"

He drew back. Kept his eyes on hers as he cupped a breast, traced the erect crest with a finger. She moaned; he thought he had never heard a more exciting sound.

"Your breasts are beautiful." He dropped his hand to her belly, curved his fingers over her warm flesh. "And this, your skin gilded with silver…" His gaze narrowed. "You are mine, sweetheart, and I have never wanted you more than I want you now."

He kissed her, parting her lips with his, kissed her throat, the slope of her breast, and when he drew the ruched pink tip into his mouth, her cry of pleasure shot through him. He teased her with his tongue. Licked. Nipped. Sucked… and suddenly there was a new taste, a taste even sweeter and richer—

Her hands flattened against his shoulders, pushed him away.

He lifted his head, saw panic in her eyes.

"I *am* hurting you," he said gruffly. "Baby, I told you. We'll stop—"

"You're not! The feel of your mouth is…is wonderful." Color leaped into her cheeks. "But I should have realized. I should have known. Sometimes, after I feed the baby, there's…there's a little milk still left. I should have warned you that…that—"

"Warned me?" He caught her wrists as she tried, again, to cover her breasts. "You're a woman, sweetheart. My woman. I love knowing that you can do this for Daniel." He paused. "For our son."

She gave a little sob, slid her hands into his hair, brought his lips to hers for a long, deep kiss and fell with him into the flames.

Dante stroked her breasts. Her belly. Her thighs. She cried out, sought his mouth. Her hand cupped his straining erection. The breath hissed through his teeth and he kicked free of his jeans.

Too fast. Way too fast. How could he, a man who was almost arrogant about his sexual control, how could he be so close to losing that control now? Because, dammit, he was.

He could feel the tightening in his scrotum, the

tension building in every muscle. He was racing to the edge, heart pounding, holding back, holding back, because his Gabriella deserved more. More of his mouth at her breasts. His hand between her thighs. His fingers parting her, finding her clitoris. More of this and this and this, he thought fiercely, as she cried out and arched off the bed.

"Please," she whispered, and he groaned, thrust into her. Deep. Hard. Fast. She reached up to him and he kissed her, rode her as she wrapped her legs around his waist.

"Dante," she sobbed. "Oh, Dante…"

She climaxed; he felt it happen, heard the trill of joy that broke from her throat, and he threw back his head and knew that what was happening to him had never happened before.

He was with her as they flew into the burning heart of the universe.

They slept in each other's arms, legs entwined, her head on his chest, his arm curved around her, his hand lightly cupping her breast.

And awoke to the darkness of the night, the wonder of being together, the sweetness of it.

The deep, hungry need for fulfillment.

He caressed her. Feathered his fingertips over her nipples. Kissed them. Stroked his hand down her body, between her legs, sought and found the very heart of her.

She moaned. Arched against his seeking hand. Used every feminine motion of her body to beg him for more. Still he hesitated. All the mysteries of a woman's body after childbirth, he had learned tonight. She said he couldn't hurt her, but for all he knew, in his ignorance, he could. Making love more than once, God, more than twice, might be a mistake.

"Are you sure you can do this?" he said, his lips a breath from hers.

She gave that wonderful laugh again, wrapped her hand around him and said, "You tell me."

He growled, rolled her on her back, lifted her leg and brought it high over his, opening her to him but entering her as slowly as he could bear.

It was agony.

Exquisite agony.

So was her soft moan of pleasure.

A shudder gripped his powerful body; he buried his face in her throat as he filled her, deeper, deeper, until he couldn't tell where he ended and she began. Until they were one. One, he thought, his heart filling with joy...

And then she moved.

His mind emptied.

She moved again and he groaned, moved with her and she cried out, sank her teeth into his shoulder and they let go together, shattered together, fell off the edge of the world together.

He held her until her breathing eased and he knew she was asleep. Then he kissed her, checked the baby monitor, smiled at the sight of his sleeping son. He drew the duvet over them both, gathered her close again.

He had never felt so complete in his life.

He slept, too.

They woke. Made love. The moon rose and set. And the night slipped away and became morning.

Gabriella opened her eyes to the soft patter of rain.

Rain, this time of year? It was too soon. Rainy season didn't come to the Pantanal until—

But she wasn't in the Pantanal. She was in Manhattan. In Dante's home.

In Dante's bed.

Memories of the long, incredible night rushed in. She tried to remember how many times they'd made love even as she chastised herself for the effort. It didn't matter... But, somehow, it did. Dante had always been an amazing lover. Tender. Savage. Giving and demanding all at once. Indefatigable. She'd been with only a couple of men before meeting him, so she was far from an expert. Still, Dante's virility was, well, amazing.

And yet last night the frequency with which he'd wanted her had shocked her.

She had wanted him, too, each time. And that had shocked her, as well, that her need for him had seemed insatiable, her desire for him endless. But then, it had always been that way with him. She'd always wanted him; even these past endless months, unable to imagine feeling a need for sex ever again, even then, if she were honest, there'd been nights she'd dreamed of Dante. Hot dreams. Dreams from which she'd awakened empty and shaken, an ache low in her belly, her breasts full and sore...

Her breasts, full and sore...

Deus! The baby! She shot a look at the baby monitor, but it showed only an empty crib. Quickly she rose from the bed. Dante's robe, the one she'd worn yesterday, was neatly draped over the back of a chair. She yanked it on, hurried to Daniel's room...

And saw Dante by the window, holding his son in his arms.

He smiled when he saw her. "Good morning, sweetheart."

"I overslept. I don't know how. The baby—"

"He's fine." He looked down. "Aren't you, buddy?"

Daniel offered an enormous grin. Dante did the same. "See? He's great."

"He must be starving…"

"Well, we were starting to think we'd have to wake you. I mean, a snack's a snack but when a guy wants his breakfast…"

"What snack?"

"He woke up at five."

"You mean, I slept through it?"

Dante smiled. "Yeah," he said huskily. "Imagine that."

She blushed, tore her eyes from his and looked at the clock. Jack and Jill were going up the hill, carrying a huge wristwatch instead of a pail of water. Her mouth fell open.

"Ten?" she said, bewildered. "It's ten in the morning?"

"It's okay. I gave him a bottle at six." Dante gave a modest shrug but it was impossible not to notice the self-satisfied smile on his face. "I diapered him, too." He shuddered. "It was, uh, an interesting experience."

She really tried not to laugh but a giggle escaped, and then another, and finally she was guffawing at the thought of her sophisticated, urbane lover changing a diaper full of poo.

Her lover, she thought, and her laughter faded. Dante was her lover again, her foolish heart was in his hands.

"Hey," he said softly, "honey, what is it?"

"Nothing," she said, and forced a smile. "Here. Give me the baby. I'll feed him."

Daniel went into her arms. She sat down in the rocker, started to open her robe…and hesitated.

"May I stay?"

Dante's voice was low and soft. No, Gabriella thought, no, he could not stay. Every act of intimacy would be that much more difficult to forget after this time together ended. This was temporary. Dante might want her in his bed but the rest—permanency, fatherhood…

"Gaby? Sweetheart, if you want me to leave—"

"No," she said, in rushed whisper. "Please. Don't go. Stay with us."

The look that swept across his face made her want to weep with happiness. He kissed her upturned face, then sat down on the floor, cross-legged. She opened her robe. The baby turned his head, latched hungrily on to her nipple. She smiled at her son, then at her lover.

And knew that this time, when Dante left her, there would be nothing left of her heart.

CHAPTER ELEVEN

IF THERE was one thing all the Orsini brothers knew, it was that no one walked a straight path through life.

There were sideroads and missteps, deep currents that threatened to suck a man under, chasms that might take a lifetime to bridge.

All the Orsinis had experienced those things.

It was how Rafe had ended up in the Army, Nick in the Marines, Falco in Special Forces. It was how Dante had found himself in the far reaches of Alaska, doing danger-ous work in the oil fields. It was, in the end, how all four of them had returned to New York, taking one hell of a deep brotherly breath and invested everything—Nick's and Rafe's savings, Falco's poker winnings and Dante's fat oil field paychecks—in what had eventually become one of the most successful private investment firms in the world.

Chasms. Deep currents. Put bluntly, jumping in with your eyes closed.

That was what Dante was thinking Monday morning, as he shaved.

He'd done that this weekend. Bringing Gabriella and Daniel to New York was one thing. Moving them into his life was another. And, yeah, he had done that, changing a guest room into a nursery, moving Gabriella from the guest suite into the master suite. She'd protested, come up with all kinds of reasons it was a mistake, and maybe because a tiny piece of him worried she might be right, he'd swept her into his arms, kissed her concerns away and switched her clothes, her makeup, all her stuff, from her room to his.

Chasms and currents, all right. And, sure, sometimes you didn't make it, but sometimes you did. And when you did... Dante smiled, turned on the water, cupped it in his hand and rinsed away the last dollops of shaving cream.

When you did, man, life was terrific.

He reached for a towel, dried off as he looked around his bathroom. A day ago it had been an austere male kingdom. Nothing on top of the long marble counter except his shaving brush, an electric razor he hardly ever used, a plain comb and brush. Everything else was in the deep drawers of the vanity. Now, little glass vials and jars, a perfume bottle, a mother-of-pearl-backed hairbrush and half a dozen other things stood on the countertops.

He ran a fingertip lightly over the hairbrush where a few strands of gold glittered among the soft bristles.

It was Gabriella's stuff. He loved seeing it here and wasn't that a hell of thing coming from a guy who had to count to ten if some woman left a tube of lipstick behind?

But Gaby was not "some woman." She was...she was special. Beautiful. Bright. Sexy. It had rained yesterday and they'd ended up spending most of it before the fireplace, reading the *Times,* tackling the crossword puzzle together. The baby, Daniel, lay on the antique Rya rug between them, cooing and smiling, kicking his arms and legs, suddenly sobbing as if his small heart would break.

"What?" Dante had said, panicked.

"He's hungry," Gabriella had replied, smiling, and she'd nursed him right there, sitting in the curve of Dante's arm, and what he'd felt, watching the baby at the breast of his woman, had almost overwhelmed him.

It had been her turn to look at him, raise her eyebrows and say, "What?"

"Nothing," he'd told her, because what happened to him when he saw her nurse the baby was too much to put into words.

Their baby.

Daniel was his.

He knew it, had known it from the start. There was no question about it. That path, the one that led through life, was, for once, straight as an arrow. He and Gabriella had been lovers, he'd made her pregnant and absolutely the road was straight…

Straight as the road that ended at a house surrounded by a white picket fence, a station wagon, a dog and a cat and…

"Dante?"

A light tap at the door startled him.

"Yes," he said. His voice sounded strange, even to him, and he cleared his throat and tried again. "Yes. Okay. Just give me a couple of minutes."

"I have a quick question."

"Yeah, well, like I said, can you wait a minute?"

Merda. He winced as the impatient words left his lips.

"Never mind. I didn't mean to disturb you—"

Ah, God, he was worse than an idiot, he thought, yanking the door open, reaching for Gabriella and drawing her into his arms even as she turned away.

"How could you ever disturb me?" he said gruffly.

"No, really, it is all right."

The hell it was. He'd hurt her; he could see it in her eyes.

"Confession time," he said, cupping her face, tilting it to his. "I am not a morning kind of guy."

The faintest of smiles tugged at the corners of her lips. "You were always a morning kind of guy," she said softly. "And you just proved it again a little while ago."

He grinned at the compliment. "Being that kind of morning guy is easy."

Her smile dimmed just a little. "I'm sure."

"Hey." Gently he threaded his fingers through her hair. "Maybe you need to know I've never asked a woman to move in with me until now."

Her eyes searched his. "Is that what you've done? Asked me to move in?"

That straight path, leading to that white picket fence, that house...

Dante blanked the picture from his mind. "Yes," he said, and kissed her.

Long moments later she sighed. "I know I had a reason for coming in here."

"Mmm," he said, slipping his hand down the back of her jeans.

"I know what it— Dante. How can I think if you...if you—"

"You have," he said solemnly, stilling the motion of his hand, "one minute for thinking."

"I'd like to tell Mrs. Janiseck to add baby cereal to her shopping list. The doctor in Bonito said I could add it to Daniel's diet when he seemed ready, and—"

"So tell her."

"Well, I was going to but she's your housekeeper and—"

"You don't have to clear things with me, honey. Just tell Mrs. Janiseck whatever you want to tell her. Come to think of it..." He took his wallet from the back pocket of his trousers, slid out a credit card and pressed it into her hand. "I should have thought of this sooner."

"No. I cannot permit you to—"

"And *I* cannot permit *you* to argue with me," he said gently. "The card is yours, Gabriella. Buy whatever you like. For the baby, for yourself. Whatever you need or want."

She looked at the card, then at him. "A loan, then. Until I am back on my feet."

He didn't want her on her feet, he wanted her in his bed, he thought, and felt heat sweep through his body.

"What?"

"Nothing. You and Mrs. Janiseck doing okay?"

"Oh, yes. She's wonderful."

Wonderful, indeed. His housekeeper hadn't so much as blinked at finding a woman and baby in his life; if anything, she'd seemed delighted.

"She has a niece, did you know that?"

"No. No, I didn't."

"Stacia. She is studying to be a teacher. She's been an *au pair* the last few summers. Mrs. Janiseck says she's excellent with babies. She suggested she could stay with Daniel—when I am out on interviews."

This entire conversation was starting to sail over his head.

"Interviews?"

"Yes. I telephoned my old agent and asked him to see if he can get me some work. Why are you frowning? I need work, Dante. I have no money and...and I already owe you a fortune."

He supposed she did need to work. Not to repay him for anything; he'd never take a dime from her, but instinct told him not to tell her that just now. But, yes, she needed to work for the same reason he did, for the fulfillment of it— except, she could feel all that, the fulfillment of just being with him. He was sure of it because it was how he felt, being with her, and what in hell was he doing, heading for the office after only a handful of days alone with his Gabriella?

"I have," he said, "a brilliant idea."

She gave a soft laugh. "Such modesty."

"We'll tell Mrs. Janiseck we'll hire Stacy—"

"Stacia."

"We'll ask Stacia if she'd like to be Daniel's nanny. I'm sure we can work out a schedule flexible enough to suit her."

"Yes, but—"

"But," he said solemnly, "you can't afford it."

She flushed. "No. I can't."

"Well, you won't have to. See, I'll employ her, not you."

"I cannot impose on you this way, Dante."

"I need the tax break," he said, lying with aplomb. Who even knew if a nanny's wages were deductible? More to the point, who gave a damn?

"So many tax breaks," she said, raising her eyebrows. "The *fazenda,* a nanny—"

His mouth captured hers. His hand delved deeper, cupping her bottom, seeking her sweet heat. She caught her breath, rose to him, wrapped her arms around his neck.

"Dante," she whispered, her lips an inch from his, "we have to talk."

He answered by scooping her into his arms, saying to hell with the office and carrying her back to bed.

An hour later he phoned his AP, told her he wouldn't be in for the week.

"Still out of town," she said, because he was using his cell and one of the best things about cells was that they didn't give away your location. "Want to give me an alternate phone number or stay with your mobile?"

"The mobile," he said casually.

It wasn't as if he were avoiding telling her he was home. Or telling his brothers. It was just that he didn't feel like explaining things just yet to them or, God forbid, his sisters and his mother. The situation—that word again—was still complicated. While he worked things out, it was probably best to keep the news about Gabriella and the baby to himself.

A man was entitled to privacy, wasn't he? Besides, he hadn't taken any time off in months.

He asked Mrs. Janiseck to invite her niece over for an interview. Stacia showed up late morning. She was charming; she had great references and when she took Daniel from Gabriella's arms, he gave her a solemn look and said, "Ba-ba-ba-ba!"

"Oh, he's babbling," Gabriella said happily. "Right on time!"

Dante felt like asking why babbling was such a big deal. He did it all the time—but he had a feeling the three women would have given him the kind of look a man did not want women to give, so he nodded wisely.

"Such a big, beautiful boy," Stacia cooed.

He could actually see the tension ease from Gabriella's shoulders.

"Okay, sweetheart," he said softly. "How about we go out for lunch?"

"Do, please," Stacia said. "That will give Daniel and me time to get acquainted."

Gabriella and Stacia talked about diapers. About formula. About a zillion things until, finally, Mrs. Janiseck clucked her tongue and shooed Dante and Gabriella gently out the door.

"Just go," she said softly. "Enjoy being together." And to Dante's amazement, she rose as high as she could in her sturdy black orthopedic shoes, grabbed his face, hauled it down to hers and planted a kiss on his cheek.

It was the kind of perfect fall day that made New Yorkers forget the hot, sticky summers and the bone-chilling winters when the snow turned into gray slush. Arms around each other, Dante and Gabriella strolled through Central Park.

She commented happily on everything. Babies. Runners. An elderly couple holding hands. People walking, and being walked by, their dogs. There was no need to ask his Gaby if she liked dogs. By the time she'd stopped to pet at least a hundred of them—okay, a slight exaggeration but not by much—by then, even he could tell that she didn't like dogs, she loved them.

When she got to her feet after a conversation with a miniature schnauzer, Dante asked the obvious question.

"Did you have a lot of dogs when you were a kid?"

She looked at him in surprise. "Oh, I never had a dog."

It was his turn to look surprised. "No dogs? On that big ranch?"

She gave a little shrug. "My father did not like dogs."

"Why not?"

Another little shrug. And, perhaps, a tiny hesitation. And then, "He just did not like them."

Something was up. Her English was taking on that just-learned-it nuance. Dante took her hand, decided to take the conversation in a new direction.

"I wanted a dog like crazy when I was growing up."

She smiled at him. "But your mother said no, no dogs in an apartment."

Had he never told her he'd grown up in a house? There was an awful lot they didn't know about each other, he thought, lacing their fingers together.

"I grew up in a house. A pretty big one, in the Village."

"But still, no dog?"

He shrugged. "Mama was convinced dogs would give us germs."

"Mama," Gabriella said, smiling.

"We're Sicilian." Dante grinned. "Calling her anything else might have won me a smack."

"And your father is Papa?"

His smile disappeared. "I never call him Papa, or Dad, or anything but Father."

"Hey. I'm sorry I—"

"No." He brought her hand to his lips and pressed a kiss to the palm. "You have a right to ask. The thing is, he's…he's—"

"Old-fashioned?"

"Old-country." A deep breath. She would surely know some of this from having read it in the papers; she'd even tossed that *famiglia* insult at him, but talking about it—that was something he never did. "Remember that Marlon Brando movie? My old man's kind of like that. The head of what he likes to refer to as a big company but in reality—"

"Dante." Gabriella stepped in front of him, laid a hand on his chest. "I don't care what he is," she said softly. "I am simply grateful that he gave you life."

Could you really feel your heart lift? The answer seemed to be yes, and right there, under the arch in the Ramble, he took Gabriella in his arms and kissed her.

Where else to take her for lunch on such a glorious day but The Boathouse?

It was early autumn but the temperature was in the low 70s, the sun was bright. Perfect for dining on the outdoor terrace beside the Central Park boat lake.

There were no tables available—but, yes, of course, there was a table for Mr. Orsini. Gabriella sat back, watching the turtles sunning themselves on a rocky outcropping. He ordered for both of them. Tuna Niçoise for her—he remembered she loved it—and a burger, well-done, for him.

"And a bottle of Pinot Grigio," he added, remembering she loved that, too, but she shook her head, glanced at the waiter, blushed and told Dante, in a low voice, that she couldn't drink because alcohol wouldn't be good for the baby.

The waiter gave a discreet smile. "Sparkling water, perhaps," he said, and Dante said yes, that would be fine.

The bottle of water arrived, along with glasses filled with ice and slices of lemon. Dante reached for Gabriella's hand.

"I wish I'd been with you when you were pregnant," he said softly. "And when you delivered. You shouldn't have been alone."

Gabriella shook her head. "I told you, I wasn't alone. Yara was there." She paused. "And my brother."

Dante watched her face, the sudden play of emotion in her eyes. "You know," he said carefully, "you never talk about him."

"There isn't much to say." Her voice trailed off; her eyes met his. There was a sudden fierce glow in them. "He is dead, but I suppose you know that."

"Sweetheart. I didn't want to make you sad. If you don't want to tell me—"

"He died of AIDS." The glow in her eyes grew even more fierce. "He was a good man, Dante. A wonderful brother."

"I'm sure he was," Dante said gently.

"Our father despised him." She gave a bitter laugh. "But

then, he despised me, too. My brother, because he was gay. Me, because I killed my mother."

"Gaby. Honey—"

The waiter arrived with their lunch. They fell silent until he'd left. Neither of them reached for a fork. At last Gabriella picked up her story.

"She died in childbirth, and our father said it was my fault." Dante clasped her hand; she gave his a tight squeeze. "I know how wrong that is now, but when I was a little girl, I believed it. Anyway, just about the time you and I—about the time we stopped seeing each other—"

"The time you found out you were carrying my baby," Dante said gruffly.

Another nod of her head. "*Sim.* My father wrote to me, a very conciliatory letter asking me to return home. He was getting old, he said, it was time to mend our relationship, he said…" She swallowed dryly. "So, considering that… that I wanted to leave New York, I went home. But he had lied to me. He was dying. He had no money—my father was a very heavy gambler. He needed someone to take care of him." She shrugged. "So I did."

"Ah, sweetheart, I'm so sorry. You needed someone to take care of you and instead—"

"I did not mind. There are things one must do in life." She lifted her head and smiled, though now there were tears in her eyes. "And a good thing came of it. I told my father I would only stay with him if he permitted my brother to move back in. Arturo was ill by then." She swallowed hard. "So Arturo and I were together again. It was wonderful. We talked and laughed and shared memories—and then my father died." Her voice broke. "And before very long, so did Arturo. And while I was still mourning him, Andre Ferrantes came to the door to tell me the bank was going to foreclose on Viera y Filho—my father had named the ranch at my brother's birth, you see, long before he could have known Arturo would be gay. And Ferrantes said— He said—"

Dante stood, pulled back her chair and kissed her. Then he drew her to her feet, dropped some bills on the table and led her from the terrace toward the door.

"How romantic," he heard a woman say.

And he thought, *Wrong*.

This, whatever was happening between them, was far more complicated than romance. It was…it was—

He clasped Gabriella's hand and hurried her from the park.

At home again, they checked on the baby.

He was sound asleep, his backside in the air.

Mrs. Janiseck left. So did Stacia. Dante took Gabriella out on the terrace. They sat close together on a love seat, his arm curved around her in the warm sun, surrounded by Izzy's flowers.

He told her all about his life. Things he'd never told anyone. His confused feelings for Cesare. His love for his brothers. For his sisters. He told her how lost he'd been at eighteen, how filled with rage because he had a father whose idea of *famiglia* had little to do with the family sitting around a dinner table and everything to do with some alien family whose existence periodically brought reporters and photographers and cops to the door.

He told her how directionless he'd been, how his brothers had said enlisting in one of the armed services would give his life structure—and how he'd known, instinctively, he needed the opportunity to find that structure in a different way.

He picked up her hand, kissed her fingertips and explained that he'd found it in Alaska, risking his not-so-precious neck in the oil fields, hiking alone whenever he could in the wilderness, camping out and watching the northern lights, listening to the mournful howl of the wolves until, at last, he'd seen his anger at life for the pettiness it was.

"So I flew home," he said. "To New York. And my brothers were starting to feel as directionless as I'd felt, now that Nick was out of the Marines, Rafe out of the Army and Falco was out of whatever in hell they had him doing in Special Forces."

And, he said, they spent hours talking. Planning. Ultimately pooled their savings and their areas of expertise in finance, where they all had done well in school and, in Falco's case, at the poker tables.

"Orsini Investments took off," he said. It still was doing well—an understatement, really, making their investors happy despite the slowed economy.

And finally he told her why he'd gone to Brazil, Cesare's bizarre request—and then the truth that he'd kept from facing.

He had gone there knowing he would not leave without searching for, and finding, her.

When he fell silent, Gabriella smiled, though her cheeks were damp with tears.

"Dante," she whispered, "Dante, *meu querido…*"

He drew her into his lap. They kissed. And touched. And when that was no longer enough, he took her to his bedroom, undressed her as slowly as if he were unwrapping a perfect gift.

An eternity later, with her lover still deep inside her as she lay sated in his arms in the afterglow of their passion, Gabriella finally faced the truth.

No matter what happened, she would always be in love with Dante Orsini.

CHAPTER TWELVE

IT WAS decades since Dante had played hooky.

He'd done it a lot in high school. Got into trouble for it, ended up on suspension once but school was dull and the world was exciting and, besides, even the principal had to admit he was too smart a kid to dump.

Or maybe the influence on the principal was fear of his old man.

Either way, he'd cut classes years back then and, yeah, at NYU, but ditching university classes wasn't the same thing, especially when you could ace the coursework without half trying.

But once he'd had his seemingly useless economics degree in hand and headed for Alaska, those easy days ended. He'd not only shown up at his job each day, he'd worked his ass off, too.

The idea had been to test himself. Get the wild streak that had driven him north out of his system. And to make a lot of money. He'd done that, too, though he'd never been quite sure why it had seemed so important except to know it represented freedom. Total and complete independence, even more so after he'd come home, invested what he'd saved along with his brothers in the company they'd started.

So, eventually, he had it all.

Freedom. Independence. And a lot of money. More money than he'd ever imagined, enough to buy pretty much anything the world had that he might possibly want.

And yet, Dante thought as he drew Gabriella into his arms on the dance floor of a tiny club in the East Village, and yet he had never truly realized that what a man most wanted carried no price tag at all.

Not just a man.

Him.

How could life change so fast? Ten days ago, ask him what made him happy and he'd have said, well, his work. His family. The call last night telling him there was a '58 Ferrari Berlinetta coming on the market in Palm Beach. And women, of course. An entire BlackBerry of them. Redheads, blondes, brunettes, all beautiful, all fun, all exciting.

For a little while, anyway.

The music went from fast to slow and easy. Not that it mattered. From the second they'd hit the dance floor, he'd held Gabriella close, his arms tightly around her, her arms around his neck, her face buried against his throat.

The truth was, nothing was as exciting as this. Gabriella, in his arms. In his life.

How could he ever have been foolish enough to have let her go?

She made him happy. And he made her happy. She'd gone from fragile and looking as if she were made of glass that might shatter, as she had in Brazil, to the woman she had been in the past. Smiling. Full of life. More beautiful than seemed possible.

She was her own woman.

And she was his.

He awoke to her softly whispered "Good morning," fell

asleep with her in his arms. He was never without her. They talked about everything under the sun, agreed on some things, agreed to disagree on others. They read the papers over breakfast, drove out to Long Island and walked the beach at Fire Island, empty and beautiful on a cool fall day.

At first Gabriella would remind him that they'd hired Stacia so she could get in touch with her agent, have him line up some interviews...

"Could that be better than this?" he'd ask her softly, and her answer was always in her kiss.

Sometimes they didn't talk at all. They just were together. He'd never before been with a woman and found the silence between them comfortable and easy.

And then there was Daniel.

He still didn't know much about kids, but even he could tell that the little guy was, well, one fine-looking baby. And, better still, brilliant. Those ba-ba-ba's had grown to include ga-ga-ga's. The kid would probably talk before he was a year old. Plus, the way he reached for that mobile above his crib, watched it with such obvious curiosity... Oh, yeah. Daniel was smart, and not only because he was his.

Which he was. Absolutely. How could he have ever doubted it?

"Dante?"

This had been the best week of his life. He was happy. Such a simple word, especially from a man who'd never thought much about his feelings, but—

"Dante!"

He blinked, looked down into Gabriella's smiling face. "What?" he said, and she gave a soft little laugh.

"We're still dancing."

"And?"

"And," she said, "the music stopped about five minutes ago."

She was right. They were alone on the dance floor, locked in each other's arms, people watching them and smiling.

"Amazing, because I could swear it's still playing."

Gabriella smiled. "Me, too."

Dante grinned, spun her in a circle, then dipped her back over his arm.

"You are *doido*," she said, laughing.

"*Doido* for you," he told her, dancing her to their table, snatching up her pashmina shawl, then waltzing her out the door. His driver spotted them almost instantly, rolled out of the No Parking zone where he'd been waiting and pulled to the curb. Dante signaled him to stay put, opened the passenger door himself and handed Gabriella inside. "Let's go home," he said. The driver nodded, closed the privacy partition and headed uptown as Gabriella snuggled into the curve of Dante's arm.

"Did you have a good time?" he said, pressing a kiss to her temple.

"Mmmm. A wonderful time." She smiled. "We'll try *salsa* next."

Dante gave a mock groan. "You just want to see me make a jerk of myself on the dance floor."

"Stop fishing for compliments, *senhor*. You're a fine dancer."

"*Salsa* means moving parts of the human body never meant to be moved."

A playful glint came into her eyes. "Ah, but I have seen you move those parts exceedingly well."

Dante drew her onto his lap. "But not on a dance floor," he said, his voice suddenly husky.

Gabriella threaded her hands into his hair and drew his face to hers.

"Perhaps we should test those moves when we get home," she whispered.

What a good thing a privacy petition was, Dante thought, and then he stopped thinking about anything but the woman in his arms.

Saturday morning, early, a courier delivered a package.

Dante insisted Gabriella watch as he opened it.

It was a long length of woven fabric with an adjustable closure. "It's a baby sling," he said, as he draped it over his shoulder and arm, then snugged Daniel securely within its soft folds. "I researched it online. Seems lots of tribal people have carried babies this way for centuries. It gives the babies a real sense of security. What do you think?"

"I think it's a great idea," she said, but what she really thought was that she was living a miracle.

The man who'd been one of New York's wildest bachelors, who had not even suspected he had a son less than two weeks ago, had become the world's most amazing father.

"You mean it?" He grinned as Daniel cooed. "Daniel, my man, what do you think?"

The baby laughed. So did Gabriella. Dante looked at her and smiled.

"I guess the vote's unanimous."

It was. She and her son both adored this man—but she couldn't tell him that. Not until he said the words she longed to hear. Instead she kissed the baby, rose on her toes and kissed her lover, too.

"Unanimous," she said brightly.

"Okay. Let's take it for a trial run. How's a trip to the Bronx Zoo sound?"

It sounded perfect, she told him. Dante smiled, handed

Daniel to her and put aside the baby sling. "Let me just check my e-mail. I haven't looked at it all week and Monday, much as I hate to do it, I'm going to have to go to work."

Her face fell; he loved the fact that it did. She didn't want him to leave. Hell, he didn't want it, either, but life had to return to normal sometime.

"Five minutes," he said softly, kissing her. "Not a second more, I promise."

But he was in his study longer than that and when he came out, she knew something had happened.

"Dante? Is everything all right?"

He assured her that it was.

It was not. His expression was closed; he was unusually silent during the drive to the zoo. Preoccupied, but by what?

Dante carried the baby in the sling as they made their way from exhibit to exhibit. He spoke to him the way he always did, as if the little guy understood every word he said about the seals and the monkeys and the giraffes.

But his behavior was subdued.

It was unsettling.

Eventually they took a break. Daniel had fallen asleep; Dante stood staring off into the distance, one hand curved around the baby, the other tucked in the pocket of his leather windbreaker.

He was quiet, his eyes impossible to read.

Gabriella felt her throat constrict.

Something was happening. What? It was as if the Dante who had gone into his study this morning had emerged a different person. He had changed. Everything had changed. She could feel it.

What if he'd decided he'd had enough? The zoo was

filled with families. Was it a graphic lesson in what his life had become?

She and the baby were both novelties. It was a crude way to put it but it was accurate. He'd never had a son before, and he'd never had a woman live with him, either. He'd made it sound like something wonderful when he'd told her that, but viewed with clinical detachment, it simply meant this experience was new for him.

Ocean kayaking had once been new to him, and back-country skiing and probably a dozen other things. Oh, she knew he cared far more for the baby than for any of that, but still, "newness" intrigued him.

It wasn't that he was self-indulgent. Or perhaps he was, just a little. It made him seem larger than life. It was one of his charms.

It also meant he was the kind of man who grew bored easily.

He'd told her that himself, just yesterday, though not in those exact words, when he'd gotten a call telling him some much-coveted kind of automobile was for sale somewhere out of state. His excitement had been palpable; he'd whooped with glee, caught her up in his arms and kissed her, and when she'd laughed and said only a man could get so worked up over a car, he'd tried to explain how it was, that he loved fast cars, that he'd been hunting after this one for a long time. And that was when he'd mentioned kayaking and skiing and all the rest, how he'd loved them and more or less still did but how cars like this one had supplanted his interest in other things.

Daniel had awakened just then, fussing for his dinner, so the conversation had ended before she could ask him the reason. Not that she had to ask.

She knew the reason.

Tides changed but the ocean was still the ocean.

Snowfall changed, but a mountain was still a mountain. Not so with automobiles. They were always different. When you grew bored with one kind, there was always another to pursue.

Was she his latest acquisition? Even more vital, was Daniel? Would her son learn to love his father only to have Dante turn into a stranger?

The thought terrified her.

Dante felt the warm weight of his sleeping son pressed against his chest.

He curved his hand over the child's bottom. He loved holding his son. The baby was so small, so trusting. He'd never imagined being a father could make a man's heart swell with pride and joy.

The zoo was full of families. Mothers, fathers, babies, kids of all ages. And them. He. Gabriella. Daniel. They were a family, too.

It was wonderful.

It was scary as hell.

And it had made him finally face the truth. Well, this—and the e-mail messages he'd found in his in-box. It was all he could think about. What was happening to Rafe...

What he was finally ready to admit was happening to him.

Had already happened to him.

Dear God, how could a man fall so hard, so fast? How could he have been blind to it? Gabriella had to feel the same way. She had to, because if she didn't...

He had to be alone with her. Take her in his arms. Tell her. Tell her—

"Gaby," he said abruptly, turning toward her, looking at the woman who held his life in her hands, "I know there's lots more to see, but—"

"Dante." Her eyes met his. "Please," she said in an unsteady whisper, "I would like to go home."

Mrs. Janiseck was off on Saturdays. So was Stacia.

As soon as they were alone, Dante cleared his throat. "Gabriella. We have to talk."

Her heart fell. "All right," she said tonelessly.

He flashed a quick smile. "I'll, ah, I'll put Daniel to bed. Why don't you, ah, why don't you start supper?"

She nodded, went into the kitchen. Actually, there was little to do. Mrs. Janiseck did almost all the cooking. Cold roast chicken and a green salad, prepared yesterday. There it was, on the top shelf in the fridge. Lovely to have it waiting, but somehow—and Gabriella knew how ridiculous the thought was—somehow, it made her feel even more a guest in Dante's life. Yes, of course, a woman to whom he had a permanent commitment would have a housekeeper and cook. Dante's income, his lifestyle, meant the woman to whom he had such a permanent commitment would have a staff to help run her home. But a woman to whom he had...

Gabriella laughed out loud, though it wasn't a happy sound.

What kind of phrase was that? 'A woman to whom he had...' Was there no word to describe what she should be to him? Not his mistress. Mistresses didn't come equipped with babies, and besides, a mistress was a woman whose lover owned the roof over her head, the food on her table, the clothes on her...

Which was exactly what she had become.

She closed the refrigerator door with a slam and went out to the terrace. It was cold outside. The city was wrapped in darkness and you could not only sense winter coming, you could feel it in the marrow of your bones.

Dante paid all her bills. Food. Daniel's clothing. Diapers. The furniture in the nursery. The rent or the mortgage, whatever it was. He paid for her clothes—she'd left so much at the *fazenda,* and she'd needed warmer things after arriving here.

It would take her years, a lifetime, to pay him back, even if her agent lined up the kind of modeling deals supermodels got, and the truth was, she'd been a successful model but not one who earned six figures a day.

He owned everything in her life and her son's life.

How had she let such a thing happen? What had become of her independence? Her sense of autonomy? Her determination, from childhood on, to rely on nobody but herself?

What had become of her responsibility to Daniel?

He deserved stability. Security. Not just financial security but the kind that came from the heart. A father's heart. She, of all people, knew how much that meant. Daniel was only a baby but already he smiled and laughed when Dante reached for him. Another few months, ba-ba-ba would turn into ma-ma-ma and da-da-da, but would Dante be there for him? Would he be there for her?

She took a deep breath. The word of the day was *commitment.*

As in forever. As in a man and a woman who were building a life together.

As in—

"Married," Dante said, and she spun toward him, heart pounding.

"What?"

He was smiling but the smile was a lie. She could see it in his eyes, the set of his mouth.

"My brother Rafe." He dug his hands into his trouser pockets as he stood beside her, his gaze on the skyline beyond the park and not on her. "When I checked my e-mail this morning, I found a couple of notes. Seems he's getting married tomorrow. Well, it turns out he's already married, some kind of quickie deal that happened in Sicily, and tomorrow, he's doing it for real. Meaning, in church where my mother can get all misty-eyed over it."

He sounded as if he were describing an *auto-da-fé* rather than a wedding but then, being burned at the stake might seem more appealing to a man like him. Was that why he'd been so distant all day?

"Oh," she said, because she had to say something. "Well, that's…that's—"

"He's been trying to reach me. The whole family has. But I've been out of touch."

He made it sound like an accusation. Gabriella narrowed her eyes.

"I did not keep you from checking your messages."

"Yeah, but who would ever expect a message like this?" Dante ran his hands through his shower-damp hair; it stood up in little black peaks. "I mean, this is crazy. He only just met this woman."

"Yes, but—"

"Marriage is a forever thing. A man needs to give it thought."

"And you assume he did not?"

"What I assume," he said, "is that I always thought a man should not leap into marriage as if he were leaping into the currents of a rampaging river."

She could feel the anger forming inside her. Or maybe it had been there all along, just waiting to surface.

"Your brother is not the only one who is leaping. The same applies to the woman."

Dante snorted with derision. "It isn't the same."

"Isn't it?" Her voice had gone from cool to frigid.

"Men are meant to be hunters. To roam. Women are meant to be gatherers. Of course it isn't the same."

Gabriella was looking at him as if he'd turned into an alien life form. Well, hell, he couldn't blame her. He knew he sounded like an idiot, but how could he not after finding Rafe's *Hey, man, I'm getting married!* e-mail in his inbox this morning? It had shaken him to the core.

Rafe, married?

It had to be a joke.

He'd phoned Rafe, got no answer, phoned Falco, got nothing there, connected with Nick who said, yeah, it was a shocker and, yeah, it was fast, and then he finally got through to Rafe who babbled like an idiot about how he'd fallen crazy in love even if he'd only married Chiara Cordiano the first time around so he could Do The Right Thing and then found he'd fallen head over heels in love.

"But marriage? So fast?" Dante had said.

And Rafe had said, yeah, why wait when you knew you'd found the right woman? A woman who loved you for what you were inside, not for what the world saw. Who loved you, just you, and could see herself growing old with you beside her. Who loved you for giving her your heart, not the things money could provide.

And in the blink of an eye, Dante had known Rafe could just as easily have been talking about him and his Gabriella.

About this "situation" that wasn't a "situation" at all but part of being deeply, totally in love.

He'd spent the day coming to grips with it, asking himself if Gabriella felt the same way, telling himself that she did, she had to, that she was not a woman who'd live with a man, sleep in his arms every night unless she loved him.

And, God, the whole thing was terrifying.

To declare his love for her, to offer his heart to her and hope she wouldn't reject it…

He'd thought about it, tried to figure out the best way to do it, delaying the moment because what would he do if she didn't feel the same and then, standing in the shower after putting Daniel to bed, the water sluicing down, he'd finally decided, okay, this was it, he'd just go out there and tell her he loved her, loved his son, that he couldn't live without them both…

"Dante," Gabriella said, and he swung toward her and caught her hands in his.

"Gaby." He spoke fast, afraid he'd lose his courage, wondering why it had taken him so long to come to his senses. "Gaby. Honey." He took a deep breath. "This thing tomorrow. My brother's wedding…" He swallowed hard; how come his mouth had gone so dry? "Taking you to it would be rough. You'd get dumped into the middle of my family and, trust me, we're not something out of a Hallmark card. My mother and my sisters would ask a million questions. My brothers wouldn't just ask questions, they'd do the Orsini version of the third degree. And my old man— Hell, where my father goes, so go the Feds. Plus, not a one of my family knows anything about this. You. Me. The baby." He paused only long enough to swallow again to moisten his throat. "So, here's the thing, Gabriella. I don't think—"

"I do not think so, either," Gabriella said. "The truth is, I would much prefer to avoid what promises to be an overly sentimental family reunion."

"What? No. See, you don't understand—"

"But I do. I understand perfectly." She drew her hands from his, gave him the kind of smile that made him understand the true meaning of a tight smile. "You say this wedding is tomorrow?"

"Right. Late morning. It'll all be over by noon."

"Excellent."

"Yes. I thought so, too. Because—"

"My attorney's name is Peter Reilly."

Dante blinked. "Huh?"

"His office is on Seventy-second Street. He handled any modeling contracts that were outside the purview of my agency."

"Gaby. What are you talking about?"

"I have been thinking, Dante. About our…our situation." *Do not cry,* she told herself fiercely. *Just because he's confirmed all your worst fears, just because he'd sooner do anything than introduce you to his family, you are not to cry!*

"Yes," he said slowly, "so have I. That's the reason I just explained things—"

"And a fine job of it you did," she said, and told herself how well she was doing. "I shall ask Peter a special favor, that he meet with us at his office tomorrow, even though it is a Sunday at, let us say, two in the afternoon."

"For what?" Dante said, totally bewildered.

This cold little speech, the frigid glare, that was what a man got for telling a woman that as rough as it was going to be, he wanted to take her to his brother's wedding? Tell his entire family he loved her? Tell them that she'd borne his child, that there would be another wedding as soon as they could get to the clerk's office Monday morning?

"For what?" he repeated, his eyes searching her face.

"For drawing up a payment schedule for what I owe you."

"What the hell are you talking about?"

"About resuming my own life," Gabriella said. "You see, I have been thinking things over. And it is time that happened. This has been very nice but—"

"Very nice?"

"You have been most kind to me. Of course, it would have been better had your attempt to buy the *fazenda* gone through."

"Better," he repeated, his voice low and dangerous. "Buying you the *fazenda* would have been better than bringing you to live with me?"

"Well, yes. It would have taken me a very long time to repay you but the *fazenda* was my home—"

"And this is not."

There was a terrible coldness in his voice. She wanted to put her arms around him, tell him that she had never been happier than she'd been the past days, that she wished, with all her heart, his home could really be her home, too...

"No," she said, struggling to hold on to what little pride she had left, "it is not."

They stared at each other while the silence of the chill night built around them.

Then Dante nodded.

"I'll want my attorney at this meeting."

"Certainly. I will give you my lawyer's address and telephone number."

"Do that."

He turned on his heel. Walked inside, grabbed his jacket, took the private elevator to the lobby and walked briskly into the night. When he got back, hours and hours later, his bed was empty.

Gabriella was in the guest suite.

Exactly where she should be, he thought grimly, and poured himself the first of the several brandies he figured he'd need before he could tumble into merciful sleep.

CHAPTER THIRTEEN

SUNDAY dawned bright and sunny.

A perfect day for a wedding, someone would probably say, but Dante knew better. It was a perfect day for a man to wake from a dream and realize he'd come within a heartbeat of putting his head in a noose.

He loved his brother, but better Rafe than him.

Dante showered, shaved, dressed and got out the door without seeing Gabriella. His mood was grim, but he wasn't sure why it should be, considering he'd barely escaped making the biggest mistake of his life. There was such a thing as carrying Doing The Right Thing too far.

He certainly hadn't been on the verge of asking her to marry him because he loved her.

Love?

Dante shuddered as he stepped from a taxi outside the unassuming little church in the Village where Rafe's wedding was to take place. Yesterday he'd done a good job of half convincing himself what he felt was love, but the truth was, love had nothing to do with it. Responsibility. That's what he felt for her. He was a decent man, she'd given birth to his child.

That was all there was to it.

Dante looked around as he straightened his tie. No cops.

No Feds. None he could spot, anyway. Rafe would, at least, be free of the kind of attention Cesare almost always received. This was Rafe's day, for better or for worse—no pun intended. He'd smile, toast his brother and his bride, then head for his meeting with Gabriella, her attorney and Sam Cohen. He'd phoned Sam at 6:00 a.m., and though Sam had grumbled, he'd said yeah, okay, he'd draw up the necessary documents—child support, child visitation— and hustle over to the two-o'clock meeting.

So, everything was a go. Have a meeting, move on with life. Today's agenda, in a nutshell.

Dante took a steadying breath, plastered what he hoped was a smile to his face and went up the stone steps into the old church.

At first he saw no one. Maybe, just maybe, Rafe had come to his senses.... Forget that. He could hear voices. His mother's, high and excited. His sisters, laughing and chattering like magpies. His brothers' low rumble. Another deep breath, and Dante headed for the small changing room where his family was gathered.

"Dante, *mio figlio,*" his mother shrieked, and embraced him in a hug that almost killed him.

"You finally got here," Anna said, but she tugged at his tie and kissed his cheek.

"We'd almost given up hope," Isabella added, but she smiled and kissed him, too.

His father gave him an inquisitive look.

"Dante."

"Father."

"Was your trip successful?"

Dante's mouth thinned. "This isn't the time to discuss it," he said coldly, and turned to Falco and Nicolo, who grinned.

"Hey, man," Falco said.

"Glad to see you made it," Nick said. "Where the hell have you been, anyway?"

"Away," Dante said.

Nick raised an eyebrow, but Rafe saved the day, grabbing him and saying, "Can you believe I'm doing this?"

Even Dante could tell the question was rhetorical. Rafe was smiling, and when he slid his arm around the waist of a beautiful, dark-haired stranger and drew her forward, the look he gave her was so filled with happiness that it put an ache in Dante's heart.

Had his eyes glowed that way each time he'd looked at Gabriella the past week? Hers had glowed when she'd turned them on him, but it had been a lie. All she'd ever wanted was that damned ranch...

"This is Chiara."

His new sister-in-law smiled shyly.

"Dante," she said softly, "I am very pleased to meet you."

She hesitated. Then she leaned in, stood on her toes and kissed his cheek.

Hell. She was starry-eyed with love, and that feeling came again, as if a hand had reached into his chest and grabbed hold of his heart. But then the organ began playing, Anna and Isabella rushed to Chiara's side and the next thing Dante knew, he was standing at the altar with his brothers.

The ceremony was brief. The women all cried. Rafe took his wife in his arms when the time came and kissed her with a tenderness that made Dante's throat tighten.

He swallowed hard. Gabriella had done one fine job, leaving him so confused that even he found today's events touching.

The reception was at their parents' home, in the big conservatory Cesare had built a couple of years ago.

Anna teased him about looking so grumpy.

"You could, at least, try looking happy," Izzy said. "This has been like a fairy tale!"

There were no fairy tales, Dante wanted to tell her, not in real life, but he smiled, said it sure was, picked up a flute of champagne and wandered over to Falco and Nick who were standing in a corner, looking out at their father's sea of withered tomato plants.

"Man," Nick said, sotto voce, "I think I'm on wedding-cake overload."

Falco agreed. "I'm glad Rafe's happy but if he tells me just once more how it's time I found myself a wife—"

Dante put the champagne flute on a table.

"How about we go someplace where nobody's gonna talk about the joys of matrimony?"

His brothers grinned.

Twenty minutes later, they were in their usual booth, the last one on the left, at The Bar.

The Bar wasn't fancy even though it was in a fancy location.

The reason was that the location had once been just a step up from a slum.

Back then, The Bar had been called O'Hearn's Tavern and was a neighborhood hangout downstairs from the hole-in-the-wall apartment Rafe had rented. But the brothers had liked the place. The beer was cold, the sandwiches and burgers were thick and cheap, and the no-nonsense ambience suited them just fine, though they'd probably have flattened anybody dumb enough to use the word *ambience* to describe the atmosphere.

Then, right about the time the four of them pooled their

resources and their skills to start Orsini Brothers, the area began to change. Tired old tenements, including the one where Rafe had lived, were gutted and reborn as pricey townhouses. An empty factory building became a high-priced club. *Bodegas* became boutiques.

Clearly, the Orsinis were about to lose their favorite watering hole.

So, they bought O'Hearn's. Stopped calling it that, started calling it, simply enough, The Bar. They had the leather booths and stools redone, the old wooden floor refinished and kept everything else unchanged: the long zinc bar, the battered wooden table tops, the thick sandwiches and burgers, the endless varieties of cold beer and ale.

Only the bartenders knew Rafe, Dante, Nick and Falco owned it. They wanted it that way. Their lives were high profile; The Bar was not…although, to their amazement, it became what was known as a "destination," which made the four of them laugh. It was where they often got together Friday nights and whenever they wanted to down a few beers, relax and talk.

Right now, though, nobody was relaxing. And that was Dante's fault.

The bar was shadowed, as always. Comfortable, as always. A Wynton Marsalis CD played softly in the background. The bartender, unasked, had brought Nick a bottle of Anchor Steam, Falco a Guinness, Dante a Belgian white. Their usual drinks, their usual booth, the usual cool jazz… but the atmosphere was tense.

Nick and Falco kept looking at each other, raising their eyebrows, rolling their eyes toward Dante.

What the hell's going on? they were saying in every way that didn't require speech, because neither of them wanted to ask. Dante's mood was, in a word, grim. His silence, his flat stare, the very set of his mouth made that painfully clear.

Still, even a brother's patience went just so far, and at last Falco decided to go for it.

"So," he said briskly, "you took the last couple of weeks off, huh?"

Dante looked up. "You got a problem with that?"

Falco's jaw shot forward. He started to answer but Nick silenced him by kicking him in the shin.

"Just asking," Nick said.

A muscle knotted in Dante's cheek. "I flew to Brazil last week. And took this week off. Okay?"

"What's doing in Brazil?"

The muscle in Dante's cheek took another jump. "I bought a ranch."

Falco and Nick looked at each other. "A ranch?"

Falco's question sounded more like "Are you nuts?" but Dante could hardly blame him. His brothers were trying to figure out what was going on. Well, hell, who could blame them? So he nodded, drank some beer, then looked across the table at the two of them.

"Correction. I almost bought a ranch. It was the old man's idea. I went down to buy it for him."

"Our old man was gonna buy a ranch?" Falco cackled. "That's a joke, right?"

"Actually," Dante said, after a beat of silence, "I ended up trying to buy it for myself."

"*You* were going to buy a ranch," Nick said, shooting Falco a worried look.

Dante drank some more beer. "Not for myself, exactly. For—for someone."

The brothers waited. Finally, Falco sighed. "Do we have to guess?"

"You remember a year ago? A little more than that. I was dating a woman."

"Wow," Nick said, "that's amazing. You, dating a—"

"Her name was Gabriella. Gabriella Reyes. A model."

Falco nodded. "Yeah. Tall. Hair a lot of different shades of gold. Spectacular legs. And what appeared to be one amazing pair of—"

"Watch your mouth," Dante growled.

His brothers raised their eyebrows.

"You want to tell us what's going on?" Nick said.

"No," Dante snarled…

And told them everything.

When he was done, nobody spoke.

He could see his brothers trying to take it all in. Hell, he'd have done the same in their place. A woman from the past. A baby. A ranch in foreclosure, a sneaky lawyer, an option that expired in twenty-four hours. It sounded like an old Western movie, except it was real.

Finally Falco cleared his throat.

"You're sure the kid is yours?"

"I'm sure."

"Because remember that time, years ago, Teresa Whatshername—"

"Gabriella is not Teresa Whatshername," Dante said sharply.

"No, no, of course she isn't. I only meant—"

"I know. Sorry. It's just— It's tough, you know?"

Nick leaned forward. "So, let me be sure I understand it all. You have a son."

"Cutest and smartest kid you ever saw," Dante said softly.

"But the woman who gave birth to him—"

"She has a name," Dante said, his voice sharp again. "Gabriella."

"Right. Gabriella. And she scammed you into buying this ranch—"

"Did I say that?"

"Well," Falco said, "you don't have to say it. From everything you told us, it's obvious."

"Nothing's obvious," Dante said coolly. "But, yeah, I bought the ranch for her." He gave a mirthless smile. "Thought I'd bought it, anyway."

"But you didn't."

"No."

"And the ranch is what she wanted."

Dante shrugged. "Yeah."

"So, no ranch. Instead, you brought her to New York. Moved her into your place. Accepted the kid as your own without asking for any proof—"

"The 'kid,'" Dante said, his tone plummeting from cool to icy, "is named Daniel. And I don't need proof. Gaby would never lie to me."

"Right," Nick said.

"She wouldn't. And I don't like the tone of your voice."

Nick nodded. Falco cleared his throat.

"And you took all these days off because…?"

A little lift of the shoulders. "It just seemed the right thing to do." Dante looked at Falco and Nick. Their expressions were benign, but something was lurking in their eyes, some truth they seemed to know and he didn't. "Gabriella was new to my place," he added. "New to the city."

"No, she isn't. She lived here. She worked here. You said so. She even knows your place, from when she dated you. So, try again, bro. You spent the time with her because…?"

Dante narrowed his eyes. "What's your point?"

Nick sighed. "I don't know, man. I mean, what could

my point possibly be? You were ready to drop five million bucks on a ranch for a woman. You acknowledged her baby as yours. You brought her home, moved her in, spent every minute with her and you tell us the relationship didn't mean a thing. Have I got the details right?"

Dante shrugged.

"You've got them right," Falco said. He looked at Dante. "Then, how come each time one of us so much as hints at her being anything but perfect, you turn purple?"

"I do not turn purple."

"He's purple now," Nick said lazily.

"He is, indeed," Falco agreed. "And we haven't even touched on why the lady's leaving you."

"No ranch. That's why."

"You don't think it could have anything to do with the fact that she suddenly realized she was living her life, living her kid's life, on your terms? That she has no money, no home, no anything here or back in Brazil that you don't graciously choose to dole out, and—"

Dante slammed down his beer bottle. "You make it sound as if I trashed her life. But that's not the way it was."

Falco narrowed his eyes. "How was it, then?" he said very quietly, and Dante's face all but crumpled.

"Oh, hell," he whispered. He looked up. "I loved her. I still do. I'm crazy for her. I want to marry her. Wake up every morning for the rest of my life with her beside me."

Nick arched an eyebrow. "But?"

"But last night, before I could tell her that, she turned cold as ice. Said it was time I met with her lawyer."

Falco nodded. "Seems to me it's one of two things happening here, bro. Either she's tired waiting for her ship to come in—"

Dante lunged for him. Falco grabbed his wrist.

"Take it easy, man, unless you think you and me taking

this outside will help calm you down." Dante didn't answer, and Falco let go of him and leaned over the table. "Or the lady loves you just the way you love her but she's got her pride, she's got the baby, and she's decided she'd rather end this on her terms than wait for you to do it."

"Why would she think that?"

"Maybe," Nick said patiently, "because you haven't said a word to her about what happens beyond today."

"Maybe," Falco added, "because of what you told us about how you broke up with her last time. The diamond earrings at dinner routine."

Dante was bewildered. "That's how we all do it."

Falco nodded. "Exactly."

"I don't know. I mean, I wanted to bring her to the wedding today. Introduce her to everybody." He gave a halfhearted laugh. "Of course, I warned her what it would be like, how rough it would be, what the old man is like, how Mama would probably go nuts learning she has a grandson, how the girls would swamp her, but before I could even finish talking, she interrupted, said she had no wish to go with me, that she wanted to discuss repaying the money she thinks she owes me…as if I'd take a dime from her."

"And how did she react to what you told her? That she'd be meeting us all at once?"

"I just told you," Dante said impatiently, "I never got that far. I just told her that— I told her that—" His face turned white. *"Merda!"*

"What?"

Dante shot to his feet. "I was preparing her for the big Orsini scene, but it must have sounded as if I were telling her there wasn't a way in hell I'd bring her with me today."

"The big Orsini scene?" Nick said, but Dante was already racing for the door.

Falco and Nick looked at each other. "He really loves her," Falco said.

"Sure seems like it."

"We could have left him in the dark."

"I know."

"But opening his eyes was the right thing to do."

"Still…"

"Still, another one bites the dust."

Nick shuddered and slipped from the booth.

"Man," Falco said, "don't tell me you're bailing, too?"

"I'm going to get us a bottle of Wild Turkey."

Falco nodded. "An excellent idea," he said, and decided they could wait until the bourbon was half-gone before they tried to figure out what in hell was happening to the Orsini brothers.

The beautiful morning had given way to a rainy afternoon. New York plus rain. A simple equation that added up to no taxis in sight.

"Hell," Dante said, and started running.

A bus plowed by, the wheels spraying him with dirty water, and pulled in at a stop when he was halfway to his destination.

"Wait," he yelled, picked up his speed. He made it to the just-closing door, slipped and tore a very expensive hole in the very expensive left leg of his very expensive trousers.

Who gave a damn?

He got off the bus at Fifty-seventh Street, dashed into the store—open, thank God—and was outside again in less than ten minutes. A taxi was just pulling to the curb, a silver-haired gentleman was about to step into it. Dante tapped him on the shoulder.

"If I don't get this cab," he said, "I might just lose the woman I love."

The old guy looked him over, from his soggy Gucci loafers to his drenched Armani suit to his rain-flattened hair. Then he smiled.

"Good luck, son," he said.

Dante figured he was going to need it.

Gabriella's attorney's office was—it figured—on the top floor of a building that housed what seemed to be a non-working elevator.

He didn't give it a second try. Instead he took the old marble steps two at a time, stopped at the top only long enough to catch his breath and run his hand through his hair. Pointless, he thought, looking down at the puddle at his feet. Then he opened the office door and walked inside. The waiting room was empty, but straight ahead, through an open door, he could see a conference table. Gathered around it were Sam Cohen, a portly bald guy in tweed who had to be Gaby's lawyer.

And Gaby.

His Gabriella.

His heart did a stutter-step. *Here you go, Orsini,* he told himself. *This is your one shot at the rest of your life.*

"Gabriella."

They all turned and stared at him. He knew he had to look pretty bad. Sam Cohen's mouth dropped open. So did the other attorney's. Gabriella turned pale. She took a quick step toward him.

"Dante," she said, "*meu amor,* what happened to—" She stopped dead. Her chin rose. "Not that I care."

But she *did* care. The look on her face, the tremor in her voice, that wonderful word, *amor*... She cared. He just had to convince her that he cared, too.

"Gaby," he said, his eyes locked to hers, "sweetheart, please. Will you come with me?"

He held out his hand, held his breath…

She walked slowly to him. She didn't take his hand.

But he knew it was a start.

It was still raining.

Gabriella was wearing a raincoat, but the rain was already turning her gold-streaked hair wet and dark.

"Where are we going?" she demanded.

"Just into the park. See? The Seventy-second Street entrance is right across the way."

She looked at him as if he'd lost his mind. "On a day like this?"

"Gaby." Dante framed her face in his hands. "Please. Come with me."

She looked at him again. His hair was plastered to his head. His beautiful dark lashes were wet. Water dripped off his Roman nose. His suit would never be the same again and his shoes…

Her heart, which had felt as heavy as a stone since last night, seemed to lift just a little in her chest.

"Gaby," he said again, and then he lowered his head to hers and kissed her, lightly, tenderly, and even as she told herself his kisses meant nothing to her, she gave a little moan at the softness of his kiss. "Sweetheart. Come with me, I beg you."

So she did.

She kicked off her shoes, because how could you run in the rain wearing four-inch heels? And this time, when he reached for her hand, she let him take it.

He led her into the park, empty of everyone but a couple of glum-looking dog walkers. The rain was coming down harder; they ran faster and now she could see they were heading for The Boathouse restaurant. Was it open? It was.

At least the lounge was, but Dante drew her straight out onto the wet, deserted terrace.

"Sir," a voice said.

Dante ignored it.

"Sir," the voice said again.

Dante turned around, said a few words she could not hear to a waiter who looked at him as if he'd gone insane, but then the man laughed, said sure, if that was what he was determined to do...

And then they were alone.

Just she and Dante, and the rain.

Just she and the man she loved, would always love, in this place where she had foolishly opened her life to him, where she had foolishly admitted, if only to herself, that she loved him.

Why had she come with him? Why had she done again that which she had vowed she would not do, let Dante sweet-talk her into something that would seem wonderful for the moment and, ultimately, leave her weeping?

"Gabriella," he said, reaching into his pocket, taking out a small blue box...

She staggered back.

"No!"

"Gaby. Sweetest Gaby..."

"What is it this time?" she said in a horrified whisper. "A diamond pin? I do not want it!"

"It isn't a pin. It isn't a goodbye gift, baby. Take it. See for yourself."

"A gift to buy me back, then? Do you truly think I would permit you to do that? That I would let you—let you buy me, as you have tried to do these past two weeks..."

"Honestly, Gabriella..."

"Honesty be damned!" She was weeping now; salty tears running down her face and mingling with the sweet rain. "You are the least honest man I know, Dante Orsini! You made me think—you made me think that someday, someday you might…you might—"

"I love you."

"You see? There you are, lying again. If you loved me— oh, *Deus,* if you only loved me…"

She began to sob. Dante caught her in his arms, whispered her name, kissed her again and again until, at last, she kissed him back.

"I hate you," she whispered.

He smiled. "Yes. I can tell."

"Honestly, Dante—"

"Honestly, Gabriella." He drew back, just enough so he could lift the tiny package between them. "This is for you, sweetheart. Only for you, forever." He kissed her again. "Please," he said softly. "Open your gift."

She opened the little blue box only to silence him, to give herself time to get her emotions under control, telling him all the while that he had wasted his money, that she did not want whatever was in that box…

What was in that box was a diamond solitaire ring.

Gabriella stared at it. Then she stared at her lover. His smile was almost as bright as the diamond.

"I love you," he said. "I adore you. I always have. I was just too much a coward to admit it." It was wet on the terrace but what did that matter? Dante went down on one knee. "Marry me, Gaby," he said softly. "And let me make you happy forever."

She laughed. She wept. And when he rose to his feet to take her in his arms and kiss her, she flung her arms around his neck and kissed him back with all the love in her heart.

EPILOGUE

THEY were married in the same little church in Greenwich Village where Raffaele and Chiara had taken their vows.

Gabriella wore her mother's wedding gown. She had discovered it tucked away in the attic of the house in which she had grown up the weekend she and Dante flew to Brazil so he could finalize the purchase of the *fazenda*, which Andre Ferrantes had finally agreed to sell to him.

Gabriella said she had all a woman could ever want, she didn't need the *fazenda* to be happy, but Dante insisted Viera y Filho had to be hers. Hers, and their son's.

So, as Dante told his brothers, he'd made Ferrantes an offer he couldn't refuse. His brothers had laughed, though in truth, the offer had simply been for two hundred thousand dollars more than Ferrantes had paid for it. The man was a bully and a brute, but he wasn't a fool.

And so, Gabriella wore her mother's wedding gown. Her new mother-in-law's veil. "A tradition, *si?*" her new sister-in-law said.

"A tradition, *sim,*" Gabriella agreed, and the women smiled as they embraced.

Raffaele, Nicolo and Falco were Dante's best men. Anna, Isabella and Chiara were Gabriella's maids of honor.

Daniel, adorable and smiling, observed the ceremony from the protective arms of his happy, weeping grandmother.

Cesare stood silent, an enigmatic smile on his face, saying nothing to anyone until late in the day, when the reception in the Orsini conservatory was coming to an end.

"Nicolo," he said, walking up to his sons, "Falco, I would like to talk to the two of you."

"Father," Falco said, "it's been a long day."

"Right," Nick said. "It's getting late. We can talk another—"

"In my study."

Falco and Nicolo looked at each other. Nick shrugged.

"What the hell," he said.

Falco nodded. "Probably the same old same old about how he's getting on in years—"

"And the safe is there, the financial records are here—"

The brothers laughed and walked to the study door. Felipe, their father's *capo,* seemed to materialize from out of nowhere.

"You first," he said to Falco.

Falco and Nick rolled their eyes. Then Falco stepped into the room, Felipe closed the door and stood outside it, arms folded.

Nick sighed, and settled in to wait.

A TOUCH OF
TEMPTATION

TARA PAMMI

To the man who started it all, my father—
for giving me my love of books,
for never holding me back,
for always believing that there was
nothing I couldn't do if I set my mind to it.

Tara Pammi can't remember a moment when she wasn't lost in a book—especially a romance, which was much more exciting than a mathematics textbook. Years later, Tara's wild imagination and love for the written word revealed what she really wanted to do. Now she pairs Alpha males who think they know everything with strong women who knock that theory and them off their feet!

CHAPTER ONE

KIMBERLY STANTON STARED at the white rectangle of plastic on the gleaming marble counter in the ladies' bathroom. Terror coated her throat as though it might come to life and take a bite out of her. It looked alien, out of place amidst the lavender potpourri, the crystal lamp settings and the glossy chrome fixtures.

The few minutes stretched like an eternity. The quiet lull of voices outside was exaggerated into distorted echoes.

Her heart beat faster and louder. A painful tug in her lower belly stole her breath. She clutched the cold granite vanity unit and clenched the muscles in her legs, willing herself to hold on.

The scariest word she had ever encountered appeared on the stick.

Pregnant.

No confusing colors or symbols that meant you had to peek again at the box discarded in terrified panic.

Simple, plain English.

Her heart leaped into her throat. Her legs shaking beneath her, she leaned against one of the stalls behind her, dipped her head low and forced herself to breathe past the deafening whoosh in her ears.

Her one mistake, which technically she had committed twice, couldn't haunt her for the rest of her life, could it?

But she couldn't change the consequences. She had never been naïve or stupid enough to wish it either.

She flicked the gleaming chrome tap open and dangled her fingers under the ice-cold water. The sound of the water hitting the sink drowned out the sound of her heartbeat, helping her focus on her breathing.

In, out. In, out...

She closed the tap. Straightening up, she was about to reach for the hand towel when she looked at the mirror and froze.

She stared at her reflection, noting the dark circles under her eyes, the lack of color in her face, the skin pulled tautly over her bones. Drops of water seeped through the thin silk of her blouse to her skin beneath.

She looked as if she was on the brink of a nervous breakdown. And maybe she was. But she didn't have time now. The breakdown had to wait. She touched the tips of her fingers to her temple and pressed. The cold from her almost numb fingers seeped into her overheated skin.

She had no time to deal with this now. She had to compartmentalize—set it aside until she was alone, until she was equipped to think logically, until the shock making her jittery all over faded into nothing more than a numbing ache.

And when it did she would assess the situation again with a clear head, take the necessary action to equip herself better to handle it. It wasn't as if she didn't have any experience with dealing with shock and pain.

Although why she had chosen this particular moment to take the test when the pregnancy kit had been burning a rectangular hole in her handbag for more than a week was anybody's guess. Or maybe she was having another momentary collapse of her rational thinking circuits.

She had been having those moments a lot lately.

She pulled her lip-gloss out of her clutch and reapplied

it with shaking fingers. She ran a hand over her suit. The silky material under her fingers rooted her back to reality.

She needed to get back out there. She needed to circulate among the guests—a specially put together group of investors she had researched for more than six months. Investors who had shown interest in her web startup *The Daily Help*.

She had a presentation to give. She had to talk them through the financial outline she had sketched for the next five years. She had to convince them to invest in *her* startup when there were a million others mushrooming every day.

She had to convince them that the recent scandal about her, Olivia and Alexander had nothing to do with the way she did business. It was a sign of how strong her business proposal was that they had even showed up, despite the scandal.

She straightened her jacket and turned toward the exit. And paused midstride.

Turning back, she picked up the plastic tube, wrapped it carefully in the wrapper she had left on the sink and threw it into the trash. She fumbled when she turned the corner, struggling to breathe past the tight ache in her gut. She placed her hand on her stomach and drew in gulps of air, waiting for the tidal wave of pain that threatened to pull her under to pass.

Striding out of the restroom, she plucked a glass of sparkling water from a passing waiter and nodded at an old friend from Harvard. She was glad she had booked this conference hall in one of the glitzy hotels in Manhattan, even though her tightfisted CFO had frowned over the expense.

Kim didn't think an evening in her company's premises—a large open space in the basement of a building in Manhattan, unstructured in every way possible—would encourage confidence on the investors' part.

She checked her Patek Philipe watch, a gift from her

father when she had graduated from Harvard, and invited everyone to join her in the conference room for the presentation.

She felt an uncharacteristic reluctance as she switched on the projector. Once she concluded the presentation she was going to be alone with her thoughts. Alone with things she couldn't postpone thinking about anymore.

It happened as she reached almost the end of her presentation.

With her laser pointer pointed at a far-off wall, instead of at her company's financial forecast on the rolled-out projector screen, she lost her train of thought—as though someone had turned off a switch in her brain.

She searched the audience for what had thrown her.

A movement—the turn of a dark head—a whisper or something else? Had she imagined it? Everything and everyone else faded into background for a few disconcerting moments. Had her equilibrium been threatened so much by her earlier discovery?

The resounding quiet tumbled her out of her brain fog. She cleared her throat, took a sip of her water and turned back to the chart on the screen. She finished the presentation, her stomach still unsettled.

The lights came on and she smiled with relief. Several hands came up as she opened the floor to questions. She could recite those figures half-asleep. Every little detail of her company was etched into her brain.

The first few were questions she had expected. Hitting her stride, she elaborated on what put her company a cut above the others, provided more details, more figures, increasing statistics and the ad revenue they had generated last year.

Even the momentary aberration of a few minutes ago couldn't mar the satisfaction she could feel running in her veins, the high of accomplishment, of her hard work bearing fruit.

She answered the last question, turned the screen off and switched on the overhead lights.

There *he* was. The reason for the strange tightening in her stomach. The cause of the prickling sensation she couldn't shed.

Diego Pereira. The man who had seduced her and walked away without a backward glance. The man whose baby she was pregnant with.

She froze on the slightly elevated podium, felt her gut falling through an endless abyss. Like the time her twin sister had dragged her on a free-fall ride in an amusement park. Except through the nauseating terror that day she had known that at some point the fall would end. So she had forced herself to sit rigid, her teeth digging painfully into the inside of her mouth, while Liv had screamed with terror and laughter.

No such assurance today. Because every time Diego stormed into her life she forgot the lesson she had learned long ago.

Her hands instinctively moved to her stomach and his gaze zeroed in on her amidst the crowd. She couldn't look at him. Couldn't look into those golden eyes that had set her up to fall. Couldn't look at that cruel face that had purposely played with her life.

She forced herself to keep her gaze straight, focused on all the other curious faces waiting to speak to her. It was the most excruciating half hour of her entire life. She could feel Diego's gaze on her back, drilling into her, looking for a weak spot—anything that he could use to cause more destruction.

At least he'd made it easy for her to avoid him, sitting in one of the chairs in the back row with his gaze focused on her.

She slipped, the heel of one of her three-inch pumps snagging on the carpet as she moved past him. Just the dark scent of him was tripping her nerves.

Why was he here? And what cruel twist of fate had brought him here the very same day she had discovered that she was pregnant?

Diego Pereira watched unmoving as Kim closed the door to the conference hall behind her, her slender body stiff with tension. She was nervous and, devil that he was, he liked it.

He flicked through the business proposal. Every little detail of her presentation was blazing in his mind, and he was impressed despite his black mood. Although he shouldn't really be surprised.

Her pitch for investment today had been specific, innovative, nothing short of exceptional. Like her company. In three years she had taken the very simple idea of an advice column into an exclusive, information-filled web portal with more than a million members and a million more waiting on shortlists for membership.

He closed his eyes and immediately the image of her assaulted him.

Dressed formally, in black trousers that showed off her long legs and a white top that hugged her upper body, she was professionalism come to life—as far as possible from the woman who had cried her pleasure in his arms just a month ago.

He had even forgotten the reason he had come to New York while he had followed her crisp, confident presentation. But the moment she had realized he was present in the audience had been his prize.

She had faltered, searched the audience. That seconds-long flicker in her focus was like a nervous scream for an average woman.

But then there was nothing average about the woman

he had married. She was beautiful, brilliant, sophisticated. She was perfection personified—and she had as much feeling as a lump of rock.

A rock he was finally through with—ready to kick out of his life. It was time to move on, and her little nervous sputter at the sight of him had gone a long way toward pacifying his bitter resentment.

He walked to an elevator and pressed the number for the tenth floor. When he reached her suite he pulled the gold-plated keycard he had bribed from the bellboy from his coat packet.

He entered the suite and closed the door behind him.

The subtle scent of lily of the valley assailed him instantly. It rocked him where he stood, dispensing a swift punch to his gut more lethal than the ones he had taken for half his life.

His lungs expanded, drawing the scent of her deep into him until it sank once again into his blood.

His body pulsed with remembered pleasure. Like a junkie getting his high.

He studied the suite, with its luxurious sitting area and mahogany desk. Her files were neatly stacked on it, her sleek state-of-the-art laptop on top of them. Her handbag—a practical but designer black leather affair—lay near the couch in the sitting area.

The suite was everything its owner was—high-class, flawless and without an ounce of warmth.

He turned at the sound of a door on his right.

Closing the door behind her, she leaned against it. A sheen of sweat danced on her forehead.

He frowned, his curiosity spiking.

Her glistening mouth trembled as she spotted him, her hands moving to her midriff.

There was a distinct lack of color to her skin. Her slender shoulders quivered as she ran the back of her hand over her forehead.

He looked at her with increasing curiosity. Her jacket was gone. A V-necked sleeveless white silk blouse showed off her toned arms. The big steel dial of her designer watch highlighted her delicate wrist. A thin gold chain dangled at her throat.

The shadow of her breasts beneath the thin silk drew his gaze.

He swallowed and pulled his eyes up. The memory of her breasts in his hands was cutting off his breath more effectively than a hand choking his windpipe. The feel of her trembling with pleasure in his hands, the erotic scent of her skin and sex—images and sensations flooded through him.

He could no more fight the assault than he could stop breathing.

Her eyes flared wide, the same heat dancing in those chocolate depths.

She was the very embodiment of perfection—always impeccably dressed, exuding the sophistication that was like a second skin to her. Yet now she looked off-balance.

He reached her, the slight sway of her lithe figure propelling him toward her. "Are you okay, *gatinha?*"

She ran her palm over her face, leaving pink fingerprints over her colorless skin. Stepping away from him, she straightened the already immaculate desk. Her fingers trembled as she picked up a pen and moved it to the side.

She was more than nervous.

"No, I'm not," she said, shrugging those elegant shoulders. The frank admission was unusual. "But that's not a surprise as I just saw *you,* is it?"

He raised a brow and sliced the distance between them. "The sight of me makes you sick?"

Her fingers clutched the edge of the desk, her knuckles

white. "The sight of you reminds me of reckless stupid behavior that I'd rather not remember."

He smiled. "Not even the good parts, where you screamed?"

Pink scoured her cheeks. The slender set of her shoulders straightened in defense. She moved to the sitting area and settled into a leather chair. "Why are you here, Diego?"

He watched with a weird fascination as she crossed her legs and looked up at him.

The nervousness he had spied just moments ago had disappeared. She sounded steady, without a hint of anger or upset. Even though the last time they had laid eyes on each other she had been half-naked in his bed, her face bereft of color as he had dressed and informed her that he was done with her.

There was no reproach in her tone for *his* behavior a month ago.

Her calm composure grated on him like the edge of a saw chipping away at wood.

She drove him to be the very worst of himself—seething with frustration, thrumming with desire—whereas she remained utterly unaffected.

He settled down on the coffee table in front of her and stretched his legs so that she was trapped between them. He flipped open the file next to him against his better instincts, to finish what he had come for. "Your proposal is brilliant."

"I don't need you to tell me that," she threw back, her chin jutting out.

He smiled. The confidence creeping back into her tone was not a surprise. When it came to her company his estranged wife was a force to be reckoned with. "Is that your standard response to a potential investor?"

She snorted, and even that was an elegant movement of her straight nose. "It's my standard response to a man who I know is intent on causing me maximum damage."

Diego frowned. "Really? Have I done that?"

She snatched the proposal from his hands and the scent of her wafted over him. He took a breath and held it fast, the muscles in his abdomen tightening.

Droga, two minutes in her company and he was…

He expelled it with the force of his self-disgust. Pleasure was *not* the reminder he needed.

"You already had your revenge, Diego. After I walked out on our marriage six years ago you refused to divorce me with the express purpose of ruining my wedding to Alexander. Then you seduced me and walked out four weeks ago. Isn't that enough?"

"Seeing that you went back to your life, didn't even falter for a second, I'm not sure."

Something flickered in her molten brown gaze as she spoke. "I propelled my sister and Alex into a scandal, putting everything Alex has worked for at risk."

"Again, *them*—not you. From where I stand nothing has gotten to you. Apparently nothing *ever* gets to you."

She ran her fingers over her nape, her gaze shying away from him. Sudden tension pulsed around her. "You left me utterly humiliated and feeling like a complete fool that morning. Is that better?"

He had wanted her anger, her pain, and it was there in her voice now, thrumming with force. But it was too little, too late. Even now it was only the prospect of her precious company having caught his interest that was forcing any emotion from her.

"Maybe," he said, shrugging off his jacket.

Her gaze flew to his, anxious. "Tell me—what do I need to say so that you'll leave my company alone? What will save it from the utter ruin you're planning?"

"I thought your confidence in your company was unshakeable? Your strategy without pitfalls?"

"Not if you make it your life's mission to destroy it," she

said. Her voice rang with accusation, anger, and beneath it all, a curious hurt. "That's what this is all about, isn't it? Anyone who crosses you, who disappoints you, you ensure their ruin. Now it's my turn."

She straightened, her hands folded at her middle. The action pushed her small breasts into prominence. He trained his gaze on her face as though his life depended on it. Maybe not his life, but his very sanity relied on his self-control.

He didn't plan to lose it again.

"Six years ago you were obsessed with revenge, driven by only one goal—to ruin your father. You didn't care who you hurt in the process. You took his small construction company and expanded it into an empire—encompassing energy generation, mining. If I were to believe the media—and knowing you personally I'm very much inclined to—you are called a bastard with alarming frequency. You crushed anything that got in your way. Including your own father." She shot up from the seat and paced the length of the room. "I don't believe in wasting precious time fighting the inevitable. So whatever you're about to do—do it. But I won't go down without a fight. My company—"

"Means everything to you, right? You should be held up as an example to anyone who doubts that women can be as unfeeling and ruthless as men," he interjected smoothly, feeling that flare of anger again.

She stared at him, her gaze puzzled. "Why do I get the feeling that that's not a compliment?"

"It's not."

Her fingers tightened on the windowsill behind her. "We're even now, Diego. Let's just leave it at that."

He moved closer. He could see his reflection in her eyes, her slender shoulders falling and rising with her rapid breathing. Her gaze moved to his mouth and he felt a roar of desire pummel through his blood. It was impossible not to remember how good she had felt, how she had wrapped her legs around him and urged him on with soft little growls.

If he kissed her she wouldn't push him away. If he ran the pad of his thumb over the pulse beating frantically at her throat she wouldn't argue. She would be putty in his hands.

Wasn't that why he felt such a physical pull toward her? Because when he touched her, when he kissed her, it was the one time he felt that he owned this woman—all of her. Her thoughts, her emotions, the core of her.

He fisted his hands. But it would prove nothing new— to him or to her. Self-disgust boiled through him for even thinking it. He had let her get to him on the island, burrow under his skin until the past six years had fallen away and he'd been standing there with her letter in hand.

Never again.

He needed a new beginning without being haunted by memories of this woman. He needed to do what he had come for and leave—*now*.

"I realized what I had done wrong the moment I left the island," he said, unable to stop himself from wringing out the last drop of satisfaction. He had never claimed to be a great man. He had been born a bastard, and to this day he *was* one. "I've come to rectify that mistake."

Kim trembled all over, an almighty buzz filling up her ears.

"A mistake?" Her throat ached as it pushed that word out.

His golden gaze gleamed, a knowing smile curving his upper lip. "I forgot a tiny detail, although it was the most important of all."

He plucked a sheaf of papers from his coat pocket and slid them on to her desk. Every inch of her tensed. The words on those familiar papers blurred.

"I need your signature on the divorce papers."

She struggled to get her synapses to fire again, to get her lungs to breathe again.

The innocuous-looking papers pierced through her defenses, inviting pain she had long ago learned not to feel. This was what she had wanted for six long years—to be able to correct the mistake she had made, to be able to forget the foolish dream that had never stood a chance.

Her palms were clammy as she picked up the papers.

"My staff at the villa were never able to locate the copies you brought."

She shivered uncontrollably at the slight curiosity in his words. *Because she had torn them up after that first night when Diego had made love to her.*

No, not *love*. Sex. Revenge sex. The this-is-what-you-walked-away-from kind. For a woman with an above average IQ, she had repeated the same mistake when it came to Diego.

She turned the papers over and over in her hands. *This was it.*

Diego would walk out of her life. She would never again have to see the foolishness she had indulged in in the name of love. What she had wanted for so long was within her grasp. Yet she couldn't perform the simple task of picking up the pen.

"You could have sent this through your lawyer," she said softly, the shock and confusion she had held in check all evening by the skin of her teeth slithering their way into her. Her stomach heaved. "You didn't have to come yourself."

He leaned against the table, all cool arrogance and casual charm. But nothing could belie the cruel satisfaction in the curve of his mouth. He wanted blood and he was circling her like a hungry shark now that he could smell it.

"And miss the chance to say goodbye for the final time?"

"You mean you wanted to see the fallout from your twisted seduction?"

"Seduction?" he said, a dark shadow falling over his features. The force of his anger slammed into her like a gale.

"Why don't you own it, like you do everything else? There *was* no seduction." He reached her before she could blink. "What does it say about us that even after six years it took us mere hours after laying eyes on each other to end up in bed? Or rather against the wall…"

Her stomach somersaulted. Her skin sizzled. He was right. Sex was all she could think of when he was close. Hot, sweltering, out-of-control, mind-blowing, biggest-mistake-of-your-life-*that-you-made-twice* sex.

She would die before she admitted how much truth there was in his words, how much more he didn't know.

She grabbed her pen and signed the first paper, her fingers shaking.

She lifted her chin and looked up at him, gathering every ugly emotion simmering beneath the surface and pouring it into her words. "It's nothing more than a stimulus and response—like Pavlov's dog. No matter how many years pass, I see you and I think of sex. Maybe because you were my first. Maybe because you are so damn good at it."

The papers slithered to the floor with a dangerous rustle. She felt his fury crackling around them. He tugged her hard against him, his body a smoldering furnace of desire.

She had angered him with her cold analogy. But it only made the void inside her deepen.

His mouth curled into a sneer. "Of course. I forgot that the cruise, those couple of months you spent with me, were nothing but a rich princess's wild, dirty rebellion, weren't they?"

She felt a strange constriction in her chest, a tightness she had nothing to fight against. A sob clawed its way up her throat.

She hated him for ruining the most precious moments of her life. For reducing them to nothing. She hated herself for thinking he had loved her six years ago, for losing her mind the moment she had seen him again four weeks ago.

For someone who had been emotionally stunted for so long, the upsurge of emotion was blinding—pulling her under, driving reason from her mind.

She bunched her fingers in his jacket, his heart thundering beneath her touch. "It's good that you're so greedy you came back for more. Because I have news for you."

CHAPTER TWO

"You have news…?" He frowned, his fingers locked in a tight grip over hers. "What, *princesa?* Do you have a new man lined up now that your sister has stolen the last one? Do you think I give a damn?"

"I'm pregnant."

He didn't move. He didn't blink. Not even a muscle twitched in his mobile face.

Hot satisfaction fueled her. She had wanted to shake his infuriating arrogance. *She had.* On its heels followed raking guilt.

Her knees buckled under her. Only Diego's hold on her was keeping her upright.

God, she hadn't meant to blurt it out like that. She hadn't even dealt with what it meant to *her,* what it implied…

What did it say about her that the only positive thing she felt about the pregnancy was that it could shock Diego like nothing else could?

After the way he had treated her she owed him nothing. And yet keeping him in the dark required a price higher than she was willing to pay.

He had provided her with the best opportunity to tell him, to get it done with. For all she knew he wouldn't even care. He had wanted revenge, he'd got it—with little scruples—and now he had divorce papers ready. And he would keep on walking.

His gaze sliced to her, searching her face. Her composure unraveled at his silence.

The roguish arrogance was gone from his face, replaced by a resolute calm. Every inch of her quaked.

"Is it mine?"

Her gut started that dangerous fall again. She needed to get herself under control. Because Diego was a master at reading her. Whatever she wished, he would do the opposite. Just to make her life harder.

She needed to play it cool. "Why do you think I'm giving *you* the good news?"

"You slept with me mere *hours* after laying eyes on me again," he said, his golden gaze betraying his fury, "while the man you were ready to marry still had his lapdog out looking for you and your twin was being your damned *placeholder* in his life."

She trembled as he walked away from her, as though he couldn't bear to breathe the same air as her.

"And you went back to him as soon as I left you. Except he was two-timing *you* just as you were doing him. So I repeat: is the baby mine?"

"That's not true. Alex and I—"

She shut her mouth with a snap, leaned back against the soft leather, trembling from head to toe. Guilt hung heavy in her stomach. The media, her father—the whole world had crucified Liv, while Kim was the one responsible for it all.

Except Diego knew where she had been and what she had been up to while Liv had pretended to be her. And of course Diego thought Kim had quietly crawled back to Alex, that nothing had changed for her. That she had jumped into his bed from Alex's and then jumped straight back.

That was untrue on so many levels.

Even before Diego had made his true intentions known

Kim had broken it off with Alexander. Only Diego didn't know that.

Her next breath filled her with his scent—dark and powerful. Her eyes flew open.

He raised a brow, watching her with hawklike intensity. "It's a simple question, *gatinha,* and sadly one only a woman can answer."

There was nothing in his tone—no nuance of sarcasm, no hint of anger or accusation—nothing that she could latch onto and feed her fury, her misery.

"Alex and I…" she whispered, feeling heat creep up her skin. "We—"

"All I need—" his words came through gritted teeth "—is your word. Not a day-by-day update on your sexual activity."

Mortification spread like wildfire inside her. Really, she needed to get a grip on herself—needed to stop blurting out things Diego had no need to know.

More information on her non-existent sex-life fell into that category without a doubt. She already had a permanent reminder of how scandalously she had behaved. And now Alex and Liv, her father—*the whole world* was going to find out…

Her gut churned again with a vicious force. "Of course it's yours."

His jaw tight, he nodded. His easy acceptance, his very lack of a reaction, sent a shiver running down her spine. She had expected him to burst out, had braced herself for an attack.

Why did he trust her so easily? He had every right to demand a paternity test. Every right to question the truth of her claim. That was what she wanted from him. That was what she expected from him.

Instead his self-possession—something she usually prided *herself* on—grated on her nerves. She was still panicking. She had blurted out the news in a petty fit of pique. Whereas he didn't even blink.

She laughed, the sound edging toward hysteria. "What? No accusations? No demands for proof? No talk of DNA tests? Just like that, Diego?"

He turned away from her to lean against the wall and closed his eyes. He ran his hand over the bump on his nose. Tension overflowed from him, filling up the huge suite, rattling like an invisible chain, reaching for her. His eyes flew open and her gaze was caught by his.

"DNA tests are for women to whom being pregnant with a rich man's child means a meal ticket to a better life. An accusation my father threw at my mother every time she showed up with me on his doorstep, begging for support."

His words vibrated with emotion. His very stillness, in contrast to the loathing in his words, was disquieting in the least. "However, with our history, I don't think that's what you're going for."

Kim tucked her head in her hands, wondering what she had started. A lump of something—she refused to call it gratitude—blocked her throat, making it harder for her to speak. He could have turned this into something ugly if he wished. *He hadn't.*

Everything within her revolted at being obligated to him for even that small display of honor. It made her weak, plunged her into useless wishing.

She couldn't let him put her in the wrong. She couldn't forget that the very reason she was in this situation was because he had orchestrated payback.

She felt the hard wall of heat from his body and stiffened.

"For a woman who fairly blazes with confidence in every walk of life, your hesitation would be funny if it wasn't the matter of a child. Are you not so sure who the father is yourself?" he whispered softly, something deadly vibrating in his tone.

"There's no doubt," she repeated.

Thinking with a rational mind, she knew she should just tell Diego the stupid truth. That she had never slept with Alexander. But then Diego would never leave the truth alone.

"Now that we have solved that particular puzzle, what do you need from me?"

It took her a moment to realize that he was waiting for an answer. A chill began to spread over her skin. "I...I don't need *anything* from you."

"Of course not." An edge crept into his tone, his gaze devouring her. Something stormy rumbled under that calm now. "Then why tell me?"

"Honestly? I wasn't thinking," she said, wondering if she was destined always to make mistakes when it came to him. "You were gloating. You were..."

"Nice to know something touches you," he said, a fire glinting in his gaze. She opened her mouth to argue and shut it just as quickly. "And if I hadn't been here to gloat? Would you have called me then?"

"That's a question I don't have to answer, because you *are* here. And stop pretending as though this means something, Diego. You were ready to walk out of my life, and I say keep on walking."

"Your arrogance in thinking that you know me is astounding, *querida*. Did I teach you nothing four weeks ago?"

His words rumbled around her, and images and sensations tumbled toward her along with them. But she refused to back down. "You take risks. Your business tactics are barely on this side of the law. The last thing you need in your life is a baby. If I had hidden this from you you would have only found more reason to hate me."

"To think for a moment I assumed that you weren't doing

this for purely selfish reasons but for the actual wellbeing of the child you're carrying…"

She flinched, the worst of her own fears crystallized by his cutting words. Her earlier dread intensified. That was what she should have immediately thought of. *The child's welfare.* "I want nothing but a divorce and an exit from you."

His laughter faded and shadowed intent filled his face. He grabbed the papers she had signed not five minutes ago and shredded them with his hands.

His calm movements twisted her gut. "Then what do you have in mind? We'll kiss each other and make up? Play happy family—"

He came closer—until she could see the gold specks in his eyes, smell the dark scent of him that scrambled her wits.

"I'm not turning my back on my child."

Panic unfurling in her stomach, she shot up from her seat. "You're out of your mind. This is not what I planned for my life—"

"I'm sure you had a list of requirements that needed to be met in order to produce the perfect offspring," he said, his words ringing with bitter satisfaction, "but it's out of your hands now."

"It is. But what I *can* control is what I do about it now. Being a mother is going to be hard enough. Dealing with you on a regular basis will just tip me over into…"

Perverse anger rose within her—perverse, irrational and completely useless. He could walk away from this. She *needed* him to walk away from this. But *she*…she had no such choice. She had a lifelong commitment. She was supposed to love this baby. She was supposed to…

"You don't want this baby?"

"Of course I don't. I'll even go so far as to say it's the

worst thing that has ever happened to me!" she shouted, the words falling off her trembling lips.

Shock flickered in his gaze, but she didn't have the energy to wish them unsaid.

"This baby is going to be a walking, talking reminder of the biggest mistake of my life. You've achieved what you wanted, Diego. You've done your worst. You have changed my life in a way I can't control. Now, please, leave me to get on with it."

Diego breathed out through his teeth and hit the punching bag again with renewed force. His right hook was beginning to fall short again. The injury to the muscle in his bicep was making itself known. The same injury that had forced him to withdraw from financially lucrative streetfights. The injury that had forced him to reach out to his father for help when he had been sixteen and unable to pay for his mother's treatment.

But he wouldn't stop now. He breathed through the vicious pain, hating himself for even remembering.

The clock on the wall behind him chimed, reminding him he'd been at it for more than two hours now.

Sweat poured down from his forehead and he shook his head to clear it off. His T-shirt was drenched through and the muscles in his arms felt like stones. Adrenaline rushed through him in waves and he was beginning to hear a faint thundering in his ears. Probably his blood whooshing. But he didn't stop.

Because even trying to drown himself in physical agony he couldn't block out Kim's words.

Stimulus and response!

Meu Deus, the woman reduced him to the lowest denominator with her infuriating logic. No one had ever got under his skin like she did. And she was carrying his baby.

The resentment that had glittered in her brown eyes pierced even the haze of his pain.

Punch.

Of course it's yours.

Thump.

It's the worst thing that has ever happened to me.

Punch.

This baby is going to be a walking, talking reminder of the biggest mistake of my life.

Thump.

Nausea whirled at the base of his throat, threatening to choke him with its intensity. He'd had enough rejection from his father to last him several lifetimes. He would be dead before he did the same to his child or became a stranger.

He took one last punch and pulled his gloves off. He picked up a bottle of water, guzzled half of it down and dumped the rest over his head. The water trickled over his face into his eyes. The biting cold did nothing to pacify the crazy roar in his head.

Because Kim had been right. He didn't want to be a father.... He wasn't fit to be a father...

He let a curse fly and went at the punching bag again, shame and disgust boiling over in his blood. Pain waves rippled up his knuckles. His skin started peeling at his continued assault.

He had no good in him. All he had was hatred, jealousy. He didn't possess a single redeeming quality that said he should even be a *part* of a child's life. He had chosen to walk the path he had with full clarity of thought—to take everything from his father that he deserved. He had known exactly what he was doing when he'd reached for that goal.

And that was what he wanted to do now, too. He wanted to take his child from Kim and walk away. Every nerve in him wanted to ensure he had full custody.

But he could not sink so low again.

He had let his hatred for his father lead him to destroy his half brother's life in the process. If not for Diego's blind obsession Eduardo would have been...

He shivered, a chill swamping him.

He couldn't risk that happening with his child. If, because of his obsession with Kim, he hurt his child in any way he wouldn't be able to live with himself. He couldn't let his anger at her drive him into making a mistake again—not anymore. Not when it could hurt his own child.

Playing happy family with Kim, seeing her every day, when she was the one weakness he had never conquered—every inch of him revolted at the very thought.

And yet he couldn't escape his responsibility. He couldn't just walk away and become a stranger to his own child.

He had a chance to change the vicious cycle of neglect and abuse he and Eduardo had gone through.

He would move mountains to make sure his child had everything he'd never had—two loving parents and a stable upbringing. Even if that meant tying himself to the woman who brought his bitterest fears to the surface.

CHAPTER THREE

KIM PULLED THE satin pillow over her head and groaned as her cell phone chirped. She hadn't gotten into bed until three in the morning, after going over the new feature on *The Daily Help* with the design architect and writing her own feature for the career advice section she did every Tuesday.

Pushing her hair out of her eyes, she looked at the digital clock on the nightstand. It was only seven. She felt a distinct lack of energy to attack the day. When her phone rang for the third time in a row she switched the Bluetooth on.

"Kim, are you okay?"

Liv.

Tension tightened in the pit of her stomach at the concern in her twin's voice. She had been putting Liv off for two weeks now.

She pushed herself up on the bed and leaned against the metallic headboard. "I'm fine. Is everything okay with you and Alex?"

"We're fine. I'm just…" Liv's uncharacteristic hesitation hung heavily between them. "God, Kim—is it true? Why the hell didn't you *tell* me?"

Kim swallowed, fear fisting her chest. "What are you talking about?"

"You've made front page headlines. Not just the scandal rags, like I did, but even the business channels on television."

"What?"

"It says you're pregnant. Are you?"

Diego.

Kim closed her eyes and breathed huge gulps of air. Obviously her refusal to have anything to do with him, her refusal even to answer his calls, meant Diego had begun playing dirty.

"Yes."

"When were you going to tell me? Are you…? I mean, are you okay with this? Does Diego know? What are you planning to *do?*"

They were all perfectly valid questions. Kim had just shoved them down forcefully.

"I'm perfectly fine, Liv. I don't have the time right now to process what it means. Once this upcoming milestone for my company has passed I'll make a list of the things I need to do." She closed her eyes, fighting for composure. "I'll even have a few sessions with Mommy Mary."

"Who is Mommy Mary?"

"The expert on all things maternal on my team."

"On *what?*"

"On what I need to learn to be the perfect mother. It's not like *we* had a good example, is it?"

"And until then you're just going to put it on the back burner?"

What else was she supposed to do? Focus on the relentlessly clammy feeling in her stomach every time her thoughts turned to the baby growing in her womb?

The stark contrast between the terrifying emptiness *she* felt and her newly pregnant CFO's glorious joy was already a constant distressing reminder that something vital was missing in her own genetic make-up.

"I can't botch this opportunity for my company by losing my focus."

"I don't know what to…" Olivia's tone rang with the

same growing exasperation Kim had sensed in their recent conversations. "Let me know if you need anything, okay?"

Kim tucked her knees close as Liv hung up. She wanted to reach out to Liv. Liv's love came with no conditions, no judgment.

But Kim—she had always been the strong one. She had had to be in order to protect first her mother and then Liv from their father's wrath.

She couldn't confide her fears in anyone. Least of all to her twin, to whom loving and caring and nurturing came so easily.

Whereas Kim had trained herself so hard to not care, not to let herself be touched by emotions. She'd had to after she had learned what her mother had planned...

Only had she accomplished it so well—just as she had everything else in life—that she felt nothing even for the child growing in her womb?

Because even after a week all she felt was utter panic at the thought of the baby. She had spent a fortune buying almost a dozen more pregnancy test kits, hoping that it had been a false positive. And every time the word "pregnant" had appeared her stomach had sunk a little lower.

Or was it because of the man who had fathered her baby? Could her anger for Diego be clouding everything else? Was this how their mother had felt? Beneath her fear of their father, had she felt nothing for her children?

Without crawling out of bed, she pulled her reading glasses on and powered up her iPad. Her heart thumped loudly. She clicked on to one of her favorite websites—one she could count on to provide news objectively.

The Daily Help's pregnant CEO Kimberly Stanton's best kept secret—a secret marriage or the identity of her unborn baby's father?

It was the first time she wasn't in the news being lauded for one of her accomplishments.

The article, for all its flaming header, didn't spend time speculating on the answer to either of the questions it posed. But suddenly she wished it did. Because the speculation it *did* enter into was much more harmful than if they had spawned stuff about her personal life.

The article highlighted the way any woman—especially one who was pregnant and with her personal life in shambles—could expect to expand her company and do it successfully.

Should investors be worried about pouring their money into a company whose CEO's first priority might not be the company itself? One who has been involved in not one but two major scandals? Could this pregnancy herald the death of the innovative startup *The Daily Help* and its brilliant CEO Kimberly Stanton's illustrious career?

She shoved the tablet away and got out of bed, her mind whirling with panic. She ran a hand over her nape, too restless to stay still. It might have been written by Kim herself, for it highlighted every little one of her insecurities—everything she had made a list of herself.

For so long she had poured everything she had into first starting her company and then into making it a financial success. She had never stopped to wonder—never had a moment of doubt when it came to her career.

She opened the calendar on her phone. Her day was full of follow-up meetings with five different investors. By the end of the day she intended to start working on putting the plans she had outlined about the expansion of her company into full gear.

She couldn't focus on any other outcome—couldn't

waste her mental energies speculating and in turn proving the contentious article right.

Only then would she deal with Diego. There was no way anyone else would have known or leaked the news to the media. She had confided in only one person.

Wasn't this what Diego had intended all along? She was a fool if she'd thought even for a moment that he wanted anything but her ruin.

Kim clicked End on her Skype call and leaned back in her chair. Her day had only gotten worse since Liv's phone call. That had been her fifth and last unsuccessful investor meeting. Not one investor was ready to wire in funds.

Whereas the invoices for the new office space she had leased, for the three new state-of-the-art servers she had ordered, for the premium health insurance she had promised her staff this year mocked her and the vast sum of numbers on the papers in front of her was giving her a headache.

She leaned her head back and rubbed the muscles knotting her neck. Her vision for her company, her team's livelihood, both were at stake because she had weakened.

Hadn't she learned more than once how much she could lose if she let herself feel?

The number of things she needed to deal with was piling up. Panic breathed through her, crushing her lungs and making a mockery of the focus that she was so much lauded for. She forced large gulps of air into her lungs.

Breathe in...out...in...out... She repeated it for a few minutes, running her fingers over the award plaques she kept next to her table, searching for something to tune out the panic.

Pull yourself together, Kim. There are people counting on you.

It was the same stern speech she had given herself at thirteen, when she had discovered her mother's packed bag one night. And the note to her father that had knocked the breath from her.

She had survived that night. She could survive anything.

She had to go on as before—for her company's sake and for her own sake. If she lost her company she had nothing. She *was* nothing.

She picked up her cell phone and dialed Alex's number. He was someone with whom she had always tossed around ideas for her business, someone she absolutely trusted. And someone she had been avoiding for the past month...

But she needed objective, unbiased advice, and Alex was the only one who would give it to her. She would exhaust every possibility if it meant she could go on with the plan for expanding her company.

Diego cursed, cold fury singing through his blood as he stared at the live webcast on his tablet. Reporters were camped with cameras and news crews in front of Kim's apartment complex in Manhattan.

He rapped on the partitioning glass and barked her address at his chauffeur.

His gaze turning back to the screen again, he frowned at a sudden roar in the ruckus. And cursed again with no satisfaction as he recognized the tall figure. Her ex had arrived. Diego could almost peek into how the press's mind would work.

The news about her pregnancy on top of the scandal last month, when her twin had been found with Kim's ex—the press would come to only one conclusion.

That the unborn child—his child—was Alexander King's.

This was not what he had intended when he'd had his head of security leak the news of her pregnancy to the media.

He stared at the tall figure of Alexander King as he

walked into the complex without faltering, despite the reporters swarming around him. Acrid jealousy burned through him. He slammed his laptop shut, closed his eyes and sought the image of Eduardo's frail body.

Which was enough to soak up the dark thoughts and send some much-needed reason into his head.

He had done this before—let his obsession consume his sense of right or wrong. He had let it blind him to the fact that Eduardo had needed his help, and instead he'd turned on him.

He couldn't do that again. This was not about what Kim could drive him to. It was about what was right for their child.

Kim took a sip of her water as Alex finished a call. She had emailed him her proposal and set up the appointment. Now she wished she had waited for the weekend. Stupid of her not to expect how much the media would make of Alex visiting her *alone* on a Friday evening at her apartment.

She had never been more ashamed of herself. It had taken everything in her to ask Alex for his help but she had no other options. A flush overtaking her, she plucked up the daily statistics report her website manager had sent her.

Based on the turnover of her company in the last quarter, and on her expansion proposal, investing in her company was a sound opportunity for any shrewd businessman. Except for the scandal she had brought on herself.

Their daily numbers, the number of questions that came into their portal and the website hits, had spiked well above average today.

But she knew, as was pointed out by the breakdown in front of her, that this was because twenty percent of the questions had been about her pregnancy, whether she was married and—worst of them all—whether she was married to the father of her baby.

She needed to make a statement soon.

Tucking his phone into his pocket, Alex turned toward her. "I'm sorry, Kim. You know how much I trust your business savvy. But, as brilliant as your plan and forecast is, I can't invest in it right now."

Her stomach turning, Kim nodded. It was exactly as she had expected: the worst.

She blinked back tears as he wrapped an arm around her. "With everything going on out there right now I just… As much as I hate to admit it, my association with your company in the current climate would only damage your credibility."

Kim nodded, the comfort he offered making her spectacular failure even harder to bear. "I know. And I'm so sorry for putting you and Liv through this—for everything. If I could I would go back to that day and do everything differently." She smiled and corrected herself. "Well, except for the part where I left you with Liv."

He laughed, and her mounting panic was blunted by the sheer joy in that sound. "You don't have to go through this alone, Kim. You should come and stay with—"

"She's not alone to deal with this. And I would think twice, if I were you, before touching my wife again."

Kim jerked around so quickly that her neck muscles groaned.

Diego stood leaning against the door of her apartment, a dark, thundering presence, and he looked at them with such obvious loathing that her mouth dried up.

Next to her, Alex stayed as calm as ever as he turned around. Just like her, he knew who was behind the leak to the media. But, gentleman that he was, he hadn't asked her one personal question.

The very antithesis of the man smoldering with anger at the door.

Mortification heating her cheeks, she met Diego's gaze.

"Don't do this, Diego. Don't make me regret ever knowing you."

He shrugged, the movement stretching the handmade grey silk tight over his muscular frame. "Don't you already? Aren't you going to introduce your husband to your ex, *querida?*"

Alex moved at her side, reaching Diego before she could blink. Her breath hitched in her throat as they both looked at each other.

"Call me anytime, and for any kind of help, Kim," Alex said.

Without another word he strolled out, closing the door behind him. The silence pulling at her stressed nerves, Kim walked past the sitting area to her kitchen, the open layout giving her an unobstructed view of Diego. She pulled a bottle of orange juice out of the refrigerator and poured it into a glass.

Diego leaned against the pillar that cut off the kitchen from the lounge. She raised the glass to her mouth and took a sip. His continued scrutiny prickled her skin. Every time she laid eyes on him she felt as if she was one step closer to a slippery slope.

"What is this? A lesson in caveman behavior?"

"I don't understand your relationship with that man."

She blinked at his soft tone. "Don't turn this around on *me*. Were you going to beat your chest and drag me to your side by my hair if he hadn't left?"

He smiled, his gaze moving to her hair. He flexed his fingers threateningly. "I've never done that before…but if anyone can push me to it, it's you."

Her mouth open, she just stared at him.

"You like throwing my background in my face, don't you? I'm not ashamed that my life began on the streets of Rio de Janeiro, that I used my fists for survival."

She glared at him, insulted by his very suggestion. "It's

got nothing to do with your background and everything to do with how you are acting now."

"True. This one's my fault. I should have expected you to go to him for help."

It was the last thing she'd expected him to say.

Calling her a few names, maybe challenging her word about the paternity of the baby as the whole world was hotly speculating—sure. But this? No. His continuing trust in her word threw her, kept her off-balance.

Or was that what he truly intended?

The doubts assailing her, the real possibility of her company falling apart, filled her veins with ice. "As you have made it your mission to destroy my life, I went crawling for help to the man whom I deceived dreadfully by sleeping with you. *Satisfied?*"

Diego let his gaze travel lazily over Kim. A long-sleeved white cotton top hugged her slim torso and the flat of her stomach, followed by tight blue jeans that encased her long legs. Her short hair was pulled back with a clip, leaving shorter tendrils teasing her cheekbones.

He believed her that the baby was his. She had nothing to gain by lying to him and everything to lose.

Except he didn't understand how, having been almost literally dragged from the altar by Diego, away from a man who was now *apparently* happily married to her twin, Kim could still share a relationship with Alexander that wasn't the least bit awkward.

Was she still pining after him? After all, she had gone to him for help. That in itself was revealing.

"I gave you a week, *gatinha*. I refuse to be ignored. I refuse to let you put your company before the baby and—"

She put her glass down with a force that splashed the juice onto her fingers. Her posture screamed with barely contained anxiety. "The baby's not going to be here for nine months. Do you expect me to sit around twiddling my thumbs until then? I'm not going to give up something I have built with sheer hard work just because I'm pregnant."

There it was again. Her complete refusal to accept that things were going to change.

"I expect you to slow down. I expect you to return my calls. I expect you to stop working sixteen-hour days." She didn't look like perfection put together today. She looked tired and stressed out. Guilt softened his words. "You look like you're ready to fall apart."

"And whose fault is that? I've been trying to minimize the damage you've caused with your dirty tricks."

"You have no idea *how* dirty I'll fight for what I want. Propelling you toward *him* wasn't what I intended, however. But I had forgotten how stubbornly independent you are."

"Careful, Diego. You sound almost jealous. And yet I know you don't give a hoot about me."

"Remember I'm an uncivilized, dirty thug," he said, with a slanted look at her. "A street-fighting Brazilian, *pequena*. Of course I'm jealous."

Kim wiped her fingers on a hand towel, feeling a flush creep up her neck.

Of course she remembered. She remembered every moment of her short-lived marriage with crystal-clear clarity. She had called him that the week before she had left him, her misery getting the better of her. It wasn't where he had come from that had bothered her. It was what she represented to him because of it that had shattered her heart.

"Why? Even *you* can see, after everything you have set in motion, how much Alex loves my sister."

He circled the pillar and neared her, frowning. "And this doesn't bother you at all?"

"What?"

"That the man you had been about to marry is now married to your twin."

"I'm incredibly happy for them. If there's one good thing that's come out of this whole debacle it's Liv and Alex."

"Only one good thing? Still not sure, then?" he queried silkily, his gaze instantly moving to her stomach.

Her spine kissed the steel refrigerator as he suddenly swallowed her space. "Any child who's the product of you and me is of course not a good thing."

"You make it sound like it's a product we designed together."

His words were soft, even amused, and yet they lanced through her. "Excuse me if I'm not the perfect vision of maternal instinct you were expecting."

He stared at her, his gaze searching hers. "Your genes needed a bit of diluting anyway, and you need a bit of softening up. All work and no play makes Kimberly a crabby girl."

"Yes, well—look where all that playing has landed me."

She sucked in a deep breath, sheer exhaustion finally catching up with her. Trust Diego to force her to face the one thing she didn't want to think about.

"We can't even have a conversation without jumping at each other's throats, Diego." Every dark fear she was trying to stay above bled into her words. "How do you think it bodes for the...the child?"

Without looking away from her he pulled her hands from behind her and tugged her gently. Stupefied, she went along, for once lacking the energy to put up a fight. With a hand at her back he guided her to the lounge and pushed her onto the couch.

He settled down on a chair opposite.

She felt the force of his look down to her toes. "You might not want this baby, but you want to do the right thing by it—right?"

She swallowed and nodded, a fist squeezing her chest. It was the only thing she was capable of at this point.

"Good. And, as much as you were hoping that I would walk away, I won't." His gaze was reassuring, his tone comforting. "Believe me, *gatinha,* that's a whole lot more than most kids ever have."

Was it?

Maybe if her mother hadn't left that night...and even when she had maybe if she had at least included Kim... would her life have been different, better, today? No, there was no point in imagining a different past or present. Being weak, trusting her heart, only led to unbearable pain. She had learned that twice already.

"Why are you jealous of Alexander?" The moment the question fell off her lips she regretted it.

His long fingers on his nape, Diego closed his eyes and then opened them slowly. His resentment was clear in the tight line of his mouth. "Alexander King has your confidence. I don't. And, having crawled out of the gutter, I find my first reaction is to hate any man who has what I want."

His stark admission pulled the rug out from under her. "You want my confidence?" She sighed. "How about you stop trying to destroy me for a minute and then we can talk?"

He leaned forward, his elbows on his knees, his expression amused. "Isn't it interesting how your company being in crisis means I'm destroying your life, but when I ruined your wedding you didn't have a word to say? So, did he agree to save your company and thus your *life?*"

His absolutely accurate assumption that her life revolved around her career and her company was beginning to grate on her nerves. She had always prided herself on her un-emotional approach. It had been a factor that had put her in direct competition with ruthless businessmen like him. "No."

He plopped his ankle on his right knee. "Is it because

you deceived him? Have you noticed how you leave *all* the men in your life with less than nice impressions?"

"Not everyone in the world is as concerned about payback as you are."

His gaze glittered for a second, but the next he was a rogue, savoring the mess he was making of her life. "So why did Mr. King refuse to be your savior?"

"Because—thanks to your tricks and my own stupidity—my image is in tatters. My company is based on the idea of a panel of experts giving women advice on any topic from health, career and fashion to politics, finance and sex. The operative word being *experts*. And, as unfair as it is, a woman who seems to *not* have her personal life together without blemish is not someone others—even other women—want advice from. It doesn't matter that nothing has changed in the way I think or in my brain matter since I learned about my pregnancy. It just is."

"But eventually the news would have come out. I just accelerated it."

He was right. It was something she would have had to face in a couple of months anyway. The sooner she dealt with all this, found a way to resolve this situation with her company, the better.

She still needed an investor, but she was not as worried about running her company as the whole world was. She could do it with her hand tied behind her back.

It was the pregnancy that was the near-constant worry scouring through her.

She had succeeded in everything she had taken up in her life. Pregnancy had to be the same, right?

If she prepared enough, if she was willing to work hard, she could do a good job at being a mother, too. She refused to think about it any other way—refused to give weight to the worry eating away at her from inside.

"What's was the point of all this, Diego?" she said, feeling incredibly tired. "Would it make you feel better if I begged you for help? Leeched money off you in the name of child support?"

"Yes."

She blinked at the vehemence in his answer.

"What I wanted was to scare away all your other investors so that you have no one else to turn to but me."

"Why?"

"It seems putting your company in crisis is the only way for me to get your attention."

Her temper flared again. "That's the second time you have mentioned my success, my company, as though it's something to be sneered at—when you pursued your *own* success with ruthless ambition. And wasn't that why you married me six years ago? Because I was smart, ambitious? Now that I'm pregnant you're asking me to put all that aside and suddenly morph into your vision of everything maternal? I never thought *you* would tout double standards."

Diego ran a hand over his nape. Just the mention of their short-lived marriage was like throwing a punch in his face. She was doing it again—getting under his skin. And it would end in only one way.

"Do you really want to go down the rabbit hole of the past, *gatinha?*"

He didn't want to argue with her. He could see very well that something about her pregnancy was stressing her out. So why didn't she make it easy on herself? If she didn't know how to, he would do it. He would drag her kicking and screaming back into his life and force her to slow down if that was what he had to do to take care of her.

He stepped over the coffee table and joined her on the couch. She scooted to the other corner. He sighed. It seemed either they argued or they screwed, and neither was what he wanted to do. Even if one option had infinitely more appeal than the other.

"I'm not asking you to give up your work. I'm asking you to acknowledge that pregnancy changes things."

Her feet tucked under her, her arms wrapped around herself, she scrunched farther into the corner. She looked absolutely defeated. "And what does *that* entail? Throwing myself a conception party and inviting the whole world?"

"You have no friends, you don't talk to your sister and you're a workaholic. You live in a fortress isolated from anyone else. That cannot continue."

"Keeping myself idle for hours on end with nothing to do is not going to turn me into *mother of the year* when the baby comes. In fact it would just…"

His patience was thinning, but there was something in her voice—a note of desperation—that snagged his attention. "Just what?"

Her stubborn silence was enough to drive his control to the edge again. Was this what he was signing up for a lifetime of?

"I will invest in your company."

Her gaze widened. Her head shook from left to right. "I'll bounce back from this."

"No, you won't." He leaned toward her, and the scent of her caressed him. "Things are different from what they were a week ago."

"Because you manipulated them to your advantage."

"I would have been dead in a ditch years ago if I didn't push things to my advantage." He smiled, enjoying her stupefied silence. "Now I've got you hooked, haven't I? I can see the gears already spinning in your head."

"What's the catch?"

"Aah… Look at us, *gatinha*. We're like an old married couple, reading each other's minds without words. If that's not a true, abiding love, then I don't know what is."

"Stop it, Diego. Why the investment now?"

"Perhaps I don't want to see your hard work go to waste?

Or I'm overcome by a consuming need to help you? I still have a soft spot for my wife?"

Kim shivered as though someone had trickled an ice cube over her spine. His taunts were painful reminders of things she had cherished once and then realized to be false. He was mocking feelings she held close to her heart, emotions she had locked up forever.

"Not funny." With each cheeky retort her anxiety spiraled higher and higher. There *had* to be a huge price to pay for this. "What do you want from me?"

"We make our marriage work. For good."

She jumped from the couch, a chill descending into her veins. He couldn't be serious. It was a twisted joke. That was all it had to be...

She swallowed at the calm in his gaze. "Now I get it. No one is allowed to say no to you, to walk away from you, without you going all *revenge of the ninja* on them. I'm not a task you failed at once and are determined to conquer."

"Let's be very clear about something, *princesa.*" The dark humor faded from his gaze, replaced by something hard and flinty. "Putting up with you, tying my life to yours again, is like signing up for a lifetime of torment. But it's a *sacrifice* I'm willing to make for my child. To provide a stable home, to give it everything I didn't have. *Nothing more.* I plan to be a hands-on parent and I will accept nothing less from you."

Bile snuck up Kim's throat. Everything within her rebelled at the thought of being tied to him. It was no better now than it had been six years ago. Then she had been his prize, his trophy, to parade before his father in his victory over a horrible childhood. Now her significance was the fact that she was going to be the mother of his child.

It shouldn't hurt. But it did. And the hurt was followed by the same raking guilt that had taken up permanent residence in her gut.

She couldn't think about what this meant for her. She had to think of the baby. She had to do what was right.

Whether she wanted to be a mother or not, whether or not she felt anything for the life growing inside her, it didn't matter. Unconditional love. She had never received it, she didn't know it, but responsibility and being strong for someone else—that she understood.

"Is this another trick so you can taunt me for the rest of my life? I won't let you use the child as some kind of pawn."

"Every inch of me wants to walk away from you. Every cell in me regrets sleeping with you. I told myself I would not waste another minute on you. But what we did has had consequences. All this is motivated by the fact that we're having a child together. A child who will have a proper father—not one who will just drop in for birthdays and pose for pictures—and a proper mother. A family. I will do everything in my power to ensure my child has everything I never had."

She swallowed, the emptiness she felt exaggerated by his words. In that moment she didn't doubt him.

Diego would do everything for their child. She could see the resolve burning in his eyes. If only he had felt a little of that toward her when they had been married. If only she felt one tenth of the emotion he felt for their child.

"We don't have to be married for that. We could share custody."

"My child is not spending half its life traveling between you and me like a soccer ball. We will be a family—a proper one."

"I'm not sleeping with you."

He laughed—the first sound he'd made that was filled with genuine amusement. "Afraid you won't be able to resist? Don't worry, Kim. I've learned that there are some things in life that can damage even dirty-fighting and wicked me. Like sleeping with you."

"Finally something we agree upon," she said loudly, trying to drown the thundering of her own heart. It figured that now he had caused maximum damage Diego had no interest in her. Why that should bother her of all the things that had happened today was beyond her.

Really, she was becoming a regular passenger on the cuckoo train.

She slid into the couch again, her knees shaking beneath her, trying to grasp the rollercoaster she was signing up for.

"So—a sexless, everlasting marriage to a man who hates me, who owns the biggest share of my company and who will no doubt find unadulterated joy in telling me what a horrible mother I make for the rest of my life? Sounds like a perfect recipe for happily-ever-after."

"Happily-ever-after? Is that what you want, *princesa?* Would you even know it if it bumped you on your over-achieving head?"

Hulking over her, he surrounded her, his gaze drilling holes into her.

"For the last time—your company is just a bargaining chip for me. I only ask that you do your best for our child. And as to sex—" his voice lowered to a sinuous whisper, his breath tickling her lips "—if you really want to change that part of the equation we can revisit it—say in a couple of years?" Dark enjoyment slashed the curve of his mouth.

She pulled her gaze upward. The whole situation she found herself in was absurdly comical. If only it wasn't her life. "A reward system? *Great.* Sex for good behavior?"

His mouth curved again, in a smile that dimpled his cheek, pure devilish amusement glittering in it. Her breath stuck in her throat. She had always loved that dimple. On any other man it would have looked effeminate. On Diego it touched his ruthless masculinity with a mischievous charm.

"See—just the way you like it. Everything reduced to a simple business transaction. Be a good little wife and you can have all the sex you want."

CHAPTER FOUR

STANDING IN FRONT of the elevator on her floor, Kim studied herself in the gleaming doors and breathed in gulps of air. So much for her hope that she might be one of the women that Mommy Mary mentioned, who had breezy pregnancies, nesting instincts and glowing skin.

Right.

What she had was nausea, exhaustion, acne—and mood swings as though she had just gotten off of antidepressants. And nothing but an unrelenting detachment at the sight or talk of anything baby-related.

Only a ninety-hour work week, with the added stress of handling PR about the new investment and the expansion of her company, had kept her from spiraling further down.

Two days after he had cornered her in her apartment Diego's legal team had contacted her own. She refused to feed her curiosity by asking where *he* was. Negotiations had been completed in a day and she now had two million dollars to sink her teeth into. It was more than she had expected in her wildest dreams.

She should be overjoyed—she had the investment and she was being awarded the prestigious Entrepreneur of the Year award by the Business Bureau Guild tonight.

But she couldn't turn her mind from thoughts of Diego. It was like a rerun of six years ago, when she had returned to New York, her heart in pieces, wondering if he would call her, if he would come after her...

Not even a month since he'd come back into her life and he was already reducing her to that pitiful self—to someone who signed up for getting hurt so easily.

Maybe she should have accepted Liv's offer to attend the awards ceremony with her and Alex. But she was still avoiding Liv and her well-meaning questions, and arriving with them would only give rise to more of the speculation that was beginning to mess with her head.

Running her company meant she always worked sixteen to eighteen hour days, and that didn't leave time for abiding friendships—or anything else for that matter. It was how she had tailored her life. And she loved it just that way.

Except for the strange tightness in her chest at the thought of the evening ahead, *alone*.

She stepped into the elevator and heard the swish of the doors closing behind her. Leaning her head against the cool mirrored surface of the wall, she fought the tears clogging her throat, a volatile rush of emotion flooding her.

In a way, the threat to her company's expansion had taken her mind off the pregnancy. Now there was nothing to do except face the void inside her. What she wouldn't give to feel one positive thing about this pregnancy...even if it was something as trivial as relief that the nausea was abating.

She reached the front lobby and asked the doorman to hail a taxi. She walked out behind him and pulled her wrap tighter around her shoulders. A black limo came to a smooth stop at the curb.

She stepped out of the way as a chauffeur opened its door. And felt Diego's presence behind her, emerging from her building.

"Ready to go?"

Her heart kicking against her ribcage, she turned around

so quickly that she almost lost her balance. Diego's hand shot out to hold her before she stumbled to the ground.

His arm around her waist, he pulled her to him, enveloping her in a purely masculine scent and hard muscles that made her feel soft all over.

Warmth flooded her, flushing out the inexplicable loneliness of a minute ago. She breathed in a big gulp of air, expanding and contracting her lungs.

Her stomach lurched in an altogether different, pleasurable way. *Why couldn't he make her nausea worse?*

Dressed in a gray Armani suit that hugged his broad shoulders, with his hair slicked back from his forehead, she wondered if he had materialized right out of her thoughts. He exuded raw magnetism, sliding her heartbeat ratcheting up and her already active hormones into overdrive.

His bronzed skin gleamed with vitality in the streetlights, his slightly bent nose and glittering eyes adding to his allure. Languid sensuality cascaded from him.

Even in the chilly New York evening she felt the heat of his perusal on her skin.

"Careful, *pequena*," he whispered.

A frisson spread in ripples from where his big palm stayed over her back. His grip on her waist tightened as he felt her shiver, the heat from his callused palm singeing her skin through the silk material.

"I know those heels are part of your image but you need to be careful."

She raised her gaze to him, tingling everywhere he touched her. She searched his face hungrily. After his absence for a week she had started believing he regretted his commitment to her—at least the personal part of it.

The moment she found her balance he let her go. As though he didn't want to touch her unless absolutely necessary. Whereas she still tingled everywhere from the briefest of contacts.

"What are you doing here?" she said loudly, trying to speak past the continued boom of her heart.

"I'm coming with you to the awards ceremony."

She closed her eyes and counted to ten, hating herself for the excitement sweeping through her. This was the result of depriving herself of basic human company. This stupid, dangerous thrill at the prospect of an evening with Diego. "Why?"

His smile seemed feral. "To see the whole world praise my wife and fall at her feet for her brilliance."

"Yeah, right. Where exactly did you come from?"

His gaze devoured her, swift and dismissive. "The penthouse."

"The penthouse? What were you doing in the penthouse?" she shot at him, regretting the question the moment she'd said it.

Was he visiting a woman up there? Did she really want to know what Diego got up to in his free time? It had been hard enough to resist gobbling up information about him in the past six years.

"Moving in," he said, with an exaggerated patience that wound her up a little more. "As will you. It will be our home. Until we figure out something more permanent."

"You moved to New York? When? Why?" She refused even to acknowledge the other suggestion he'd slipped in. Equal parts of dread and hope thrummed through her. Because, despite every protest she made with Diego close, the knot in her stomach about her pregnancy relented just a little.

"Why do you think I've moved here?" His mouth twitched. "Have you noticed your brilliance deserts you when I'm around?"

"There's nothing new about that, is there?" She sighed. Really, it was better to accept it than fight it. "For every inch you move closer it's like my IQ drops a few points.

My brain works *sooo* much better with a continent separating us."

He took a step closer and she could smell the scent of his soap and skin combined. Her heart raced. She made a *ca-ching* sound. "Down five points."

His gaze alight with laughter, he ate up a little more of the space between them. She felt the heat of his body tease her skin, tug lower in her belly.

She made another sound with her mouth. Only it emerged croaky and faint this time. "Down five more."

He neared her, tugged at her wrap, which was trailing toward the ground, and tucked it neatly around her bare shoulders. Encompassed by his wide frame, she felt the world around her fall away. His fingers grazed her nape in the barest of touches and lingered. Need rippled across her, every inch of her hyper-sensitive to his nearness.

She wet her lips. "Annndddd...I'll probably spell my own name wrong if you ask me now."

Throwing back his head, he laughed. It was such a heart-felt sound that she couldn't help but smile, too. And marvel at the breathtaking beauty of the man. She felt the most atavistic thrill, like a cavewoman—the very thing she had accused him of being—that he was choosing to spend the evening with her.

He moved away from her, his mouth still curved. "We want you functioning with your normal brilliance tonight, right?"

She should be glad he had some kind of control, because apparently she had none when it came to him. Swallowing her body's frustrated groan, she looked away from him. "Have you really moved to New York?"

He studied her with a lingering intensity. The laughter waned from his face. "Aah...you thought I wasn't coming back."

"I went by your past record." She gave voice to the

thought that wouldn't leave her alone. "Of course I forgot that this time you have something precious to come back for."

He closed his eyes for an infinitesimal moment, his posture throwing off angry energy. When he spoke, his gaze was flat, his voice soft with suppressed emotions. "Are you accusing me of something, *pequena?*"

She shook her head. She was too much of a coward to hear what she already knew—that she hadn't mattered enough for him to come after her six years ago.

With his hand at her back, he nudged her toward the waiting limo.

She settled into the seat, scrambling to get her wits together. Acknowledging that her common sense went on a hike when he was close was something; mooning over him was another. She crossed her legs. Her dress rode up to her thighs and she tugged the fabric down, heat tightening her cheeks. Watching her like a vulture, Diego didn't miss anything. She pulled her wrap tighter and sat straight, like a rigid statue.

One glance in the tinted windows was enough to throw her further equilibrium.

She was due for a haircut, which meant her hair didn't have the blunt look she preferred but curled around her face in that annoying way. And she hadn't had the strength, for once, to straighten it to its usual glossy look. She had applied a little foundation and her usual lip gloss. But she looked pale after another sleepless night. She plumped her hair with her fingers on one side, so that a curl covered it.

She fidgeted in her seat and pulled the edges of her wrap together. *Again.* She should have changed, even if it had meant she would be late. Because the dress just...*clung* too much. The fabric cupped her breasts tight. One could probably even make out the shape of her...

Damn it. Nothing about the evening felt right.

Diego's attention didn't waver from her for a second.

She looked at him and uttered the first thing that came into her head. "Do I look okay?"

"Excuse me?"

"It's a simple question, Diego."

"Really? I didn't think you needed assurance in any walk of life."

"Well, you're wrong. I have lots of moments where I think I might just break," she said, with a catch she couldn't hide, "and this pregnancy is bringing out the worst in every way possible—mood swings, nausea. And you're not making it easy by..."

He pulled her hand into his and squeezed. His touch anchored her—a small but infinitely comforting gesture. "Tell me how I can help."

"For starters you can tell me—" she sucked in a deep breath "—how I look."

His gaze flicked to her, roguish amusement glinting in it. "Okay. Take off that wrap."

Her mouth clamped shut, Kim sat rigid, her hands fisted in her lap.

"Do you want my opinion or not?"

"Yes."

He grabbed the edge of her cashmere wrap and pulled it.

His gaze traveled over her slowly, methodically, from her hair to her shoulders, left bare by the strapless beige silk dress which hugged every curve. She sucked in her breath as it hovered over her midriff.

It felt like forever before it moved to her bare legs and her feet clad in Prada pumps.

He cleared his throat. "You look *different*," he finally said.

Of course he was going to squeeze the moment for everything. "What kind of different?"

Amusement glinted in his gaze. "Are you fishing for a compliment, *minha esposinha?*"

"Maybe... And stop calling me your wife." She smoothed her hands over her thighs. The soft, lush silk only heightened her anxiety. "This is not me. I much prefer—"

"Conservatively cut clothes that say 'look at my brain, not at my breasts.'"

Did he miss *anything?* "I have to present the right image, work harder than a man for the same level of respect. Not everyone in the business world is as forthcoming as you are with their confidence in my capabilities—much less their...money..." she finished slowly, realizing how much truth there was in her words.

She knew firsthand how ruthless a businessman he was, that the only allowances he made were for hard work. He might have invested in her company in the most twisted way possible, but he hadn't had to. If he'd truly wanted to leave her with no options he could have really let it all go down the drain...

"Thank you for your investment—for your trust in me," she said, trying to breathe past the tightness in her chest.

He shrugged. "Only a fool would doubt your company's success, or your ability to run it whatever your personal life." His gaze moved over her again quickly. "Although I have to tell you it doesn't really work."

She blinked, her skin tingling at his appraisal. "What doesn't?"

He smiled, apparently finding her stupidity very amusing. "Whatever you wear—even those trousers and shirts that you are so fond of—it doesn't hide the fact that you're hot."

Something latent uncoiled in his gaze—a spark—but was gone before the meaning of his words even sank in. How did he do that? How was he so effortlessly able to look at her with so much desire in his eyes and in the next bank it down to nothing?

She stared at his dark head as he powered up his tablet.

She had thought nothing had changed in him in six years. She was wrong. A lot had—and not just his success.

The man she had married had been a passionate twenty-one-year-old, quick to anger and to love. His emotions had simmered on the surface almost like a glow, a blaze of un-diluted energy that lured everyone toward him.

His drive to succeed, his determination to squash any-thing that lay in his way—she had understood *that* ambi-tion. But this new, refined man…he had a disconcerting calm, a control to him, that gave no clue as to what was simmering beneath the surface. Unless he told her with that piercing honesty.

She had expected him to question her about the preg-nancy. He hadn't. She had expected him to walk away with-out a backward glance. He hadn't. And on top of that he was really here, in New York. Because he wanted to give their marriage a real try.

She couldn't get the measure of him because everything she had taken for granted before was now hidden beneath a veneer of sophisticated charm, of polite courtesy.

But she knew the man beneath it, and she didn't buy that façade for a second. If she lowered her guard, if she let him into her life any more than she absolutely had to, she had a feeling he would only strike again. And this time she wouldn't be able to walk away unscathed.

A scowl on his face, he flicked the tablet off. He leaned forward in a sudden movement, his jaw tight. "So, why the change in how you dress?"

She had a feeling he'd meant to say something else—as if he was working to control himself first. "It's a friend's design. I agreed to do her a favor and wear it tonight. Except she tricked me and didn't deliver it until an hour ago. She knew I wouldn't—"

"You wouldn't wear it otherwise? Smart woman," he said. "She knows that the only way to get you to do something for others is to trick you or to manipulate you."

His words pricked her with quiet efficiency. "Is this what you mean by creating a happy environment to raise a kid? Throwing continuous barbs at me? Because I've seen that marriage. I'm a product of that marriage. And, believe me, it only screws up the kids."

She leaned back against the seat, feeling as fragile as a piece of glass. How stupid had she been to believe even for a moment that there could be truce between them? Six years of separation wasn't enough to thaw this anger between them. Or the attraction, for that matter.

"I had…I *have* every intention of making this work."

His words weren't bereft of emotion now. On the contrary, they vibrated with a dark intensity that gave her goosebumps.

"Except you make it so hard to be civilized with you."

"What are you talking about?"

He raised the tablet toward her. "I just watched the coverage of your press statement."

"And?"

"You left out the most important part. *Again.*"

"I don't know what you're talking about. My statement was concise. I followed the details of the investment contract, just as your legal team dictated, and I stopped it from downgrading into Twenty Questions about my personal life."

"Your personal life," he said softly, "is not just yours anymore."

She waited for him to elaborate. Unknown dread pooled in her gut.

The limo came to a stop in front of the plush New York

Plaza Hotel, where the awards ceremony was being held. She could hear the hushed roar of the crowd outside.

Before she could blink he opened a small velvet box.

Drawing a painful breath, she tucked herself farther into her seat, her heart pounding behind her ribcage. He'd done this on purpose—waited until the last minute.

The diamond twinkled in the dark, every cut and glitter of it breathtaking in its princess setting. There was an accompanying band of white gold, exquisitely simple in contrast to the glittering diamond.

Alarm twisted her stomach into a knot. That simple band might very well be an invisible shackle, binding her to him. And it could unlock every impossible hope, every dangerous dream she had so ruthlessly squashed to survive. "I don't want to wear it. I don't know what you think this achieves…"

Her words faltered as he gently tugged her hand into his and slipped the rings on her finger. They were cold, heavy against her skin, yet she felt branded.

"It puts a stop to the dirty speculation about you…about my child."

"What does it matter what the world thinks?"

"Do you know when the first time my mother took me to see my father was?"

Every other thought fled her mind. She just stared at him. She knew he didn't like talking about his childhood. And she hadn't pushed him six years ago.

"I was six. We stood outside his house for three hours before he even met with us. Then she took me again when I was seven. Every year she would drag me to his doorstep, hoping this time he would accept me as his son. I grew up hearing the neighborhood's taunts—*bastard* and so much more. She wanted a different life for me, a better one, but I never cared. I didn't think he owed me anything. Until she ended up in the hospital."

A cloud of dark anger surrounded him in proportion to the incredible cruelty of his father's treatment. A knot twisted in her own gut. Could she blame him for how much he had hated his father? Because she knew, firsthand, what a parent's negligence, even indifference, could do to a child. "How old were you?"

He blinked as though suddenly realizing she was there. "Sixteen. Her body was weakened by years and years of hard labor and not enough food. I couldn't pay for her treatment, and she'd made me promise I wouldn't go back to the street gangs. So I went to see him. By myself for the first time."

Her gut churned, the subdued violence in him raising the hairs on her neck. Sixteen years old—he had been nothing but a child himself. Suddenly she had a feeling where this was going. She understood what had angered him so much. Guilt spiraled through her.

"I went to the offices of his construction company. I begged him to pay for her treatment. I told him I would work for him for the rest of my life. He had his bodyguard drag me by my collar and throw me out. She died that night. And I swore I would take everything from him. I didn't stop until I destroyed him."

"Diego, how would I—?"

"There is very little I have asked of you or will ever ask of you. But when it comes to our child I won't settle. I will never be that boy who was denied his rights ever again." He shrugged—a casual movement, in complete control of himself. "I want my child to be recognized as mine. You had the perfect chance to do that at your press statement. You didn't. So now we will do it my way."

Diego let his fingers linger around Kim's as she stepped out of the limo and joined him on the red carpet in front of the New York Plaza.

He felt her fingers stiffen in his, her body already taut as a tightly wound spring.

For a minute everything around him, all the ruckus, faded away as he let himself indulge in the gloriously sensuous figure she made by his side.

The cream-colored dress drew a straight line, covering her breasts, but it was the sexiest sight he had ever seen. His fingers fanned out of their own volition over her back. The cut of the dress was such that it didn't begin again until the upper curve of her buttock.

Everything in him that was barely restrained roared at the silky feel of her skin.

Desire was a hard knot in his belly, messing with his thinking. As it had been in the limo. It was hard enough to resist her when she dressed in trousers and jackets, even though they didn't hide the sensuality of the woman beneath.

At least *he* had never been able to buy into the frosty business façade. Maybe because he knew the passion that lurked beneath her composed, perfect exterior.

But dressed as she was now, every curve and dip delineated so sexily, her long legs in those heels… He had a better chance of stopping breathing than controlling his hunger for her.

Her wrap slipped and a creamy shoulder glistened in the camera flashlights. A simple chain with a teardrop diamond pendant glittered at the juncture of her breasts. He swallowed, heat flexing in his muscles, pumping him for action, and pulled his gaze away.

A roar erupted around them as they turned together and mounted the carpeted steps. Flashes exploded in their faces, a frenzy of questions in the air around them.

Her press statement about a new investor for her company, against all the odds, had been sensational enough. The fact that it was him hadn't gone unnoticed by the media.

But of course she hadn't answered their questions. Which meant the task was left to him. More fool him that he had believed even for a minute she would do the right thing. That she would give him what he deserved without him having to fight for it.

It was good that he'd fought his whole life for every little thing—from the roof over his head, to every single morsel of food.

He had fought for his mother, he had fought for himself, and now he would fight for his unborn child.

He tightened his grip around Kim as she faltered, her mouth stiff with the smile she'd pasted on, her chin tilted high. It was but a momentary fracture in her perfection, not noticed by anyone but him.

The media were like bloodhounds after her, rejoicing in even a little crack in the pedestal of perfection that Kimberly Stanton stood on.

Nothing would give him more satisfaction than fracturing that pedestal, breaking the woman, so that all of her was undone at his hands. Except it would require a price from him, too, a piece of his soul, and he was damned if he'd let her take anything more from him.

"Ms. Stanton, is it true that you were still married when you were engaged to your twin's husband?"

"Who is the father of your child?"

"Are you seeing Mr. Pereira now?"

Diego heard her startled gasp amidst the rumble and forced her to stop beside him. Had she not expected this? Had she no idea how hungry the media was for a story—*any story*—about her?

He leaned over the thick rope that contained the press, toward the microphones thrust into his face. "It is Mrs. Pereira," he said, and paused, waiting for his words to sink in. He turned toward Kim and smiled. He bent and kissed her cheek. The shock in her gaze was visible only to him.

The softness of her skin burned an imprint on his mouth and he turned toward the flashing cameras again. "And we're very happy to begin our life together again, with our baby on the way."

The crowd went ballistic. He hadn't expected any less.

"You guys are married?"

"Reunited after six years."

He pulled her tighter toward him, every action hungrily raked over by the crowd. She felt like a ticking bomb that could go off at any minute.

"My wife realized her mistake and came back to me on the eve of her wedding."

"You are happy to be together?"

"Incredibly happy," he said, tongue in cheek. "Like we've never been apart."

Kim turned to him, her face devoid of any color. "You bastard," she hissed at him.

He deftly pulled her away from the uproar his statement had caused, dark satisfaction heating his blood. His arms around her slender waist were literally keeping her upright as he and his wife climbed the stairs.

An incredible high buzzed through his veins. Possessive triumph sang in his blood.

His wife.

He had waited for this moment for a long time. To be able to shout to the world that Kim was his wife and have her accept it.

The fact that he had arrived at it through foul means and six years late didn't diminish his victory one bit.

He'd learned a long time ago that playing fair would give him nothing but a bruised body and a broken heart.

CHAPTER FIVE

IT WAS THE worst evening of Kim's life.

It shouldn't have been.

The awards ceremony was being held in the huge banquet hall at the Plaza, the food was delicious and she was rubbing shoulders with great business minds.

Yet in between avoiding Liv's curious gaze, fielding congratulations from her peers, which were *not* over her being chosen for the prestigious award, Kim had never wanted to escape more.

She had realized two minutes after they had walked in that Diego's infuriating statement to the press had given new meaning to the term fairy-tale ending. It wasn't enough that the incredible mockery of his statement—something she would have cherished in an alternative life—haunted her, pricked her.

With the news of his two-million-dollar investment in her company coupled with his revelation that he was the father of her child *and* that they were married, he'd suddenly become her knight in shining armor.

No matter that the same crowd—the same media—had called him a monster just days ago, for his predatory tactics when it came to new businesses, for the way he had recently used a man's gambling losses to take ownership of an island off of Brazil's coast. An ecological paradise, no less, which he was allegedly going to mine and destroy for its precious metals.

Her mouth hurt from the contented smile she forced to her lips as more people congratulated her for the fact that she had landed on her feet with Diego.

She didn't know what infuriated her more—Diego's charming smiles and the intimate glances he threw her way in the face of everyone's prurient curiosity about them, or the educated crowd's insulting joy that she finally had her act together.

As if Diego's very presence in her life could somehow make her brain work better. She laughed at the irony of it.

By the time the awards presentation was over and her speech delivered—which had left a sour taste in her mouth—all she wanted was to escape the crowd, sink into her marble bathtub and lose her mind in a crossword puzzle.

But her torment was nowhere near over yet.

His grip on her wrist unyielding, Diego pulled her onto the dance floor. His hands around her waist, he enveloped her in a hard wall of heat until he filled her vision and the invigorating scent of him was all she could breathe.

He had held her at arm's length ever since she had blurted out the news of her pregnancy. The sudden intimacy of his embrace now toppled her equilibrium, and her flesh sighed against his hardness.

Her skin tingled when his callused fingers moved over her back at images and sensations she'd rather not remember: the feel of those calluses on the sensitive skin of her thighs, the muscles in his back bunching under her fingers... Her body reveled in the memories his nearness evoked.

She sucked in a sharp breath, willing herself not to melt into his arms, not to enjoy it so much. Because all this was for show. He was playing to the media, leaving no doubt in anyone's mind about them, leaving her no way out.

At least no way out with her life still intact.

He studied her, curious amusement playing on his mouth. "You're not enjoying the evening?"

She pulled her head back and glared at him. "I've never been more disappointed in my entire life. I'm the same person with the same faculties I had yesterday. And yet *you* get lauded for sweeping me off my feet."

A smile curved his lush mouth, and infuriated her further.

"You weren't this upset even when I trapped you at the island."

"I don't like being thought an incompetent idiot," she said, gritting her teeth.

His mouth narrowed with displeasure. "You mean you don't like even the *illusion* that you're in love? You have your investment, your company's reputation is intact and you have my total support with the pregnancy. I don't see what's bothering you so much."

Put like that, she sounded the very epitome of selfishness. But she couldn't quiet the increasing panic that things were slowly but surely slipping out of her control. That Diego was stripping away everything she needed to survive. Whatever his intentions, the truth was that he would bring her down to her knees, plunge her into the same whirlpool of crippling hope, if she wasn't on guard.

"There's no need for this pretense that we're living a happily-ever-after. As if this is *Romeo and Juliet Reunited*."

"No? Have you thought of how this might have affected your sister and her life? Being continually mobbed by the media speculating on how she felt about her sister carrying her husband's child?"

Her mouth fell open. "Liv always knew the truth."

"Does it mean it doesn't bother her? Hurt her? Cast a dirty shadow on her marriage? What about Alexander King? You went straight to him for help, and you claim guilt for having deceived him, but did you think for a minute what this twisted speculation might do to him? Do you care that you've asked them to pay a high price just because it raises your hackles to be tied to me?

Shame flooded her within, and her gaze wavered away from him. God, every word out of his mouth was true. She had been avoiding Liv, worried she would know that Kim was barely keeping it together.

"Did you give a moment's thought to me? Or have you, in your usual selfish fashion, neglected to think of anyone else but you?"

"How would I know how you felt about this? Until a couple of hours ago I didn't know how cruelly your father had treated you, or how your mother died. You never told me anything. Once we were off that ship you kept me in a bubble, as if…" She met his gaze, the disbelief spiking there halting her words.

But would she have behaved differently even if she had known?

He frowned, and she had a feeling he was thinking the same.

"The truth is that it scrapes at you that you're not able to reduce this pregnancy and my involvement in it into something tangible." Frustration glimmered in his gaze. "Anything that makes an average woman happy breaks *you* out in hives."

"Your fault if you thought me average."

"No, I didn't think you average—or this warped either. You cover it all up with your perfection."

She mocked a pout, her heart crawling into her throat. Only Diego could reach the horrific truth with a few careless words. The muscles in her face hurt with the effort to keep the smile intact, even though inside everything had crumbled under his attack.

But she couldn't let him or their marriage mean anything

to her. He had already proved her worst fear true once. If she let her guard down, if she let herself care, she would just break this time. "Does that mean you don't want a perfect wife anymore?"

His fingers tightened over her hipbones, a fierce scowl bunching his forehead. "You're the one obsessed with perfection. Not me. And I never wanted a perfect wife either."

"You mean *now?*"

"What?"

"Now that you've achieved all this status, this wealth, now that you've proved yourself to your father and the whole world, you don't need a trophy wife for an accessory *now*. Not like you did six years ago."

His hand stole up her back, his fingers curling possessively around her nape. Her skin seared as though branded. The entire world around them fell away in that moment. As did the veneer of his sophistication. A curse fell from his lips and she colored. Even her little grasp of Portuguese was enough for her to understand.

"You don't want to wear my ring. You didn't want to acknowledge the baby as mine. However much I want to give this marriage a try, you're determined to make this warfare. Maybe working sixteen-hour days with no social life is beginning to fry your brain and corrupt your memories."

He whispered in her ear. It was a low growl, every word pulsing with the slow burn of his anger.

"Because I was not the one that walked away. You knew when you married me what I came from. When we got off the cruise, when the dirty reality of my roots, my life, began to creep in, you didn't want me anymore. So don't you *dare* blame me for the past."

Diego set Kim away from him, his muscles pumping with furious energy. He needed to walk away right that moment, before he did something stupid.

Like kissing her senseless or driving his fist into the nearest wall.

This was the woman who had looked back at him calmly after he'd slept with her and then discarded her as if she was garbage. This was the woman who had then quietly slunk back to her life, to her waiting fiancé, calmly dismissed any thought of him and gone on with her life.

Nothing touched her—not the fact that he was back, not the fact that she was carrying his child. How many times did he need to learn the same lesson?

How *dared* she place the blame for their failed marriage at his feet?

And yet he could swear he had seen sadness lurking in her eyes as she had called herself a trophy wife, felt her shiver as if her words were leaching out the warmth.

He was about to walk out of the hall, away from the crowd, when someone tapped him on the shoulder. He turned around, his control razor-thin.

Beautiful brown eyes—open, smiling, similar to Kim's and yet so different—greeted him. *Olivia King.*

She wore a red knee-length dress. A ruby pendant hung at her neck. Where Kim's hair was cut into a sophisticated blunt style, Olivia's hair was long and curly and wild. There was nothing drastically different from the way Kim was dressed, especially tonight in a dress uncharacteristic of her. And there was the same sensuous vitality to Olivia that was muted but so much more appealing in Kim.

"Hello, Diego," she said, with very little hesitation in her expression.

He raised a brow at her familiarity. She waved a hand at him and moved closer. The gesture, her very movement, lacked the grace and the innate poise he expected from that face. It stunned him into a moment's silence.

"Sorry to be crowding you on the dance floor like this, but I have to take my chance now. You're the father of my niece or nephew—" a smile split her mouth "—and I only have a few moments before Alexander chews my head off for butting in."

His anger thawing, Diego took the hand she offered boldly.

Where Kim wore her sophistication, her brilliance, like an armor that no one could pierce, Olivia's irreverence, her open smile, was the pull. Her emotions were right there in her smiling gaze.

A man wouldn't look into those eyes and wonder if she was his salvation or his purgatory. He wouldn't have to spend a lifetime wondering if he was banging his head against a rock.

They looked exactly the same and yet were so different. He found it highly disconcerting and illuminating. Because he didn't feel the least bit of attraction toward her.

He frowned. "A chance at what, Mrs. King?"

Her gaze twinkled. "Call me Liv. My chance to talk to you. Everyone's talking about your statement to the press, and Kim hasn't been very…forthcoming about you."

"No?" Just like that his ire rose again. "Let's just say I'm your perfect sister's dirty little secret."

His gaze sought the woman in question and found her immediately. Kim was standing at a table, talking to Alexander.

They were peas in a pod, those two. So similar in everything. And yet Alexander King had walked away from Kim, entrenched himself in scandal for Olivia.

"Which you've made sure is not a secret or dirty anymore," Olivia said, with the initial warmth fleeing from her words.

He flicked his gaze back to her. "Waiting for your sister to do the right thing was a futile exercise."

A little frown appeared in her brow. "My sister…" She

hesitated, as though choosing her words carefully. "She's always kept her feelings and her fears to herself."

"You mean she *has* any under that brilliance?"

Her brow furrowing, Olivia continued, "Kim always had to be the strong one—for my mother and for me. It was the only way to survive—the only way she could protect me."

"From whom?" he said, before he could stop himself. He rubbed his nape, feeling tension curl into his muscles. Damn his wife and his ever-spiraling curiosity about her. "You know what? All I care about is that she does the right thing by my child."

He couldn't keep his resentment out of his words.

Olivia nodded. "Look, all I wanted to say was that I'm glad you and Kim are working things out."

"Do you know, if looks could kill, I would have died a few times from your husband's wrath in the past few minutes?"

She glanced to where they stood—her husband and his wife. "Please ignore Alexander." She bent toward him, and though she stood at a perfectly respectable distance to someone standing on the other side of the room, it looked as though she was too close to Diego. "He's a bit possessive when it comes to me."

She had sidled closer to him just to get a rise out of her husband. On cue, the frown on the other man's brow deepened across the banquet hall. Diego smiled despite everything. "He doesn't like me very much."

She smiled. "My husband has a very rigid sense of right and wrong."

"*Really?* And yet he carried on with you while pretending to be married to her? Traded her for you without a moment's—?"

Her gaze flashed with anger. "Alexander and Kim—what they shared was not a real relationship. Even before she knew about us, after her time with you on the island, she broke it off with him. I mean, they never even—"

Kim had broken it off with Alexander? When? He felt as though he'd had his breath knocked out of him. "Never even what, Olivia?"

Olivia's look was more calculated now, gauging if he was trustworthy. "Did you mean what you said to the press? About a new beginning with Kim?"

"Yes."

"Alexander and Kim never had a physical relationship."

Diego felt as if a curtain was falling away from his eyes. Primal satisfaction filled his veins even as he wondered why his perfect wife would hide something like that from him. Especially when he had accused her of being unemotional and unaffected by how easily she had gone back to Alexander.

But of course Kim offered nothing of herself. Truth or anything else. Frustration erupted through him.

True, he had given her the perfect reason to believe him the enemy. And that had to change if their marriage had a chance of being anything but a battleground.

He looked up at Olivia just as she stiffened next to him. Within seconds the color fled from her animated face and her gaze was stricken with fear. Diego turned to see where her gaze was trained.

Their father, Jeremiah Stanton, was shaking hands with someone.

His gaze instantly zeroing on his wife, Alexander cut his way across the crowd toward them, his stride purposeful.

Even Diego felt a flash of anxiety at the fear that filled Olivia's eyes. "Olivia? Are you all right?"

She glanced up at him, her gaze glittering with pain. "Sorry. Old habits die hard." She bent toward him, the very picture of anxiety. "You have to find Kim immediately— okay?"

"What are you talking about?"

"My father," she said, glancing at him and turning away quickly. "I know his wrath when he's displeased better than anyone. He won't like what the media's been saying about her."

"I don't either."

"You don't understand. He will rip into her for this. Whatever issues you have with her, tonight just…just take care of her."

Her muscles quivering, Kim paced the quiet corner of the banquet hall.

Every inch of her wanted to confront Diego, challenge every arrogant word he had uttered about six years ago. She could take anything he tossed at her—his tactics to control her company, his manipulations. But she couldn't stand his latest accusations. His background had never bothered her—not then, not now. As if she had *ever* assumed that she was better than him, as if she hadn't given it *everything* she had in her—until he had turned her into his prize trophy.

She turned toward the banquet hall, determined to have it out with him right there. And then she saw her father at the edge of the crowd, walking toward her, wearing the fiercest scowl she had ever seen.

With her father being out of country for the past month she had almost forgotten about him. They hadn't had their twice-weekly lunch, and of course he had only flown in today. Which meant this was the first he'd be hearing about everything.

She smiled as he neared her, a feeling of failure threading through her. She ran a hand over her stomach, unable to stop herself. Anger fell off him in dark waves. Which wasn't unusual—except before it had always been targeted at Liv.

She bent her cheek toward him as she always did, but he

didn't kiss it. Straightening up, she met his gaze. The fury pulsing in it curled into dread in her stomach.

"Have you lost your goddamned mind, Kimberly?" His words were low and yet his wrath was a tangible thing around them. "I'm gone for a month and not only have you screwed up your life, but your company too?"

She drew a sharp breath in. "Dad, I understand how awful this must sound to you, but I'm trying my best to control the damage. I'm so sorry you had to hear about it like this."

"Are you? Wherever I turn I'm smacked in the face with news that both my daughters are indiscriminate…" His gaze flicked to her. "Are you really no better than Olivia?"

She shook her head, hating the disappointment in his words. "For the last time—Liv did nothing wrong. And, yes, I know that I've messed up, but the truth is that I—".

"Unless you can tell me that everything I've heard so far is false there's nothing you can say."

His gaze flayed her, eroding her already thin composure.

"You run away from your wedding, you get yourself pregnant by God-knows-who… After everything I taught you you've proved that you're no better than the trash your mother was. These are *not* the actions of the daughter I raised—the daughter I've always been proud of."

Her heart sinking to her feet, Kim clutched at his hands. She was *not* like her mother. She was *not* weak. "He's not just someone I picked up, Dad," she said, for the first time acknowledging that very fact to herself, too. She had walked away from the hurt Diego had caused her six years ago, given up on a foolish dream, but it didn't mean she was impervious to his sudden reappearance in her life.

"Is it true, then?"

"What?"

"You married him six years ago? He's the father of your…*child?*"

She nodded. "Diego is the baby's father. And, yes, our marriage is valid."

"Then you'd better work it out with him and clean up this mess. The last thing I want is a bastard grandchild."

She flinched at his cutting words. "I will, Dad. I promise. Will I see you—?"

He shook his head, his denial absolute. "Don't call me until you've kept yourself out of the news for a while. And if you can't clean it up you're just as dead to me as your sister is."

Nodding, Kim sagged against the wall as he walked away without a backward glance. She exhaled a long breath, tears prickling behind her eyes. It had to be the damned hormones again. Because her father's reaction should not be a surprise. She had seen it enough times with Liv.

She had let so many people down recently—Liv, Alex, her father *and* herself. Apparently Diego was the only one who didn't care about the consequences. She turned her head and saw him standing there, watching her father go, rage mirrored in his golden gaze.

Diego couldn't believe his own eyes. His ears rang with those softly delivered yet harsh words. It was nothing a father should ever say to his child, and Diego himself had had more than his share of nasty words from his own father.

His temper frayed to the edge. Every inch of him wanted to turn around, find Jeremiah Stanton and pound his fists into the older man.

In another lifetime he wouldn't have given it another thought. He would have worked through his fury the only way he knew how. But he was not that man anymore. He had promised his mother that he would remove the violence that had been part of his life for so long as a member of a street gang.

Even though keeping his promise was the hardest thing at moments like this.

Kim looked frazzled. Her dress had more color than her face. He wrapped a hand around her shoulders and the shocking thing was that she let him. He felt her shiver and a curse fell from his lips. "Are you okay?"

Her brown eyes drank him in silently. The very absence of hurt in them jarred through him. "I'm perfectly fine."

"You were apologizing to him while he uttered the foulest words and yet you flay me for lesser sins?"

He felt her smile against his arm. Holding her like this was pure torture but he couldn't let go.

"That's just the way my father is."

He reared back, frowning. "He laid into you in the middle of a crowd. For what? Because you slept with me? Because you're pregnant? Because you let your control slip for one night? You're twenty-five, you're the CEO of your own company." He frowned as another thought came bursting in. "Are you saying he's always been like this?"

"Yes, but it was usually aimed at my mother and then Liv."

His breath left him in a sharp hiss. "But not you? Ever?"

"I never gave him the chance—never let him find fault with me. I did everything he asked me to and I excelled at it."

"So you're not upset?" he said, disbelief ringing through him.

"I'm upset that I gave him any reason. But you already know that I regret my actions four weeks ago."

"You're *defending* him?"

"My father is responsible for all the success I have achieved. If he hadn't continually pushed me, I would have—I would *be*—nothing. This is his way of warning me to not let it all go down the drain."

"You make one mistake—*if* it can be called that—and he tears you apart? Don't you see—?"

"You're reading too much into this, Diego."

Her mouth was a study in resignation that mocked his anger.

"I've always known that his approval comes with conditions."

"I saw fear in Olivia's eyes. Are you saying he didn't put it there?"

She glanced past him, her gaze riddled with anxiety. "Yes, he did," she said. "Do you know where she is?"

Fisting his hands, Diego reined in another curse. She wasn't upset for herself but for her twin. "Alexander's with her."

"I always tried my best to protect Liv," she said, with a hint of pleading in her tone, as if she needed to explain herself. "The only way to do that was to play peacekeeper by not giving him any more reason to lose it."

Why was it her job to protect Olivia? He kept those words to himself through sheer will. "So of course you had to become everything perfect?"

"Why do you say that like it's a—" she glared at him "—curse? How is he any different from you?"

"Your father is a bully of the worst sort," he said through gritted teeth. "I fought in street-gangs, yes, but I used my fists for survival. If that's what you think about me—"

"No. I didn't mean that you're a bully." She looked at him, her expression pleading. "I meant he's no different from anyone else in his expectations of me. He's just upfront about it. My accomplishments, my capabilities, are the things that draw people to me. Nothing else..." She swallowed, as if she found it hard to speak the words. "It's why you married me six years ago, it's why Alex picked me for his wife and it's what my father's approval of me is based on."

There it was again—that accusation. As though he hadn't...

She swayed and he caught her, questions tumbling through his head.

His throat felt raw at her matter-of-fact admission. But buried beneath it there had been... *hurt.* Her attachment to her company, her isolated lifestyle... Suddenly his perspective shifted, as though he had been looking at her until now through a dirtied window.

"I think I've had enough excitement for the night," she said softly, puncturing his thoughts. Her fingers clasped his arm. "Can we leave?"

He nodded and guided her toward the exit, his palm staying on her back. He couldn't tear his gaze from her, however.

She looked breathtakingly beautiful, every curve and dip of her sexy body outlined in that damned dress, every step she took grace embodied.

Whether it was her disconcerting statement, or the weary look in her eyes, he didn't see the aggravatingly prickly woman she had become.

Instead she reminded him of the night he had met her, on the cruise ship six years ago. The memory stole through him like an insidious drug, catching him unawares.

She had been standing alone on the deck, away from the rest of the crowd. Wind had been whipping her hair; her green knee-length dress had been molded against her slender figure.

None of the usual festivities that attracted a nineteen-year-old—dancing or drinking—had grabbed her interest. She had looked utterly alone, heart-wrenchingly alluring, driving every dormant instinct of his to the surface. He had observed her for over an hour before he had approached her.

They had done no more than exchange their names that night, but he had spent over two hours teasing a smile from her. And when she had smiled he had found the most thrilling, satisfying joy in it. He had felt on top of the world.

That was how she looked now.

Infinitely fragile and unraveled, as if the tiniest pressure might splinter her perfection apart. She *was* hurt by her father's outbursts, though for the wrong reasons.

That flash of vulnerability shredded the anger and scorn with which he had covered up his desire. He had only deceived himself that it was all gone. Need and something more sinuous glided through his veins.

He wanted to grab her by those dainty shoulders and shake her until she realized she didn't need her father's approval, conditional or otherwise. He wanted to kiss her just as much as he wanted to provoke her, until her beautiful eyes sparkled with that infuriating combination of logic and desire. But he couldn't—not if he wanted to keep his sanity intact.

He couldn't fight the feeling that he knew very little about the woman he had married six years ago. Her statement that what she'd represented to him was the reason why he had wanted her pricked like a thorn in his side.

What if there was more to why she had left him? Was he culpable too? And, if he was, why didn't the aggravating woman call him on it?

CHAPTER SIX

K IM SLID FROM the luxurious bed in Diego's spare bedroom—
or one of the *six* spare bedrooms. She cast a glance toward
the digital alarm clock on the nightstand. It was only five
minutes past seven.

Diego's housekeeper, Anna, had mentioned a pool out
on the terrace. She needed to burn off some of her restless energy.

Walking into the closet, which was the size of her living
room, she searched for her swimsuit. By the time Kim had
returned from work the day after she had moved in, Anna
had unpacked everything for her.

Spotting the trendy one-piece she had bought recently,
Kim tugged off her pajamas and tank top.

She knew why she felt so restless. Coordinating her
move into Diego's penthouse to be when he was out of the
country had felt like the best idea. Except now she couldn't
dwell on anything else.

Would he be pleased? What if he had changed his mind?
She had been on tenterhooks for days after the awards ceremony, waiting for him to manipulate something, anything,
in order to get her to move.

But he had surprised her with a strangely disappoint-
ing silence.

His words at the awards ceremony wouldn't leave her
alone, though. Neither had she been able to get Liv's face,

when she had waylaid her on the steps of the Plaza, out of her head. Liv had clutched at Kim's hand, concern pinching her mobile mouth.

Her every action, every word, since she had learned of her pregnancy had been directed by the selfish need to protect herself, to make sure she didn't reveal the slightest weakness in front of Diego. She had conveniently pushed Liv away, refused to share anything, uncaring of how worried she might be.

When had she stopped caring about everyone else's feelings along with her own? When had the lines between being strong and selfishness blurred? Would she continue to push Diego away because he was the one man who had the power to hurt her, to drive her to weakness?

Would she do that when she had the child too? Would she put her own well-being first always? Would she put herself before her child as her own mother had done?

The questions had tied her up in knots. So before she lost her nerve and remembered the million reasons why it was a bad idea she had called Anna and informed her she was moving in.

She pulled her robe on and pushed her feet into comfy slippers. It took her a few minutes of walking through the long corridor to reach the lushly carpeted foyer.

She reached the grand salon and sighed. Huge pillars stood in the room, supporting high ceilings. The room could have housed her entire apartment. Pristine white marble floors gleamed beneath her slippered feet, and the glass walls all around offered three-hundred-and-sixty-degree views of midtown Manhattan and the southern end of Central Park.

Contemporary art graced the walls. She smiled as she recognized a couple of artists native to Brazil.

It was the spectacular luxury she had expected from a man with Diego's assets, and yet it was different. There was no ostentation here or anywhere else in the penthouse. Just a quiet, simmering elegance—a flash of bright red here and there, a candid portrait of a street-fighter on the streets of Rio de Janeiro reflecting Diego's passionate nature.

The best feature, however, was that it was so big she needn't ever see Diego unless required.

Feeling a lightness that had been missing for several weeks, she walked through the salon toward the terrace.

She stepped into the covered part of the L-shaped space and a shape emerged from the shadows. She had expected it to be only Anna and her for another night.

A quiet gasp escaping her, she stepped back. A teenager, his bulging biceps inked with elaborate tattoos, one of which looked eerily familiar, met her gaze. Her mouth fell open as he moved toward her and the light from the salon behind her illuminated his face.

The left side of his rugged face was covered in blue and purple bruises. His hair was cropped close to his scalp. A naughty smile split his severely cut mouth, which had blood crusted on it. "You are Diego's wife?"

Between his thick accent and his swollen lip Kim was barely able to understand him. She nodded, a different kind of shiver overtaking her now.

He stepped in front of her when she moved, leaving only just enough space between them. His gaze traveled over her leisurely in a defiant, purposeful scrutiny that she assumed was meant to make her nervous.

With every inch of her headspace taken up by thoughts of Diego, she wasn't.

"I'm Miguel," he said, still sporting that smile, which was just short of lascivious. "If you get...*bored* with Diego..." He finished his sentence with a wink and a subtle thrust of his hips that left no doubt in her mind. "Call me. I will treat you right."

She stood stiffly without blinking. "Nice to meet you,

Miguel," she threw at him, refusing to show how much his presence had spooked her.

She stepped onto the rooftop terrace, her head spinning with questions—which fled her mind at the sight in front of her.

The vast terrace was illuminated with little solar lights lined up against the floor. The rest of the light came from the spectacular skyscrapers of Manhattan around them. The effect was breathtakingly simple and just the peace she wanted.

There was a fire pit with comfy-looking recliners to her left, and a small bar with a glass top. But it was the perimeter of the pool that caught and held her attention.

A hot tub was on one side, with a couple of loungers on the other.

She walked toward the pool like a moth drifting to light—until the splash-splash of long, powerful strokes punctured the silence.

It took her a moment to realize that half the pool stretched past the terrace, overhanging the streets of New York. Her heart thudded like a tribal drumbeat, her gaze searching for the powerful figure in the water.

Not that she needed to see him to know that it was Diego. Only *he* could find swimming in a pool that edged twenty stories into the sky relaxing.

She was about to turn around, ready to flee, when he swam to the edge of the pool facing her and stood.

His wet hair clung to his scalp, outlining the strong angles of his face. Water sluiced enticingly over biceps that flexed while holding him up. His gaze ran over her, sweeping thoroughly from the top of her mussed hair to the opening of her robe and her bare legs. "Is everything okay?"

She folded her arms around her midriff. "Yes, everything's fine. I just…"

"Did you come up for a swim?"

"What? No. I....." She clasped the sash of her robe, moving to the balls of her feet, ready to run.

She sighed. This was her reality now. Seeing Diego in all his glorious forms, apparently counting up her points on his weird reward system for sex. She smiled at the absurdity that she was actually keeping count.

How desperate was she?

"I did come for a swim," she said, trying hard to keep her gaze on his face. And not trail down his wet, sexy body. "But not from my own apartment."

He pushed at the water dripping from his forehead with his hand. His frown grew. "From where, then?"

"Didn't Anna tell you? I moved in when you went to... Well, wherever it is that you went."

Luckily he didn't seem to have noticed the curiosity in her words.

With an agility that was a beauty to watch he pulled himself up in a single movement. And of course he was naked.

She gasped and closed her eyes. But the sight of his chest and midriff, velvet skin rippling over toned muscles, was etched into her mind. A twang shot through to her sex. She squeezed her thighs—which didn't help at all.

The man was knock-your-knees-out-from-under-you sexy. Was it any wonder he'd always been able to scramble her senses as easily as he did?

"You can open your eyes now."

She did.

A white towel was wrapped low on his hips. He walked around the pool, reaching the bar on her right in silence. The muscles in his back moved sinuously as he poured himself a drink and quickly guzzled it down.

A faint hum began thrumming over her skin. Even the thin silk of her robe felt oppressive.

The tattoo on his back, right under his shoulderblades, glimmered under the low lights. A memory rose to the surface, heating her already warm skin. She had traced that ink with her fingers first and then with her tongue, fascinated by the ripple and play of his muscles at her actions.

Six years on she shivered as sensations from that long-forgotten night touched her just as powerfully.

She moved without realizing it to where he stood, and ran a finger over the wing of the eagle.

He jerked, the muscles in his back bunching tight. As if she had touched him with a hot poker. He faced her before she could blink, his scowl fierce.

She jerked her hand back. "That tattoo…" She licked her lips, her cheeks tightening, "That eagle shape… The teenager I just met—he has—"

Suddenly he was so close that she could smell the scent of him, see the evening stubble on his jaw, feel the warmth of his body. His scowl deepened. "Miguel?" He looked back inside. "Did you run into him? Did he say anything wrong to you?"

"Not really," she said, hurrying to reassure him. "I just didn't spot him until he stepped out of the dark. I didn't know anyone else was here, or that you were back."

His frown grew. He moved away from her, his movements edgy. "Anything more?"

She shook her head belatedly.

Heat unfurled in the pit of her stomach as he turned to the side, dropped his towel casually and pulled up a pair of black sweatpants. She caught a glimpse of tight butt and rock-hard thighs.

Her heart raced. The stretchy fabric of her swimsuit was chafing everywhere it touched. She needed that swim even more than before.

He turned around to face her, his expression serious. With his glorious rippling chest close enough to touch, it was hard to focus on his face.

"I'll arrange something else for him. He's already upset

Anna in the few hours he's been here. Probably why she forgot to mention you were here. He won't harm you, but I know how nervous you get around people from that background."

Hurt splintered through her, knocking the breath out of her. Maybe it was because she hadn't been prepared to see him tonight. Maybe it was her hormones again. She glared at him, finding it hard to speak. "Did I say that?" Her words rang in the silence. "I wouldn't even have mentioned him if you weren't flashing that tattoo. I knew this was a bad idea. You might have the best intentions, but you'll never—"

"Wait." His long fingers clasped her wrist and pulled her to him.

She fell into him with a soft thump that made her sigh. Her fingers landed on his chest. The thump-thump of his heart was as loud as her own. He was hard and hot and all she wanted to do was curl into him. Even when he flayed her with his words.

She closed her eyes, lacking the strength not to care about his opinion.

"I didn't mean to upset you." He pulled her chin up and she opened her eyes. His hands on her waist were a languid weight, searing her. "This is our home and I want you to feel safe and be happy here."

Something warm and gooey bloomed inside her chest. She took a deep breath as if she could capture it there. A tingling warmth spread through her—something she remembered from the cruise. For the first time in her life she had felt cherished.

His fingers lingered on her cheek. "The last time our marriage fell apart it was just us." Just as easily he took the warmth away. "This time we have someone else to think of... Do you understand?"

She nodded, swallowing her disappointment. She strove to sound just as casual as he did. "It doesn't bother me. This place is so huge anyway I don't have to even see you if I don't want to, right?" His expression didn't relax. "And... thanks for thinking of me."

He was right. This wasn't about what either of them wanted.

At his quick nod, she grabbed his wrist. The hair on his forearms tickled her fingers. "I appreciate your support since I...since we found out about the—" she needed to stop choking on the word *baby* "—the pregnancy. You've been...great about it, and I...well, I haven't."

His gaze moved to her mouth and lingered. The need to feel his mouth on hers, the need to touch him, rose inside her.

It wasn't the blaze of lust that had driven reason from her head a few weeks ago. Now it was more of a slow, soft burn that always smoldered beneath her skin. It was an insidious longing more dangerous than pure lust.

He extracted his hand from hers as though he couldn't wait to get away. Her heart sinking to her toes, she suddenly realized she wanted his company. Just for a few more minutes. Even if it meant prolonging her own torment.

So she said the first thing that popped into her head. "What happened to Miguel's face?"

He stopped and turned around, surprise flickering in his gaze. Was her interest in the teenager, in what went on in Diego's life, so shocking? *Really,* she wasn't the one with corrupt memories of their short marriage.

"It was his initiation into a street-gang last week. With everything else going on I wasn't able to stop it."

Because he had been dealing with *her.* "He's got the same tattoo as you do. Is it the same street-gang you were a part of?"

For a second the same sensuous memory of that long-ago night flared in his gaze, the pupils turning molten gold. "Yes," he said, in that clipped *whatever* tone of voice.

Turning away from her, he grabbed a white tee shirt and pulled it on. It was a silent version of *show over, move on.*

Something within her rebelled. His calm dismissal was beginning to annoy the hell out of her. Before he could walk away she moved closer to him, effectively blocking him.

"So you got him out of the street-gang?"

"Yes—kicking and screaming."

"He didn't want to come with you?"

He shook his head. "What I forced him to leave behind is the only life he knows. And I need to keep an eye on him. Like I said, he won't harm you. But he's got a grudge against me."

She slid to a lounger and crossed her legs. "Now it all makes sense."

He plunked down on the one next to her. "What do you mean?"

She felt him still and hid a smile. Perverse satisfaction filled her. He wasn't as unaffected by their situation as he made out. "Of course at first I thought it was…you know…the appeal of the *sexy older woman* and all," she said, tongue-in-cheek. She was rewarded by his begrudging grunt. "But now I see it was partly to get back at you. Although I have to admit even with half his face covered in bruises he's quite the looker. He made me a very interesting offer."

He pounced on her like a predator on his prey. One minute they were sitting on two separate loungers, the next he was on hers, his muscular thighs on either side of her, trapping her neatly. His broad shoulders filled up her vision. The very air she breathed was filled with the scent of him.

"You said he didn't say anything." His words were a low growl.

"I meant he didn't say anything threatening."

"What *did* he say to you?"

Diego had been like this with her before, too. And, for

all the time she had spent learning to be self-sufficient, his protective attitude had had her melting like butter under the sun. She smiled, just enjoying the moment. "Stop acting all grouchy caveman over the fact that he talked to me and I will tell you."

Diego closed his eyes, gripped the edge of the lounger and counted to ten. On two he remembered her laughing face. Five—her long, bare, toned legs. On eight the silk robe clinging to her skin, ending several inches above her knees. The luscious picture she made was etched onto his retinas.

Meu Deus, the temptation she presented—walking around his home, making his space her own—was more than he could handle tonight. Even though it was exactly what he had asked her to do.

His trip to Rio de Janeiro, seeing his half brother in the clinic—just a shell remaining of the boy he had once been—it beat down on him like a relentless wave determined to drown him. He knew what to expect, and yet every time the sight of Eduardo kicked him in the gut.

Now he had Miguel to contend with, too. He really couldn't afford to make mistakes in handling the teenager.

And throw in his enticingly sexy wife—parading in a swimsuit, no less—he knew where he would slip up.

He must have truly misplaced his marbles to have suggested that she move in, to think that he could keep his libido in check with her under the same roof.

He would see her in the mornings, all mussed up and unraveled, the way he liked her best. And before he went to bed. The sensuous scent of the woman would be absorbed into every inch of his living space. He hoped his child appreciated the torture he was going through for his or her sake.

"Diego?"

Her voice in front of him was tentative, testing, her fingers on his infinitely tempting. He swallowed a groan. The mischievous note in her voice was gliding like velvet over his skin.

Drawing another bracing breath, he opened his eyes. "Tell me what he said."

"Something about calling him if I ever got bored with you."

"It's not a joke, *gatinha*. Women, like bikes and land, are possessions jealously guarded in that world. Coming onto you is a challenge thrown at *me*."

She frowned, studying him with interest. "But you were from the same background and you never treated me like that. In fact it was the oppo…" Her gaze flickered to him, wary.

Something tightened in his chest. "How *did* I treat you?"

The slender line of her shoulders trembled. "Like I was a princess."

"And yet you…?"

No. He didn't want to turn this into a battle again.

"That was my mother's doing," he said. "Any little good I have in me, she gave it to me. By the time I was ten I had seen how horribly my father treated her, as if life wasn't hard enough for her as a single mother. She would have peeled my hide if I was anything but respectful toward a woman."

Laughter lit up her eyes. "I would have loved to see that."

Her smile wound around him. He couldn't breathe for a second. "And *you*… I could never…"

"What?" She scooted closer and clutched his hands. "Please tell me."

He brought her hand to his mouth and kissed the palm. The scent of her tickled his nostrils. "That cruise… I went on it to amuse Eduardo. You were like this exquisite gift that somehow landed in my lap. That first week I was even afraid to touch you. I was terrified that I would somehow mar you."

She shied her gaze away from him, but not before he saw the incredulous look in her eyes.

"Is that why you took forever to kiss me?" she asked with a laugh.

He didn't buy it. She was struggling under the weight of what he had said. *Why, when she had known how much he had loved her?*

"I mean, I might as well have been wearing a T-shirt that said Take My Virginity that first week."

Laughter barreled out of him. "I don't remember you coming onto me that hard."

"That's not a surprise. Every woman on that cruise ship wanted a bite of the GMM. I had very stiff competition—especially from that hot dancer."

Wasn't *she* full of surprises? "What's GMM?"

A blush dusted her cheeks pink. "Glorious Man Meat."

"Aah...I'm very honored."

"Liv's term. Two minutes after meeting you I finally got what she meant." A naughty smile—a very rare sight—split her mouth. "Though now, what with you all old, out of shape and with this whole daddy-in-the-making thing—" her gaze caressed his body in a swift sweep, belying her words "—I think we can pass the title of GMM on to Miguel," she finished with a dreamy sigh.

The little cat was needling him on purpose. But it was this cheeky, smiling side of her that got to him. He leaned into her and clasped her face with his hands.

Before he could think better of it, he touched his mouth to hers.

The barest of contacts was enough to spread a wildfire of need inside him. With a groan that was torn out of him, he pulled her close and devoured the lushness of her mouth.

Her fingers dug into his arms. She mewled against his

mouth, a sound made deep in her throat that slithered over his skin.

He half dragged her into his lap, his hands spanning her thin waist, seeking and searching the curve of her breasts.

Droga, but she was all soft and warm, the stretchy fabric of her swimsuit no barrier. He closed his hands over her covered breasts, felt the tightened nipples grazing his palms. He rubbed his palms up and down and her mouth opened on a soft moan.

"*Meu Deus,* I touch you and you blow up like TNT..."

He plunged his tongue inside her mouth and licked the inseam. He felt lightheaded with desire, every drop of blood flowing south.

He pressed wet kisses down to her neck—just as the two floodlights on the opposite sides of the terrace came on, drowning them in bright light.

With a gasp, Kim slid off his lap. Her lips were swollen and pink, her hair all mussed up. Their gazes met in silence for a second, before both of them burst out laughing.

"I'm thinking that was Miguel, right?" she said, her smile still in place.

Her taste lingering on his mouth, he nodded. "Sorry."

"No, it's good he stopped us when he did. Of course I *did* earn my kiss, but you don't want to give me too many points."

He raised a brow.

A teasing glint appeared in her eyes. "Remember? Sexual points for good behavior? You kissed me because I moved in, right? Like a dutiful little wife? Or was that just you forgetting your own—?"

He made a quick lunge to catch her, but she was too fast this time. With lithe grace she moved to the other side of the lounger. Her robe half dangled around her elbows, giving him a perfect view of her swimsuit-clad body.

Holding his stomach tight, he sucked in a sharp breath. His wife was hot. There was no other word for it.

Like everything else she wore, the swimsuit was modest, a one-piece in hot pink. But it showcased the swell of her high breasts, the dip of her dainty waist...which would soon be rounded...the slight flare of her hips and long legs that went on forever. The memory of how she had wrapped them around him while he had thrust into her, her tight heat clenching him. He was rock-hard just thinking about it.

Which meant it was time to walk away, however painful the simple act was.

She tied the sash on her robe, stepping back as he reached her. He raised his hands. "Stay and have your swim," he said. "I need to have a talk with Miguel anyway."

She waylaid him again. If she kept touching him like that, one of these days he wasn't going to be able to walk away. "I forgot to ask—how is Eduardo?"

Just hearing his half brother's name felt as if someone had stuck a knife in his side. He stilled, the ball of guilt around his neck threatening to choke the life out of him. He had lived through busted kneecaps, broken bones and so much more, but this clawing, crippling guilt—it was going to gouge him alive from inside out.

"I'm surprised he's not still following you around. He worshipped you."

Every word out of her mouth was true, and every single word dug into his skin like the sharp end of a knife.

"Diego?"

He jerked back from her. "He's in a rehabilitation clinic in Sao Paulo."

"What? Why?"

Eduardo was the best kind of reminder as to how far Diego could go when he was obsessed with something—when he let something he wanted have control over him.

Then, it had been pursuit of his wealth. Now it could be the woman in front of him, waiting for an answer.

"He's receiving treatment for a cocaine addiction."

"Eduardo used cocaine? But he used to be so... That's awful. He was always so sweet and kind to me."

Kind and sweet. They were the perfect words to describe Eduardo.

Fisting his hands, Diego rocked on his heels, bile filling his throat.

His half brother had been a nice kid, weak at heart, forever bullied by the man who had fathered them—which Diego had learned too late. Diego should have protected him. Instead Diego had been the one who nudged him that last step toward his own self-destruction.

But he wouldn't give up. He would never give up on him. If Eduardo didn't have the will to fight for his life anymore Diego would fight for him. He would use every cent he had, would wield all his power, if it meant he could get his half brother back.

CHAPTER SEVEN

K<small>IM SCRUNCHED HER</small> eyes closed and tried to recall all the
literature she had been reading over the past month. With
little Jennie wailing in her arms and that image from her
afternoon appointment flashing before her eyes it was all
a blur. *There were two. She wasn't even equipped for one.*

Telling Laura, her company's design architect, that she
would look after little Jennie for a couple of hours had
seemed like a good idea. She had been reading all about
how to take care of a baby for almost a month. So of course
she was ready for a ground test, right?

Wrong.

Sweat beaded her brow. Her arms were starting to ache
a little bit.

She bent her knees and picked up the cheat sheet she had
made out of Laura's instructions, even though she knew
them by heart.

She had warmed the pumped milk to precisely the exact
temperature, tested it on her wrist, had fed Jennie and even
tried to burp her. And then she'd put her down for a nap.
Not a minute early or late.

The nap had lasted ten minutes, ending in a loud wail.
According to Laura's schedule Jennie should have napped
for at least an hour.

Tucking the baby tighter against her chest, she swung a
little from side to side, imitating what she had seen Laura

do when she had brought the baby to the company's premises a couple of times.

Her chubby cheeks scrunched up tight, Jennie wailed louder. The muscles in Kim's arms quivered until she shook all over. Even her head was beginning to pound now.

She increased the pace of her walk, tension tugging her skin tight. She should call Laura and take Jennie back to her. Every hysterical inch of her wanted to. *Will you desert your child when it gets hard?* the annoyingly logical part of her asked.

No, she couldn't accept failure—yet.

She heard the door open and turned around. Why hadn't she thought of Anna?

Diego stood in the doorway, frowning.

Her heart sank to her feet, dismay making her weak-kneed.

His gaze amused, he checked his watch.

"Was I gone *that* long?"

"You said you were going to Sao Paulo."

They both spoke at the same time.

His mouth tightened. As it did every time their conversation skated anywhere near Eduardo. "My trip got postponed."

Her shoulders felt as if there were metal rods tied to them, crushing her with their weight. The last thing she needed was for Diego to see her abysmal failure.

"What's with the baby?"

"She's—"

"Laura's. I know. She had her with her last week."

She nodded, insecurities sawing at her throat. Of course he remembered Jennie from that one visit—while Kim had always scrambled even to remember her name.

He had picked her up one evening last week from work—a strangely domestic but comforting gesture—and she had been forced to introduce her staff to him. All forty of them—from their sixty-year-old office manager Karen to nineteen-year-old intern Amy—had mooned over him. *And* informed her with a sigh the next morning that they understood her actions perfectly.

"Kim?"

She sighed. Jennie's little mewls were picking up volume again. "I offered to look after her for a few hours."

A single eyebrow shot into his hairline. "Why?"

She raised her voice to be heard over the infant's cries. "I decided to take myself on a test drive, and Laura's the only one with a baby."

"You're *practicing* because you're pregnant?"

"Something like that."

"Isn't that a little extreme?"

"I believe in being prepared."

"Prepared for what?"

She pushed her hair out of her face with her free hand, trying to ignore his gaze drilling into her.

"I…I don't know what's wrong with her. She won't calm down." Hitching Jennie up with her one hand, she wiped her forehead. "I've fed her, changed her and tried to burp her. I'm running out of ideas except to take her back."

She looked around the cozy sitting area she had taken over for the evening, taking in the untouched protein shake, the dirty diaper on the rug, Jennie's blanket trailing over the edge of the designer leather couch…

But it was the clawing urge to take Jennie back to Laura and pretend the evening had never happened that gutted her.

Tears burned in the back of her throat, gathering momentum like a storm.

Dear God, how was she…?

Diego's hard frame in front of her pulled her to a stop.

Jennie's wails were becoming incessant, her little face scrunched up tight. Kim's heart sank to the floor. She was ready to bawl her *own* eyes out.

She raised her gaze to Diego, her neck stiff, her forearms strained to the point of shaking. "She won't stop crying, Diego."

He took Jennie from her, his movements infinitely gentle. The little girl fit on his forearm with room to spare.

Kim's heart lurched into her throat.

With curious ease he held Jennie high in the cradle of his arms, her pink dress contrasting against his rough, large hands. "Might be because you're holding her too tight and she can feel your tension."

"That's not true. She was crying long before I picked her up…"

The infant immediately stopped crying, as though confirming Diego's statement. He swung the cradle of his arms left to right, gently, his gaze never moving from Jennie.

Kim froze as he cooed to her. It was the most wonderful sight she had ever seen.

"Babies are very sensitive to our own moods and personalities."

His soft words landed like a slap on her. "What the hell does *that* mean?"

The look he threw her, puzzled and doubting, pierced through the last shred of her composure.

"It means that she can sense that you're nervous—*wound up.*" His gaze drilled into her. "*Overwrought, stressed out…* do you want me to go on? What *you* feel is setting *her* off. If you just—"

"I get it—okay!" she said, practically shouting.

Every muscle in her trembled, and her chest was so tight that it was an effort to breathe. As long as it had just been in her head it had still been bearable. Given voice like that, it tore through her.

"She can sense that I don't care, that I want to be doing anything but looking after her. That's it, right?"

* * *

Diego lowered the sleeping infant into the tiny bassinet and tucked her in tight. The little girl settled in without a whisper, and he rubbed his thumb over a plump cheek.

A soft, sleepy gurgle erupted from the baby's tiny mouth.

Whatever his past sins, the new life that was coming was a precious gift. If only he could figure out what was worrying Kim.

Familiar frustration spiked through him. The past few weeks they had fallen into a somewhat torturous routine of sorts. With each passing day and every single minute they spent in each other's company—and this was with both of them avidly trying to keep it to a minimum—he had realized how hard it was to keep his hands to himself. Especially when he had begun to see glimpses of the girl he had fallen in love with so long ago.

She still hadn't cut down her work hours, but she *had* spent the last Sunday home watching a soccer game with him and Miguel. Who, interestingly, had said more to her than he had to Diego.

He might even say she was slowly letting her guard down with him. Except when Anna or he brought up the pregnancy.

Then she immediately retreated behind that shell of hers. She refused to share what was on her mind. And yet more than once he had seen her reading articles on motherhood on her tablet, lost in deep thought.

And tonight she had borrowed a baby. Because she had known he would be out for the night.

Foreboding inched across his skin. Once he had been too involved in his own world and had neglected Eduardo when he had needed him. He wasn't going to make the same mistake again. He was going to get to the root of what was bothering her tonight.

He eyed her across the room. She was plumping the

same pillow on the couch, her shoulders stiff with tension, her punches into it increasing steadily, until her jabs were vicious and accompanied by soft grunts.

He reached her quickly, meaning to catch her before she buried whatever was troubling her under grating self-sufficiency. With a hand on her shoulder, he turned her around. "If you're imagining that to be my face," he said, "let me…"

She let him look at her for only a second before she pushed away from him. But what he had seen in that second was enough to stun Diego.

Tears filled her huge brown eyes.

His breath felt as if it had been knocked out of him— as if someone had clocked his jaw. He had never seen her tears. Not when he had humiliated her, not when he had threatened her company, not even when her father had shredded her.

With an arm thrown around her waist he tugged her hard against him and locked her there. She was plastered to him from shoulder to thigh. Her soft flesh shuddered and rearranged itself against him.

"Let me go."

"Shhh…" he whispered near her ear, knowing that she was extra-sensitive to any touch there. "I just want to look at you."

Her hands against his chest, she glared at him, her tears unshed.

Every inch of her was taut, like a tightly wound spring, and a slow tremor was inching through her. Something had shaken her up badly. He tightened his arms around her, waiting for the tremors to pass.

Dark blue shadows danced under her huge eyes. Her hair was not the sleek polished silk that gleamed every time she moved her face in that arrogant, thoroughly sexy way of hers. Instead it curled around her face, lending a false vulnerability to the sharp angles of her face.

But the fact that she was close to exhaustion was written in the dull pallor of her skin, in the pinched look stamped upon her features.

His ire rose to the surface again, and he didn't fool himself that he was worried for his unborn child. The anxiety that he couldn't purge from his system, the anger that had his muscles quivering for action, was all for *her*.

Despite his best intentions he just couldn't *not* care about her.

He moved his hand up from her waist to her nape and dug his fingers into her hair, held her tight.

His grip didn't hurt her. He knew that. But he needed that hold on her for a second—the deceptive illusion of control over her, over her emotions.

Because she reduced him to what he'd been born to.

All the trappings of wealth, all the polish he had acquired in the past six years, fell away, reducing him to what he was at his core. Someone who had been born into the gutter and craved a better life that had remained out of his grasp for so long.

There was always a part of her that remained unreachable, unattainable to him, as though he still didn't make the cut.

He trailed his gaze over her, from the well-worn Harvard T-shirt that hugged her breasts to the low slung sweatpants that left a strip of flesh bare at her midriff.

"You can't stop shivering. You look awful," he said.

Pushing away from him, she glanced down over herself. Distaste marred her brow. "I spent last night at work and I didn't have time for a shower when I came back."

"Aren't you working enough without taking on baby-sitting?"

She glanced at Jennie and trembled again. "I just… I

wanted to see if I could handle her for a few hours." The resigned curve of her mouth tugged at him.

"*Meu Deus,* what is the matter with you?"

Silence.

He frowned, resisting the urge to shake her by her shoulders. He had never seen her so defeated, never heard that self-deprecating tone in her words. He picked her up and settled down into the recliner with her in his lap. The fact that she sagged into him without a protest alarmed the hell out of him.

"You look like you're ready to tip over. Answer my question, *pequena.* What's going on?"

She tucked her knees in closer. Tears rolled over her cheeks. "There are two, Diego."

He raked his mind. "Two... *Two what, gatinha?*"

"Two heartbeats."

He pushed her chin up none too gently. *"What?"*

A shadow descended on her face, her skin a tight mask over the fine bones. "I went to see the doctor today for a routine checkup. She thought it best to do an ultrasound. There are two... Diego, there are twins."

His mouth slack, Diego couldn't believe her words. Incredible joy flushed through him. He was going to be a father to not one but two babies. He had no breath left in him. He felt lightheaded, as if nothing could mar his happiness anymore. He was going to have a family—a proper one—with *two* babies looking to him for everything.

He shivered at the magnitude of what it meant.

It had been a shock when he had first learned of the baby, but now all he felt was exceptionally blessed. As if for the first time in as far as he could remember he had a chance to be something good, to build something good—as if life had finally handed him a good turn.

Gathering Kim tight in his arms, he pressed a kiss to her upturned mouth and tasted her tears.

He pulled back from her, the worry etched into her pinched mouth, the sheer terror in her gaze, puncturing his own joy.

"That's why you brought Jennie over? Why you're practicing?"

He cupped her jaw, forcing her to look at him. His mouth felt dry. Words were hitching in his throat. He palmed her back, up and down, looking for words to do this right.

Because he had never been in this position of offering comfort or strength to her—ever. She had never leaned on him for anything. Her unwavering strength was both incredibly amazing and annoying at the same time.

"This is not something where we practice for perfection, *gatinha,*" he said softly, anxious to remove anything negative from his words. "We just try to do our best."

"But that's not enough, is it? Good intentions and effort can't make up for what's missing. You told me once your mother had never been able to scrape enough money to feed you properly, but you didn't care, did you? Because you knew that she loved you."

"As will you love our children. I told you before—we don't have to be perfect parents; we just have to love them enough—"

She fought against his grip again, a whimper escaping her. That pained sound sent a shiver racing up his spine.

"Whatever is paining you, I swear I will help you through it, *gatinha*. Tell me, what is—?"

"I'm not good with babies." Her words sounded as if they were tortured, as if they were ripped from her. "I'll never be, so it's a good thing you're here. Or else our kids might never stop crying—might turn out just like me, hating their mother."

Something squeezed in his chest and he released a hard breath, shoving aside his own conflicted emotions for the minute.

"And the fact that you're exhausted has nothing to do with it?"

She bit her lip. Her uncertainty—something he had never seen—was a shock to his system.

"How do you feel about being a full-time stay-at-home daddy?"

He smiled even as stark fear gripped him. "And what will *you* do?"

"I'll do everything else." She ran her tongue over her lips, her brow tied into that line that it got when she was in full-on thinking mode. "I'll work, I'll clean, I'll cook. I'll even—" She stopped, as though she had just caught on to the desperation in her words. Her tears spilled over from her eyes, her slender shoulders trembling under the weight of perplexing grief. "I don't feel anything, Diego."

His heart stopped for a minute, if that was possible. "What does that mean?"

"For the babies. I don't feel *anything*."

He sucked in a breath, the anguish he spied in her gaze sending waves of powerlessness hurling through him.

"Except this relentless void, there's nothing inside of me when I think of them," she said, rushing over her words as though she couldn't stop them anymore. "I should look forward to it now, at least. I should be used to it by now. At first I thought it was because I was angry with you. Because you were the father. It's not. *It is me.* All I can think is how I wish it was anyone but me. *Every waking moment.* I can't bear to look at myself because I'm afraid I will see changes I don't want to. My team is more excited about this than I am. The ultrasound technician was more excited than I was when we looked at them. *And now there are two.* What if I never feel anything for them? What if all these years of...? What if I never love them? They'll realize that, won't they? God, I would just curl up and die if they—"

"Shh…" Diego swallowed past the tears sawing at his throat and hugged her tight, pouring everything he couldn't say into the embrace. He couldn't bear to see her like this. This pain—her pain—it hammered at him with the quiet efficiency of a hundred blows.

How blithely had he assumed she didn't give a damn about anything but herself? How easily had he let her rejection of him color everything else? How easily had he let his own hangups blind him to her pain?

Her cutting indifference every time she had mentioned the pregnancy had been the perfect cover for this terrifying panic beneath. Regret skewered through him.

He pressed his mouth to her temple and breathed her scent in. He had no idea if it was for his or her benefit. "You built a million-dollar company from nothing but your talent and your hard work. Don't tell me your failure with Jennie tonight means you won't love our children."

Her upper body bowed forward, her forehead coming to rest on his shoulder as though the fight was literally deflating her. "I've spent years cauterizing myself against feeling anything. I think I did it so well that nothing can reach me now."

"That's nonsense." Diego wrapped his hands around her and tucked her closer to him. "You care about your sister. You told me you tried your best to protect her from your father's wrath. I'm sure once the babies come you—"

"I'm the reason Liv suffered so much at my dad's hands. It was my responsibility to protect her. Nothing else."

"What are you talking about?"

"You think you're the only one who has a monopoly on guilt?"

Frustration boiled through Diego as defiance crept back into her tone. Her shields fell back into place, the pain shoved away beneath layers and layers of indifference. His hold over her was just as fleeting as always.

* * *

Feeling Diego stiffen against her, Kim slid out of his reach. Her knees threatened to collapse under her, but anything was better than the cocoon of his embrace.

It had felt so good. The temptation to buy into his words that everything would be fine, the need to dump the bitterest truth in his lap, had been dangerous.

Except she was sure there would be nothing but distaste left on his face if she did that. She would take his anger anytime.

That was what living with him was doing to her—slowly but surely eroding everything she had learned to survive.

"How come you're so good at it?" she threw at him, the pain dulling to a slow ache.

For now there was nothing to do but wait. That was the part that was slowly driving her crazy. There wasn't a way to *make* herself feel. There was no switch to turn it on.

"I'm not. But Marissa always has a baby attached to her hip, and I think I've picked up a thing or two in all these years."

An image of a laughing, petite brunette flashed in front of Kim's eyes. Her mouth burned with the acidic taste of jealousy. Until now she had held on, pretended even to herself that he didn't matter to her, that falling into his bed four weeks ago had been nothing but a mistake.

"Marissa?"

He nodded slowly, a flat, hardened look replacing the tenderness she had seen seconds ago, as though he resented Kim even uttering her name. Not as though. *He hated it.* It was there in the way his stance stiffened, in the way he turned away from her.

"You were…?" Kim swallowed, forcing the lump in her throat down, that acidic taste burning her mouth. "You've been with *her* all these—?"

He shrugged. "Over the years Marissa and I have always

drifted toward each other. In between deserting spouses, deaths and even..." His gaze fell to Jennie and his mouth curved into a little smile. "She's nothing if not maternal."

The last sentence was like driving a knife into her already torn-up gut. "But you're not with her anymore because of me?"

His gaze collided with her. "Because you're pregnant with my child."

Kim flinched.

"When I learned of your wedding I was furious. Marissa didn't like my reaction. She gave me an ultimatum. I had to finish things with you if I wanted a life with her."

"But that means you..." She blinked. "You didn't come to the island to sed...to sleep with me?" She corrected herself at the last minute.

The arrogant resolve in his eyes dissolved and she sucked in a sharp breath.

"No. I wanted to see you one last time, to show you what I had become. To throw the divorce papers in your face and walk away. Instead I saw you and lost my mind again."

Bitter disappointment knuckled her in the gut. How pathetic was it that she felt cheated because Diego hadn't come to find her for some elaborate revenge scheme? That she hadn't merited even that much of his energy?

Exactly as she hadn't with her own mother.

She bit out a laugh. It was either that or dissolve into tears. "And I fell pregnant and ruined your plans...and hers."

He shot up from the couch and materialized in front of her. "It would be so much easier if I could blame you, but we were both there."

"Oh *please*. Will you stop with the whole honorable act? I would much prefer seeing the hatred in your eyes than looking for things that are not there."

"*I* hurt her, Kim. Not you. The one thing she asked of me was to finish things with you. Because of my insane obsession with you, because of my refusal to leave you alone—" every word out of his mouth reverberated with bitter disgust, and the depth of it slammed into her "—I…I broke her heart, and there's no way to fix it. I have to live with that guilt my entire life."

He stepped away from her as though he couldn't bear to be near her now Marissa had been mentioned, as though even looking at her compounded his guilt.

"I'll send Anna down. She will look after Jennie," he said, halting with his hand on the doorhandle. "Make sure you eat something and get some sleep. Think of the babies, if nothing else."

She sank to the couch as he closed the door behind him. She had hated him for setting her up, for ruthlessly walking away, but he had paid the price for their reckless passion just as she had.

She wished with every cell in her being that he was the ruthless man she had thought him. Because the man he was underneath—kind and thoughtful—how was she supposed to resist him?

He could have thrown her ineptitude in her face, laughed at her fears. Wasn't that why she had been stewing in it by herself? But he hadn't.

He had held her, hugged her, tried to make her feel better. He had been genuinely concerned for her. He could make it so easy for her to depend on him, to bask in his concern, to fall deeper and deeper…

That was if she wasn't *already* in exactly the situation she had fought so hard against.

Her legs shook as she hugged herself. She needed Diego in her life. No, she *wanted* Diego in her life. But the gnawing, terrifying truth was that nothing but his honor was keeping him there.

Nothing about *her* was keeping him there.

CHAPTER EIGHT

IT WAS, WITHOUT doubt, a sex party.

Diego had no other name for it. His thoughts had swung from mild curiosity to full-blown agitation when a six-foot bouncer had checked his ID at the entrance and announced that admittance cost ten thousand dollars.

He had spent the better part of the evening trying to find Kim. It was half past ten now, and this was where her colleague had finally directed him to.

The party was in full swing in a two-floor Manhattan loft that had taken him several phone calls to locate. He scowled and moved past a waitress dressed in a French maid's costume serving hors d'oeuvres.

Soft, sultry music streamed through the richly carpeted foyer from cleverly hidden sub-woofers. Pink neon lights strategically placed on the low ceiling bathed the lounge, illuminating the retro-style furniture and a bar. It was very elegantly done, with a high-class Parisian feel to it.

The lower floor was dotted with futons against the retro chic walls, and in the corner a thin, exotically dressed woman was working massage oil into a naked man's back. On the other side of the full bar was a huge dance floor, where at least twenty men and women were softly bumping into one another.

He gritted his teeth and loosened his tie. What the hell was Kim doing *here*? Was this to compensate for the vulnerability she hadn't been able to hide yesterday? Or was it an act of defiance to rile him up because he had organized her day today?

He glanced up the curving staircase toward the more expansive upper floor. Every muscle in him tightened as his gaze fell on more than one couple getting hot and heavy up there, their moans adding to the soulful music downstairs.

A sudden chill hit Diego. Which floor was Kim on?

Running a hand over his nape, he moved toward the dimly lit lounge. He had no idea what he would do if he didn't find her on the lower floor. Already every base instinct in him was riled up at the very fact that she was here, of all places.

If he found her with... No, that thought didn't even bear thinking.

He reached the outer edge of the dance floor, searching for her. He froze at the edge of the crowd as he finally located her. She was right in the center of the crowd, her hands behind her head, moving in perfect rhythm to the music, while a smartly dressed man had his hands around her waist.

His blood roared in his veins. *Mine,* the barely civilized part in him growled.

She was only dancing, he reminded himself, before he gave in to the urge to beat the crap out of the man touching her. A caveman—just as she had called him.

He slowly walked the perimeter of the crowd.

Her eyes closed, her legs bent, she was moving with an irresistible combination of grace and sensuality that lit a fire in his blood. Every muscle in his body tightened with a razor-edged hunger.

Her hair shone like raw silk. Her mouth was painted a vivid dark red, almost black, like nothing he'd ever seen on her before. Usually her lips shimmered with the barest gloss. A black leather dress hugged every inch of her—

cupping her breasts high, barely covering her buttocks. The dress left her shoulders bare, and the exposed curves of her breasts were the sexiest sight he had ever seen.

She'd done the rest of her face differently, too, heavier make-up than he had ever seen. Usually the lack of make-up only served to heighten the no-nonsense, made-of-ice vibe she projected.

It was the opposite today—that outfit, her make-up, everything signaled sexual availability, grabbing attention and keeping it there. Was that why she was here? What had prompted this out-of-character interest in a sex party, of all things?

She looked like his darkest fantasy come true.

Lust knuckled him in the gut. All he wanted to do was pull the dress down until her breasts fell into his hands, past her hips until she was laid bare for him, and then plunge into her until neither of them could catch their breath, until the roar in his blood stopped.

He moved closer to her without blinking, his heart pounding in his ribcage, his skin thrumming with need. Her gaze lit upon him and shock flashed in it. Good—she'd recognized him.

He stepped on the raised platform and roughly collared the guy dancing with her, moved him out of the way. He palmed her face and tilted it up roughly. "Are you high?"

"What?" Even her question sounded uneven. "Of course not."

He sniffed her. Nothing but the erotic scent of her skin met his nostrils. His jeans felt incredibly tight. It was all he could do to stop from pressing into her. If he did, he didn't think he could stop. "Are you drunk?" he said, noting a hoarse note in his own words.

She shook her head, something dangerous inching into her gaze. She ran a hand over her midriff, drawing Diego's gaze to the dress again. "If you're just going to spoil my fun…"

He blocked her as she turned away from him, the forward momentum pushing her breasts to graze against his chest. He clamped his fingers around her arm and tugged her.

She turned to face him. A strip of light illuminated the lush curve of her mouth, leaving the rest of her face in shadow. "What are you doing?"

He bent his head and tugged her lip with his teeth. Molten heat exploded in every nerve. His cock ached hard. Her hissing breath felt like music to his ears. "Taking you home."

She dug her heels in and he loosened his hold. "I'm not ready to leave yet."

"Yes, you are."

To hell with all his rules, and with sanity and with whatever crap he had spun to keep things rational between them.

She was *his*—whether she knew it or not, whether she liked it or not. And not just because she was going to be the mother of his children.

Kim pulled the flaps of Diego's leather jacket tighter around her and stepped out of the limo. A gust of wind barreled into her. She folded her hands against her midriff, her mouth falling open as she realized why the drive from the party had taken so long. Diego had been talking non-stop on his cell phone, effectively silencing any questions she had.

They were at a private airstrip. The ground crew was finishing up its prep, and the aircraft was being revved up. A tremor traveled up and down her spine.

She walked toward Diego, who was still talking on his phone.

His gaze traveled the length of her once again, intractable.

"What's going on?"

He clicked his phone shut. "I have something urgent to take care of."

Her stomach tightened. "So go. I'll even bid you good-bye with a smile."

"You're coming with me. You can laze in a spa, swim in a beach, shop for maternity clothes...among other things."

Her skin sizzled at the double intonation on the last bit.

"Everything you *should* be doing."

Her breath hitched in her throat at the resolve in his gaze. "You like lording it over me, don't you? I'm not going anywhere with you."

He took a step toward her and backed her against the limo. He pulled her hand into his and twined their fingers. She felt his touch to the tip of her toes.

"I was worried about you. I am still. So shut up and accept it."

Her heart thumped inside her ribcage. Gooey warmth flooded through her. No one had ever worried about her. *Ever.* It had been her job to worry for as long as she could remember.

She had worried about her mom first, shielded her from her father. And after she had walked out she had tried her best to protect Liv from her dad's wrath. No one had ever seen past the veneer of her perfection to the emptiness beneath—even Liv, who cared about her....

With his thumb and forefinger he rubbed over her fore-head. "Stop thinking so much. You will stay with me so that I can keep an eye on you."

"Why?"

"You didn't seem yourself last night. Or just now."

"Last night I was hormonal. Tonight I'm horny."

Liquid fire blazed in his gaze.

"Those are the only colors on my rainbow lately."

He laughed, the sexy dimple in his cheek winking at her.

"Hormonal and horny women *need* looking after."

It had been a very strange day on so many accounts.

Once the janitor had locked her out of her company's premises she had returned to her apartment, fuming with disbelief. Because for the past six years she had worked every Saturday except the day she had gone to her wedding.

By the time she had finished every last scrap of the delicious sandwich Anna had given her, taking away her laptop in the process, and with her usual intelligence deserting her, Kim had realized too late that everything had been orchestrated by Diego.

Total lack of sleep last night meant she had zonked out for the rest of the day.

"I came to check on you twice and you were sleeping. Anyone with a little sense can see your body needs rest. Why do I have to force you to it?"

She flushed, unbidden warmth spurting in her. He had checked on her. *Twice.* She should resent his high-handed attitude; she should at least offer token resistance. But she couldn't muster a protest past the warm fuzzies filling her up.

When had anyone ever checked on her? This was the same strangely weakening, cared-for sensation that had driven her to marry him six years ago. She had stupidly wanted that feeling to last forever.

"And what were you doing *there,* of all places?"

He sounded so aggravated that she smiled. "I was going crazy after sleeping straight through the day. So I made a list of all the things I need to get ready before the babies come. Then I—"

He tapped her temple with one long finger. "I'm going to cure you of your overthinking if it's the last thing I do."

"Then I got thinking of all the things I won't get to do anymore *when* the babies arrive."

"And going to a sex club was one of them?" His frown deepened into a full-fledged scowl. "What else was on it?"

The flare of interest in his gaze goaded her. Last night had been terrifying on so many levels. Right at that moment she would do anything to see what he felt for her reflected there. Even if it was just lust.

"Sex with a stranger was number two and sex in a public place number three. I thought I could shoot two birds with one—"

He tilted forward, all two hundred pounds of hulking, turned-on, prime male focused on her. A tingle started deep in her lower back and began inching its way all over. Her palms slapped onto his chest as he angled his lower body closer.

"You're pushing me on purpose, *pequena*. Are you ready for the consequences?"

His rock-hard thigh lodged in between her thighs, sparking an ache in that exact spot. A whimper clawing out of her, she pushed at him. The feel of hard muscles and the thundering of his heart under her fingers was just as torturous.

The heat uncoiling in his gaze made mincemeat of her. "Okay, fine. I made that up," she said, cupping his jaw. "I…I didn't know what to do with myself. But if you're going to rearrange my everyday life the least you can do is…"

His gaze locked on her mouth and he relented the pressure of his thigh just a little. "What?"

"Let me enjoy it the way I want to."

"Coward."

A slow smile—one that should come with a health warning—curved his mouth, digging deep grooves into his face. Glorious warmth unraveled inside her. She loved it when he looked at her like that, when he smiled like that. As if she was the only one in the world who could put it there.

It was wishful thinking at best, dangerous indulgence at worst, but she couldn't fight the feeling.

"It kills you to ask, doesn't it? To admit, even if only for a second, you wanted to see me?"

She smiled, incapable of resisting him at that moment. "I did call your secretary. She had no idea when you would be back. So I took Carla's offer."

"The sex expert on your team? Carla was there too?"

She smacked his chest with the back of her hand at the exaggerated interest in his words.

A car pulled up alongside their limo, the headlights illuminating the airstrip.

Miguel stepped out of the dark sedan. He opened the trunk and pulled out a pretty pink suitcase which, even in the low light, looked familiar.

Her jaw hit her chest. "That's mine."

"I had Anna pack some of your things." He nodded at Miguel, who disappeared back into the car without a word to Kim. "Let's go."

He was serious. He was taking her away on a holiday. She shouldn't be so happy about it, but she was. "But I—"

"You're taking a few days off. Do you want to spend it alone? Maybe interview some more nannies? Borrow another baby? Dodge more calls from Olivia?"

Heat tightened her cheeks. She was getting more than a little obsessive in her *Planning for Pregnancy* phase. As if she could somehow make up for lacking the most necessary part of it. And, judging by the way Diego was looking at her, he knew that she was slowly going insane.

For the first time in her life she didn't want to be alone. She didn't have any strength left.

"I can't just leave like that, Diego. I run a company. My laptop—"

He turned around. "It's in there," he said, with a nod toward another bag she hadn't noticed before.

Her laptop case. She hated it when anyone touched it. Her most precious possession was in there.

She moved to take it from him but he held it behind him.

"I'm warning you again. This is a vacation. Mary and Amber have already been informed."

Her assistant and her VP of Operations.

"I will send this back with Miguel unless you agree that your time on it will be limited."

"*Limited?* What does that mean?" she said, hurrying behind him.

He paused at the foot of the plane's stairs, one hand extended toward her. "You'll be allowed one hour every day on that laptop."

Reaching him, she paused. "What am I supposed to do for the rest of the day?"

His hand clasping hers, he smiled, the very devil lurking in his gaze. "I'm sure we will find something enjoyable."

She waited until they were settled into the flight and she had picked at her dinner before she started looking around her seat.

Without asking, Diego knew what she was looking for. He couldn't believe it. The woman really was a workaholic.

"Where's my laptop case?" she threw at him, meeting his gaze.

"It should be somewhere here." Her expression anxious, she unbuckled her seat belt and stood up.

He leaned forward and grabbed her hand, stopping her. "This is what I'm talking about. What is so important that you need it *now?*"

With her other hand she pushed at his hold. "I don't." She looked almost panicky. "I just... I want to make sure it doesn't get misplaced."

He stared at her for a few seconds before replying, "It's in the rear cabin."

After a few minutes he followed her there, unable to keep his mind on anything else.

She knelt by the small side table next to the bed and unzipped the case. Smiling, he hunkered down on his knees next to her.

"What are you looking for?"

Her gaze wide, she froze with her hand inside the case. "Oh, just a…an old CD of songs I made a while ago. I want to upload it to my iPod and I…" She swallowed as he didn't budge. "I would prefer to do it alone."

He laughed. "Send me on my way so that you can work? *No*."

"Never mind." She began zipping it closed. "I don't think the CD's in here anyway."

He grabbed the leather case from her.

Her hand shaking, she tugged it back. "No, Diego… Don't…"

"You are acting *really* strange," he murmured, and tugged the zipper open.

A bulging envelope fell out—a faded one, with a logo he instantly recognized. It was from a photo studio in Rio where he'd used to have his pictures developed long ago.

Where she had gone to have the pictures developed from the disposable cameras she and Eduardo had carried on that cruise.

She grabbed it and tucked her hand behind her jerkily.

He met her gaze, his chest incredibly tight. The last thing he wanted was to remember the pain he had felt when she had walked out. Not when they were finally starting over again, even if not with a clean slate.

The memory brushed his words with a harsh edge. "I'm surprised you didn't burn them all a long time ago."

Hurt flashed in her gaze. Still on her haunches, she moved away from him, as though she was shielding a precious commodity. "They're catalogued under 'Mistakes Never to Be Repeated.'"

"Why do you have them in your laptop case?"

Her answer was extremely reluctant. "When I packed my stuff to be moved I put them in there, to keep at work."

So that he didn't see them even by accident.

Anger burning through him, he made a quick move. The envelope fell from her arms, scattering pictures all around him. Every one of them showed Kim and him, happy, smiling, the world around them faded to nothing.

He grabbed a couple and crumpled them in his hand.

She gasped and plucked at his hand, her fingers digging into his bunched fist. "No… What are you doing?"

"I'm going to do what you should have done—tear them and trash them."

She was trembling. "Don't you dare."

He grabbed another one, seething inside. He was about to rip it in half, when she clamped his wrist, her grip strong as a vise.

She shook her head, hot anger burning in her eyes. "Stop it, Diego."

He let the picture go and pulled her toward him. "Why did you leave?"

"What?"

"It's a question I should have asked years ago."

"Believe me, the answer won't make you happy."

With a grunt, she tried to pry his fingers open. Her nails, even though blunt, dug into his knuckles. He didn't care, and apparently neither did she.

"Let it go, Diego."

"No. Not unless you answer my question. And truth this time."

"I've never lied to you."

"You've never told me the truth either. Like the fact that you never slept with Alexander."

Her gaze flashed to him even while her fingers still jabbed at his. "Is that it? You want to know how many men I've slept with in my life? Two—you first, and then this other guy a year after I left you, because I couldn't forget you. But it was horrible. There—are you happy?"

A red haze descended in front of his eyes. "What is supposed to make me happy? The fact that you would do anything to wipe me from your mind? Everything you give me—whether your word, or your promise, or even a damn kiss—I have to fight you for it. But you know what? I've fought for everything in my life and I fight dirty. So, unless you want me to rip up every picture I see here…"

Her efforts doubled. She scooted closer to him on her knees, stretched to her full height and then tilted her head to see the picture he was holding. "God, Diego, don't you dare—"

He pulled away from her and raised his hand, looked at the picture, too.

His stomach churned with a vicious force.

This one had been taken the night after he'd had sex… no, had made love to her. However much he tried, it was a night he couldn't cheapen. Not even in his thoughts.

Did she feel the same? Was that why the picture was so important to her? He was sick and tired of second-guessing.

He held it with both his hands. There was a small tear in the picture already.

She slammed into him as she tried to reach it. "Give it back, Diego…"

"No."

"Fine."

She didn't shout. And yet her words vibrated with raw pain and utter desolation.

"I left because you turned me into a prize to parade before your father—into some trophy that was a victory over your childhood."

"You said I treated you like a princess."

"Yes—a princess dressed up in glittery clothes and exhibited for the status she provided. Anyone who asked, you recited my accomplishments as though it was my résumé. You were obsessed with taking over your father's company. You spent every waking minute devising ways to get more access, more information. I...I loved you, and you broke my heart."

"How is that possible? I was ready to move so that you could go to Harvard. I wanted to give you everything you had before I—"

"I didn't want money or a grand life. I didn't want to go back to Harvard. I wanted to stay with you."

Diego's head swam with each word she uttered. "What?"

"I tried to tell you that last week. All I cared about was being with you. You didn't spend a single minute with me. We spent every evening at some gala or charity event. During the day you disappeared to God knows where. You made all these plans for how we would live our lives in New York....I didn't want that life. When I met you I was running away from that life. Liv was gone and I felt so utterly alone. I went on that cruise on an impulse and I met you. No one's ever looked at me like you did that fortnight, like there was something to me beyond... But in the end, you were the same as anyone else."

Diego forced himself to breathe past the heaviness in his throat. She clamped his wrist again, but her grip was slippery, her fingers shaking. She breathed in slowly, softly, as though it took a lot of effort.

"That picture..." Her words were low, heavy, desolate. "It represents the happiest time of my life, Diego. The only happy time. So, *please,* give it back."

His heart crawling into his throat, Diego dropped the picture. She picked it up from the floor, and the others with it, and tucked them back into the envelope hurriedly, as though she didn't trust his temper.

He had done everything she had blamed him for and more. He had come to his own conclusions about why she had left him, let it fester inside. He had let his own insecurities color her actions. He had destroyed his happiness with his own hands…

All in pursuit of the very wealth and status that had robbed him of the two people who had truly loved him, who had cared about him.

He lifted her chin, his hands shaking with impotent rage. That familiar guilt clawed through him. Another person he'd hurt, another black mark on the increasing roster of his sins.

He palmed her cheek, tracing the jutting angles of her cheekbones with his fingers. Words rushed out of him on a wave of powerlessness that pricked his muscles.

"I did love you. I couldn't bear the thought of not seeing you again once we were off that ship. That's why I married you. I…I was obsessed with defeating my father, yes, but I never meant to hurt you. But of course neither of us had enough faith in the other, did we? You didn't have enough to tell me the truth, and I didn't have enough to drag you back to me."

"Why didn't you?"

Fury such as he had never heard, rattled in her words. But she didn't wait for his answer.

He should have gone after her. But he had been able to see nothing past what he had termed as her rejection of him. He had driven himself to new, ruthless heights, manipulated and eventually driven Eduardo over the cliff.

All because she had made him realize the bitter truth that he had shoved beneath his fight for survival—that he would never be enough.

CHAPTER NINE

KIM STEPPED OUT of the shower stall in the luxurious rear cabin. She loved the circular space with its vanity lighting, but the hot water hadn't helped.

Tugging on satin shorts and a matching silk top, she put her robe back on and tied the sash. She eyed the huge bed anxiously. She trailed her fingers over the soft Egyptian cotton.

Were they going to share a bed when they couldn't even bear to look at each other?

She put a trembling hand to her forehead. Her racing thoughts were giving her a dull ache. The only time someone had put her first and she had run away from it. She wanted to go out and... What? Apologize for being a coward who had ruined their lives?

Her cell phone chirped an alarm. It was time for her multi-vitamin. She pushed at the strange sparkly bag that sat on top of her handbag with a little grunt. The bag slipped, its contents slipping onto the lush carpet at her feet. It was the goody bag from the sex party earlier that night.

She stared, aghast, at the tasteful assortment of favors scattered against the elegant rug.

Pink fur handcuffs, what were surely painful nipple clamps, two bottles of strawberry and chocolate-flavored massage oil, a contraption in shocking pink made in the shape of a...

It was a vibrator.

A sound—a cross between a gasp and a moan—escaped her. Heat pumped to her cheeks. Excitement dried her mouth. She stared at the doorway, a wild idea taking root in her.

She had had enough of his stupid rewards system. She was going to go for the jackpot.

She picked up the vibrator and settled on to a small settee facing away from the entrance to the main cabin. The smooth silicone was soft and yet hard in her hand. Sucking in a quick breath, she clicked the small button on the side.

A soft whir filled the cabin.

She didn't know what drove her to it. Maybe it was the horny part of her that she had no control over. Maybe it was the self-loathing running through her veins because she was still a coward who, instead of walking up to Diego and kissing him, as every cell in her wanted to, only dared to sit in here and play sexual peekaboo with him.

She didn't care.

She leaned against the wall, tugged her robe open and pushed it back over her shoulders.

Her PJs were nothing to write a Victoria's Secret catalog about, but at least the spaghetti strap top and the shorts were satin, in a cute shade of peach with little bows. They were not dull or boring, as Diego had said.

Her shorts exposed her legs which, thanks to Carla, she had gotten waxed for the party. Her toenails, painted the same sexy pink as the vibrator, gleamed against the cream leather couch.

The grooved velvet handle offered a sturdy grip as she held the vibrating head of it against her smooth calf. It tickled her skin and a giggle escaped her.

Laughing, she dragged the vibrating head upward from her calf. The thump-thump of her heart as she heard movement in the main cabin gobbled up the calming whir of the device.

She stalled as she reached her knee and pulled it back down. Up and down she moved it, covering a little more ground on the way up every time.

A tingle started sweeping up the base of her neck, across her face, spreading all over her skin. A shocking wetness dampened her panties. Even her palm felt slippery on the handle.

Her mouth dried up.

Because her clammy palm had nothing to do with what the device in her hand was doing to her body and everything to do with the thundering presence of the man looming at the entrance to the cabin, looking down at her from behind.

She could feel his gaze on her, daring her to raise her head and meet his gaze.

She could feel his hardened breathing in the way oxygen was swiftly depleted around her.

She could feel his arousal in the way her body reacted to his presence, in the way it was feeding off the desire he was emanating, even if she couldn't hear it or see it.

Her heart hammered. Her legs shook. Every muscle in her body trembled with an almost feverish chill. It was a good thing she had sat on the couch or she would have melted into a puddle of longing at his feet.

Bending her head, she moved the vibrating tip up past her knee this time. Her already sensitized skin vibrated with a thrumming awareness.

She reached the halfway point up her thigh.

He didn't interrupt her.

She let her boneless right leg collapse to the side, opening up her inner thigh to her hand. Her breathing quickened, the scent of arousal filling the scant air in the cabin.

He didn't make a sound.

The vibrating head reached the sensitive skin of her inner thigh. Heat crept along every inch of her skin as she moved the head a little more. Heat pooled at her sex.

He didn't move in his stance.

Her boldness had a shelf life of a few minutes at best, and it was fast running out. Sitting there, open in front of him, even with her shorts covering her aching flesh, she felt the most erotic thrill begin in her lower belly.

Over the past few seconds this had morphed into a battle of wills. He was calling her bluff, daring her to continue. And she was damned if she'd give in. She wanted his hands on her body, his fingers on her aching flesh, and she would settle for nothing less.

Refusing to look up, she moved her wrist another inch, up under the hem of her shorts. It was nowhere near where she wanted it.

She threw her head back, closed her eyes and imagined it to be his long fingers crawling up her thigh, propelling her toward ecstasy. A moan began inching its way up all the way from her lower back and she let it out.

The sound was erotic, thrilling to her own ears.

Rough hands seized the vibrator from her boneless fingers. Her eyes fell open, her body whimpering with unfulfilled desire.

His golden gaze glittering dark with fire, he loomed over her, color bleeding into his cheeks.

The desire uncoiling in his gaze was enough to scare her back into her shell—where it was safe, where she didn't risk anything.

No.

A muscle jumped in his jaw as he flipped off the vibrator and threw it across the cabin. It landed with a thud.

She pulled herself to a kneeling position. The robe slid from her arms. "You better have a good reason for throwing that away."

Tension smoldered around them, tightening every muscle in her into a quivering mass of anticipation.

"What the hell do you think you're doing?" His accent was thickened, his words rolling over each other.

She ran a hand over her throat. His gaze followed the movement hungrily. "With the *blast from the past* episode we've just had, I figured it would be forever before you wanted to touch me again, so I was taking matters—"

He pulled her flush against him, until her breasts were crushed against the solid musculature of his chest. It was heaven. It was hell. It was everything she wanted with crystal-clear clarity.

"Do you want me to touch you?"

"Yes." She dragged his hand to her chest, her heart racing. Her breasts cried out for his touch. "Here." She dragged it down to her stomach. "And here." She pulled it farther down to the juncture of her thighs. "Everywhere. Nothing but your touch will erase this pain—"

He plundered her mouth with his, swallowing her words. His lips were hard against her, grinding into her with savage need, forcing her to open up to him.

With a moan that never left her throat she gripped his shoulders and opened her mouth. He plunged his tongue into her—fast, ardent strokes that sent arrows of need shooting lower.

Molten desire pooled between her legs and she tried to squeeze them closer.

But his thigh was lodged between hers. And, God, he was so deliciously hard. She rubbed against his rock-hard muscles, groaning, whimpering.

She wanted him so much, needed him so much, and she was going to let him fill her inside out, fill every inch of her, with him, with his scent, with his touch, until the regrets gouging holes inside her were gone.

*Because she wanted another chance at this. She wanted
another chance with Diego.*

Diego had never felt such all-consuming desire as he did
for this woman. Need prickled along his skin, making his
erection an instrument in self-torture. Seeing her with that
blasted vibrator in her hand, her legs open in sinful invitation, was enough to push him to the edge of his control.

And he had never had much to begin with. Not when
it came to her.

He plunged his tongue into her mouth with all the finesse
of an impatient teenager. He licked the inseam, nipped at
the sensitive flesh.

There was no tentativeness in her either. In fact the bold
strokes of her tongue against his own had him thrusting his
hips into her soft stomach like a randy animal.

Meu Deus, she tasted like sunshine and strawberries and
the decadent promise of wild, hot sex. A hint of lily of the
valley clung to her skin and filled his nostrils.

A loud whimper emanated from her when he sucked on
her tongue. Her hands crawled up his nape into his hair.
When she tugged his lower lip between her teeth he shuddered violently, jerking his lower body into hers.

The groove of her legs cradled his erection perfectly
as she rubbed herself against him. Heat gathered low at
the base of his back, balling up into unbearable need in
his shaft.

How could anything that felt so good be bad?

He wanted to take her right there. Because she was his
and she wanted him, and it was the one place where there
was only truth between them.

He slipped his hands under the flimsy satin of her top.
Her skin, silky soft and warm to the touch, slithered like
velvet under his rough palms. Her breathing was harsh; her
soft gasps and groans were goading him on.

He was about to tug the silky strap off her shoulder when she shook her head and pulled back.

He growled instantly, like a wild animal denied its prey at the last moment.

The next minute her hands were on the fly of his jeans. He groaned—more of a request this time than a demand— as she undid the button.

His teeth were on edge as his jeans gave in. And she wrapped her long fingers around his shaft.

With a guttural groan, he pushed into her hand, blood roaring in his veins.

His eyes flicked open when her hand stopped its mind-bending caresses.

Sweat gleaming on her brow, she was trying to tug her shorts down, but her fingers kept slipping on the satin hem. She tugged a little more and the sight of black panties peeking out from under the hemline sent his blood pressure skyrocketing.

Every inch of his body was coiled tight, anticipating the pleasure, remembering how tight and wet and good she had felt around him the last time. She tugged her top off and lust blinded him.

But it was the sight of her stomach that cleared his vision. She wasn't showing much yet, but her midriff wasn't flat either. And it stopped him in his tracks.

He didn't want to force her against the wall and be done in a minute, which he was very close to doing. This could not be about slaking his lust. He didn't want to lose control as he had done the last time. Not now. Not ever again.

Because once they did this he wouldn't stop with tonight. He wanted her in his bed for the rest of their lives. If he kept control of his sanity, if he held himself back, maybe there was hope for a civilized relationship with her after all. That was what it had to be, for the sake of his children.

He wanted *her* to lose control, he wanted *her* mindless

with pleasure and he wanted her begging for release. This time he wanted to savor every inch of her, wanted to linger over her body. This time he wanted all of her revealed to him.

"I want you inside me *now,* Diego. Please…" she said, her words a sensuous whisper.

Gritting his teeth, he clasped her wrists and stopped her. "No."

Kim blinked, felt a tightening in her throat.

It was the cruelest word in the English language. She sagged against him, her breath coming in choppy little puffs. It was a good thing his hard body was still supporting her or she would have sagged to the floor. She hid her face in his rising and falling chest, loath to reveal the tears burning at the backs of her eyelids.

He lifted her into his arms. Only when he lowered her onto the bed, on top of the covers, did she open her eyes again. He stood over her, his tight features set into a stony mask of spine-tingling…*resolve.* That was the only word for it.

What she saw in the tight set of his mouth, in the lingering heat in his hungry gaze, set all her internal alarms ringing.

His jaw set, he trailed his gaze over her slowly, from the top of her hair to her pink toenails, without missing an inch in the process. Something flitted into it and a flutter began in the pit of her stomach.

She was still clothed, even though the upper curves of her breasts were visible over her bra and her shorts were bunched up against her upper thighs.

He disappeared and then reappeared on the bed in the blink of an eye. With something in his hand. "Take off your clothes."

Her breaths came quick and rushed. The pink handcuffs

looked absolutely flimsy in his large hands. An unrelenting throb, a tremble, started in her. Pushing back with her heel, she tried to roll away from him. He didn't let her.

With her ankle in his free hand, he flicked his wrist and she slid down the bed, her legs now trapped between his knees.

A dark smile full of sinful promises curved his mouth. The handcuffs dangled in the air above her. "I want to see every inch of you, lick and kiss every inch of your skin. I want you incoherent with pleasure."

She shook her head, her mouth dry as a desert. His words had the most arousing effect on her. A slow, wicked pull began pulsing at her sex and she clutched her thighs together.

It wasn't enough that she had surrendered. She had to surrender *everything*. His words and her thoughts collided, her mind and her body clashed, even as an illicit thrill shot through her.

"No."

He shrugged, sitting back on his haunches. "My way or no way. Last offer, *gatinha*. Give up your control or I'm walking out the door."

There was a savage satisfaction, a grating pride in his words, that irked her.

She wanted to say, *Fine.* Slide off the bed and walk away. The word trembled on her lips. The sensible part of her was screaming at her to walk away. But what had all these years of being careful and logical brought her?

A crushing loneliness and nothing else.

She nodded, unable to give words to her acceptance.

His teeth were bared in a smile, gleaming with unabashed hunger.

Sliding back on the bed, trembling with a host of conflicting emotions, she unhooked her bra and shrugged it off.

A hungry groan was torn out of Diego and it shuddered around them.

He seemed to freeze right in front of her, drinking her in. Need knotted her nipples and moved incessantly lower. Gritting her jaw, she lay back against the bed and slowly peeled off her shorts in one movement.

He leaned forward and she drew in a sharp breath, her fingers halting on the edge of her panties. He clasped her wrists and tugged her arms upward. His shirt grazed her nipples, setting her skin ablaze. The hem of his jeans rubbed against her belly. She groaned and almost bucked off the bed, the delicious friction setting her skin on fire.

He neatly clamped her wrists with the handcuffs and moved back to his knees. "Turn around and lie facedown," he threw at her roughly, before sliding off the bed.

She bristled at his command, even though the hoarse note in his words, the way he moved away from her as though he didn't trust himself, sent a wave of feminine power rippling through her.

CHAPTER TEN

"CHOCOLATE OR STRAWBERRY?"

The question from across the room was fraught with unsatisfied hunger, mirroring her own. The soft Egyptian cotton chafed against her breasts and her skin. She let out a shaky breath.

"I have a choice?"

Silence—waiting, threatening—met her.

She shut her eyes, clutched the sheets with her fingers and mumbled "Chocolate..." Every second he didn't touch her was reducing her into a mindless state of anticipation and need.

She didn't know what she had expected—didn't know what his question even meant. It was definitely *not* the hot slide of his oil-slick palms over her back.

The massage oil.

She groaned as he rubbed at the knots in her shoulder. The scent of dark chocolate combined with his own, infiltrating every pore of her. His calluses abraded her skin, sparking tiny pinpricks of pleasure all over.

Done with the knots in her shoulders, his hands moved down, over her lower back, lower still to her buttocks. She closed her eyes and savored the sensation as they traveled over her buttocks, her thighs, her calves and even her feet.

They pulled and kneaded, rubbed and stroked, until every muscle in her was pliant and boneless. Her throat was raw with the sounds she made. She felt as if she was floating on clouds.

But he didn't stop.

And suddenly the tempo of his touch changed.

A different kind of pleasure slithered over her skin. Her mouth dried up. Her breath hitched in her throat.

Even his breathing seemed different, shallower, the strokes of his fingers more calculated.

A heat flush was overtaking every inch of her as he pushed her thighs the tiniest inch apart.

His slick hands molded over her thigh muscles. With new tension replacing old knots, she breathed hard. He tugged her panties down. She shuddered and struggled to move.

"Relax, *pequena*."

His command was gruff, curt.

She felt the slide of his hot mouth, open and scorching against the base of her spine. She moaned—a guttural sound that filled the cabin.

He scraped his teeth over one buttock. She clenched her thighs, trying to catch the ache there. With his huge palm between her thighs, he didn't give her that satisfaction.

She whimpered, ready to beg. "Please, Diego...just—"

"No, *gatinha*. Remember—my rules, my way."

His words elicited an erotic thrill from her that she had no way to control. Sliding his left hand beneath her tummy, he pulled her up a little, while his right hand steadily but slowly crept toward her sex.

An electric current sizzled along her nerves. She bit her lower lip hard, striving to catch the groan that was tearing out of her.

"Let go of your lip," he ordered, his voice guttural.

She shook her head in denial, or something like it.

He snuck a finger into her sex. Millions of nerve endings flared to life.

She flinched from the pleasure and then shivered all over, her toes curling into the bed.

Dear God, what was he doing to her?

She was draped over his hand like a rag doll, *everything* open and visible to him. She had never felt so vulnerable and so out of control. And yet she couldn't wait for him to do whatever he wanted with her.

His hand reached her curls, delved through her folds. She was aching for his touch, for the pressure that would send her over.

"*Droga,* but you're so wet and ready."

A scream built in her chest and she trembled from head to toe. "Please, Diego…" she whispered on a sob.

Another finger joined the first inside her sheath. She rubbed herself into his touch and heard his groan.

His fingers reached finally and stroked her clitoris. "Come for me, *gatinha.*"

She opened her mouth and breathed in jerkily. Pleasure built as he moved his fingers faster, inside and out, the heel of his palm rubbing against her with every movement. She closed her eyes, heat gathering momentum in her pelvic muscles, her groans sounding erotic.

Until he pressed down with his thumb and forefinger and set fire to that aching bundle of nerves.

She cried out as she orgasmed violently, white lights exploding behind her eyes, her breath hitching somewhere between the base of her throat and her lungs, her body fraying with the assault of pleasure, her mind utterly soaked with satisfaction.

The sound of her climax, rasping and throaty, wrenched a tormented answering shudder from Diego. He placed his palm on her lower back as the tremors in her body slowly subsided and then pulled her up to her knees gently. The scent of her arousal was thick in the air he breathed. Her skin was warm to the touch, with a faint sheen of sweat on it. Her locked hands lay in front of her. Her neck was thrown back against his shoulder.

His erection nestled into the curve of her buttocks. He rubbed himself against her and groaned, his shaft aching with need.

She felt so breakable in his rough hands, and the receding shudders in her slender body, her nudity, revealed a fragility that she hid under her perfection.

He pressed an open-mouthed kiss just above the indent of her buttocks and she tautened like an arrow. She tasted of chocolate and sweat. He trailed kisses upward, tasting and licking her, until he reached the graceful curve of her neck.

He opened his mouth and bit the tender flesh there. A moan rumbled out of her. She struggled against the handcuffs.

"Unlock them, Diego."

Her words were a raw, needy whisper. His stomach muscles tightened into hard rocks.

"I like you like this, *minha esposinha*," he said, uncaring that he sounded like the dirty thug he was. He pushed her hair away from her face and licked the seam of her ear.

Her response was a delicious tremble. "You're still fully dressed."

He moved his right forearm until his palm lay flat against her belly. She sucked in a sharp breath. He pushed her back onto the bed and joined her, lying on his side. She went without a sound. He laughed.

A delicate pink dusting her cheeks, she tried to cross her arms over her breasts and the triangle of curls that stole his breath.

She glared at him. "What?"

"I really like you all pliant and naked like this. All mine to do whatever I want with."

"Undo the cuffs, Diego," she said, with a hint of pleading in her words now.

He smiled and slid his palm up toward one breast,
kneaded the soft flesh.

She closed her eyes on a long exhale and twisted to the
side. As if she would deny him access. He stood up from
the bed and eyed the dips and valleys of her body, need
yanking relentlessly at his groin.

He shed his clothes quietly and rejoined her on the bed.

"Are your breasts already fuller, *gatinha?*" he asked, his
words slurring around his tongue. "You're not quite showing, but I see the signs." He kissed the curve of her hip.
"Here." He planted another one on her stomach. "Here."

Her gaze flew open, stroked over his naked body with
a swift greed that set his teeth on edge. "You're still pun-
ishing me for walking away, aren't you?"

"I'm not. I adore seeing you naked, searching for the
small little changes in your body that my children might
already be causing."

She swallowed visibly, her gaze filled with a dark fear.

"I prefer to lie in bed with you and savor every inch of
you instead of screwing you against the wall."

A single tear rolled out of her eye and he caught it with
his mouth. It knocked the breath from his lungs. He palmed
her face and forced her to look at him. "If you want me to
stop—?"

She shook her head, the remaining unshed tears making her eyes twinkle like precious stones. "I'm…*glad* that
it's your children inside me, Diego."

He felt a strange tightness in his chest as he captured
her mouth again. Even the erotic pull of her mouth wasn't
enough to dilute the disappointment that slashed through
him. He'd had the feeling she had meant to say something
else. But, as usual, she had kept it to herself.

And why the hell was he hanging on to each word of

hers like a faithful little dog? He needed to keep this on *his* terms.

He palmed her breast and felt a shudder go through him as the pebbled tip rasped against his palm. Her moan, almost bordering on a sob, filled his ears. His fingers looked worse than rough around the puckered nipple. He flicked it with the pad of his thumb and she pushed herself into his hand.

He kept his gaze on her, the sounds she made at the back of her throat, the lust that she couldn't hide from him, bleeding into the air around him, giving him unparalleled satisfaction.

She was his wife. She was going to be the mother of his children. This strong, brilliant, stubborn woman, who was worried that she didn't care about the babies in her womb, she needed him, needed something only he could give her.

In that moment she was unraveled at his touch, a hair trigger away from exploding with pleasure again.

Desire was a feral pounding in his veins. He hardened a little more, heat billowing from his very skin.

Nothing but her short gasp could have stopped him, so intent was he on losing his mind in her body and its softness.

"What is it, *pequena?*"

Her gaze took a few seconds to focus on him. She wiggled her handcuffed wrists and scrunched her nose. "They're beginning to hurt now."

He unlocked them instantly.

The next moment was a blur to his lust-soaked brain. As soon as he took the handcuffs off her she rolled away from him.

But he was in no mood for games or smiles. Somewhere between rubbing oil onto her body and seeing her naked he had begun losing control of himself again, started losing a small part of himself again. And he was damned if he'd let her take anything he wasn't willing to give.

"Come here, Kim," he said arrogantly.

Her gaze widened. She hadn't obviously missed the dark edge to his words. But of course she didn't heed his warning. She never did. It was always a battle of wills with her.

"Make me."

Kim squealed as Diego trapped her neatly on the bed. She threw punches. Not one fazed him. She even aimed her leg for a swift kick. It was too late.

He held her beneath him, his body a blazing furnace of tightly controlled desire.

He bent his mouth and took her nipple in his mouth. She lost the capacity for all coherent thought. He suckled at it—deep, long pulls that instantly sent pangs of need arrowing down to her sex—while his erection throbbed against her thighs.

She bucked off the bed, a throaty moan ripped from her throat. She snuck her hands into Diego's hair and held him there. He softly blew on the nipple and turned his attention to the other one. He rolled it between his fingers, rasped his stubble against the sensitive underside. She was ready to climax again.

She moved her legs restlessly and the rasp of his hair-roughened leg against hers sent sensations spiraling inside her. He closed his lips on the nipple and tugged it between his teeth. It was beyond bearable, bordering on pain-pleasure.

"I want to touch you, Diego," she pleaded, pushing him back, her hands on his shoulders. He didn't budge an inch.

He continued the assault with his mouth, trailing hot, wet kisses between her breasts, toward her stomach. Every inch of her skin that he kissed felt as if it was waking up from a long slumber.

The minute she felt his breath on her thighs she decided enough was enough. She rolled to slip from under him, a smile stretching her mouth from ear to ear.

Before he could stop her, she pushed him back on the bed and lay atop him from head to toe, her breath shaking in and out of her. Their mingled groans filled the silent cabin.

The rasp of her skin against his, the friction, was incomparable. Her breasts rubbed against his chest. His erection pressed into her belly. Her legs tangled with his.

Without giving him a moment to breathe, she pressed her mouth to his.

And she didn't do it tenderly. She gave the kiss everything she had in her, infusing her touch with every little emotion she had never been able to put into words and never could. She traced his lush lower lip with her tongue, nipped the moist inside, sucked his tongue into her mouth, rubbing herself against him like a cat.

God, whatever she did, she couldn't stop rubbing against him.

He breathed out on a hiss, his muscles shifting and pressing into her.

"You're going to be the death of me," he whispered as she dragged her mouth down to his neck.

He sounded utterly on edge, and she liked him like that. She bit his nipple and his fingers tightened on her arms.

She moved down and the friction of their sweat-slick bodies threatened to drive her crazy. She rubbed herself over his erection. He growled.

She dragged the tip of her tongue over the hard ridges of his stomach. He roared.

She clasped her fingers around his shaft and slid her fist up and down. Sweat shimmered on his brow. He jerked his hips into her touch, his stuttering breathing filling her ears. She bent and licked the swollen head, the taste and scent of him sending pulsing tingles straight to her wet core.

She laid her palm flat against his flinching abdominal muscles and licked the head again.

His upper body shot up off the bed, and before she could blink he'd tugged her boneless body until she was straddling him.

He grabbed her hips and entered her—slowly, hotly, precisely—until all she could feel was his possession. She clamped her arms around him so his face burrowed into her breasts as he pulled himself up.

A billion nerves jumped into life as their hips bumped into each other.

She dug the tips of her fingers demandingly into his rock-hard shoulders. She opened her eyes, ready to beg for more—and froze.

His gaze was studying her raptly, glittering with raw intensity, as though he saw into her very soul and found her disappointingly wanting. It was a sensation she couldn't shed, a feeling she couldn't shake.

But she was damned if she'd let it spoil the most precious moment of her life.

She kissed his mouth and moved swiftly off him.

And pushed herself back onto him.

They both groaned, the sounds needy, desperate, on edge.

She bent her head and bit his shoulder, digging her teeth into the muscle none too gently. It was all the signal he needed, apparently.

With a rough groan he reversed their positions, until he was on top of her. Throwing her legs over his shoulders, he thrust into her, harder, faster, until neither of them could see clearly, until neither could even breathe properly, until their bodies were ready to jump out of their shells.

She came with an unchecked scream that was torn out of her on a surge of need. Pleasure rocked through her—

waves and waves of unrelenting pressure that splintered and spread through every inch of her.

With one final thrust, Diego collapsed over her.

Eventually, even though it felt like forever, the pleasure waves receded, bringing in their wake painful realization. As though there was always a price for such life-altering joy as she had found in his arms.

She was in love with Diego. She always would be.

Had she ever been out of love with him really? It was a simple truth, as simple and soul-wrenching as the babies growing inside her.

Every inch of her wanted to retreat, hide, until she could come to terms with the terrifying truth. She needed to prepare herself, needed to set expectations for herself. She couldn't let it make her weak.

She couldn't let her love for him define her existence.

Diego felt Kim stiffen even before he pulled out of her. But he refused to let her hide from him. Not after the most intense orgasm of his life.

But when had it been anything less than explosive with her?

Still joined with her, he tumbled onto his back and pulled her with him until they were both lying sideways. He cupped her breast and kissed the upper curve of it, unable to resist the urge.

She opened her eyes with a helpless moan, dark chocolate pools swimming with desire. And yet there was a shadow of retreat, too.

"No, no, no," he whispered, putting his free hand on her temple and pressing.

She half smiled, every bit of it reluctant and torn from her. "No, what?"

He tapped her temple with his finger. "No thinking."

The shadows disappeared from her gaze and her mouth curved into a wide smile. He felt something loosen in his gut.

"No thinking, huh? That's like asking you…"

He raised his brow, urging her on.

"Like asking you to not be *sexy*." She raked her nails over his abdomen and he sighed with pleasure. "Although if you are naked like this I can't *actually* think."

He laughed. He really liked her like this. And not just because she was naked and sexy and it drove him crazy with desire. But because an inherent part of her—a side of her he rarely if ever saw—was exposed to him when they made love.

This intimacy, he realized slowly, was something she guarded closely—as she did all her feelings. It was something she had shared only with him. Primal satisfaction beat through him at the realization.

"Then we will be naked all the time. I mean, if that's what it takes to have a happy marriage I'm up for it."

She laughed, and the rich sound surrounded him.

He moved his hands toward her breasts and cupped them. "You were right. All this sophistication—it's just on the outside. Beneath it I'm an old-fashioned, chauvinistic man."

"Yeah?" she said, challenge glinting in her gaze. But her gaze dropped as he flicked a hard nipple with his fingers, her breathing becoming sharp.

"Yeah. I would like my wife to not think too much—even if she *is* one of the most brilliant women I have ever met. I would like to protect my wife from the big, bad world—even though she's the strongest woman I have ever met. I would like to be the only man—or the only *equipment*," he amended quickly, and she laughed, "that is allowed to touch her. I would like to be the only one who can—"

"Tie her up in knots? Make her forget right or wrong?

Turn her world upside down and generally plunge her life into chaos?"

His heart pounded so hard in his chest that he wondered if it would burst out of him.

"You already do all that and more to me, Diego."

Before he could pull in his next breath she pushed him onto his back and straddled him. With sure movements she wrapped his fingers around him and guided him inside her wetness as though she had blurted out too much…as though she didn't want him to linger over her words.

Once she started to move over him, her high breasts moving softly with her movements, her eyes drooping to half-mast with need, he forgot everything but the lust driving him to the edge.

He thrust upward in rhythm with her movements, he pulled himself up as her tempo increased. He pulled her nipple into his mouth and tugged at it with his teeth.

And she exploded around him, her muscles contracting and pulling at him. He thrust one more time into her and hit his own orgasm. He jerked his hips into her for every inch of pleasure she could give him, but something else was fueling the pleasure breaking out all over him.

CHAPTER ELEVEN

SITTING ON THE terrace overlooking the Brazilian coast, Kim ran her hands over her bare arms. The evening sky glittered with stars and the breeze carried a hint of the exotic flowers that were native to the island, which was an ecological paradise.

The past ten days she had spent here had flown by in a whirl, and they had been the best days of her life.

She saw Diego most days, except when he made trips to Rio di Janeiro. He made a lot of those—even though he was often back before she'd realized he was gone.

He didn't inform her about his schedule and she was still too new at this…whatever *this* was—to ask him to share. But the time they did spend together was becoming more and more precious to her.

Two days into their stay she had taken a trip around the island with Miguel, who had joined them a day after they arrived. She had met four young men, ranging from Miguel's eighteen-year-old best friend to a hulking brute of a boy whose age was indeterminate. And that was when she'd realized the truth.

Diego was doing everything he possibly could to get as many kids out of the street gang he himself had been a part of and bring them here. He was giving them honest work to do, showing them a different way of life. Some came willingly in search of a something better, and some, like

Miguel, who had seen too much violence already, didn't believe a better world existed.

She had thought Diego obsessed with wealth, determined to take everything he thought the world had denied him. She couldn't have been more wrong. She'd felt an insane urge to shout to the world what an honorable man he was, how wrong the media's perception of him was. So she had started a project with Miguel's help, excited to be doing something for Diego.

He might think himself damned, but with each passing second Kim could only see the good, the honor in Diego. And fall deeper into love with him.

Only being in love was just as horrible as she remembered it to be.

Not that she didn't enjoy the attention he showered on her. She had never been so pampered in her life. Forget pampered—no one had ever even so much as cooked a meal for her.

She walked on white beaches every day, swam in the infinity pool that edged from the villa into the ocean, napped for an hour every afternoon. The third day after their arrival Diego had even taken her on a hot air balloon ride over the island. It had been the most wonderful time she'd had.

He had shown her the exotic flora on the island, the place where construction had begun on a house for the teenagers he was bringing over. They had even seen Miguel and the other kids playing soccer on a vast expanse of untouched land.

Anything she asked for, she had it in a few hours—like the state-of-the-art camcorder she had requested.

He even had Miguel watch over her when he was busy, and the little punk seized her laptop every day after an hour, as though she was on the clock.

It had taken a couple of days but she had gotten over her panic about her company. Her staff were experts at what they did; of course they could manage without her for a couple of weeks.

She should feel on top of the world. And she did in those split seconds when she could stop obsessing and let the tight leash she kept on herself go.

Her day, from dawn to dusk, was spent wondering why he didn't kiss her again, what was stopping her from crawling into his bed—wherever it was that he slept. She was tired of waiting for him to make a move when all she wanted was to surround herself with him.

She wanted him, and she was pretty sure, from the way his hungry gaze ate her up, he wanted her. Tonight she would...

All her intentions disintegrated into dust when he walked onto the terrace. With his BFF in tow.

Jealousy burned like a blaze in her chest. She trembled from head to toe. The strength of it was feral. It pummeled her muscles into action and she got up in a sudden movement that made her lightheaded. She clutched at the wrought-iron railing.

Just the sight of him with Marissa was enough to burn a hole through her heart.

For the first time in over a week Kim had no appetite for dinner. Even though Anna had prepared everything the way Kim liked.

She smiled and nodded, answered with yes or no for the first half hour, pushing her food halfheartedly around on her plate. The other woman—or *was* she the other woman in this case?—was nothing but polite, inquiring after Kim's health, how she was enjoying her stay on the island.

There was only so much Marissa could do to squelch the awkwardness while Kim stayed resolutely mute. But what could she say?

She felt such an influx of emotions—jealousy roped

with guilt that she had destroyed this woman's life with one single action, a hot rush of anger toward Diego for subjecting them all to this—she was literally stupefied into speechlessness.

Eventually Marissa switched to Portuguese, and Kim was almost grateful for the snub. She waited another ten minutes before she excused herself and fled back to the terrace.

Loneliness churned through her and she suddenly missed Liv with an ache. She needed her irrepressible twin so much right now. Because her life was in tatters if *this* was how being in love was going to feel.

A soaring high one minute and a gut-wrenching low the next.

It was early evening the next day when Diego found Kim walking along the beach, a couple of miles from the villa. He made a quick call.

This part of the island was even more untouched than the other side. Pristine white sands, turquoise waters—he loved this view. This island was the one thing he owned that gave him the utmost satisfaction and joy at what he had achieved in life.

It was a place with nothing but sky and acres of land around him. The one thing he had craved for so long. Somewhere that wasn't a ditch to call his own. Now Miguel, and others like him, could enjoy the freedom that came from knowing their very lives *didn't* depend on their ability to throw punches and fight dirty.

Not that he had ever stopped. Now it was just for different things.

Today the view didn't hold his interest. And he had a feeling the quiet contentment he had felt over the past week or so had been more to do with the solitary figure half a mile in front of him than his success in purchasing the island that he had wanted for so long.

To break that spell he had brought Marissa. He could have caught up with her on his next trip to Rio. But he knew she'd wanted to see the island. And he was loath to change anything in his life just because Kim was in it now.

That was the only way to keep this in check. Only Kim had looked as if he had slapped her last night.

It had taken everything he'd had in him to not chase after her when she had left for the terrace halfway through dinner. Instead he had spent the evening with Marissa, going over the last few legalities. Even her update that visa issues were now taken care of for two more boys like Miguel hadn't been enough to keep his mind from Kim.

And yet he had fought the pull.

He didn't even have a clear idea why. As each day passed with her he had felt an increasing sense of uncertainty creeping into his thoughts. As to how much he enjoyed her company, how much he looked forward to seeing her in the morning, how much he enjoyed it when she pored over a financial report with him and came up with a solution in two minutes flat.

He had learned early on that anything that felt that good always came with a high price.

He tucked his hands into the pockets of his trousers and came to a standstill, watching her. Not his heart, though. It pounded extra hard in his chest.

The utter silence, punctured only by the ocean's waves, cocooned them, weaving its own magic.

She stood barefoot in the sand, the ocean lapping at her feet.

Her slender back, skin glowing in the sun, was pure temptation marred only by two yellow strings tied at the neck and then down lower. His gaze followed the curve of her back to the dip. A sarong-style wrap hugged her pert behind. Her long legs were only visible again from her knees.

He released a shaky breath. He had purposely pulled himself back these past few days, held back through sheer will. He didn't want to fall headlong into his desire for her again, to forget the right and wrong of the situation—forget himself.

He wanted the comfortable camaraderie they had slipped into to last. He wanted something stable for his children, and for the first time since she had told him that she was pregnant, for the first time on this island, he felt the goodness of what they had in his bones.

This felt right. This felt good. And he would do anything to keep it like that.

The line of her shoulders tightened infinitesimally. Her hands wrapped around herself and she stiffened, holding herself aloof from the world.

It was enough to burst the bubble of tranquility he had felt just a second ago. Tension curled his muscles and his mind geared up for whatever fight she was going to throw his way, his body exulting in the thrill shooting through his blood.

She turned and met his gaze.

He felt the intensity of her look as if she had run those long fingers over him. His muscles were flexing and rearing for her touch. Lust rocketed through him, tightening every muscle with fiery need.

Her lustrous hair slapped across her face. Her bikini top cupped her breasts just as he wanted to. He couldn't deny they were looking rounder. She had put on some weight, was losing that gaunt, over-worked look. And she had that first blush of pregnancy he had overheard Anna mentioning to her.

It was in the slight flare of her hips, in the fullness of her breasts, in the healthy flush of her skin. Her stomach, though not yet round, was beginning to grow. He trailed his gaze over her, enjoying the sheer eroticism of looking at her.

She was the sexiest woman he had ever seen, and her innate modesty made her even more appealing. Even now she was oblivious to her effect on him, on his self-control, as her overactive mind whizzed through something.

"Do you miss being with her?"

Diego blinked. For a second he didn't understand her question. "*Droga,* I knew I shouldn't have left you alone for so long. You're ripe for a fight, aren't you?"

"That's ridiculous."

"You are much more comfortable when we're fighting, when you can peg me into whatever box you can. We have been laughing, generally enjoying each other's company, for over a week now. So of *course* it's time to draw the lines again."

"I...I'm serious, Diego."

He didn't miss whatever it was he had once shared with Marissa. It had been a comfortable relationship they had both fallen into whenever something had gone wrong in their lives—the one good thing that had stood firm despite every hardship they had faced.

He just wished he had realized sooner that it had meant so much more to Marissa than it had to him. What he felt for Kim—a crazy obsession that knew no right or wrong—he had never had with any other woman in life.

Nothing like the fizzle of anticipation roaring in his blood as she came closer, nor the tightening in his gut every time he thought he had finally reached the core of her and then she retreated behind her shell again.

She came to a halt right in front of him. Her scent teased his nostrils. Hot arousal was inching across his skin.

"You don't have to spare my feelings. I can take it," she said.

Curiosity blazed like a forest fire through him. "Does that mean it would hurt you if I said I do miss her?"

"Yes," she replied, her mouth a tight line.

Was it downright sadistic of him to *enjoy* the fact that she could be hurt by his actions? That he had a hold over her, however tenuous?

"I couldn't trust myself to not lose it right in front of her. That's why I left. I will understand if you…want me to leave."

He cursed—a filthy word his mother would have washed out his mouth for. "What the hell does that mean?" At her grating silence, he answered. "I don't miss her."

"Then why is she here? Who are you trying to punish by pushing us all together? Yourself or me?"

He frowned. "You want me to cut her out of my life? Tell her she has no part in it now that you are here? She's the one person who has stood by me my whole life. Whether I was a success or a failure, whether I was being a sanctimonious bastard or not. What do you expect me to do? Tell her—?"

Kim shook her head, feeling sick to her stomach. She got it now. Marissa was the *constant* whereas Kim was the *variable*—the one who could disappear from his life any minute.

Maybe even the one he could leave behind when he didn't want her anymore?

"I don't know," she said, her anxiety spilling into her words. "All I want to know is whether you'll give this… *us*…a real chance or not."

"And bringing a friend of mine here means I won't?" He smiled. "Is this you being jealous, *gatinha?*"

Kim flinched. "I'm sorry. I don't know what came over me. I have no right to—"

He tugged her around. "Yes, you do. You have every right to ask me whatever you want to. You might not always like the answer. It could be worse than what you lose by keeping silent. Why do you *do* that?"

"What?"

"Walk away silently."

She tried to shy her gaze away from him. "I don't know what you're talking about."

"Yes, you do. Even last time on the island, when I said I was done with you, you didn't utter a word. You should have called me a bastard right then. Instead you left without a word. You fight more for your company than you do for yourself."

"If I don't ask anything of you, don't expect anything of you, you can't hurt me."

He shook his head. "It is never that simple."

"It's the only way to survive."

"Who hurt you?"

She tried to turn away from him but he wouldn't let her. This was not a conversation she wanted to have. "No one hurt me, Diego. However, you will be disgusted by the depths of selfishness I can fall to."

His hands locking her in place, he looked into her eyes. "Nothing you do or have done will ever make me despise you. Make me angry, yes. Drive me crazy, yes... But disgust me...? *No.* Haven't I showed you that already?"

"The night before my mother left I found her note."

"A note?"

Every inch of her shook just remembering that night. "It was one line. Addressed to my father. She was leaving him and taking Liv with her."

Leaving her behind.

She had gone to her mother's room to check on her, to inform her of what her father had planned for the next day, to tell her that she had taken care of everything needed for a small party at their house.

Instead she had found a small bag sitting on the floor

of the closet. It had contained her mother's jewelry, cash, her passport and—the thing that had sent a shiver down Kim's spine—Liv's passport. For a frantic minute she had emptied the bag, looking for her own passport, her lungs constricting painfully.

It hadn't been in that bag.

Wondering if her mother had made a mistake, her head reeling from what it meant, she had walked to the bed and found the note scribbled on her mother's stationery.

It had been the worst moment in her life—sitting there, wondering what she had done wrong, how she could have acted any different, why her mother would choose to take Liv but not her...

Her vision blurred. The same confusion, the same utter desolation sprang inside her at the memory. The words she hadn't dared to speak aloud, the thoughts that wouldn't leave her alone even after all these years, the fears she hadn't shared with another soul, poured out of her on a wave of uncontrollable pain.

"For as long as I can remember I did everything I could to shield her from my father. I always stayed strong for her. I stayed by her bed when she was ill. I never once asked her for anything, Diego. And in the end she—" her voice broke, her insides twisting into a mass of pain.

Diego's rough palms on her cheeks, the familiarly comforting scent of him, pulled her out of the depths of despair. He forced her to look at him.

"Tell me you confronted her, Kim. Tell me you demanded to know why."

"No. And I didn't beg her to take me, too, if that's what you want to hear." Her throat felt as if pieces of glass were stuck in it. "I threatened to go to my father with the note if she went anywhere near Liv. I stayed awake by Liv's side all night. And my mother...she...left sometime during the night. But you're right. I *am* an unfeeling, selfish bitch."

"You did nothing wrong." His words were a frustrated growl.

"No? You see, I was determined to not let her rob the one person who loved me from my life. Except you know what...?"

His stomach churning with a vicious force, Diego watched Kim. She walked away from him, trembling from head to toe, her words vibrating with pain.

"Liv paid for it. With our mother gone, my father turned his corrosive, controlling attention to *her*."

"You can't blame yourself for that. You were a child."

"He made her life miserable every single minute of every single day, Diego," she said, her fists locked by her sides. "There—are you disgusted now?"

How could he hate her for surviving when he would have done the same? She'd lived her life with the cards she had been dealt and made no excuses for it.

She slipped from him before he could tell her how much he understood, how that kind of hurt never died down.

She could have hated Olivia after her mother left. But she had been strong for both of them, had tried to shield her from their father when she had been nothing more than a teenager herself. And she thought there was nothing in her that felt...

He tugged her closer and wrapped his hands around her. She didn't relax immediately. He tightened his hold.

She smelled of the ocean and lemons and something undeniably *her*.

He stood holding her like that, running his fingers over her back. So many things rushed through him. Utter amazement at her strength robbed him of his ability to speak.

Walking away from her mother, from her father, from him—it was the only way she had survived.

A lump in his throat cut off his breath and he relaxed his hold on her.

Handling her was no different from handling a hurt teen-ager like Miguel, really. Miguel lashed out at the world in order to live through his pain, whereas Kim internalized everything to survive—pushed her own feelings and de-sires so deep inside she had pretty much cauterized herself against any hurt.

If his childhood had been hell, hers had been no better. Just a different kind of hell.

"You remind me of Miguel," he whispered, breathing her scent deep into his lungs.

She looked up at him, reluctance filling her gaze. "I don't know what to make of that."

"Whenever I see him in pain I want to hunt down ev-eryone that's hurt him. It's the same way I feel right now. Instead of protecting you, your mother used you and Ol-ivia as shields against her husband. She was not fit to be a mother. And I will throttle you if you compare yourself to her again."

Tears glazed her eyes.

He moved his palm to her stomach and felt his heart kick inside his chest. "Except I've never wanted to kiss Miguel, as I want to do you, every waking minute."

Kim blinked back the tears that prickled behind her eyes. His tenderness was unraveling her and she was terrified she would never be whole again, never be strong again.

Day by day, word by word, he had slowly peeled away all her armor. Her emotions were spilling and overflowing. It was both terrifying and exciting.

She shivered and scrunched closer to him. His arms were steel bands around her, his body a furnace of need and want. And for the first time in her life she felt wanted. As if her wishes mattered, as if *she* mattered. And not for her brains, for her accomplishments, but for the person she was beneath all that—scared and hurt and frozen.

She moved in his embrace and pressed her mouth to his chest. He rumbled beneath her touch.

"Come with me," he whispered.

Her smaller hand encompassed by his, she let him tug her whichever way he wanted.

They walked for about five minutes, the sand crunching under their feet.

She came to a sudden halt, dragging Diego to a stop along with her. Dusk was beginning to streak the sky orange above them and a custom-made cabana, its dark oak gleaming in the fading sunlight, stood about two feet from them, big enough to accommodate two people.

And narrow enough to squish them together.

Pristine white cotton sheets covered the opening, contrasting richly against the dark oak. Heat uncurled low in her belly, her legs threatening to collapse under her.

And that wasn't all.

A small table was set up in front of the cabana, with candles and dinner for two. A pink cardboard box with a small bow also sat on it. The curly "A" on top of it looked very familiar...

His hard body shifting behind her, Diego wrapped his arms around her, his strong legs supporting her own.

"That's a box from Angelina's in Paris." It was her favorite patisserie on the Champs d'Elysées.

Suddenly she knew what was in it. She turned to him, laughter bubbling out of her.

"Anna told me you've mentioned their pastries once or twice."

She met his laughing gaze. "How about a million times?"

"Happy Anniversary, *minha esposinha.*"

Her breath hitched in her throat. It was the first thing that had hit her when she'd woken up this morning—the reason why she had wandered away so far from the villa.

It was the one date she had always taken off and spent at her apartment, reliving that day.

She nodded, struggling to speak past the lump cutting off her breath. Stretching on her toes, she pressed into him until his erection rubbed against her bottom.

He groaned and hugged her tighter.

"I don't want the pastry."

He licked the seam of her ear. Her skin was too fraught with need to contain her.

"What *do* you want, *querida?* Whatever it is, I will bring it to you."

"You," she said clearly, loud enough for anyone in the vicinity to hear. It wasn't all she actually wanted to say, though. "I want *you,* Diego."

Without waiting for his answer she dragged him toward the cabana, intent on showing him with her actions everything she still wasn't brave enough to put into words.

They tore off each other's clothes with frenzied movements, as though they were both aware of how fragile, how precious this moment of perfection was.

Pushing her back into the soft mattress, Diego stretched out on top of her, his taut muscles a heavenly weight over her. His mouth, his tongue, his caresses, *he* was everywhere—kissing her, licking her, tasting her, generally reducing her body to a writhing mass of sensations and needs. He didn't give her a minute to breathe.

She cried out loud, the raw sound clawing its way out of her throat, when he pulled her nipple deep into his mouth and suckled at it. His rough fingers tweaked its twin, and twangs of hot pleasure shot down between her legs.

He smelled of the ocean, his muscles taut and shifting under her touch. She sobbed incoherently when he rubbed her aching core with the heel of his palm while his mouth trailed wet kisses around her navel. Pleasure coiled low in her belly, tugging every nerve-ending inside her along for the ride. Her whole body was unfolding mindlessly in tune with his erotic strokes.

His hair-roughened legs rubbing against hers, he reversed their positions with one smooth movement until she was straddling him.

Her sex quivered with need as his erection rubbed against her folds, and a shiver inched its way all over her skin.

Putting her weight on her thighs, she resisted.

His face was all severe planes and rough angles in the fading light. His choppy breath bounced off of her skin, giving her goosebumps.

His mouth was tight, his gaze drugged with desire. "This is not the time for one of your arguments, *gatinha*."

She smiled at the way his words rolled over each other, his accent creeping into his words. She placed her palms on his thighs and the rock-hard muscles clenched under her touch.

He groaned—a guttural, painful sound—as she drew her palms upward a little, until the pads of her fingers were idly tracing the length of his erection.

Her mouth dry, she forced herself to put her thoughts into words. "I want you on top of me." Pushing her hands into her hair, she stretched innocently.

His gaze moved to her breasts. Naked hunger was etched into his face. "Why?"

She slid off him and stretched alongside him. He immediately turned toward her. "I'm going to start showing in a little while." He moved his palm to her stomach. "And I...we...in the coming months it's going to be awkward."

He frowned. "So you won't want to have sex anymore? Because being near you and not having it will kill me."

She laughed. God, she would never have enough of his piercing honesty. "I will. But today I want your weight over me as you enter me. I want to feel every inch of you plastered to me."

He didn't say anything. He just pulled her wrists up with one hand and kissed her mouth, plundering her. Kneeled between her legs. Pulled one leg over his shoulder. Covered every inch of her with him as he thrust into her.

She was already wet and ready for him. But something more than pure lust sang in her veins. Her breasts shifted against his chest as he moved inside her. Her stomach groaned under the weight of his muscles. Sweat beaded over his forehead and she licked his shoulder when he thrust again.

It was hard and crushing. Her breathing was ragged, her skin ablaze with need. The delicious friction of his thrusts awakened a billion nerve-endings in her groin muscles.

Sharp bursts of pleasure crested over her. Desire pooled low and intense in her pelvis. She sensed his control slipping, his desire taking over, just as hers did, and each thrust was more desperate and less measured. Each sound he made was rougher and filled with a delicious lack of control.

When they hit their climaxes and pleasure broke out all over her she knew nothing was going to protect her heart now. How stupid she had been to think she still had control over this—that she could withstand it without losing herself.

Her heart was Diego's now—*whatever* he wanted to do with it. And she couldn't help but hope, after everything they had been through together, that he wouldn't trample it.

CHAPTER TWELVE

IT HAPPENED WHEN they had almost reached the villa. The fact that it had been near midnight by the time they had finished with each other, *and* with dinner at the secluded spot, meant that the loud, strident peal from his cell phone shattered the peace, the moment of perfection.

Diego froze next to her, bringing them both to a grinding halt even before he picked it up. He literally froze—his body next to her and his hand around hers going from delicious warmth to dreadful cold in a second. The jarring tune blared again, and Kim realized why she had felt a shiver go down her spine that first time.

That ringtone was different from his usual one. Which meant he had set it up for a particular call. And he seemed to expect the worst.

He shifted to the side, almost as though hiding himself from her, and picked up his phone.

The conversation lasted two minutes—tops.

A curse flew from his mouth and Kim flinched. With a growl that had the little hairs on her neck standing, he hurled his cell phone. It fell into the ocean and sank in seconds with a little gurgle.

Leaving the most deafening silence around them.

His emotions floated over him like a dark cloud that cut off the intense physical connection she had felt with him only a few minutes ago. Like a signal of extreme danger to anyone who dared approach him.

Foreboding inched over her, her skin chilly in the balmy night air.

He stared into the ocean, his shoulders rattling.

She reached him quietly where he stood, with tension and aggression pouring out of every sinew of him. "Diego, what's going on?"

"He's dead."

The words landed around them with the intensity of an earthquake that shook everything. She swayed for a second, her gut trembling. She dug her toes into the sand, blindly seeking to root herself. "Who?" she asked, wishing her instincts could be wrong.

"Eduardo."

The anguish in him wound itself around her. "I'm so sorry, Diego."

"Multiple organ failure killed him."

"I—"

"But they are wrong."

Her tongue wouldn't move to form the words she wanted to ask. She was so terrified of everything crumbling. "What do you mean?"

"*I'm* the one who killed him. As surely as if I put my hands on his throat and choked the life out of him."

Kim gasped. The self-loathing in his words was unbearable to hear. The need to comfort him pounded in her blood. "What are you talking about? Eduardo loved you."

"And I used his love, his trust in me, to my advantage. He was already crumbling under the weight of my father's expectations. And you know what I did? I befriended him under false pretenses, gained access to the company's information and pulled it out from under him. My father had no choice but to hand it over to me. I told myself Eduardo was barely keeping it together anyway. And then, when you left, I wanted blood. I went from driven to obsessed. Instead of helping him, I pushed him into his own destruction. I should have known Eduardo was already using— should have known how close he was to breaking. By the time I did it was already too late. Are you *still* glad that it's my children you're carrying, *gatinha?*"

The words dug their claws into her.

"I am. Because you're not that man anymore, Diego. You never were. I see how you are with Miguel, what you've gone through to pull him from that life. Whatever culpability you have in Eduardo's death—if you have any—you have paid for it a million times over."

She moved toward him and folded her arms around his middle from behind. A tremor shook him and it crashed into her, his raw anguish churning her stomach.

Innocence. They had both never had it. And even without realizing it they had been drawn to each other. For the first time she felt the loss of it as keenly as he did.

She pressed her mouth to his shoulders, felt him shudder under her touch, felt his rock-hard muscles relax against her. Felt him pull in a breath with the utmost effort.

She wanted to do everything she could to ease his pain. The intensity of how much she wanted to rocked through her. For a second she thought he might let her share his pain—for once let *her* support *him*.

"You have to forgive yourself. If you don't you'll—"

He walked away from her without a word.

His silence whipped at her hope. The weight of his guilt was a crushing weight on her own shoulders, even if he said it wasn't her fault.

Kim stood there watching him go, her hold on him just as slippery as the sandbanks holding the ocean at bay.

Kim didn't see Diego over the next couple of days. It was Miguel who informed her that he had gone to Sao Paulo to bury Eduardo, and that Marissa was by his side. It was Miguel who didn't leave her side for a minute, as though he could understand her mounting confusion.

Marissa was the one person Diego hadn't shut out of his grief. His friend had stayed by his side while Kim had watched from afar.

It hurt like nothing else in her life had—like a nail stuck under her skin, gouging into her flesh. And there was nothing she could do to change it

Would it be like this forever? She hated that feeling from the depths of her soul—hated that her happiness, her very state of mind, was dependent on whether Diego would ever smile at her again.

It was the same vicious circle of hell she had gone through when she had found her mother's note. What could she have done differently? What could she change within herself? It was a powerless, clawing feeling she couldn't shed.

She blinked back tears, disgusted by the feeble feelings. She missed him every minute of every day with an intensity that stole the breath from her lungs.

How could she live like this forever? Wanting to be more, needing to be more to him, but knowing that she could never change it?

She knew they had formed a bond in the past days. She knew, for all that her life had been an emotional desert, that what they shared had been special. But he would never love her. She would never amount to anything other than the mother of his children.

It was a truth she had already known, except now it felt excruciatingly unbearable.

Pain constricted her chest. Her lungs were collapsing under its crushing weight. She sank to her knees on the hardwood floor in her bedroom and hugged herself.

She couldn't live with him like this—forever wondering, waiting for the moment he decided she wasn't worth it, the moment he decided he was done with her.

Because he would. Sooner or later he would decide he only wanted his children. She would go mad waiting for that moment.

She had wanted this chance with him, but she didn't want it at the cost of losing her sanity, her will.

Diego couldn't believe the evidence of his own eyes. His gut kept falling lower and lower as he methodically checked each room through the villa. He left her room for last—like a coward postponing the moment of truth.

She has gone.

Miguel had texted him almost two hours ago. Because Miguel, unlike his pilot and the rest of the staff, had known something was wrong, had known her swift departure was something Diego wouldn't have agreed to if his life had depended on it.

Lost in his own world on the other side of the island, pushing himself through another rigorous workout, Diego had seen it too late.

His heart, if it was possible, felt as if it had come to a screeching halt. Because he had instantly known it wasn't a work emergency, as she had claimed to everyone else, or a tantrum because he had been avoiding her since he had heard Eduardo's news.

Kim didn't throw tantrums. She didn't argue, and she didn't fight back—she left quietly, as though he wasn't even worth a goodbye.

His helicopter was gone, his pilot was gone and Kim was gone. And yet he couldn't crush the fleck of hope holding him together.

It was the most pathetic feeling that had ever run through him. Right up there with the hope that had fluttered every time his mother had trotted him down to his father's house to beg for his help.

He arrived at the suite she had been using. The sheer curtains at the French windows flew in the silence. Crickets chirped outside on the veranda.

She hadn't left the room as spotless as she usually did. A couple of paperbacks were still on the bed.

The scent she used, lily of the valley, fluttered over the breeze toward him. Knocked him in the gut like a kick to his insides. He breathed deeply, trying to get the knot in his belly to relent.

A strange sense of déjà-vu descended on him. He looked at the bathroom, his heart in his throat, waiting for her to emerge from it as she had in the hotel suite that day. She would come out and turn her nose up at him. Challenge him. Rile him. And kiss him.

Breathing through the pain, he reminded himself that it would crest soon. It had to.

It didn't.

He rammed his fist into the nearby wall and roared a pithy curse.

Despite his best efforts, he was right where she had left him six years ago—he still wasn't enough for her. Why else would she leave without a word?

In the wake of that crushing realization came waves of roaring fury and unrelenting pain. He was damned if he'd let her go.

He would move heaven and earth to drag her back into his life. He would spend every last dollar he had and more on suing her for custody, using any legal means he had to tie her to him. He would destroy everything he had built— destroy himself if that was the price to make her his again.

He wanted her back in his life. And he would fall as low as needed.

* * *

He had just hung up with his lawyer when Miguel entered his office. He cast a long look at Diego, threw a file on his table, switched on the flatscreen TV and left.

Diego was about to turn off the TV when a familiar sight stopped him in his tracks. The pristine white beaches, the turquoise waters as a background, with Miguel in the forefront, were *here*—on the island.

Stunned, he settled into the couch.

The documentary started with Miguel being asked questions about his past life. Diego could see the resentment in his face, past hurt playing shadows in his dark gaze, the effort it cost him to answer those questions.

He shivered as he realized it was Kim answering the questions. She walked Miguel through every tough question, her tone gentle as he revealed his horrible past

The questions then focused on his current life. His chest tightened and a warm energy flew in Diego's veins as she probed Miguel on how Diego had taken Miguel out of the street gang in Rio di Janeiro, how Diego had worked long days to get through to Miguel that violence wasn't the answer, how Diego had brought him to this island...

Tears burned in Diego's eyes as the short feature went on. As Kim interviewed the other two kids who had joined them last week.

And then it was her smiling face that filled his huge screen.

"The world should know of Diego Pereira's efforts to get these kids out of violent street gangs and toward a better life."

Her statement reverberated within him, shaking the rigid fear at the core of him loose.

He switched the television off, his heart pounding. She thought the world should know what he was doing. But he had never wanted the world's applause, the world's validation.

He had wanted it from *her,* had craved it. He had wanted to be worthy of the strong, brilliant, beautiful woman she was.

Feeling as though he was coming apart, he opened the file that Miguel had tossed at him.

The contents of the file blew him away. There were detailed plans for the infrastructure required to run a shelter for kids recovering from drug problems. There was a list of healthcare workers who had expertise in working with kids like Eduardo. A list of legalities and forms that needed to be fulfilled in order to begin such a program right there on the island.

It was detailed, precise and exactly what he had had in mind when he had bought the island. He had never revealed his plans to her. She couldn't have created a file that made her loss more apparent.

Every inch of him ached at the emptiness he felt. Had she been horrified by what he had driven Eduardo to?

Seeing Eduardo's body, seeing his own father, whom he had hated for so many years, his hatred blazing just as ever, had broken the hold he had kept on himself—had shown him what he couldn't achieve through wealth or power, however hard he fought.

All his life he had fought for everything he had. But he hadn't been able to make his mother happy before she died, he had never received his father's acknowledgment or praise and he hadn't been able to save Eduardo.

If he did anything to manipulate Kim now, if he fell any lower—even if it was because he loved her—he would probably only destroy her, as he had done Eduardo, and she had already suffered enough.

He closed his eyes and threw his head back. Grief

scratched at his throat, and his muscles were burning with the need to fight, to bring her back into his life.

But he couldn't.

He couldn't force her to love him—not as he loved her. With every breath in him. With every cell in him. And letting her go meant letting go of the dream he had looked for with her and his children.

He had no doubt she would love their babies, whatever her fears.

In the end, after everything he had done to get to this stage in life, he was terrifyingly powerless again—and alone with it all.

CHAPTER THIRTEEN

"ARE YOU GOING to avoid me for the rest of our lives?"

Kim drew a sharp breath, her fork freezing midway to her mouth, as Liv's words flew across the lounge like loaded missiles. She had been back in New York for a week now and had been dreading confrontation. But this wasn't one she had prepared herself for.

She had forgotten that Liv still had a key to her apartment. And she had been so lost in her own thoughts that she hadn't even heard the front door being opened.

Liv joined her at the dining table, her gaze brimming with concern—and something else. *Almost fear.*

"Hey, Liv."

She lifted her fork to her mouth and took a bite of pasta. She chewed on it, forcing herself to keep at bay the nausea that had been threatening all day. It had become worse the moment she had returned—as though her body had gone into fully fledged revolt the minute she had got off the plane from the island.

Away from Diego.

Liv pulled a chair out, sat down at the table and studied her.

"You look like hell, Kim. You shouldn't look like this."

Kim nodded, and ran her palm over her midriff. She raised her head and met Liv's gaze. "I just haven't been sleeping well. I have been taking good care of myself, Liv," she said guiltily. "I've cut down my hours. I've been eating lots." She pushed her chair back and hugged Liv. Hard. "*You* look wonderful, though."

Liv's arms tightened around her. "Please tell me this is just you being hormonal. Because you're scaring me."

Kim bit her lip, striving to hold back the raw ache in her throat. "You and Alex okay?" she said softly. Every time she saw one of them she felt the knot of guilt in her stomach relent a little. As different as they were, Alex was the perfect man for her sister.

If Diego hadn't stopped her Alex wouldn't have fallen in love with Liv, and *she* wouldn't have the babies growing in her womb... A shiver went over her.

"I'm not here to talk about Alexander and me."

Kim laughed and pulled back from her. "That means you're fighting again?"

Liv shrugged. "He's angry that I forged his signature on Emily's parental release form so that she can screen-test for a movie role," she replied, a guilty blush stealing into her cheeks.

"*You forged his...?* God, Liv. I know how he is about his sister. How *could* you?"

"Acting's in her blood, Kim. She was going to do it whether he agreed or not. And Alexander...*when he loves someone*...it's just so..." She hesitated, a little shiver spewing into her words. "Emily doesn't realize how easily she can hurt him. And I would rather he be pissed off with me than—"

"Than be hurt by her?" Kim finished for Liv, her gut folding in on itself.

She stared at her twin, a fog falling away from her eyes. They looked similar, yet they were so different on the inside. Even before their mother had left Liv had always somehow understood their mother's pain.

Hadn't that always been the difference between them?

Liv's ability to put everything she loved before herself? To take that leap again and again, even if it pained her? To risk everything for love?

Kim had always assumed that *she* was the stronger one—the one in control, the one with no weaknesses. What if her strength had only been a self-delusion? Was she a coward after all? A coward who didn't believe herself worthy of being loved?

She had been so sure she loved Diego, but apparently only if there were no risks involved, only if she was sure that he would return her feelings.

"I'm worried about you, Kim," Liv said. "Alexander told me you asked him to recommend a good custody lawyer. And yesterday Diego came to see me."

"He did what?" Kim's fork clattered to the table. "He was in New York?" And he hadn't even called her.

Liv nodded, worry creasing her brow. "He…he wanted me to give you something. He said he didn't want you to open it alone. I think he's worried about you. When I asked him why he didn't do it himself, he said he was done running after you."

Liv opened her handbag and pulled out an envelope from it.

Fear curled up in her stomach and Kim braced herself.

He hadn't called her. He hadn't responded to her email. Every second of every day for the past week she had been on tenterhooks, waiting to hear something, *anything* from him. And she had a terrifying feeling about the contents of that envelope.

He was going to sue her for custody. He was going to take the babies away from her.

Just the passing thought was enough to plunge her into an abyss of panic. Her hands moved to her stomach and she shuddered. Her lungs felt as if they were seizing up on her.

She sagged to the floor and tucked her head between her legs.

Her palm on Kim's back, Liv whispered something, but Kim could hear nothing past the terror clawing through her. She couldn't even bear the thought of being forced to part with her children, the thought of not seeing them every day for the rest of her life.

How cold-hearted had her mother been to walk away so easily from them? Kim couldn't imagine making that choice if her life depended on it.

Maybe she would have a little girl with a golden gaze and a distinct nose like Diego's, and a boy with jet-black hair and a penchant for fighting. She would love her kids no matter what life threw at her. She would spend every minute...

A choked sound fell from her mouth.

There it was. The connection. The joy she had wanted to feel for so long. She closed her eyes and gripped the feeling closer to her heart. She curled up on the floor and gave in to the tears scratching her throat.

She couldn't share it with Diego. Couldn't tell him of the joy overflowing within her at the thought of the children they had created together. Couldn't tell him she finally understood what he had experienced from the minute she had told him about the pregnancy.

And now he was going to take them away from her.

Liv joined her on the floor and hugged her. "God, Kim. What are you doing to yourself?"

Kim wiped her tears and steadied herself. At least now she had the strength to fight for her kids—she couldn't expect Diego to give up his rights, but she was damned if she would either.

"If you don't want to open this now—"

She shook her head. "No. Better to get this over with..."

Casting her a worried look, Liv tore the envelope. Her mouth tight, she scanned the documents rapidly.

"This is a motion to start divorce proceedings. You're to have full custody and there's a note requesting minimum visitation rights to the...*children?*"

Kim gasped, every inch of her trembling with relief and shock.

"Wait... What does he mean *children?* Oh my God, you're having twins?"

Clutching Liv's hand, Kim nodded. Her vision was blurred. Her head felt dizzy. Delayed shock was setting in.

He was divorcing her. He was giving her full custody...

Liv skimmed through the papers in her hand again. "He will never contest your custody rights in any way. He..."

Saliva pooled in Kim's mouth, followed by a wave of nausea pushing its way up her throat. She kept her hand on her stomach.

Liv threw the papers on the table and knelt in front of her. She squeezed Kim's fingers, her gaze filled with shock. "It's so strange, isn't it? After everything he did to get you into his life, he's agreeing to all this."

An empty chill pervaded Kim's limbs, sucking out every ounce of emotion from her. *This was it.* "He's finally given up on me."

"What?"

"He's finally realized I'm not worthy of him after all."

Liv shook her head violently. "That's BS, and you know it."

Kim wiped her tears with the back of her hand. The sooner she accepted the truth, the better now. She missed Diego as if she had a hole in her heart, but she would tailor her life better for her kids. Starting with telling Liv the truth.

"I lied to you, Liv. All those years ago when Mom left."

Liv stared at her, her gaze searching Kim's. Fear clouded her eyes. "What?"

"I found her note the previous night. She was going to take you with her."

"She didn't say a word to me."

"Because I stopped her. I threatened to tell Dad if she even touched you. I was selfish. I couldn't bear the fact that she would take you from me. I couldn't—"

"You didn't ask her why she wasn't taking *you?*"

"Everything that Dad did to you—it was my fault. If you had left with her... She *did* love you, Liv. You should know that."

Her twin laughed, the sound full of bitterness. "Isn't it weird how you're blind to what she was?" She clasped Kim's cheeks, her own eyes full of tears now. "You can't blame yourself. You did everything in your power to shield me from Dad. And Mom didn't love you *or* me—not enough. The moment you threatened her escape she decided I wasn't worth it either. Don't you see? She wasn't strong enough for that. She was never strong enough for us."

Kim's heart felt as if it was bursting with emotion. The love shining in Liv's eyes was enough to pull the last bit of wool from her eyes.

God, she had been such a fool. She had let guilt and pain rob so much from her. Her mother hadn't robbed it from her. She had done that to herself. And now she was letting her fear rob her of Diego, wasn't she? Failing herself even before she took the leap?

"And even if she had been, do you think I'd have gone with her? Left you behind?" Now her sister's words vibrated with pain. "You are my sister. You're all I had—all I *have*. What I don't get is why you have let it hurt you so much. All these years you just accepted her decision, you let it weigh everything you've done."

"What was I supposed to do?"

"You are supposed to fight for yourself. You shouldn't have let her cowardly decision have so much power over you. You always fought for me. You stood up to Dad every time he came at me. Why do you think you deserve any less?"

Kim's tears ran over her cheeks as she stared at Liv. She had no answer. It was what she was doing again with Diego. Instead of fighting for herself—fighting for her love— instead of fighting for her *babies* she was walking away to protect herself.

So what if he didn't love her? So what if he only wanted their marriage to work for the sake of the children? He took care of her, he pampered her, he understood her stubbornness and he had stood by her when she had been crumbling. It was more affection than she had ever received from anyone.

She scrubbed her cheeks and grabbed the papers from the table. "You're right. I am going to fight for myself." Her stomach churned with fear, but she couldn't let it stop her now. Her fingers shaking, she tore the documents Liv had brought into so many pieces. "Can you please call Alex? I need transportation."

Her eyes wide, Liv laughed as she followed her into her bedroom. Kim plucked at her suitcase, which she still hadn't emptied, opened it, threw the clothes into a pile and started throwing others in. Mostly shorts and tank tops, nightwear.

She slipped her laptop into its case, tucked in the power cord, followed by her cell phone charger and her wallet. She quickly called her assistant, informed her of her travel plans and hung up while the woman was still struggling to grapple with what she'd just been told.

After three years of non-stop work, Kim knew her team was obviously surprised that she was now taking vacations so frequently. But they were an expertly trained team, and she could do her job from wherever Diego was just as easily as she could in New York.

She made another call to her VP of Operations and informed her she should start a headhunt for another CEO. Effective immediately, she was going to cut down her hours. And when the time came she would need maternity leave, too.

Excitement mixed with fear thrummed through her veins, making her a little light-headed.

Liv stopped her with a hand on her shoulder. "Whoa… Kim…. Slow down." Her mobile mouth was frozen in shock. "Wow, you're really doing this."

"Yep, and I can't stop, Liv," she said, walking back into the kitchen and throwing her multivitamins into her handbag. "I have to keep moving, I have to get on a plane before I start thinking. Diego was right. I should get a device that stops my brain from overthinking."

"He said that?"

Kim nodded, the memory of his smile lending her courage.

"Alex's pilot should be ready in half an hour. Do you want me to come with you? Bring Alexander to take on Diego?"

A laugh barreled out of her and Kim kissed Liv's cheek. Hugged her again.

"No. I'm going to be fine. Whether in the name of revenge or my pregnancy, Diego always fought for us." She had to believe that and she had to do the same. "If he hadn't cared he could have sued for custody. After all the things I told him he still trusted me enough, believed in me enough, that I would love our children. He's fought for our relationship with everything he has in him. Now it's time I do the same." She clasped Liv's hands in hers, her throat closing up again. "We're good, aren't we?"

Liv nodded and kissed her cheek again. "Of course. Whatever happens, you always have me."

CHAPTER FOURTEEN

Diego had no idea how long he had been pushing himself in the huge state-of-the-art gym that he'd had specially built on the island. His muscles groaned under the rigor he was putting himself through. It felt as if his flesh had morphed into points of torture and then turned inward.

But he couldn't stop. He hadn't been able to stop for the past week, since Kim had left. He had flown back and forth to New York within a day, worked from morning to evening and then punished himself with a brutal workout each evening, so that when he went to bed he hoped to be so exhausted that sleep came.

It hadn't worked. Even with his body turning into a bruising pulp he couldn't fall asleep. He was beginning to feel like a ticking bomb.

The days stretched torturously ahead of him, with memories of Kim pricking into him wherever he turned.

He was beginning to hate the island, after everything he had done to own it.

He'd seen Miguel and Anna poke their heads in a couple of times at the entrance to the gym.

They were worried about him. He got that. But nothing could puncture his need for physical pain right now. Nothing else could numb the emptiness he felt inside.

* * *

It was midnight by the time he walked toward his bedroom. He had showered at the gym, yelled his head off at Anna and Miguel when they'd tried to talk to him and then wandered on the beach for more than a couple of hours.

And he still wasn't tired. Every nerve in him was strung tight. Olivia would have gone to see Kim yesterday. She would have handed her his documents. He couldn't breathe for the ball of pain that was hanging around his neck.

He froze at the entrance to his bedroom.

A breeze flew in from the ocean. The French doors were wide open. The lamp was turned on, the feeble light from it illuminating the woman snoring softly in the center of his king bed.

He felt as if a tornado had hit him in the gut and then tossed him around.

How long had she been waiting for him? When had she arrived?

She was lying on her side, her knees tucked into her chest. Her arms were wrapped around herself. He didn't question why she had returned. He didn't question why she was in his bedroom, of all the rooms in the villa. They hadn't shared a bed even when she had been here.

Kim was back. The woman he loved with every breath in him was back.

He walked toward the bed, his gaze unblinking. His chest tightened and he realized the tight sensation was fear. Every inch of him was shaking with spine-chilling fear. He loved this woman so much and he was afraid to blink. He was afraid she would disappear if he did.

He climbed on to the bed slowly and pulled the cotton covers over her sleeping form.

She wore a silk sleeveless gown in dark blue that clung to the small bump at her stomach and just about covered her knees. The lace neckline fluttered over her breasts with every breeze that flew in through the door. He greedily looked over her, from her hair, which was a mess, to her painted toes.

Her long eyelashes cast shadows on her cheeks. Dark blue circles hung under her eyes. He muttered a soft curse.

Droga, that gaunt look was back in her face again. He rubbed the pad of his thumb over her cheek, his breath hovering in his throat. And then, and only then, did he breathe air into his lungs again.

He ran his fingers over her toned arms. The skin was so soft and silky that he was afraid he would mark her with his rough fingers. His hand shaking, he pulled back.

He was never going to let her go. He had ripped out his own heart to let her go once. He couldn't do it again.

Even if he had to handcuff her to this very bed. Even if he had to spend the rest of his life tearing away her defenses piece by piece.

He didn't care anymore if she loved him or not, if she was as crazy about him as he was about her. All he wanted was to spend his life with her, looking after her, loving her, telling her every single day how much he wanted her, how much he needed her.

He stretched out next to her, feeling the weight on his shoulders dissolve into nothingness. Calm floated over him. His sore body felt lighter. He would just sit here, stay with her, watch over her.

He turned onto his side and pressed his mouth to her temple, breathed in her scent. And closed his eyes.

Sleep hit his eyelids with the force of a hurricane dragging him under, as though it hadn't eluded him at all for that whole torturous week.

Kim drifted awake suddenly, instantly registering the warm, comforting weight around her waist. It was the same feeling all over, actually. From her hair to her toes she felt as if she was encased in the most delicious embrace ever.

She opened sleep-heavy eyes. The lamp she had turned on was still lit, and Diego's sleeping face filled her vision. A soft gasp escaped her mouth. It was his arm that hung around her middle.

Her heart went from a quiet drone to a thundering pace in a mere second.

For a few minutes she just looked at him to her heart's content. He wore shorts and nothing else. She swallowed as her gaze drifted over his long, hair-roughened legs. His abdomen was a ridge of hard muscles, with a line of hair that disappeared into his shorts.

His powerfully built chest rose and fell with his even breathing. The groove where his neck met his shoulders invited her touch. She fisted her hands, her gaze on his face now.

His mouth was a lush line in repose, his features etched with the passion and kindness that made this man. How stupid had she been to walk away from him?

Taking a deep breath, she lifted the arm around her middle and twined her fingers with his long ones. She heard him breathe in on a soft hiss and froze. With a frown, she pulled his hand up and saw the raw knuckles. The skin was broken in several places and crusted with blood.

Tears hit her eyes with a brutal force. She lifted his hand to her mouth and kissed the center of his palm. She dragged her mouth over the rough calluses, learning and loving every inch of him anew.

His breathing altered from its soft rhythm to a sharp intake of breath. She froze with the tips of his fingers on her mouth.

Their gazes collided. Her fingers tightened around his. "You have to stop fighting Miguel and whoever else you are."

Warmth filtered into his gaze. "I wasn't fighting."

She fought to keep the tears at bay. "Then what is this?"

He shrugged.

"It hurts when I see you hurt, Diego. I don't ever want to see *this,*" she said loudly, pointing his own fingers in his face, "again."

She couldn't keep the demand out of her tone.

She expected him to mock her, question her, tease her at least.

He said nothing, his gaze raking her face hungrily. His silent nod was too much to bear.

He scooted closer, his body an inviting fortress of pulsing heat and so much more. He still didn't say anything, didn't ask her anything. Just held her, his leg thrown over hers, his open palm on her back.

She pulled his hand to her face.

He obliged her without a word, his long fingers fanning out from her temples to her mouth. She kissed every finger, every ridge and mound of his palm.

She shivered as a sob built in her chest.

She drew a painful breath and tucked her face into his chest. She kissed him, the thundering boom of his heart the only sound filling her ears. "I've torn up the divorce papers. I never want to see them again in this lifetime. I'm never leaving you again, Diego. *Ever.*"

She felt his silent nod as he pulled her against him, his arms tight bands around her. *Why didn't he say anything?* His agonizing silence, compared to his usually mocking, challenging, probing self, was beginning to breathe crippling fear into her limbs.

Her throat was choked up with all the words she wanted to say, her strength once again leaving her in her moment of need. But she had to do this. She had to tell him, had to show him her heart.

She struggled against him and he loosened his hold.

Using his strength, she pulled herself up. She laughed, the sound tinged with her fear. She breathed hard, her hands going to her small belly. "I'm already a little clumsy."

He stayed on his side, propped by his elbow, his gaze on her belly. "You've begun to show."

She laughed, her tears finally spilling from her eyes. *He was still speaking to her. It was more than she deserved.* "Every day is making a difference."

"Can I touch you?"

"You don't have to ask," she whispered, wondering if she had already lost him. Because Diego never asked. He manipulated her, he tricked her, he bargained with her. It was the only way she had ever given him anything, the only way she had let him see anything. And his solemn request now pierced her.

He placed his hand on her belly, his huge palm almost spanning the small bump.

She placed her hand atop his and he glanced up toward her. "Aren't you going to ask me why I came back?"

The warmth disappeared from his gaze. He pulled himself up with a smooth movement and joined her against the headboard. "No."

She held his hand tightly, drawing strength from it. One question swirled on the tip of her tongue, gouging into her. Every instinct inside her told her to embrace the silence again, to let it go. If she didn't ask, she couldn't be hurt by his answer. If she didn't ask, she could…

She was short-changing herself again.

"I…I would like to ask *you* something. And I want you to give me an honest answer, okay?"

He nodded, his gaze never leaving hers.

Her throat almost seized up. There was a hot prickle of tears at the backs of her eyes. "You… Why did you take Marissa with you? I… It was the cruelest thing you could have done to me. I knew Eduardo. I would have come with you…"

He touched his mouth to her temple. "Shh…I never meant to hurt you."

His fingers tightened around hers. He didn't smile, but she saw the softening in his eyes. Because he understood how big it was for her just to ask.

"I wanted to take you with me. All I wanted was to hear you say again and again that you weren't disgusted by what I had done, that I was a better man than I already was." His words were soft, yet loaded with emotion. "But, Eduardo, he was always a good reminder to me of what I could become if I let something matter to me too much. Leaving without you was a matter of denying myself, proving to myself that I didn't need you. Marissa…when she requested if she could come I couldn't say no."

"I want to share both good and bad with you, Diego. I want to be the one you lean on when…" She took a deep breath. "I meant what I said before. I'm never leaving again."

A fire licked into life in his gaze. "That's good to know."

"Why are you being like this?"

"What is it you want from me? I will do it."

"You have given up on me."

Fresh tears spilled from her eyes, but she wiped them with determination. This was only one day—the beginning. She would spend this entire lifetime and more waiting for his love. Because this man—he meant everything to her. And she wasn't going to hide how she felt for him either.

"I'm in love with you, Diego." She rushed over words that should be said slowly, softly, without waiting for his reaction. She could do this only one way. "I've always been in love with you. I was an idiot before. I'm going to spend the rest of my life fighting for us, proving to you that I'm worth it. All I ask is—"

In a second he was kneeling over her, his legs on either side of hers. And then he kissed her. She moaned and wrapped her hands around his nape. Gave his kiss everything she had in her. He wasn't gentle with her. His hand in her hair kept her where he wanted her as his tongue plunged into her mouth.

Heat blasted all over her as he pushed up her nightgown with rough hands. His hands cupped her breasts and she whimpered at the pleasure sparking all over.

"Diego, wait…" she managed to say, even as arousal stole through her, lighting an insatiable fire in her body.

He halted, his breathing rough, his palms spread out over her thighs. His face was tight with guilt. "Did I hurt you?"

She laughed and cupped his jaw, her breathing still nowhere near normal. "I won't break, Diego. I want nothing more than to feel you inside me." Stealing her fingers into his hair, she pressed an open-mouthed kiss to his lips. Warmth stole through her. Diego's groan added to it. "But I… You haven't said anything. I understand if you're angry, if you're—"

"Angry?" he said, and the very emotion he was denying crept into his tone. "Try gut-twisting emptiness. I've never been more alone, felt more alone in my life than the past week. Everything I have achieved, everything I have—it means nothing without you."

Her heart leaped into her throat. She felt dizzy—as though someone had sucked out the oxygen from around them.

He touched his forehead to hers. "I love you so much, *minha esposinha*." His words reverberated with pain. His features were stark and menacing. "And if you leave me again it will destroy the little good there is in me. It almost did this time."

Her heart felt as if it would burst out of her chest. Kim wrapped her arms around him and hugged him so tight that her breathing stuttered. It was more than she had ever hoped for. "You love me?"

His gaze was filled with pain. "I can survive if I lose all this wealth, I have survived rejection from pretty much everyone in my life, but I can't survive losing you. When you left, for a few moments all I could think was that you had gone because everything I had done wasn't enough. *I* wasn't enough."

"No, Diego. Don't say that. You're the most wonderful man I've ever met. I just couldn't bear to be by your side thinking that you would never love me. It hurt so much that you turned away from me. I wanted to ask you. I wanted to…" She shivered and he kissed her temple. "It was nothing to do with you, Diego. I was weak. I…"

"You're stubborn, arrogant, you drive me to the worst of myself and you're so damn hard to get through to sometimes. But you're the toughest woman I know and I love you for everything you are."

He settled his palm on her belly and she wondered if she would combust from the pride, from the acceptance, from the love in his words.

"I can't think of a better, stronger mother for my children."

This fierce, passionate man loved her. She would count herself lucky for the rest of her days. "You really think that, don't you? I couldn't believe you trusted me enough to…"

"Of course I do. You might not feel that connection, but I have no doubt that you'll love our children."

Kim smiled and hid her face in the crook of his elbow, his words washing over her with a warmth she wanted to keep close. She would tell him in a minute. She would tell him how much joy now flew through her just at the thought of their little family.

"Will you promise me you will never stop fighting for

me and you will never give up on me? Even when I don't believe I'm worthy of you?" she said, fear stealing through her.

He met her gaze and smiled, his hands tight against her waist. And the tenderness in it stole through her. "We will always fight for each other. We will never let ourselves settle for anything less than we deserve. It's a promise, *gatinha*."

Olivia laughed as strong arms engulfed her from behind and pulled her hard into a body she would know in her sleep. She clamped Alexander's arms with her fingers, tucking herself even tighter into his embrace.

She should have known he would follow her to Diego's island.

"You left without telling me," he whispered near her ear, his hands holding her hard at her ribcage.

Liv closed her eyes and breathed the essence of him, every inch of her trembling with that same happiness that had marked her life the past couple of months.

"I was worried about her," she said, nodding toward Kim.

Kim and Diego were walking hand in hand at the edge of the water on the beach, lost in each other. Liv couldn't stop smiling at how Diego's hand never left her twin, how Kim hadn't stopped smiling ever since Liv had gotten here.

Alexander kissed her jaw, his hands inching under her T-shirt until they found bare skin. She sucked in a breath at the weight of his palm.

"There's no need, is there?" he asked.

"No need," Liv repeated, knowing that he understood. "He loves her, Alexander. Like she deserves to be loved." She swallowed the tears in her throat. This was a time to rejoice. "I've never seen her so happy and glowing. And did you know she's having—?"

He turned her around, his blue gaze eating her up with

a hungry intensity that started an ache in her own body. It was always like that.

But he looked haunted, with deep grooves pinching his mouth. "You got on a plane without telling me after we had a God-awful fight, Liv. You weren't answering your phone. I asked Emily. She thought it was really funny that I didn't know where my wife was before she told me. I think my heart stopped for a few moments."

The edge in his words, the way he was holding her so tight... Liv frowned. Damn her and her impulsive head. "I left my phone by accident. And I should have realized Emily would play with you first. I *was* really worried about Kim. And I'm sorry about Emily. I know I shouldn't interfere, but—"

He pressed a soft kiss to her mouth, his hands capturing her face. The love that shone in his gaze took her breath away. "I think I know why you did that. It's a strange feeling to be protected by my ferocious wife. I love you, Liv," he whispered.

God, she would never tire of hearing him say it.

"And I'm glad Kim has found happiness."

Liv nodded and returned his kiss, her own joy making her light-headed. She twined her fingers with his and tugged him forward. "It's time you met Diego properly, don't you think?"

She laughed when he raised his brows in an exaggerated way. Her husband and her twin's husband were just as different as she and Kim were.

Life was going to be really interesting for them, but full of laughter and love.

* * * * *